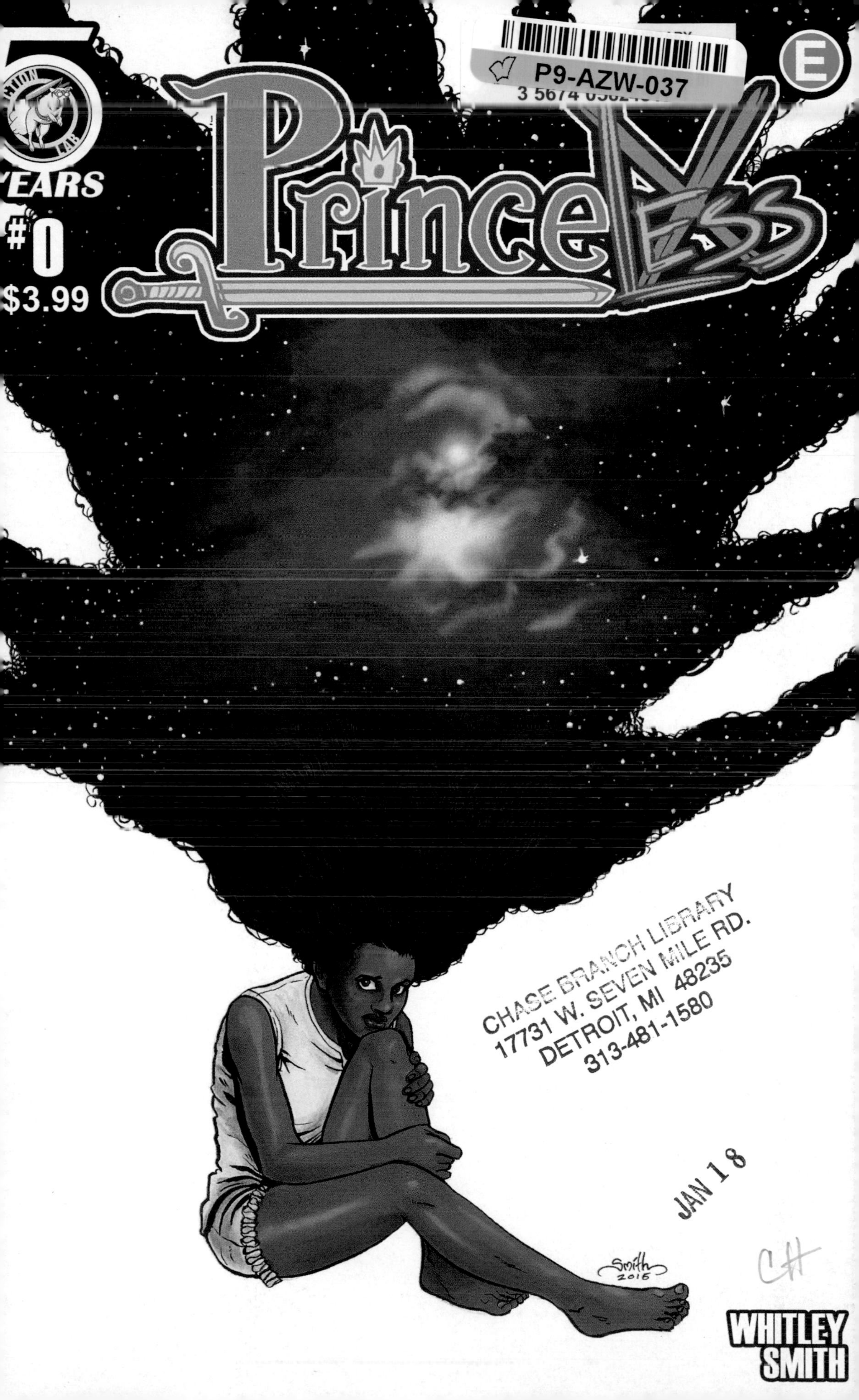
YEARS
#0
$3.99
Princeless
E
SMITH 2015
WHITLEY
SMITH

FROM ALL-AGES TO MATURE READERS
ACTION LAB HAS YOU COVERED.

 **Appropriate for everyone.**

 **Appropriate for age 9 and up. Absent of profanity or adult content.**

 **Suggested for 12 and Up. Comics with this rating are comparable to a PG-13 movie rating. Recommended for our teen and young adult readers.**

 **Appropriate for older teens. Similar to Teen, but featuring more mature themes and/or more graphic imagery.**

Contains extreme viloence and some nudity. Basically the Rated-R of comics.

 FIND YOUR NEW FAVORITE COMICS.

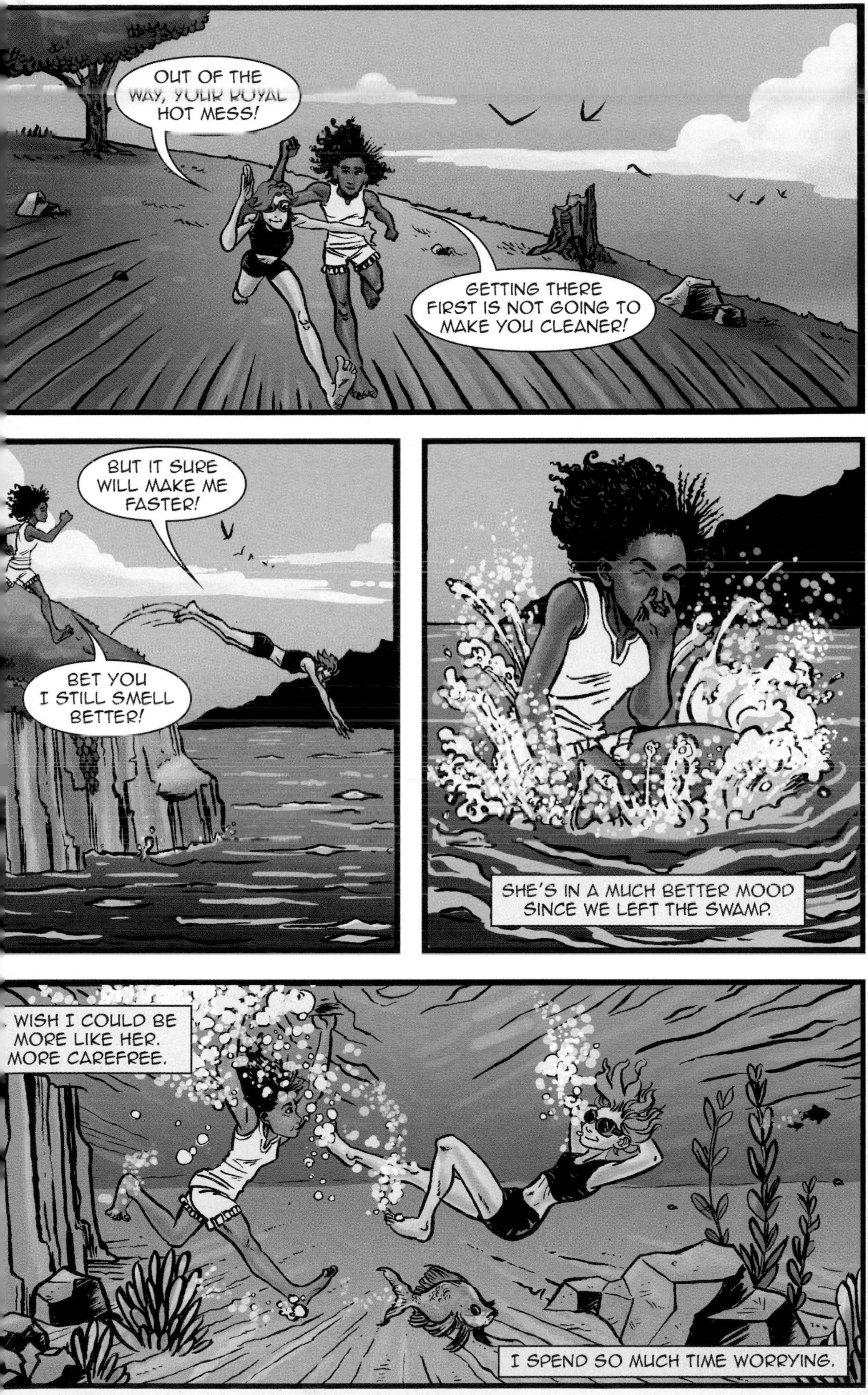
OUT OF THE WAY, YOUR ROYAL HOT MESS!
GETTING THERE FIRST IS NOT GOING TO MAKE YOU CLEANER!
BUT IT SURE WILL MAKE ME FASTER!
BET YOU I STILL SMELL BETTER!
SHE'S IN A MUCH BETTER MOOD SINCE WE LEFT THE SWAMP.
WISH I COULD BE MORE LIKE HER. MORE CAREFREE.
I SPEND SO MUCH TIME WORRYING.

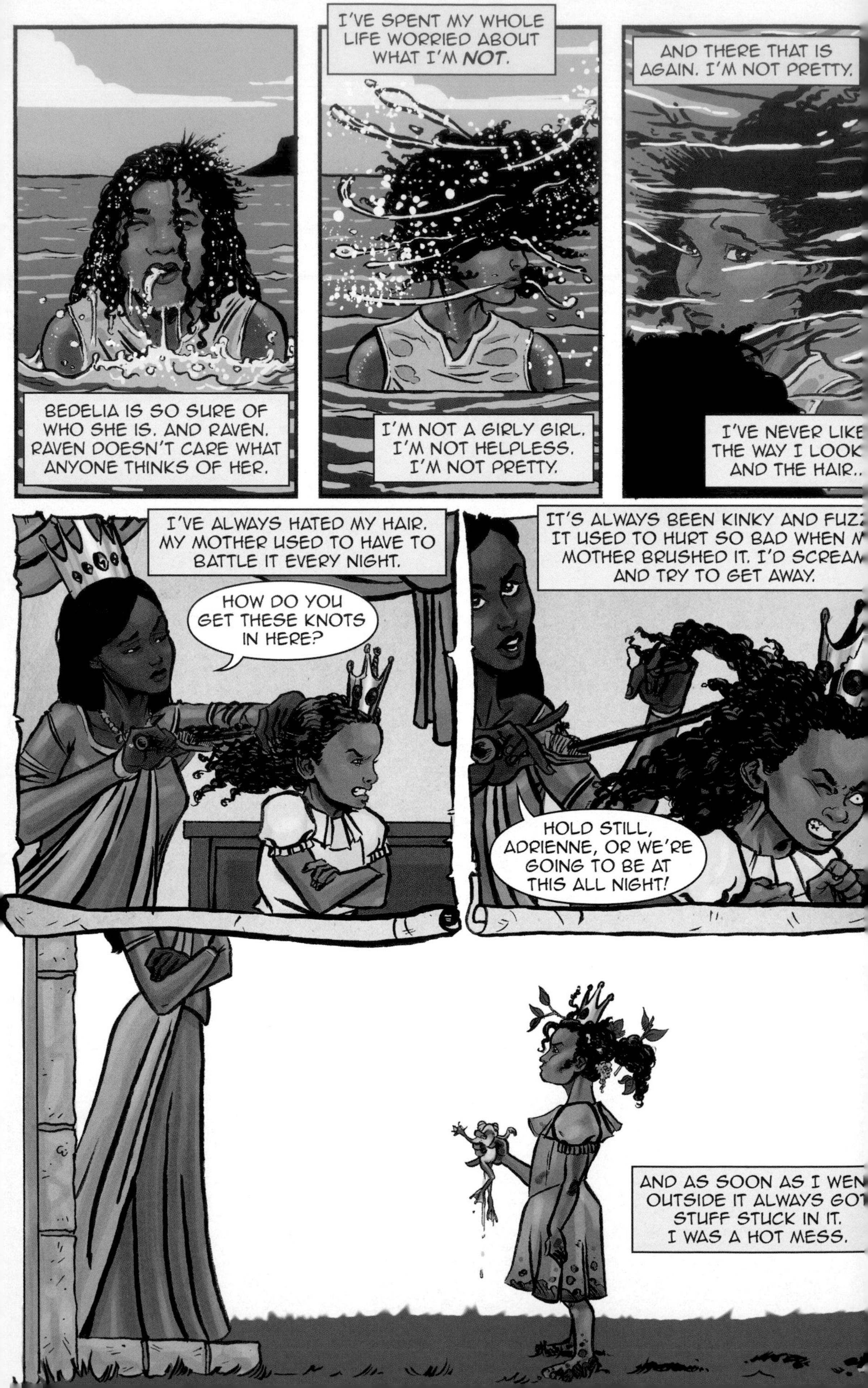
BEDELIA IS SO SURE OF WHO SHE IS. AND RAVEN. RAVEN DOESN'T CARE WHAT ANYONE THINKS OF HER.
I'VE SPENT MY WHOLE LIFE WORRIED ABOUT WHAT I'M ***NOT***.
I'M NOT A GIRLY GIRL. I'M NOT HELPLESS. I'M NOT PRETTY.
AND THERE THAT IS AGAIN. I'M NOT PRETTY.
I'VE NEVER LIKE THE WAY I LOOK AND THE HAIR..
I'VE ALWAYS HATED MY HAIR. MY MOTHER USED TO HAVE TO BATTLE IT EVERY NIGHT.
HOW DO YOU GET THESE KNOTS IN HERE?
IT'S ALWAYS BEEN KINKY AND FUZ IT USED TO HURT SO BAD WHEN M MOTHER BRUSHED IT. I'D SCREAM AND TRY TO GET AWAY.
HOLD STILL, ADRIENNE, OR WE'RE GOING TO BE AT THIS ALL NIGHT!
AND AS SOON AS I WEN OUTSIDE IT ALWAYS GOT STUFF STUCK IN IT. I WAS A HOT MESS.

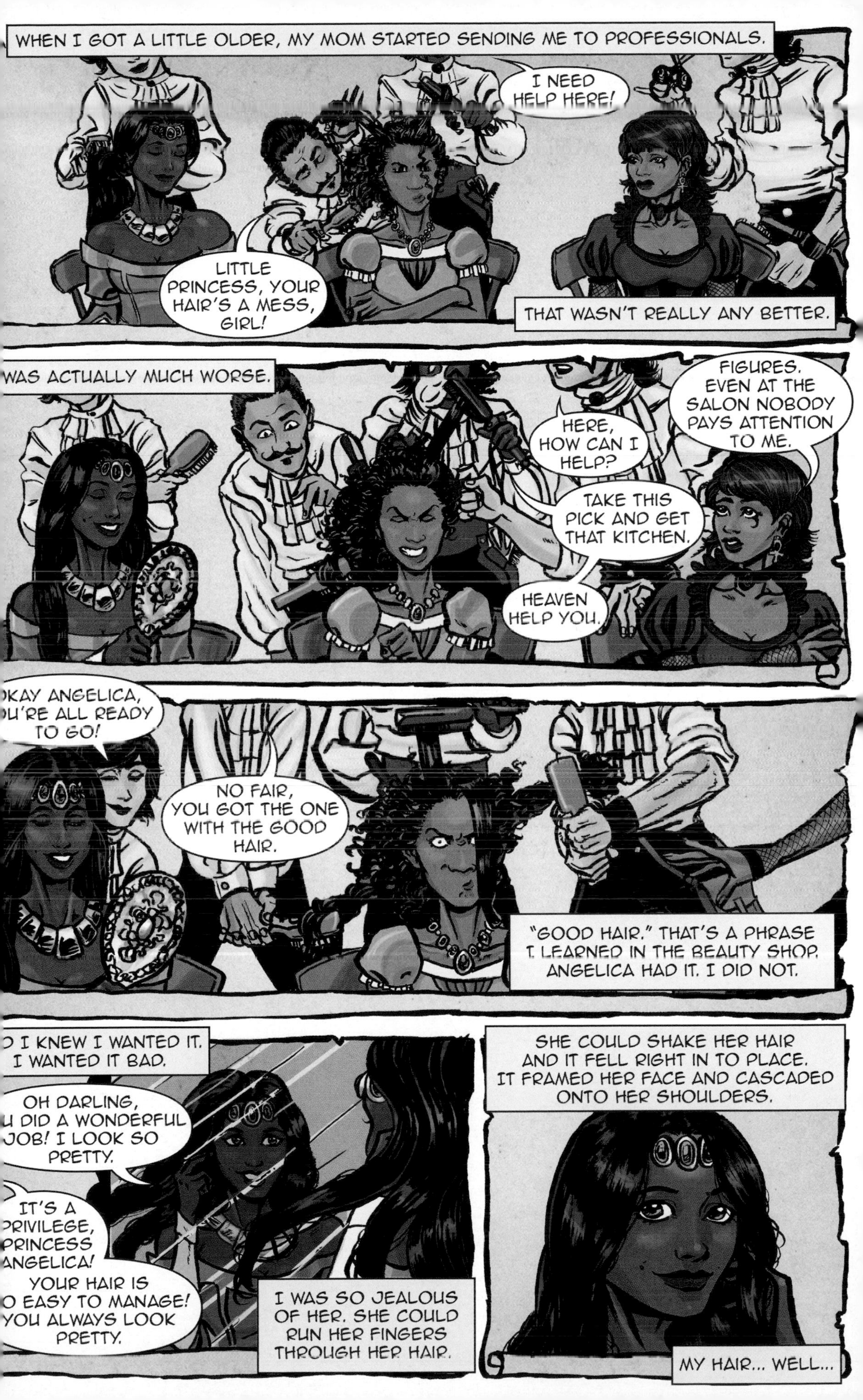
WHEN I GOT A LITTLE OLDER, MY MOM STARTED SENDING ME TO PROFESSIONALS.
I NEED HELP HERE!
LITTLE PRINCESS, YOUR HAIR'S A MESS, GIRL!
THAT WASN'T REALLY ANY BETTER.
WAS ACTUALLY MUCH WORSE.
HERE, HOW CAN I HELP?
FIGURES. EVEN AT THE SALON NOBODY PAYS ATTENTION TO ME.
TAKE THIS PICK AND GET THAT KITCHEN.
HEAVEN HELP YOU.
KAY ANGELICA, U'RE ALL READY TO GO!
NO FAIR, YOU GOT THE ONE WITH THE GOOD HAIR.
"GOOD HAIR." THAT'S A PHRASE I LEARNED IN THE BEAUTY SHOP. ANGELICA HAD IT. I DID NOT.
I KNEW I WANTED IT. I WANTED IT BAD.
OH DARLING, U DID A WONDERFUL JOB! I LOOK SO PRETTY.
IT'S A PRIVILEGE, PRINCESS ANGELICA! YOUR HAIR IS O EASY TO MANAGE! YOU ALWAYS LOOK PRETTY.
I WAS SO JEALOUS OF HER. SHE COULD RUN HER FINGERS THROUGH HER HAIR.
SHE COULD SHAKE HER HAIR AND IT FELL RIGHT IN TO PLACE. IT FRAMED HER FACE AND CASCADED ONTO HER SHOULDERS.
MY HAIR... WELL...

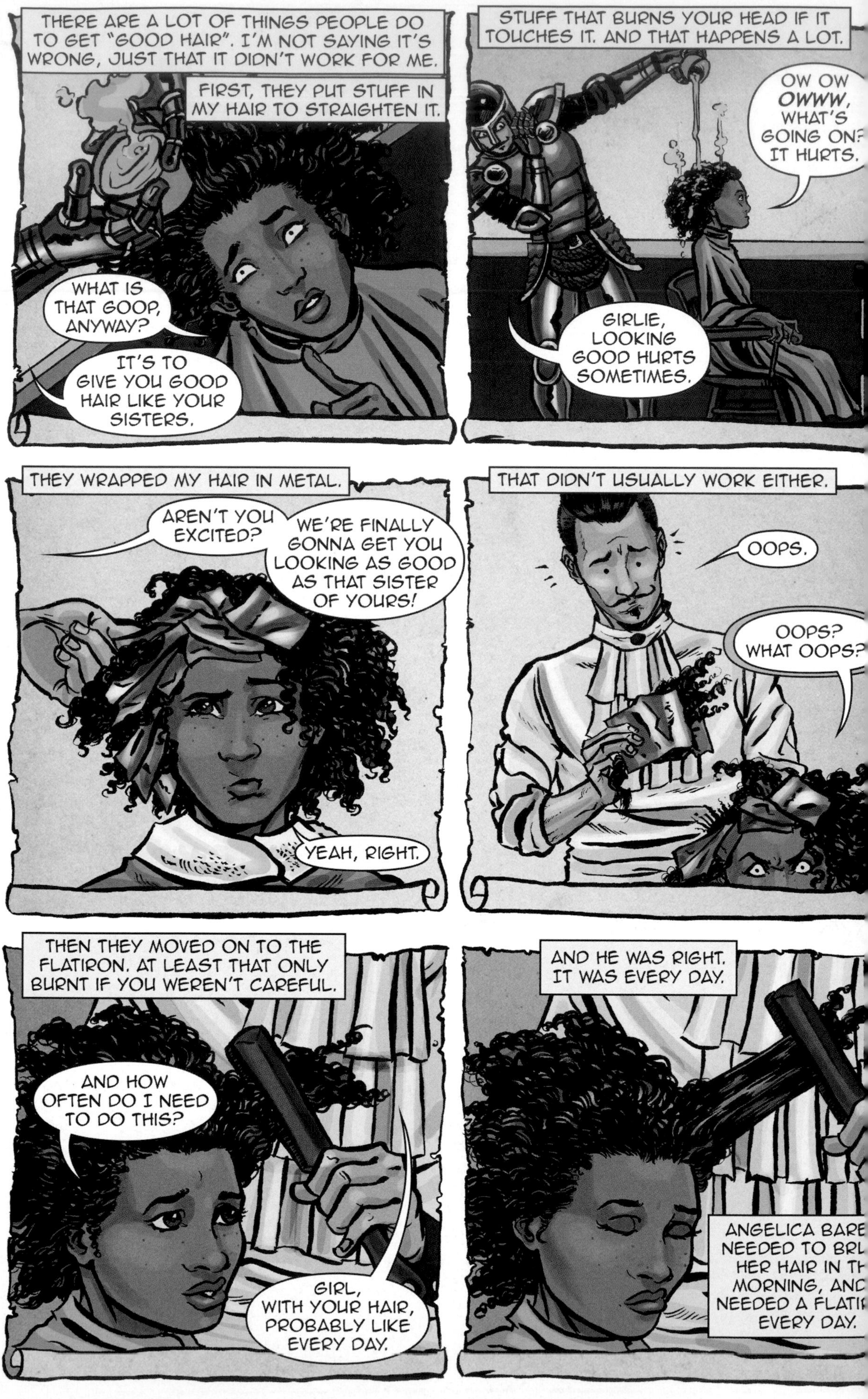
THERE ARE A LOT OF THINGS PEOPLE DO TO GET "GOOD HAIR". I'M NOT SAYING IT'S WRONG, JUST THAT IT DIDN'T WORK FOR ME.
FIRST, THEY PUT STUFF IN MY HAIR TO STRAIGHTEN IT.
WHAT IS THAT GOOP, ANYWAY?
IT'S TO GIVE YOU GOOD HAIR LIKE YOUR SISTERS.
STUFF THAT BURNS YOUR HEAD IF IT TOUCHES IT. AND THAT HAPPENS A LOT.
OW OW OWWW, WHAT'S GOING ON? IT HURTS.
GIRLIE, LOOKING GOOD HURTS SOMETIMES.
THEY WRAPPED MY HAIR IN METAL.
AREN'T YOU EXCITED?
WE'RE FINALLY GONNA GET YOU LOOKING AS GOOD AS THAT SISTER OF YOURS!
YEAH, RIGHT.
THAT DIDN'T USUALLY WORK EITHER.
OOPS.
OOPS? WHAT OOPS?
THEN THEY MOVED ON TO THE FLATIRON. AT LEAST THAT ONLY BURNT IF YOU WEREN'T CAREFUL.
AND HOW OFTEN DO I NEED TO DO THIS?
GIRL, WITH YOUR HAIR, PROBABLY LIKE EVERY DAY.
AND HE WAS RIGHT. IT WAS EVERY DAY.

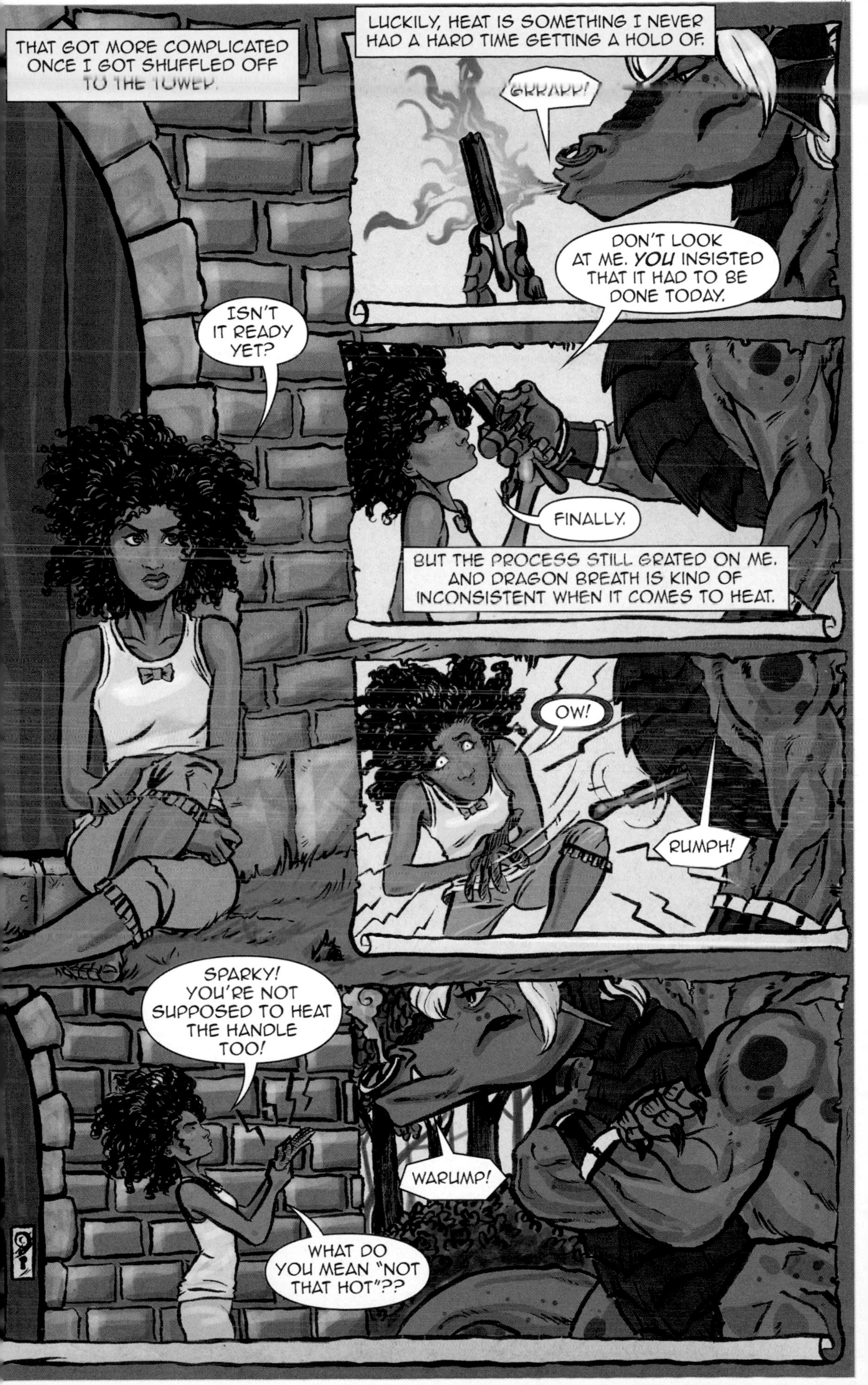
THAT GOT MORE COMPLICATED ONCE I GOT SHUFFLED OFF TO THE TOWER.
LUCKILY, HEAT IS SOMETHING I NEVER HAD A HARD TIME GETTING A HOLD OF.
GRRAPP!
ISN'T IT READY YET?
DON'T LOOK AT ME. *YOU* INSISTED THAT IT HAD TO BE DONE TODAY.
FINALLY.
BUT THE PROCESS STILL GRATED ON ME. AND DRAGON BREATH IS KIND OF INCONSISTENT WHEN IT COMES TO HEAT.
OW!
RUMPH!
SPARKY! YOU'RE NOT SUPPOSED TO HEAT THE HANDLE TOO!
WARUMP!
WHAT DO YOU MEAN "NOT THAT HOT"??

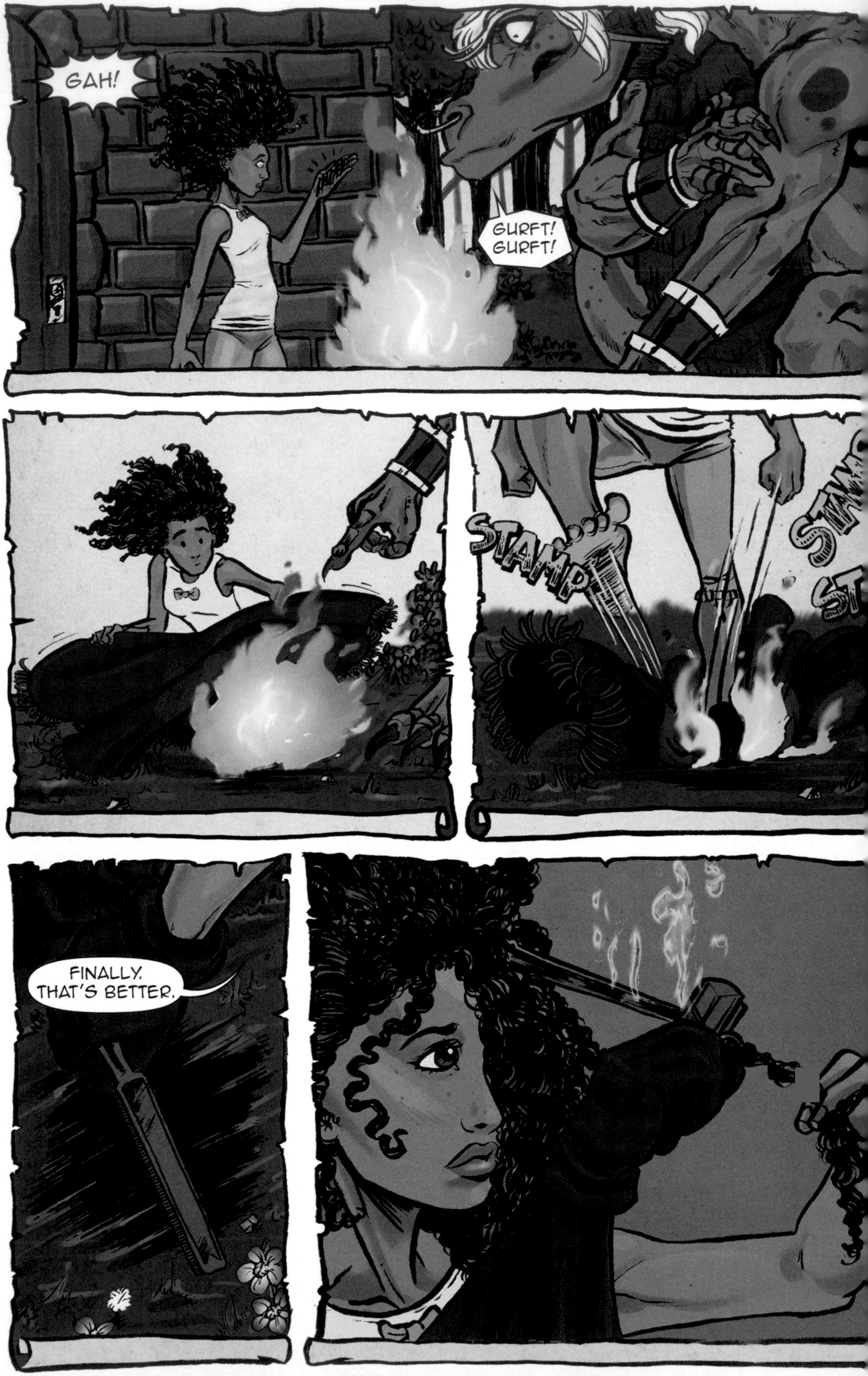
GAH!
GURFT! GURFT!
STAMP
FINALLY. THAT'S BETTER.

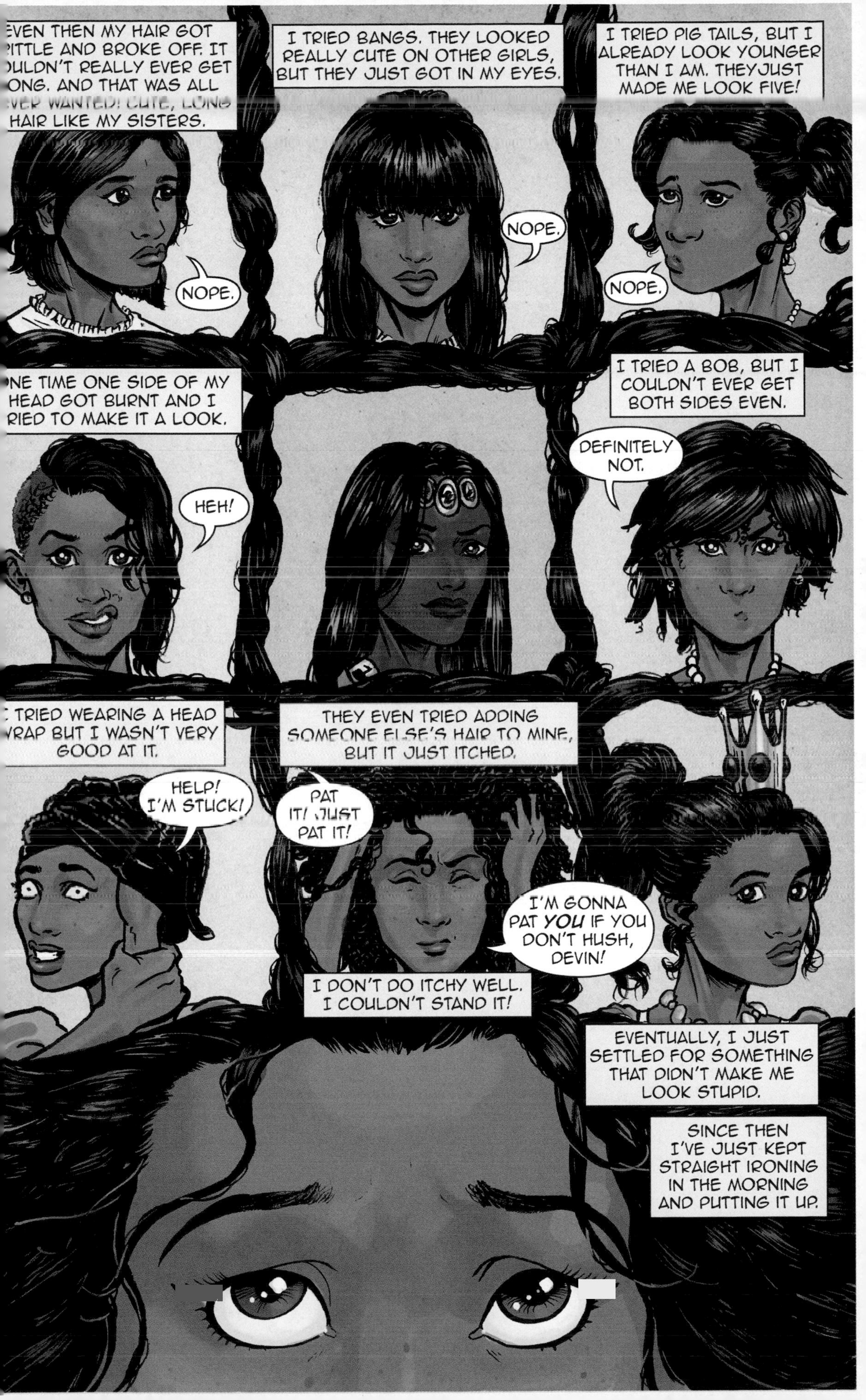
EVEN THEN MY HAIR GOT ITTLE AND BROKE OFF. IT OULDN'T REALLY EVER GET ONG. AND THAT WAS ALL EVER WANTED! CUTE, LONG HAIR LIKE MY SISTERS.
NOPE.
I TRIED BANGS. THEY LOOKED REALLY CUTE ON OTHER GIRLS, BUT THEY JUST GOT IN MY EYES.
NOPE.
I TRIED PIG TAILS, BUT I ALREADY LOOK YOUNGER THAN I AM. THEYJUST MADE ME LOOK FIVE!
NOPE.
NE TIME ONE SIDE OF MY HEAD GOT BURNT AND I RIED TO MAKE IT A LOOK.
HEH!
I TRIED A BOB, BUT I COULDN'T EVER GET BOTH SIDES EVEN.
DEFINITELY NOT.
TRIED WEARING A HEAD RAP BUT I WASN'T VERY GOOD AT IT.
HELP! I'M STUCK!
THEY EVEN TRIED ADDING SOMEONE ELSE'S HAIR TO MINE, BUT IT JUST ITCHED.
PAT IT! JUST PAT IT!
I'M GONNA PAT YOU IF YOU DON'T HUSH, DEVIN!
I DON'T DO ITCHY WELL. I COULDN'T STAND IT!
EVENTUALLY, I JUST SETTLED FOR SOMETHING THAT DIDN'T MAKE ME LOOK STUPID.
SINCE THEN I'VE JUST KEPT STRAIGHT IRONING IN THE MORNING AND PUTTING IT UP.

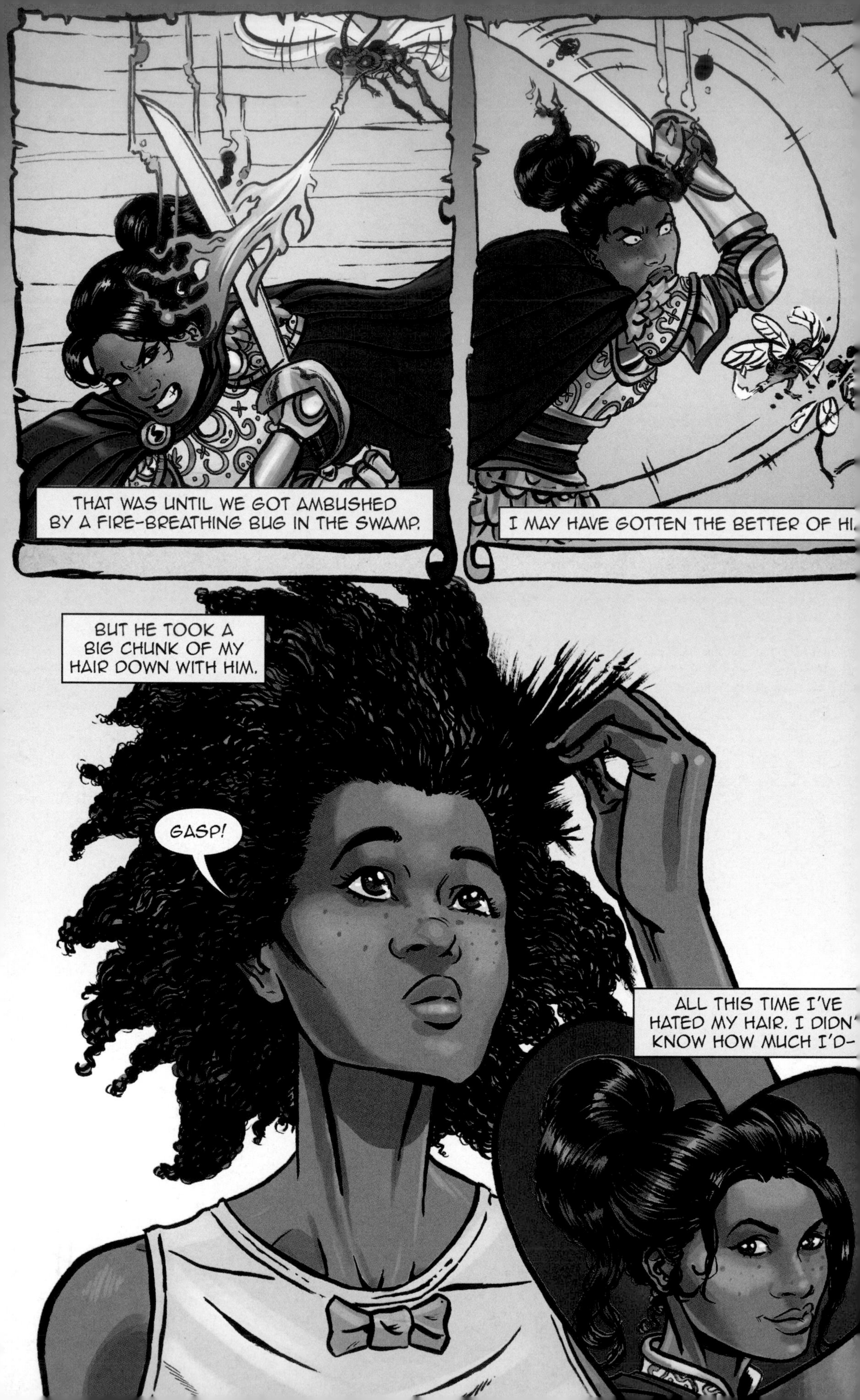
THAT WAS UNTIL WE GOT AMBUSHED BY A FIRE-BREATHING BUG IN THE SWAMP.
I MAY HAVE GOTTEN THE BETTER OF HI
BUT HE TOOK A BIG CHUNK OF MY HAIR DOWN WITH HIM.
GASP!
ALL THIS TIME I'VE HATED MY HAIR. I DIDN' KNOW HOW MUCH I'D-

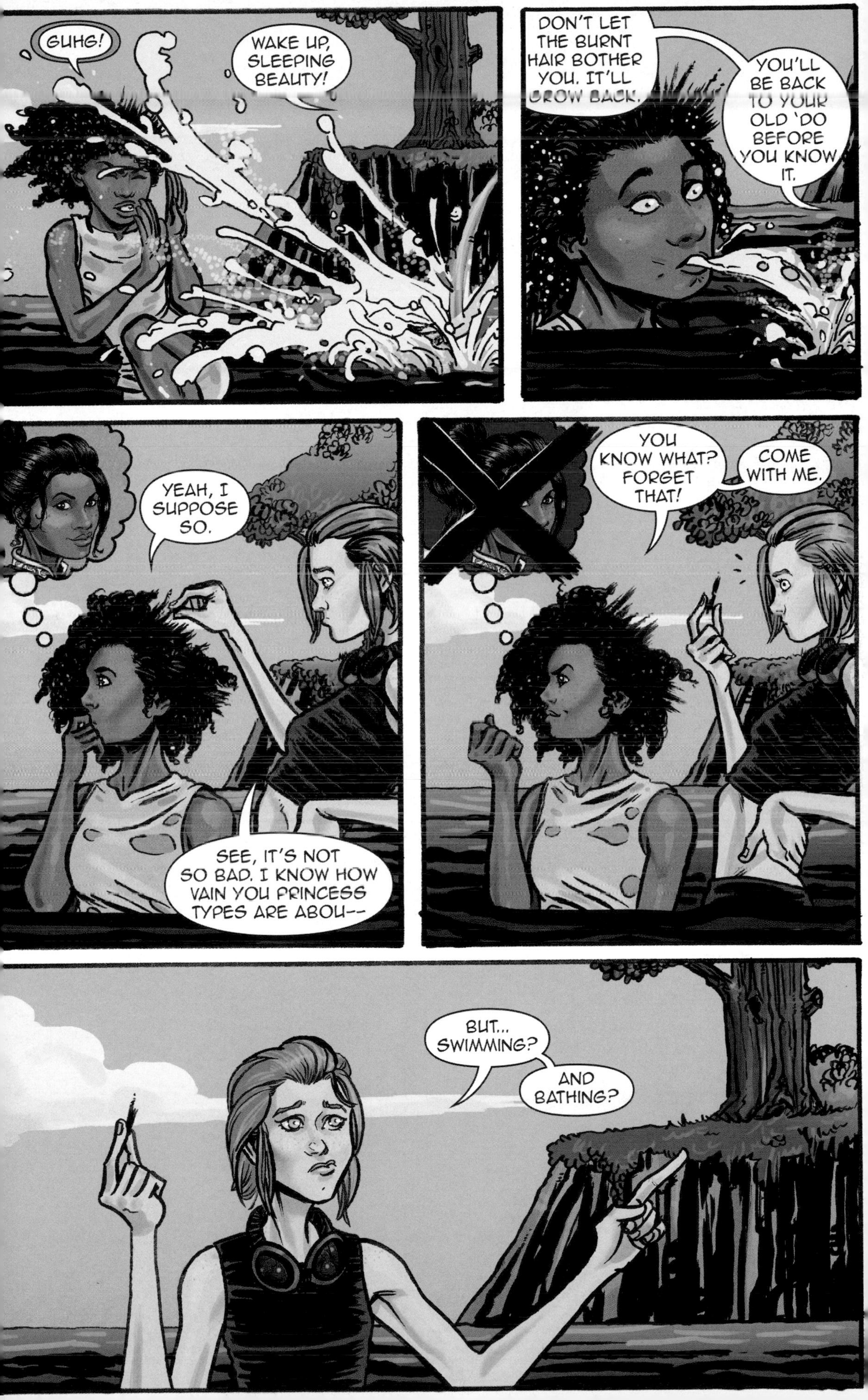
GUHG!
WAKE UP, SLEEPING BEAUTY!
DON'T LET THE BURNT HAIR BOTHER YOU. IT'LL GROW BACK.
YOU'LL BE BACK TO YOUR OLD 'DO BEFORE YOU KNOW IT.
YEAH, I SUPPOSE SO.
SEE, IT'S NOT SO BAD. I KNOW HOW VAIN YOU PRINCESS TYPES ARE ABOU--
YOU KNOW WHAT? FORGET THAT!
COME WITH ME.
BUT... SWIMMING?
AND BATHING?

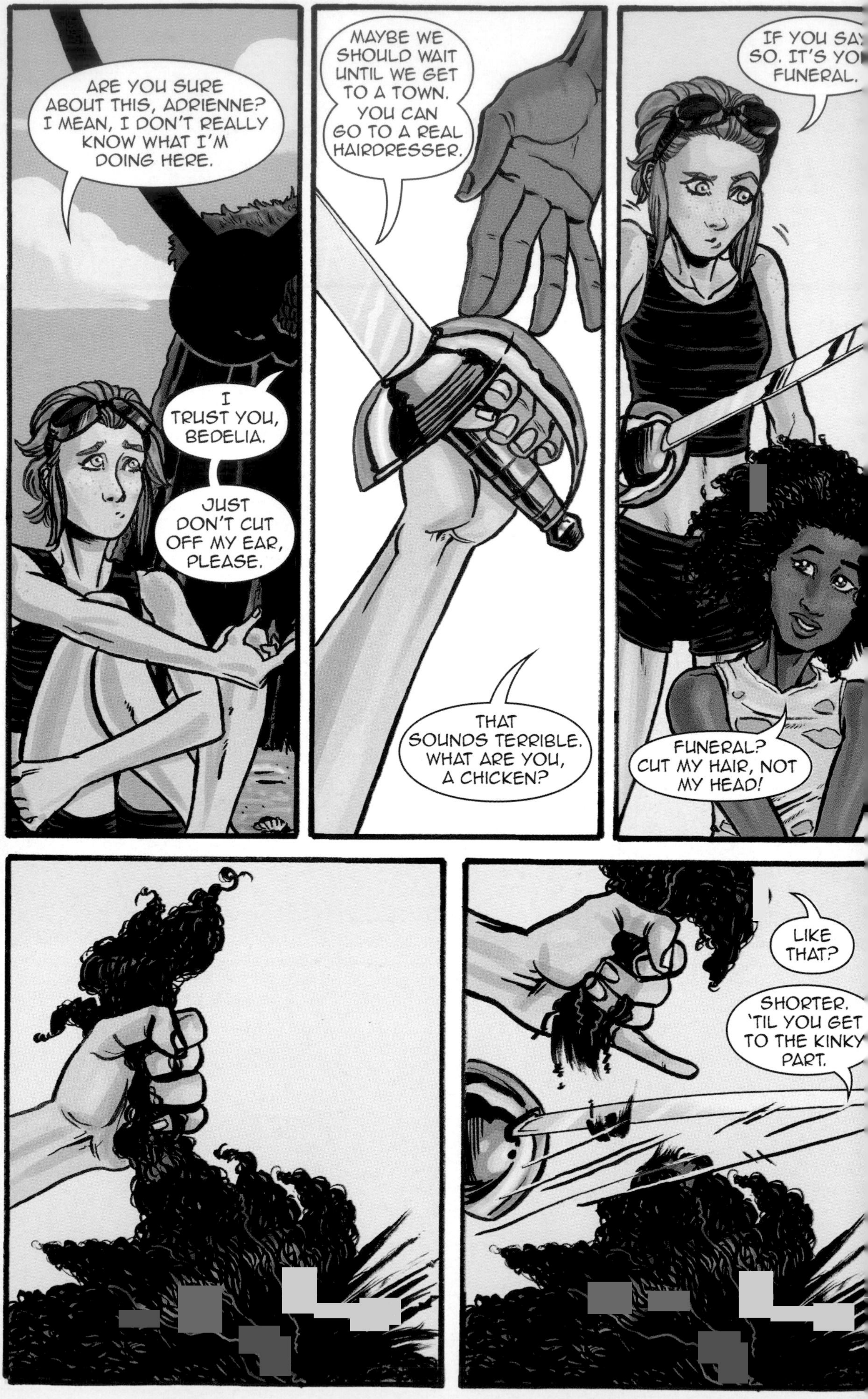
ARE YOU SURE ABOUT THIS, ADRIENNE? I MEAN, I DON'T REALLY KNOW WHAT I'M DOING HERE.
I TRUST YOU, BEDELIA.
JUST DON'T CUT OFF MY EAR, PLEASE.
MAYBE WE SHOULD WAIT UNTIL WE GET TO A TOWN. YOU CAN GO TO A REAL HAIRDRESSER.
THAT SOUNDS TERRIBLE. WHAT ARE YOU, A CHICKEN?
IF YOU SA
SO. IT'S YO
FUNERAL.
FUNERAL? CUT MY HAIR, NOT MY HEAD!
LIKE THAT?
SHORTER. 'TIL YOU GET TO THE KINKY PART.

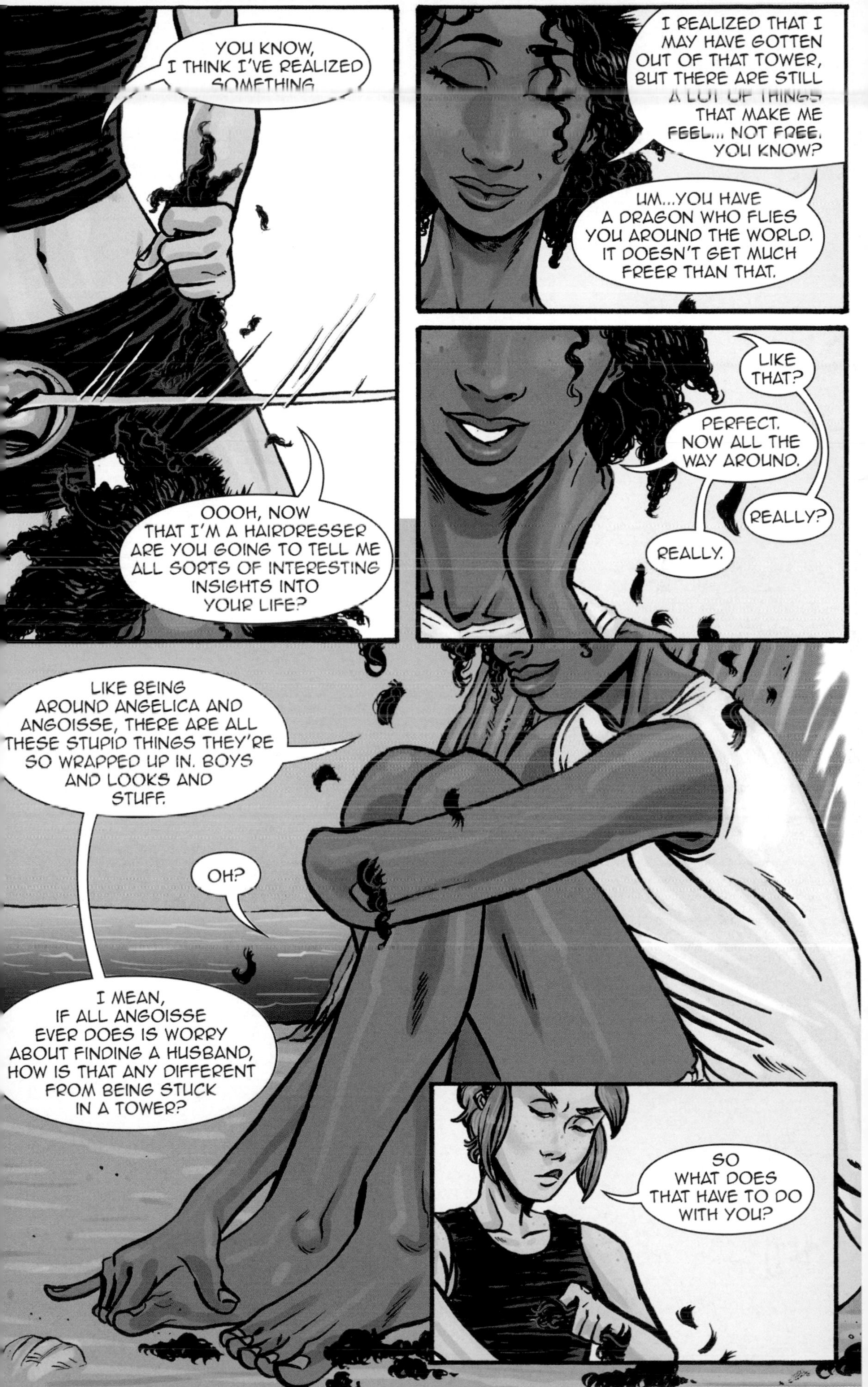
YOU KNOW, I THINK I'VE REALIZED SOMETHING.
OOOH, NOW THAT I'M A HAIRDRESSER ARE YOU GOING TO TELL ME ALL SORTS OF INTERESTING INSIGHTS INTO YOUR LIFE?
I REALIZED THAT I MAY HAVE GOTTEN OUT OF THAT TOWER, BUT THERE ARE STILL A LOT OF THINGS THAT MAKE ME FEEL... NOT FREE. YOU KNOW?
UM...YOU HAVE A DRAGON WHO FLIES YOU AROUND THE WORLD. IT DOESN'T GET MUCH FREER THAN THAT.
LIKE THAT?
PERFECT. NOW ALL THE WAY AROUND.
REALLY?
REALLY.
LIKE BEING AROUND ANGELICA AND ANGOISSE, THERE ARE ALL THESE STUPID THINGS THEY'RE SO WRAPPED UP IN. BOYS AND LOOKS AND STUFF.
OH?
I MEAN, IF ALL ANGOISSE EVER DOES IS WORRY ABOUT FINDING A HUSBAND, HOW IS THAT ANY DIFFERENT FROM BEING STUCK IN A TOWER?
SO WHAT DOES THAT HAVE TO DO WITH YOU?

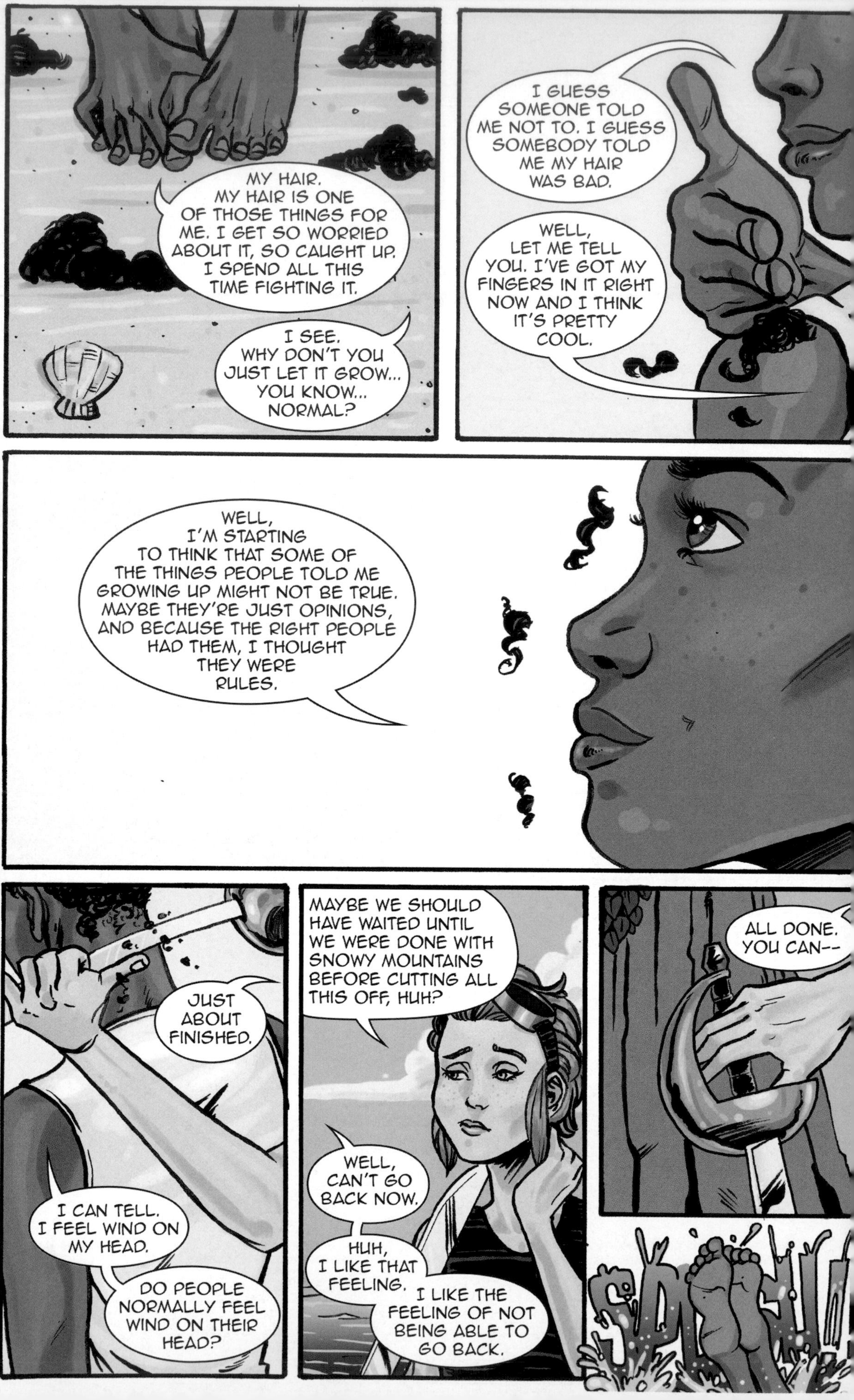
MY HAIR. MY HAIR IS ONE OF THOSE THINGS FOR ME. I GET SO WORRIED ABOUT IT, SO CAUGHT UP. I SPEND ALL THIS TIME FIGHTING IT.
I SEE. WHY DON'T YOU JUST LET IT GROW... YOU KNOW... NORMAL?
I GUESS SOMEONE TOLD ME NOT TO. I GUESS SOMEBODY TOLD ME MY HAIR WAS BAD.
WELL, LET ME TELL YOU. I'VE GOT MY FINGERS IN IT RIGHT NOW AND I THINK IT'S PRETTY COOL.
WELL, I'M STARTING TO THINK THAT SOME OF THE THINGS PEOPLE TOLD ME GROWING UP MIGHT NOT BE TRUE. MAYBE THEY'RE JUST OPINIONS, AND BECAUSE THE RIGHT PEOPLE HAD THEM, I THOUGHT THEY WERE RULES.
JUST ABOUT FINISHED.
I CAN TELL. I FEEL WIND ON MY HEAD.
DO PEOPLE NORMALLY FEEL WIND ON THEIR HEAD?
MAYBE WE SHOULD HAVE WAITED UNTIL WE WERE DONE WITH SNOWY MOUNTAINS BEFORE CUTTING ALL THIS OFF, HUH?
WELL, CAN'T GO BACK NOW.
HUH, I LIKE THAT FEELING.
I LIKE THE FEELING OF NOT BEING ABLE TO GO BACK.
ALL DONE. YOU CAN--

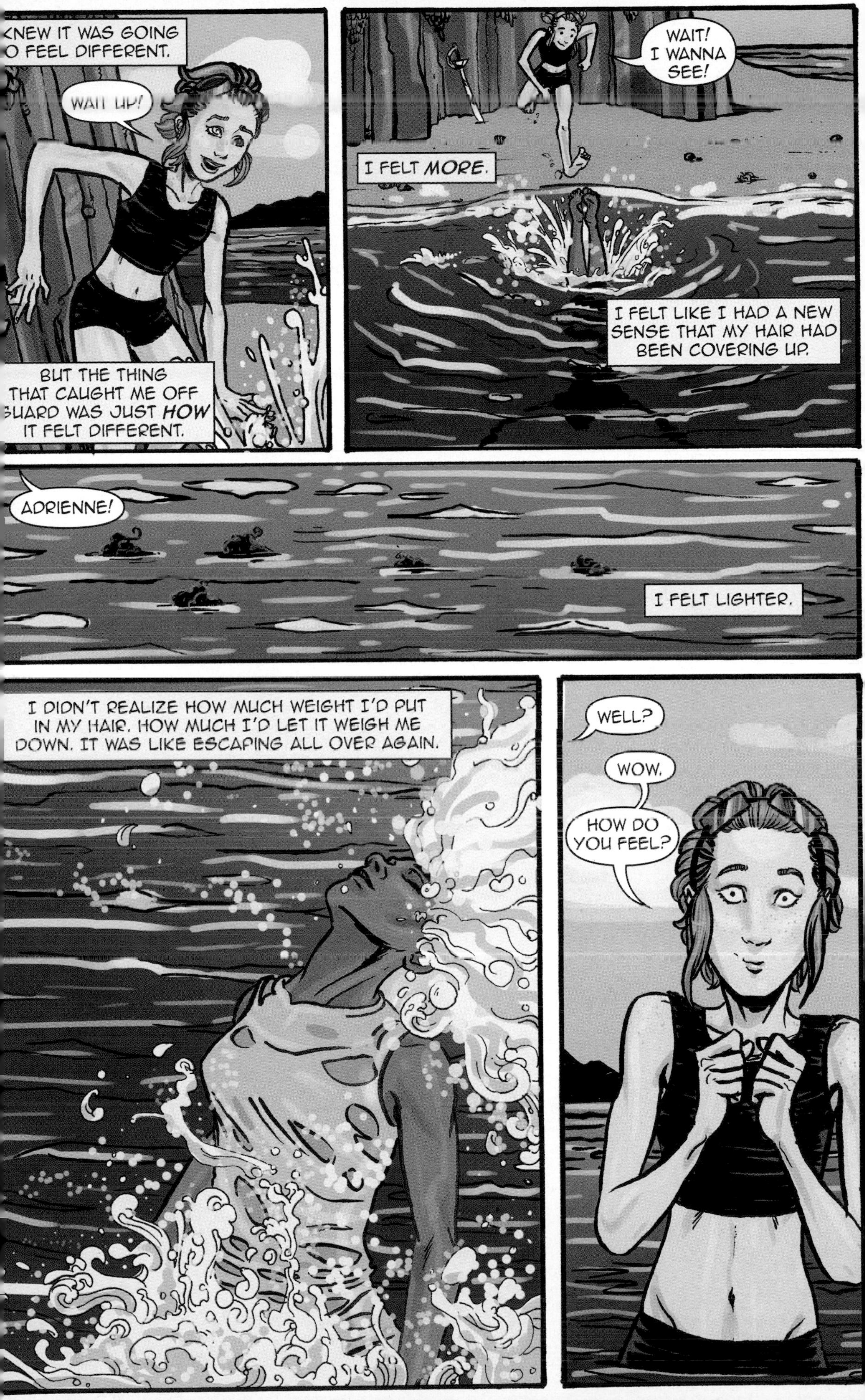
KNEW IT WAS GOING
O FEEL DIFFERENT.
WAIT UP!
BUT THE THING THAT CAUGHT ME OFF GUARD WAS JUST *HOW* IT FELT DIFFERENT.
WAIT! I WANNA SEE!
I FELT *MORE*.
I FELT LIKE I HAD A NEW SENSE THAT MY HAIR HAD BEEN COVERING UP.
ADRIENNE!
I FELT LIGHTER.
I DIDN'T REALIZE HOW MUCH WEIGHT I'D PUT IN MY HAIR. HOW MUCH I'D LET IT WEIGH ME DOWN. IT WAS LIKE ESCAPING ALL OVER AGAIN.
WELL?
WOW.
HOW DO YOU FEEL?

Written by Jeremy Whitley   Illustrated by Alex Smith   Lettered by Emily Spura

Bryan Seaton: Publisher • Kevin Freeman: President • Dave Dwonch: Creative Director • Shawn Gabborin: Editor In Chief
Jamal Igle: Vice-President of Marketing • Vito Delsante: Director of Marketing • Jim Dietz: Social Media Director
Nicole DAndria: Script Editor • Chad Cicconi: Black Sheep • Colleen Boyd: Submissions Editor

PRINCELESS: MAKE YOURSELF #0, December 2015. Copyright Jeremy Whitley, 2015. Published by Action Lab Comics. All rights reserved. All characters are fictional. Any likeness to anyone li
or dead is purely coincidental. No part of this publication may be reproduced or transmitted without permission, except for small excerpts for review purposes. First Printing. Printed in Can

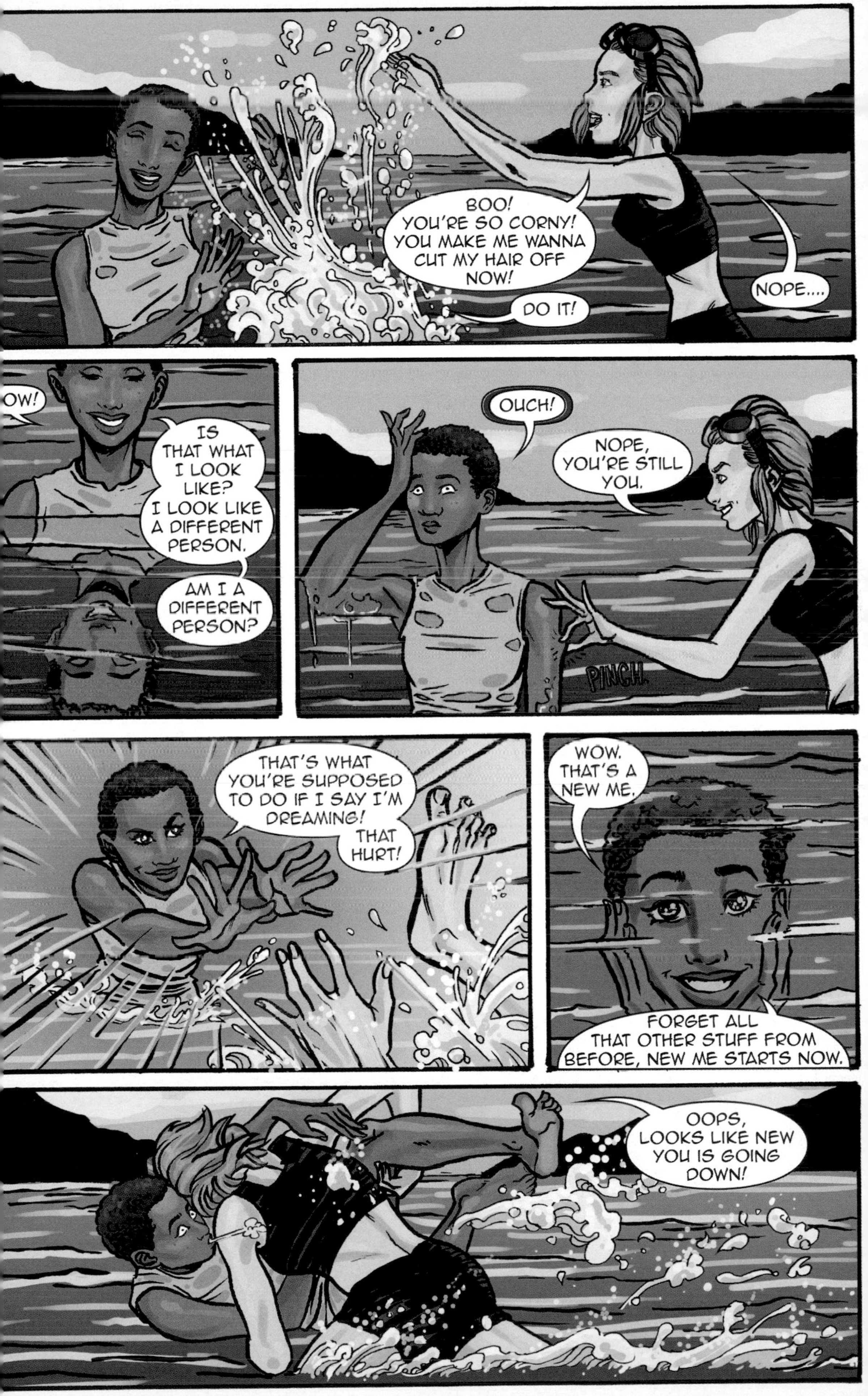
BOO! YOU'RE SO CORNY! YOU MAKE ME WANNA CUT MY HAIR OFF NOW!
DO IT!
NOPE....
OW!
IS THAT WHAT I LOOK LIKE? I LOOK LIKE A DIFFERENT PERSON.
AM I A DIFFERENT PERSON?
OUCH!
NOPE, YOU'RE STILL YOU.
PINCH
THAT'S WHAT YOU'RE SUPPOSED TO DO IF I SAY I'M DREAMING!
THAT HURT!
WOW. THAT'S A NEW ME.
FORGET ALL THAT OTHER STUFF FROM BEFORE, NEW ME STARTS NOW.
OOPS, LOOKS LIKE NEW YOU IS GOING DOWN!

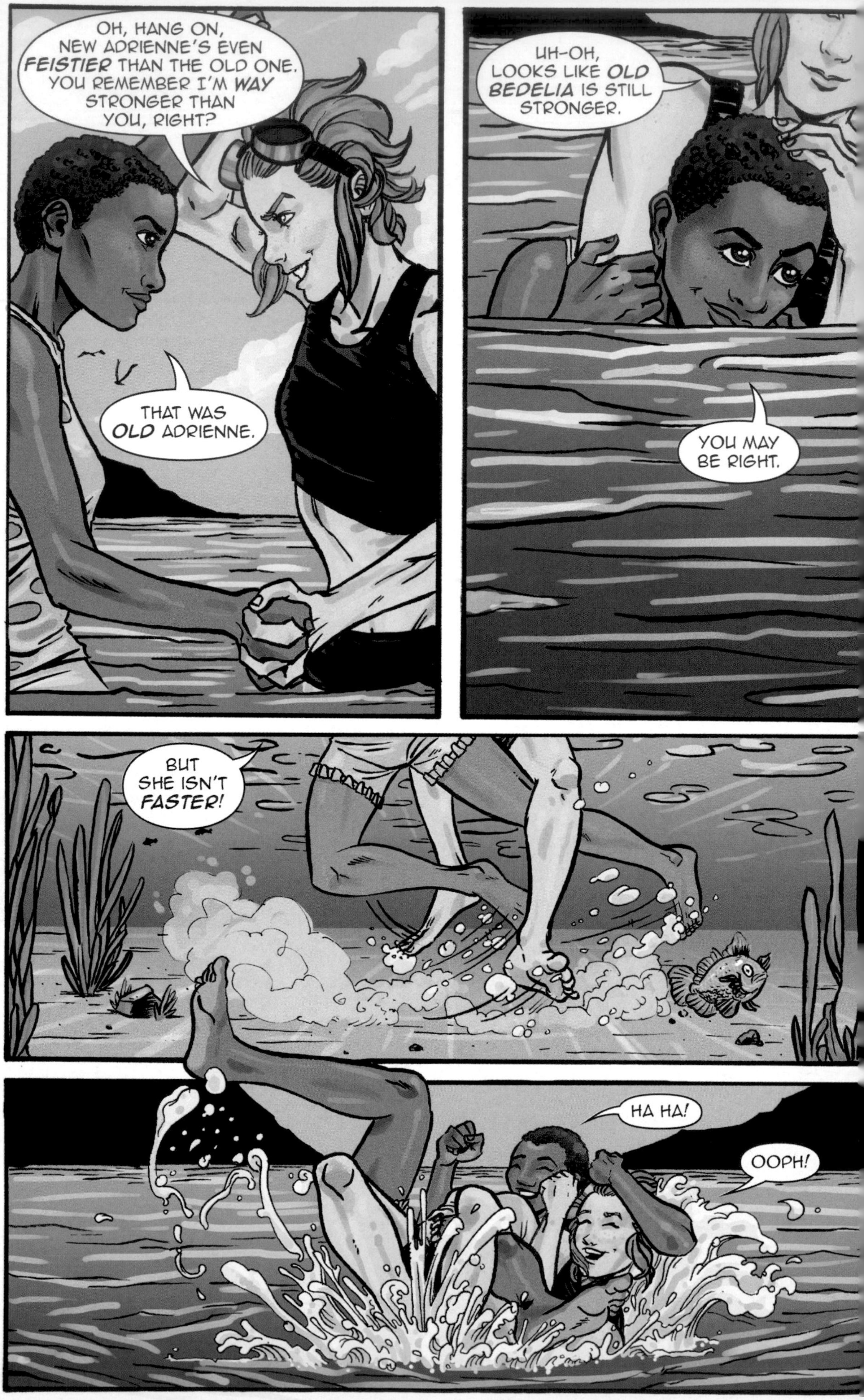
OH, HANG ON, NEW ADRIENNE'S EVEN FEISTIER THAN THE OLD ONE. YOU REMEMBER I'M WAY STRONGER THAN YOU, RIGHT?
THAT WAS OLD ADRIENNE.
UH-OH, LOOKS LIKE OLD BEDELIA IS STILL STRONGER.
YOU MAY BE RIGHT.
BUT SHE ISN'T FASTER!
HA HA!
OOPH!

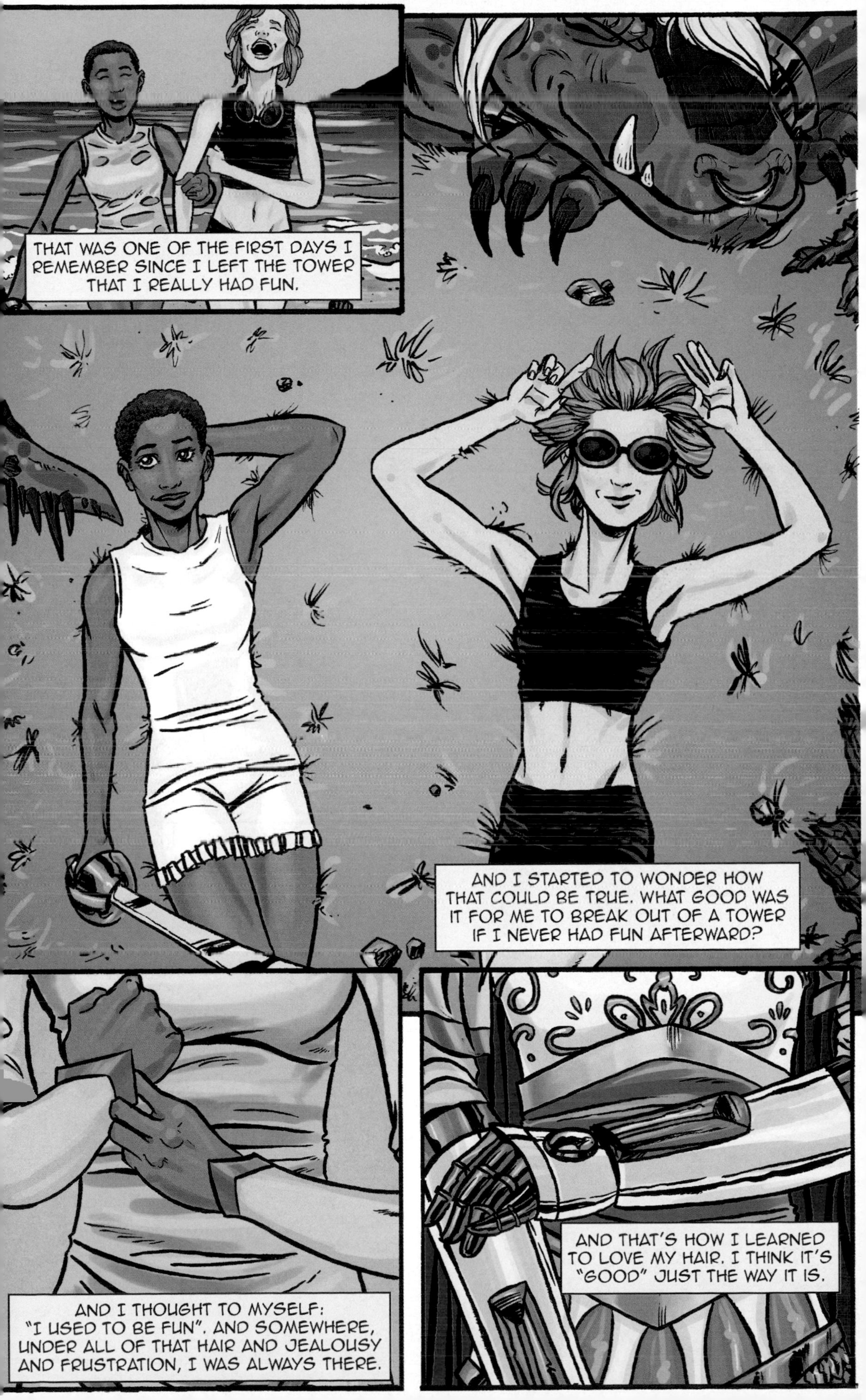
THAT WAS ONE OF THE FIRST DAYS I REMEMBER SINCE I LEFT THE TOWER THAT I REALLY HAD FUN.
AND I STARTED TO WONDER HOW THAT COULD BE TRUE. WHAT GOOD WAS IT FOR ME TO BREAK OUT OF A TOWER IF I NEVER HAD FUN AFTERWARD?
AND I THOUGHT TO MYSELF: "I USED TO BE FUN". AND SOMEWHERE, UNDER ALL OF THAT HAIR AND JEALOUSY AND FRUSTRATION, I WAS ALWAYS THERE.
AND THAT'S HOW I LEARNED TO LOVE MY HAIR. I THINK IT'S "GOOD" JUST THE WAY IT IS.

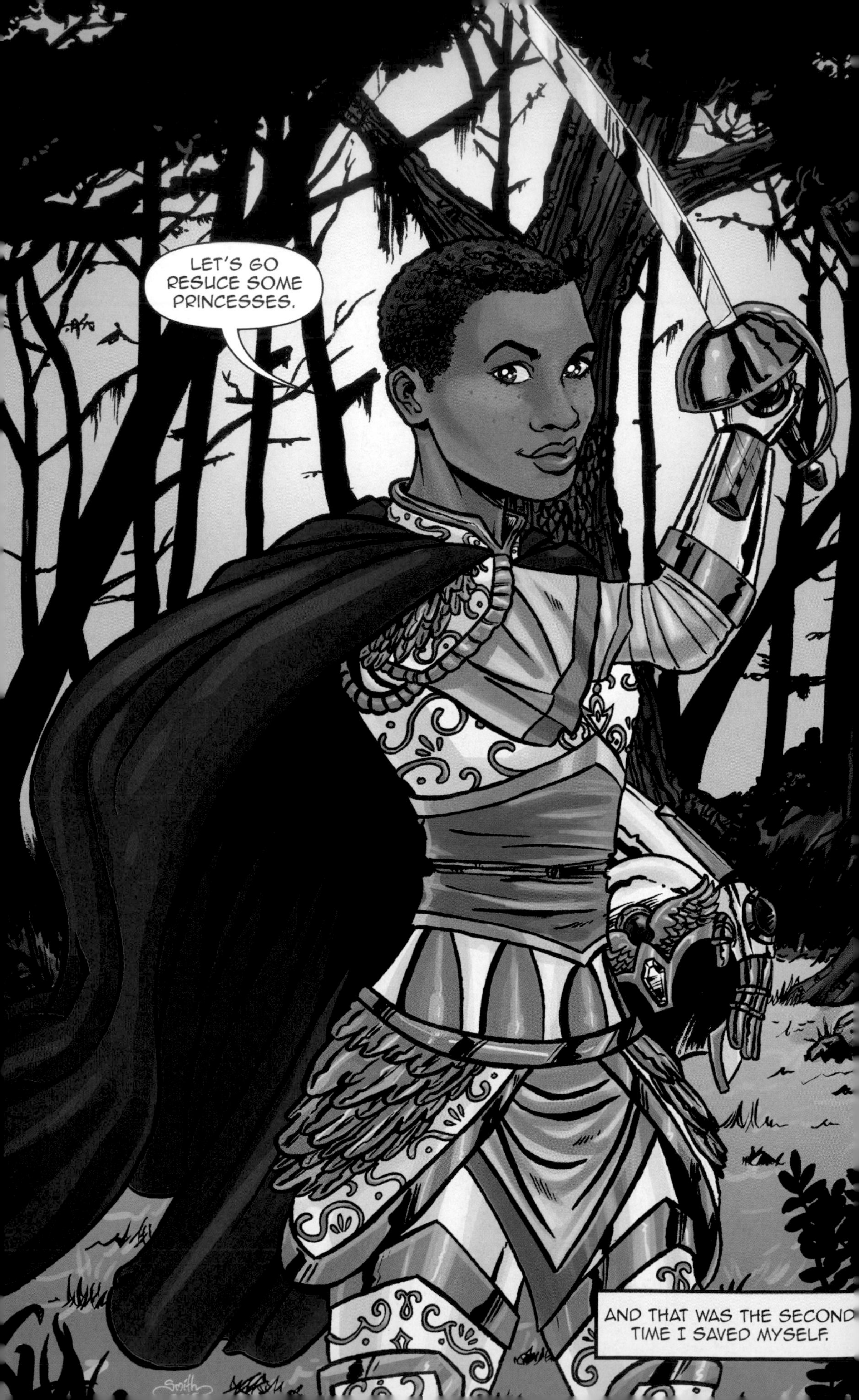
LET'S GO RESUCE SOME PRINCESSES.
AND THAT WAS THE SECOND TIME I SAVED MYSELF.

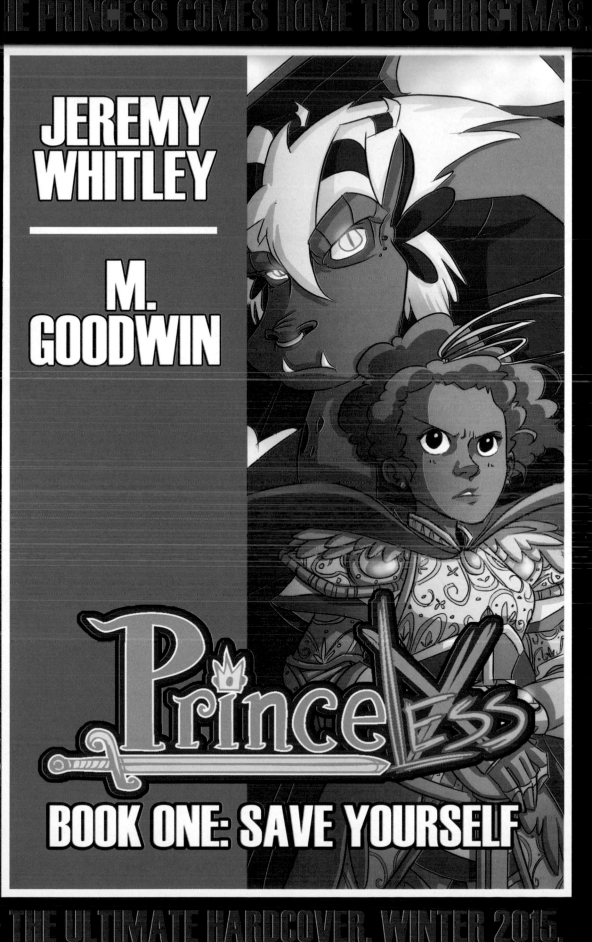

ACTION LAB

JEREMY WHITLEY & EMILY MARTIN
AWARD WINNING SERIES CONTINU[ES]

Prince*less*

VOLUME 4: BE YOURSELF

AVAILABLE IN FINER STORES EVERYWHE[RE]

Angoisse Ashe, the oft-forgotten middle sister of the Ashe royal family, is locked in a castle deep in the swamp. Not only is her castle guarded by zombies, but the swamp is full of dangerous hazards. Everything from quicksand to goblins to swamp monsters to... VAMPIRES! But does that give Adrienne pause? Unfortunately not, as she and Bedelia dive head-first into their most dangerous adventure yet!

FROM SUSAN BENEVILLE & BRIAN HESS

awake

AVAILABLE IN FINER STORES EVERYWHERE

Twelve year-old Regn has the power to wake and heal planets. But, on her first mission, she lands on Gremon where she discovers an angry planet tearing itself apart, an irresponsible big brother, and a greedy baron who stokes the chaos for his own benefit. Her power may not be enough when she comes face-to-face with the planet's consciousness.

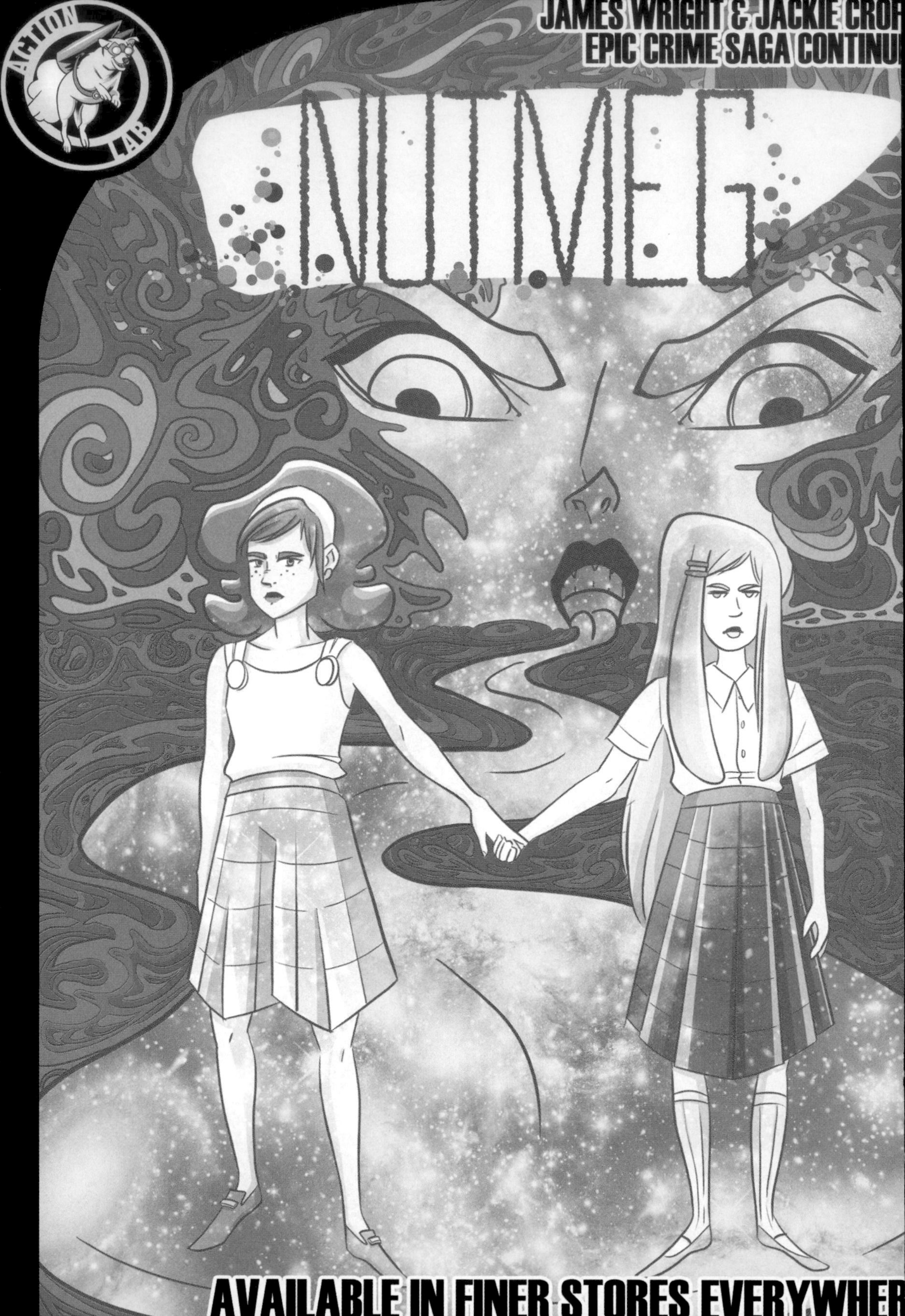
ACTION LAB
JAMES WRIGHT & JACKIE CROF
EPIC CRIME SAGA CONTINU
NUTMEG
AVAILABLE IN FINER STORES EVERYWHER

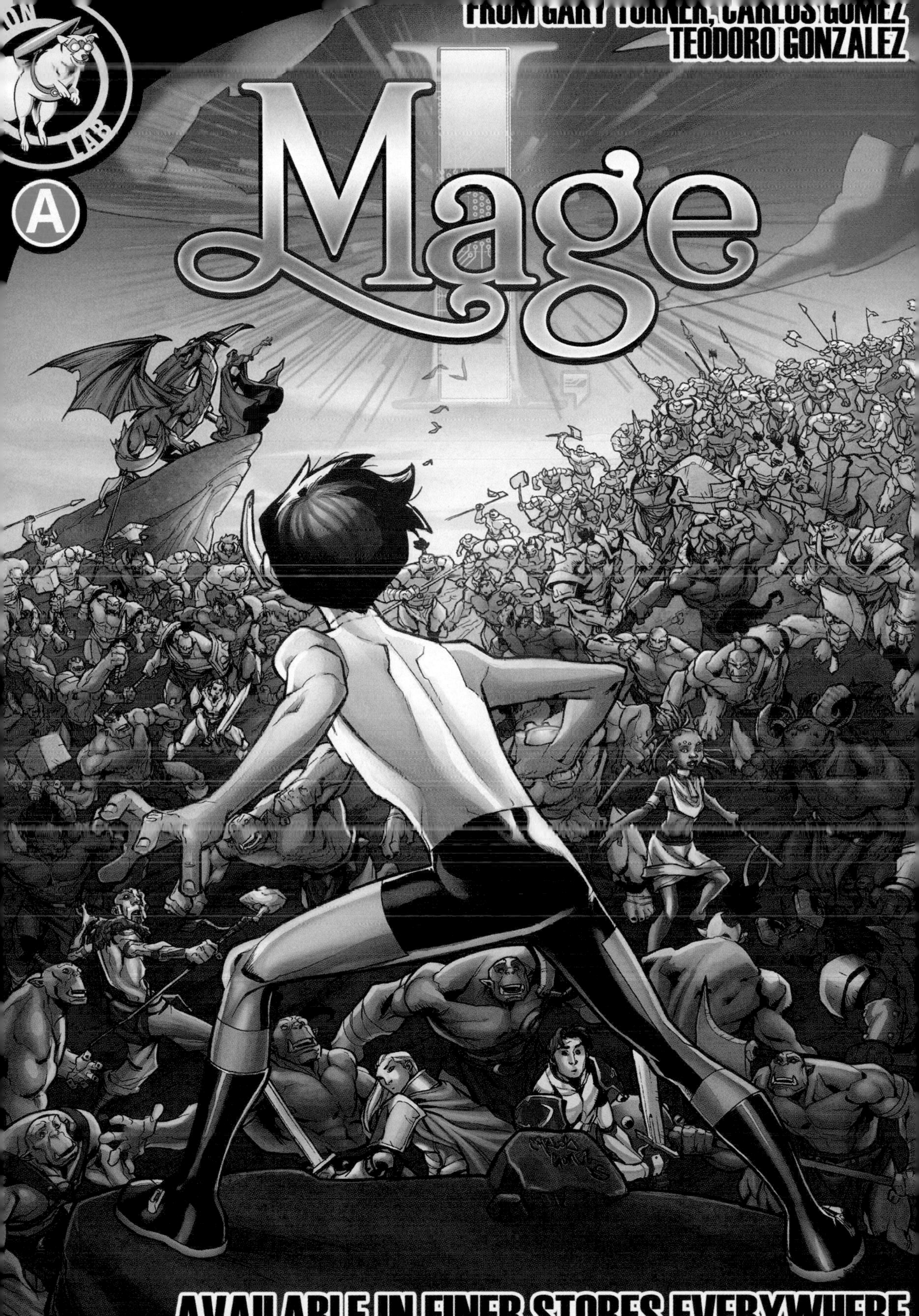

FROM GARY TURNER, CARLOS GOMEZ
TEODORO GONZALEZ

Mage

AVAILABLE IN FINER STORES EVERYWHERE

Kai and his family are on with a scientific mission to study a primitive world of magic when an unforeseen accident devastates their vessel, leaving Kai separated from the rest of the crew. Now, with the protection of a loading dock robot, an apprentice magi and her quirky mentor, Kai must survive on a world very different from his own!

After the tragic events of last issue, Cyrus Perkins has gone from aimless Taxi Cab Driver to amateur Detective. Teaming with Michael, the ghost boy trapped in his car, Cyrus speeds into mystery, danger, and a conspiracy too twisted for words!

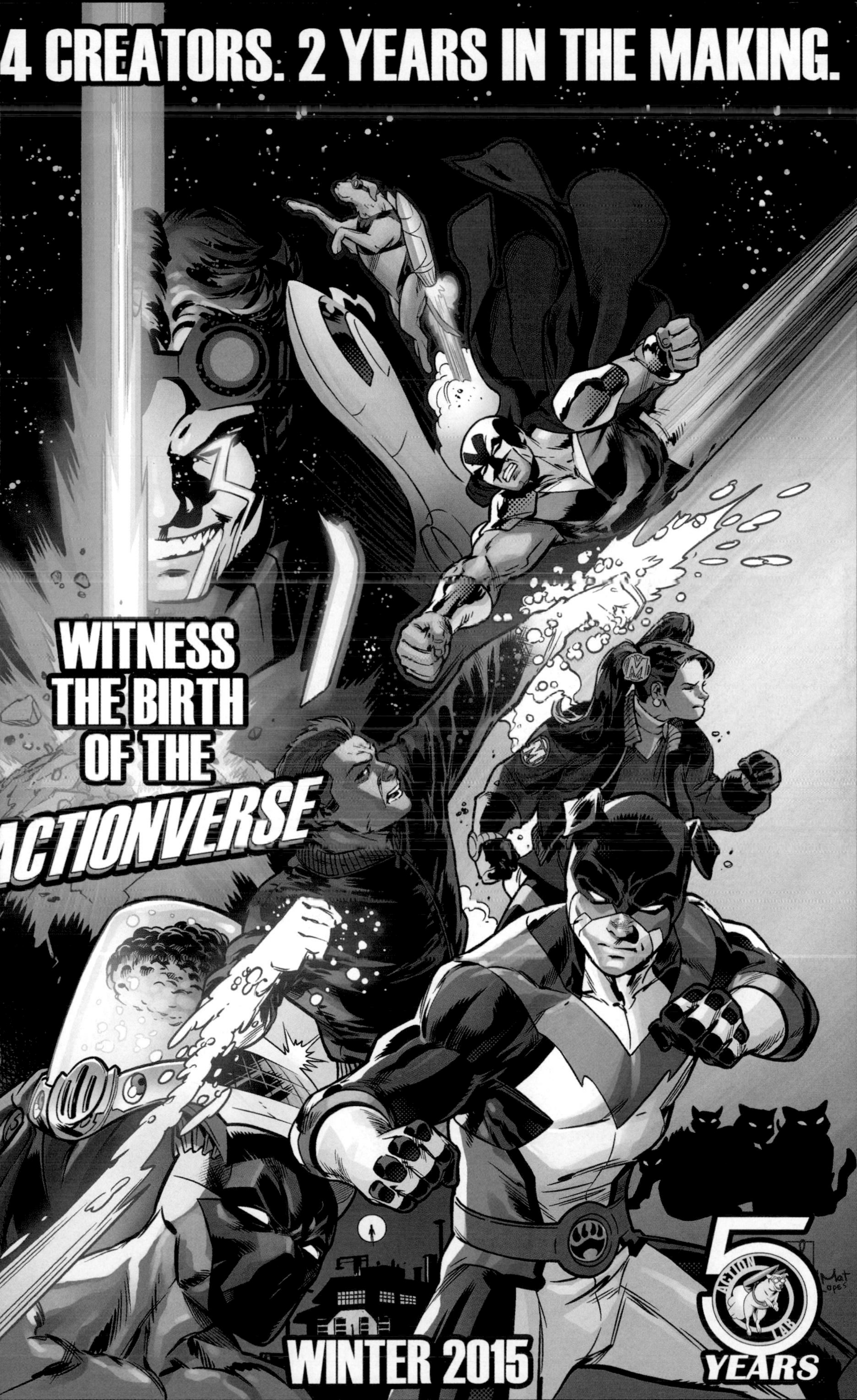
4 CREATORS. 2 YEARS IN THE MAKING.
WITNESS THE BIRTH OF THE ACTIONVERSE
WINTER 2015
5 YEARS
ACTION LAB

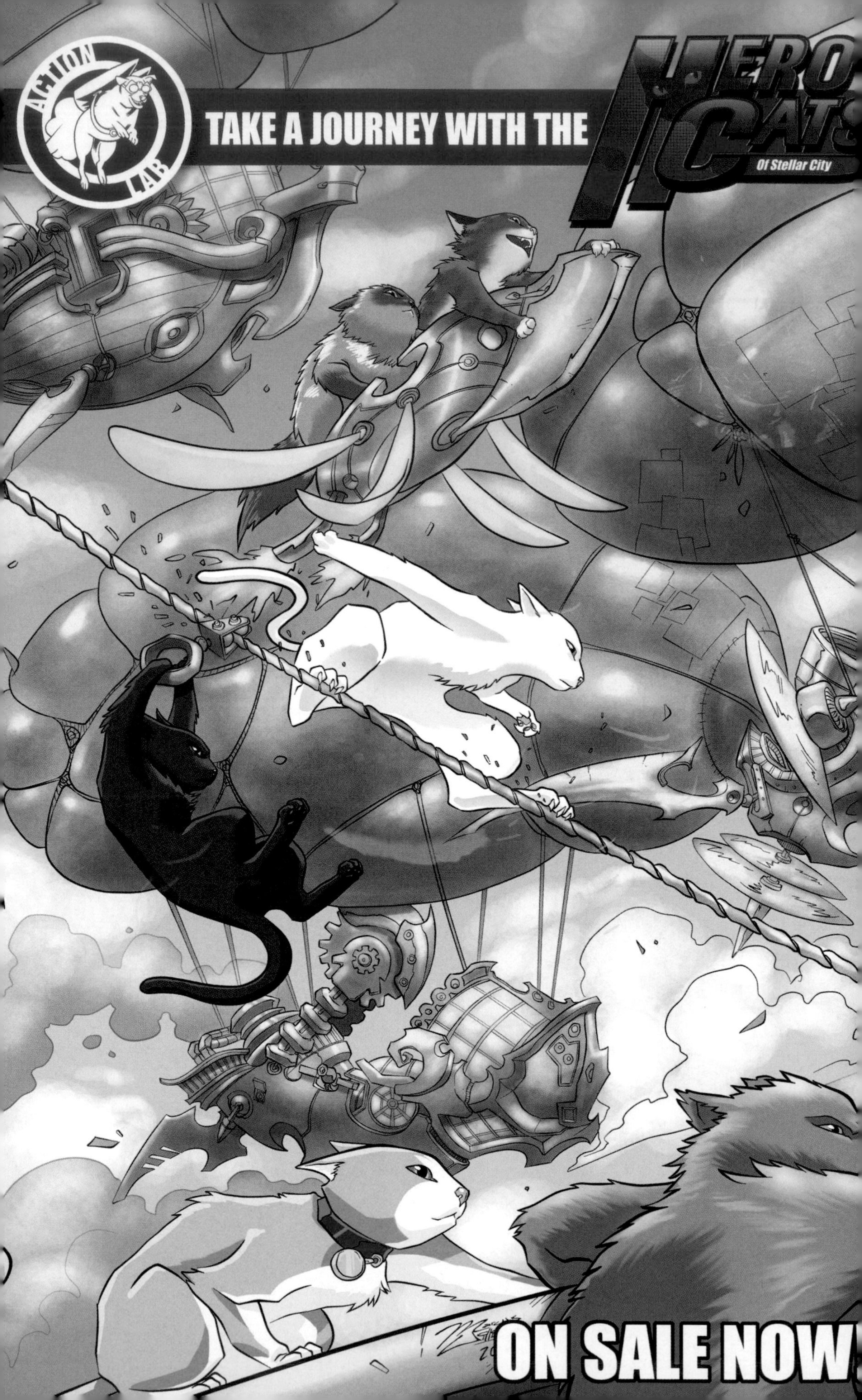
TAKE A JOURNEY WITH THE
HERO CATS
Of Stellar City
ON SALE NOW!

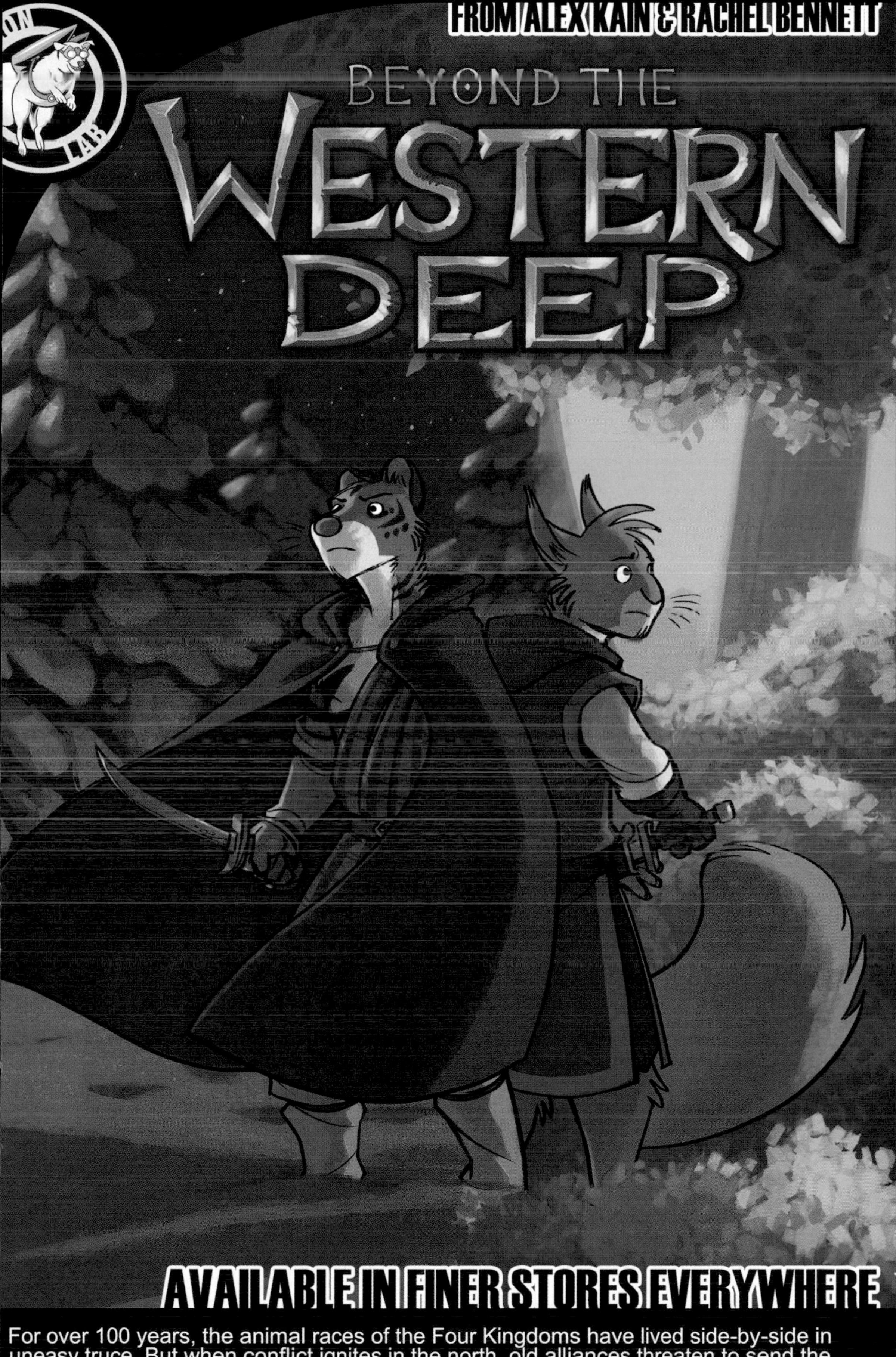
FROM ALEX KAIN & RACHEL BENNETT
LAB
BEYOND THE
WESTERN
DEEP
AVAILABLE IN FINER STORES EVERYWHERE

For over 100 years, the animal races of the Four Kingdoms have lived side-by-side in uneasy truce. But when conflict ignites in the north, old alliances threaten to send the world into chaos. Experience the beginnings of an epic all-ages fantasy in this first collected volume!

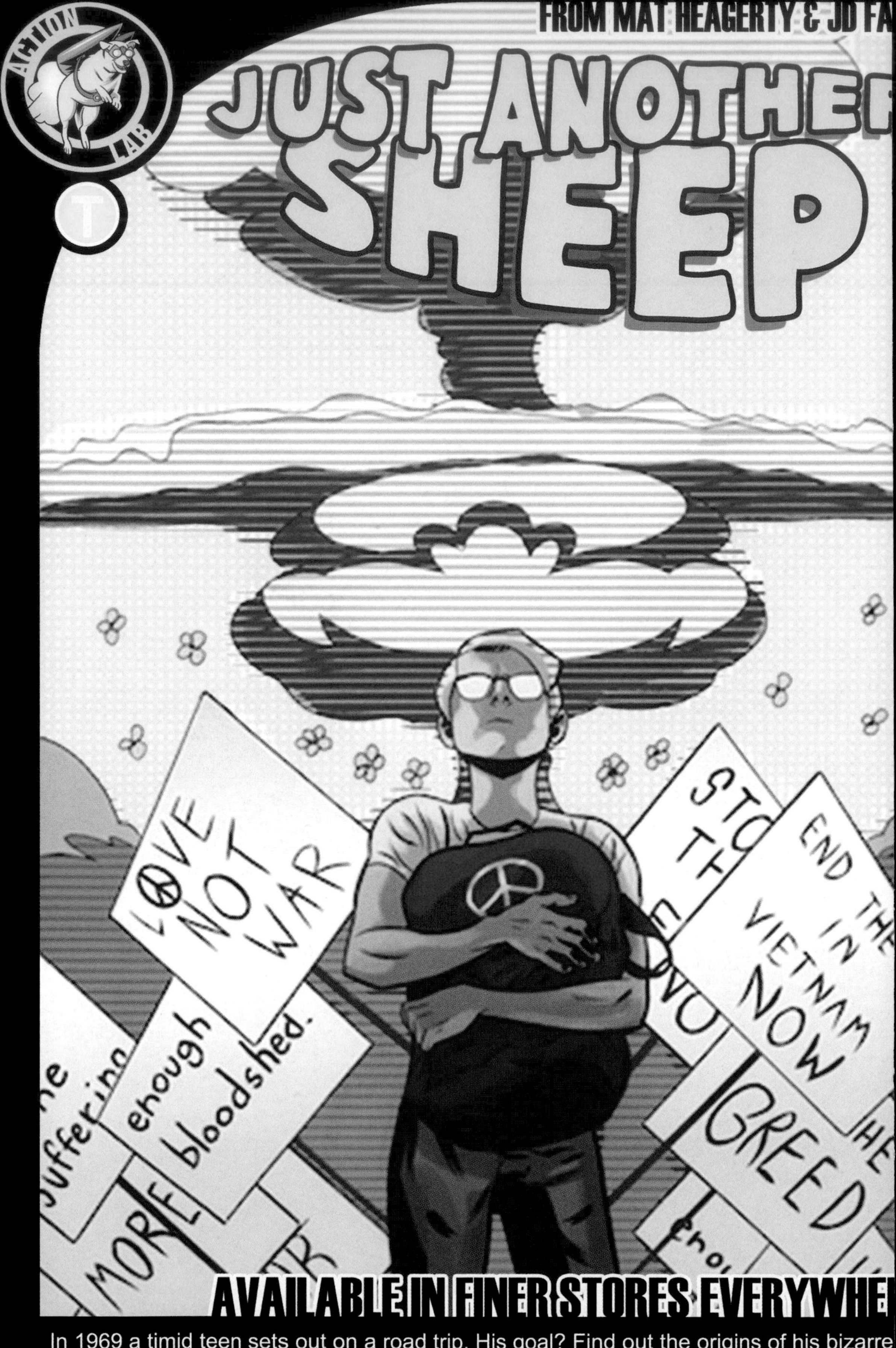

FROM MAT HEAGERTY & JD FA
JUST ANOTHE
SHEEP
LOVE NOT WAR
enough bloodshed.
suffering
MORE
STO
END THE IN VIETNAM NOW
GREED
AVAILABLE IN FINER STORES EVERYWHE

In 1969 a timid teen sets out on a road trip. His goal? Find out the origins of his bizarre super human abilities. Always the follower, his trip is derailed when he befriends a group of extremist war protesters.

ADAPTING THE EDGAR ALLAN POE CLASSIC!

THE CASK OF MONTIC:LLADO

AVAILABLE IN FINER STORES EVERYWHERE

"The thousand injuries of Fortunato I had borne as I best could, but when he ventured upon insult, I vowed revenge." A new adaptation of Edgar Allan Poe's most famous tale of wine, friendship and betrayal. Includes an exciting first look at pages from the upcoming sequel to the Poe classic, The House of Montresor!

READ MORE NOW

Princeless: Make Yourself - Action Lab
www.actionlabcomics.com

00011

7 02382 69115 8

ACTIONLABCOMICS.COM

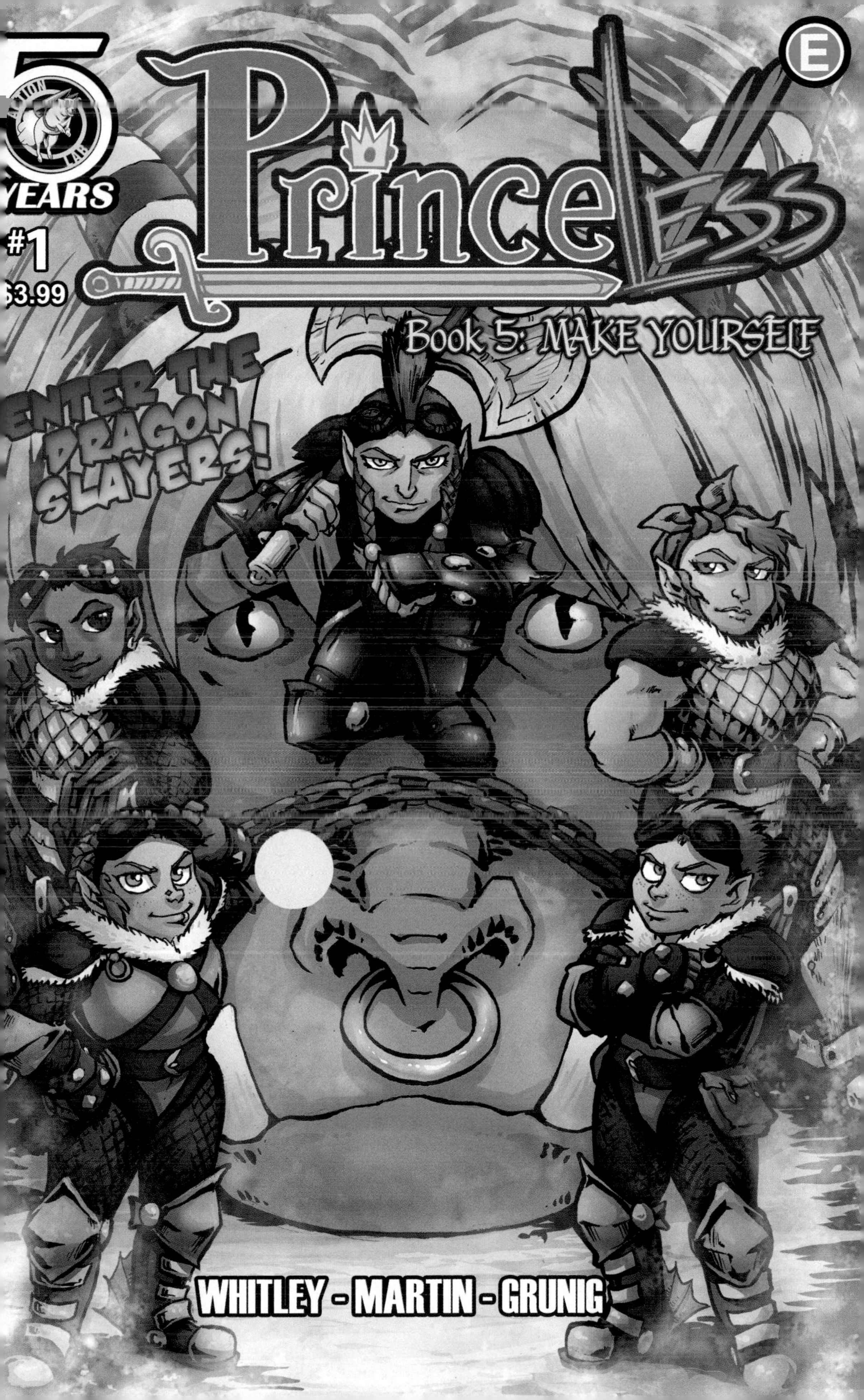
5 YEARS
ACTION LAB
#1
$3.99
E
Princeless
Book 5: MAKE YOURSELF
ENTER THE DRAGON SLAYERS!
WHITLEY - MARTIN - GRUNIG

FROM ALL-AGES TO MATURE READERS ACTION LAB HAS YOU COVERED.

 **Appropriate for everyone.**

 **Appropriate for age 9 and up. Absent of profanity or adult content.**

 **Suggested for 12 and Up. Comics with this rating are comparable to a PG-13 movie rating. Recommended for our teen and young adult readers.**

 **Appropriate for older teens. Similar to Teen, but featuring more mature themes and/or more graphic imagery.**

 **Contains extreme violence and some nudity. Basically the Rated-R of comics.**

 FIND YOUR NEW FAVORITE COMICS.

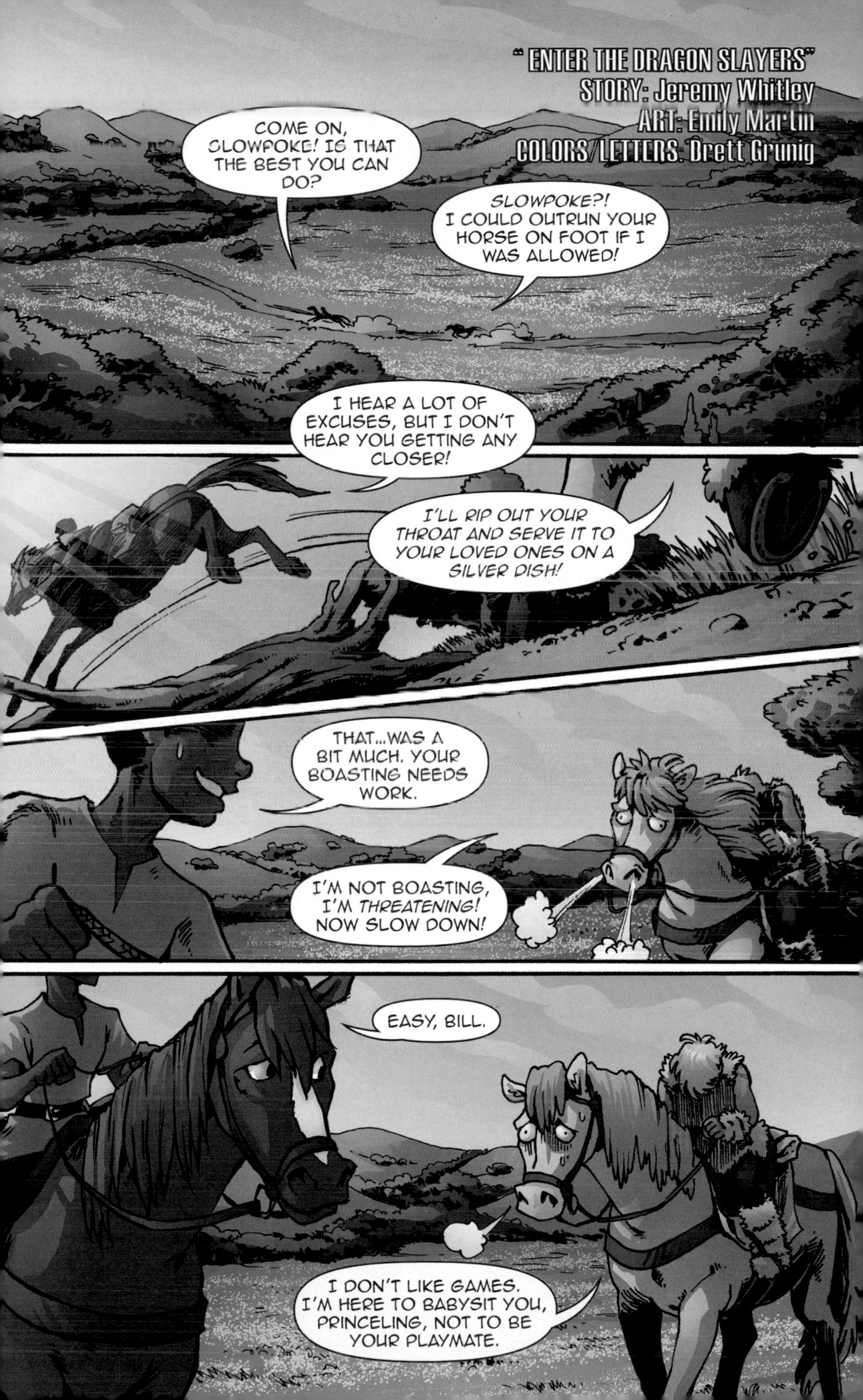
"ENTER THE DRAGON SLAYERS"
STORY: Jeremy Whitley
ART: Emily Martin
COLORS/LETTERS: Brett Grunig
COME ON, SLOWPOKE! IS THAT THE BEST YOU CAN DO?
SLOWPOKE?! I COULD OUTRUN YOUR HORSE ON FOOT IF I WAS ALLOWED!
I HEAR A LOT OF EXCUSES, BUT I DON'T HEAR YOU GETTING ANY CLOSER!
I'LL RIP OUT YOUR THROAT AND SERVE IT TO YOUR LOVED ONES ON A SILVER DISH!
THAT...WAS A BIT MUCH. YOUR BOASTING NEEDS WORK.
I'M NOT BOASTING, I'M THREATENING! NOW SLOW DOWN!
EASY, BILL.
I DON'T LIKE GAMES. I'M HERE TO BABYSIT YOU, PRINCELING, NOT TO BE YOUR PLAYMATE.

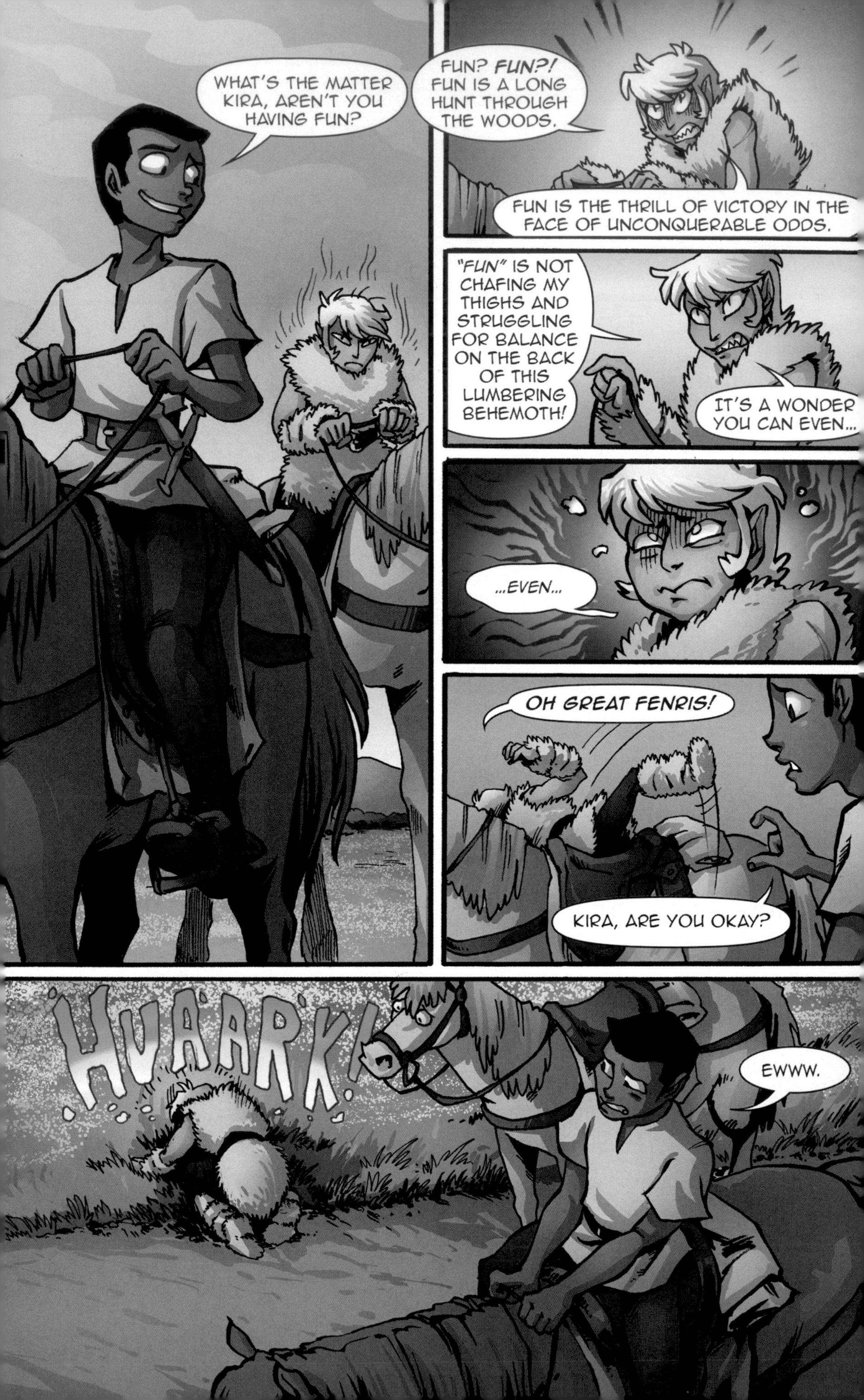
WHAT'S THE MATTER KIRA, AREN'T YOU HAVING FUN?
FUN? FUN?! FUN IS A LONG HUNT THROUGH THE WOODS.
FUN IS THE THRILL OF VICTORY IN THE FACE OF UNCONQUERABLE ODDS.
"FUN" IS NOT CHAFING MY THIGHS AND STRUGGLING FOR BALANCE ON THE BACK OF THIS LUMBERING BEHEMOTH!
IT'S A WONDER YOU CAN EVEN...
...EVEN...
OH GREAT FENRIS!
KIRA, ARE YOU OKAY?
HUAARK!
EWWW.

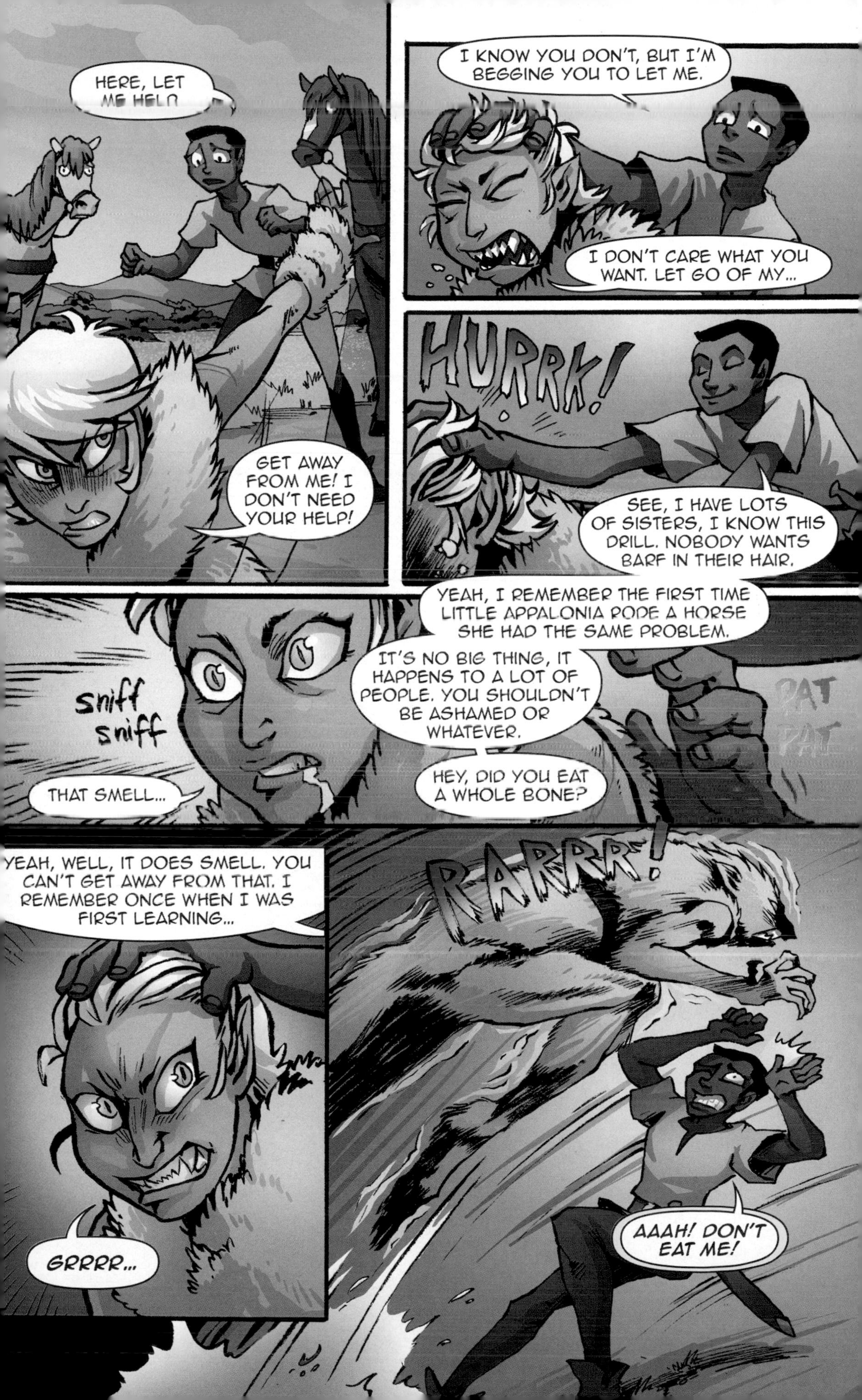
HERE, LET
GET AWAY FROM ME! I DON'T NEED YOUR HELP!
I KNOW YOU DON'T, BUT I'M BEGGING YOU TO LET ME.
I DON'T CARE WHAT YOU WANT. LET GO OF MY...
HURRK!
SEE, I HAVE LOTS OF SISTERS, I KNOW THIS DRILL. NOBODY WANTS BARF IN THEIR HAIR.
YEAH, I REMEMBER THE FIRST TIME LITTLE APPALONIA RODE A HORSE SHE HAD THE SAME PROBLEM.
IT'S NO BIG THING, IT HAPPENS TO A LOT OF PEOPLE. YOU SHOULDN'T BE ASHAMED OR WHATEVER.
PAT PAT
sniff sniff
THAT SMELL...
HEY, DID YOU EAT A WHOLE BONE?
YEAH, WELL, IT DOES SMELL. YOU CAN'T GET AWAY FROM THAT. I REMEMBER ONCE WHEN I WAS FIRST LEARNING...
GRRRR...
RARRR!
AAAH! DON'T EAT ME!

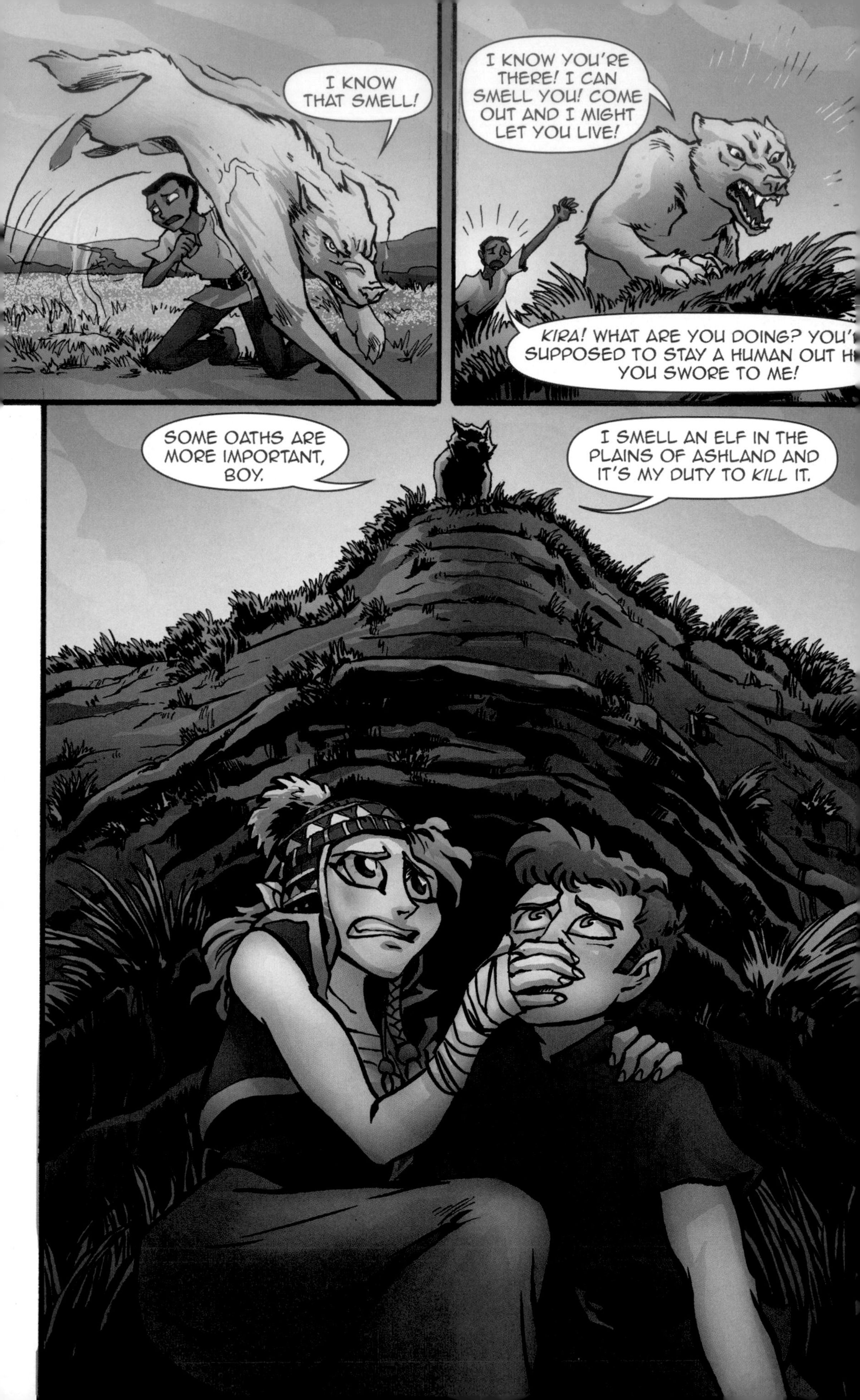
I KNOW THAT SMELL!
I KNOW YOU'RE THERE! I CAN SMELL YOU! COME OUT AND I MIGHT LET YOU LIVE!
KIRA! WHAT ARE YOU DOING? YOU'
SUPPOSED TO STAY A HUMAN OUT H
YOU SWORE TO ME!
SOME OATHS ARE MORE IMPORTANT, BOY.
I SMELL AN ELF IN THE PLAINS OF ASHLAND AND IT'S MY DUTY TO *KILL* IT.

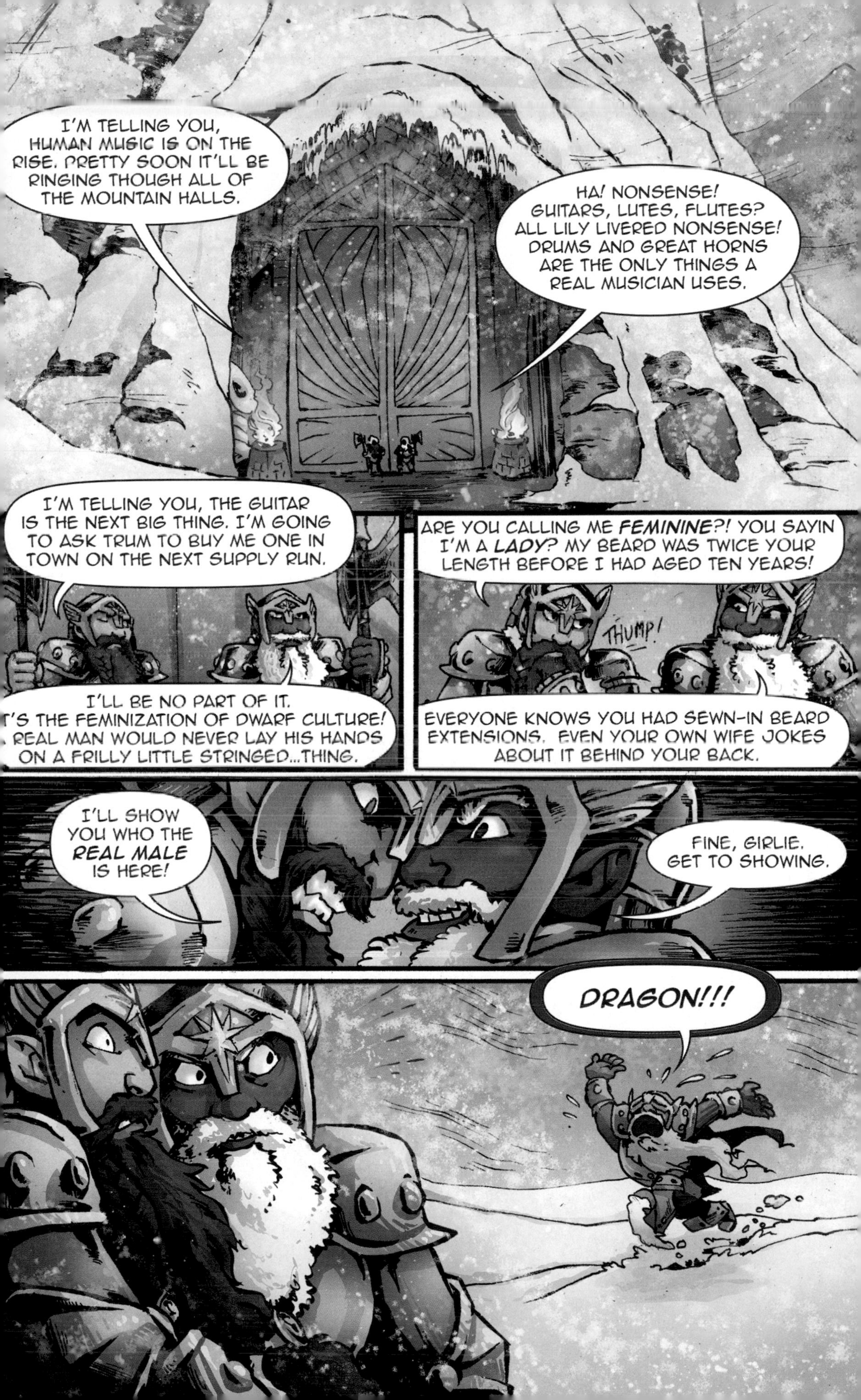

I'M TELLING YOU, HUMAN MUSIC IS ON THE RISE. PRETTY SOON IT'LL BE RINGING THOUGH ALL OF THE MOUNTAIN HALLS.
HA! NONSENSE! GUITARS, LUTES, FLUTES? ALL LILY LIVERED NONSENSE! DRUMS AND GREAT HORNS ARE THE ONLY THINGS A REAL MUSICIAN USES.
I'M TELLING YOU, THE GUITAR IS THE NEXT BIG THING. I'M GOING TO ASK TRUM TO BUY ME ONE IN TOWN ON THE NEXT SUPPLY RUN.
I'LL BE NO PART OF IT. T'S THE FEMINIZATION OF DWARF CULTURE! REAL MAN WOULD NEVER LAY HIS HANDS ON A FRILLY LITTLE STRINGED...THING.
ARE YOU CALLING ME FEMININE?! YOU SAYIN I'M A LADY? MY BEARD WAS TWICE YOUR LENGTH BEFORE I HAD AGED TEN YEARS!
THUMP!
EVERYONE KNOWS YOU HAD SEWN-IN BEARD EXTENSIONS. EVEN YOUR OWN WIFE JOKES ABOUT IT BEHIND YOUR BACK.
I'LL SHOW YOU WHO THE REAL MALE IS HERE!
FINE, GIRLIE. GET TO SHOWING.
DRAGON!!!

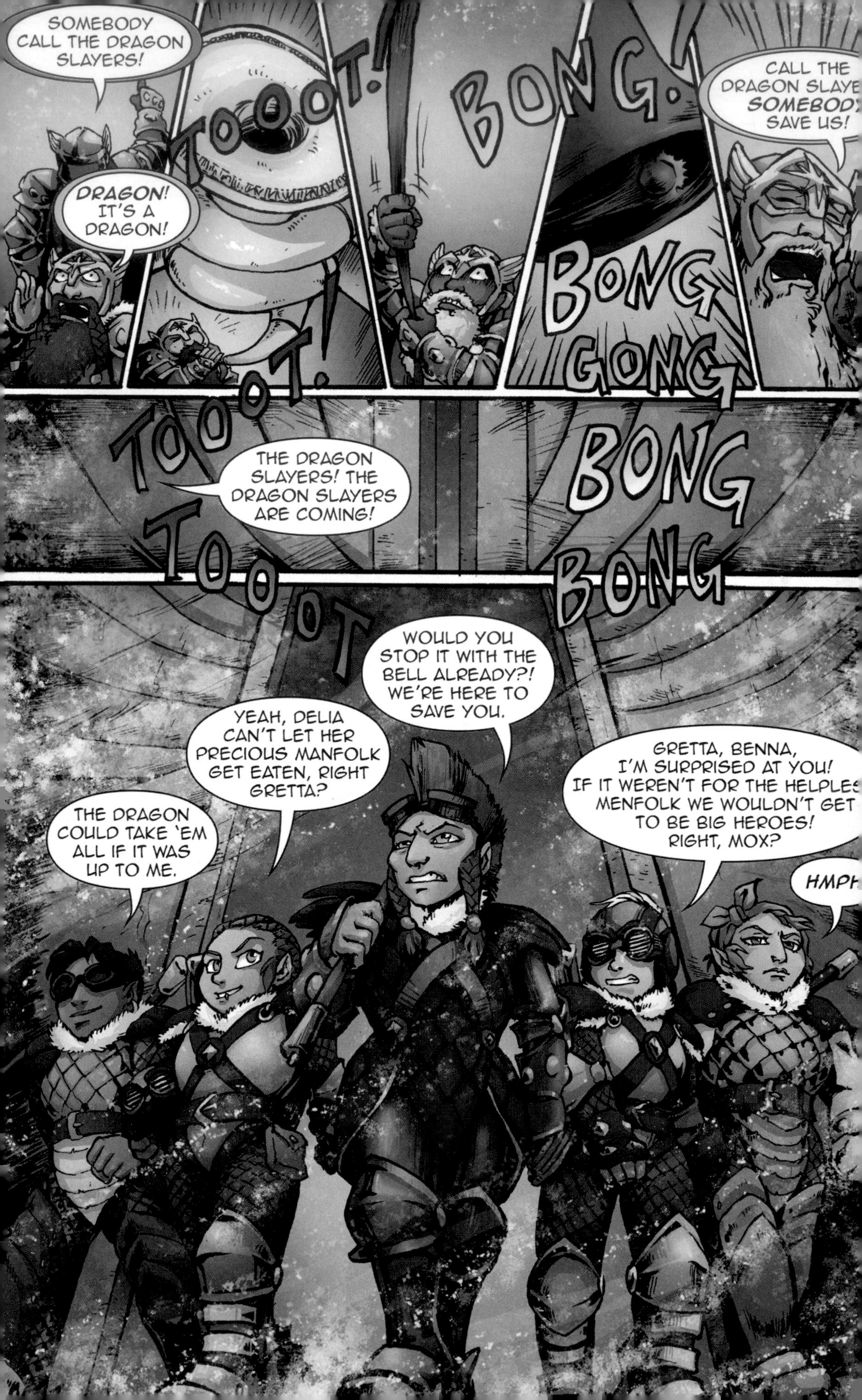
SOMEBODY CALL THE DRAGON SLAYERS!
DRAGON! IT'S A DRAGON!
TOOOT!
TOOOT!
BONG!
BONG GONG
CALL THE DRAGON SLAYE SOMEBOD SAVE US!
TOOOT
THE DRAGON SLAYERS! THE DRAGON SLAYERS ARE COMING!
TOOOT
BONG
BONG
WOULD YOU STOP IT WITH THE BELL ALREADY?! WE'RE HERE TO SAVE YOU.
YEAH, DELIA CAN'T LET HER PRECIOUS MANFOLK GET EATEN, RIGHT GRETTA?
THE DRAGON COULD TAKE 'EM ALL IF IT WAS UP TO ME.
GRETTA, BENNA, I'M SURPRISED AT YOU! IF IT WEREN'T FOR THE HELPLES MENFOLK WE WOULDN'T GET TO BE BIG HEROES! RIGHT, MOX?
HMPH

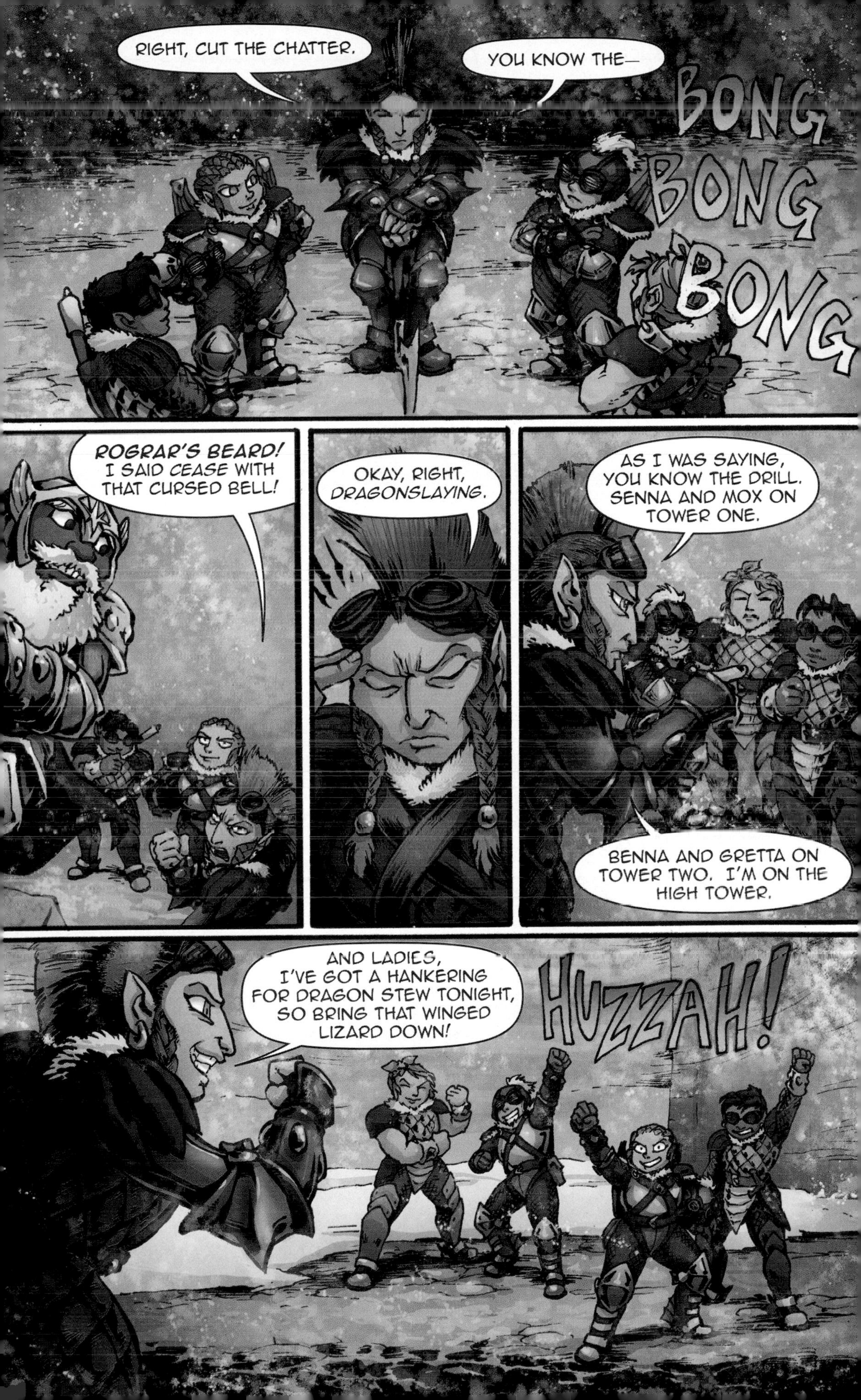
RIGHT, CUT THE CHATTER.
YOU KNOW THE—
BONG
BONG
BONG
BONG
ROGRAR'S BEARD! I SAID CEASE WITH THAT CURSED BELL!
OKAY, RIGHT, DRAGONSLAYING.
AS I WAS SAYING, YOU KNOW THE DRILL. SENNA AND MOX ON TOWER ONE.
BENNA AND GRETTA ON TOWER TWO. I'M ON THE HIGH TOWER.
AND LADIES, I'VE GOT A HANKERING FOR DRAGON STEW TONIGHT, SO BRING THAT WINGED LIZARD DOWN!
HUZZAH!

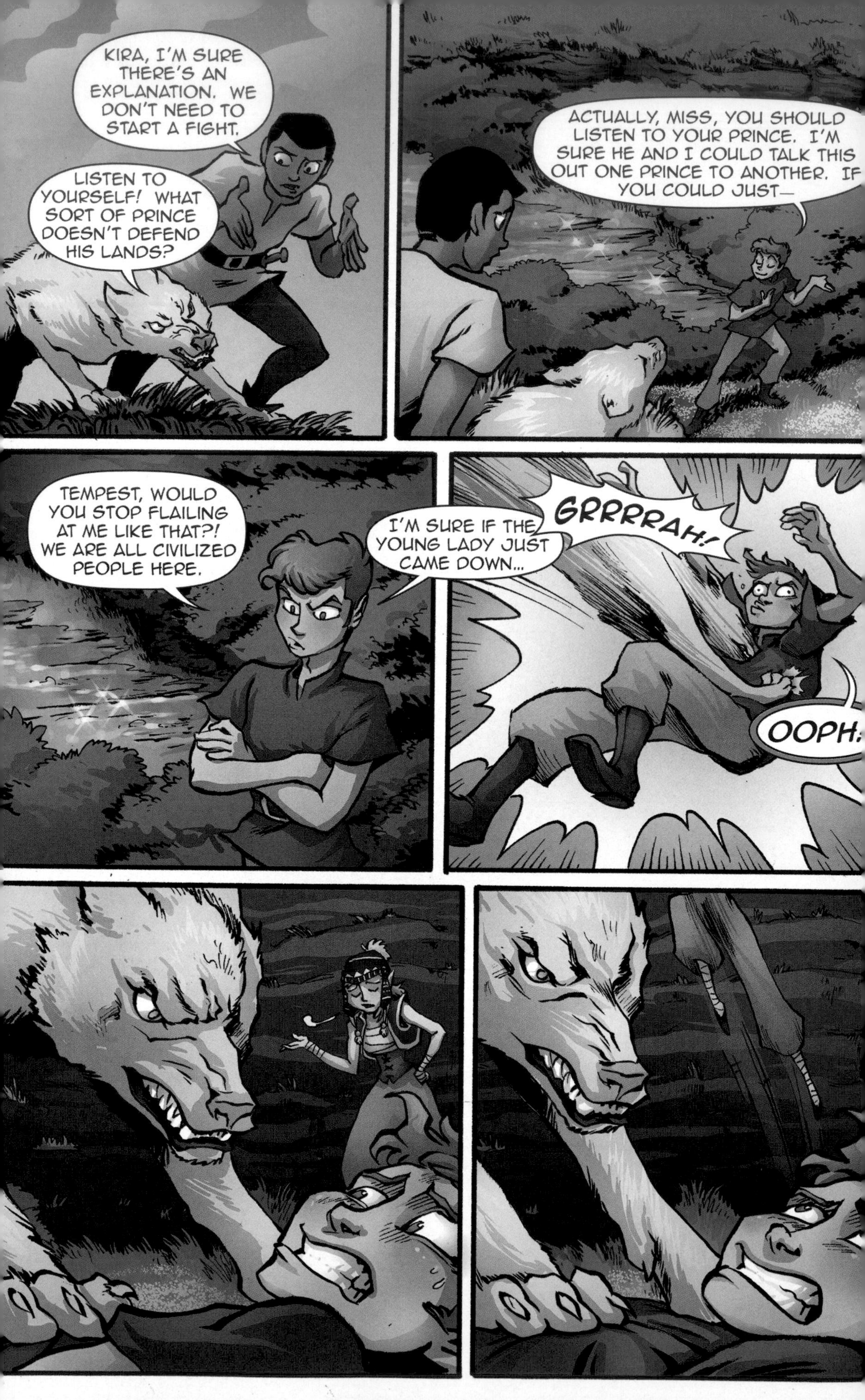
KIRA, I'M SURE THERE'S AN EXPLANATION. WE DON'T NEED TO START A FIGHT.
LISTEN TO YOURSELF! WHAT SORT OF PRINCE DOESN'T DEFEND HIS LANDS?
ACTUALLY, MISS, YOU SHOULD LISTEN TO YOUR PRINCE. I'M SURE HE AND I COULD TALK THIS OUT ONE PRINCE TO ANOTHER. IF YOU COULD JUST—
TEMPEST, WOULD YOU STOP FLAILING AT ME LIKE THAT?! WE ARE ALL CIVILIZED PEOPLE HERE.
I'M SURE IF THE YOUNG LADY JUST CAME DOWN...
GRRRRAH!
OOPH!

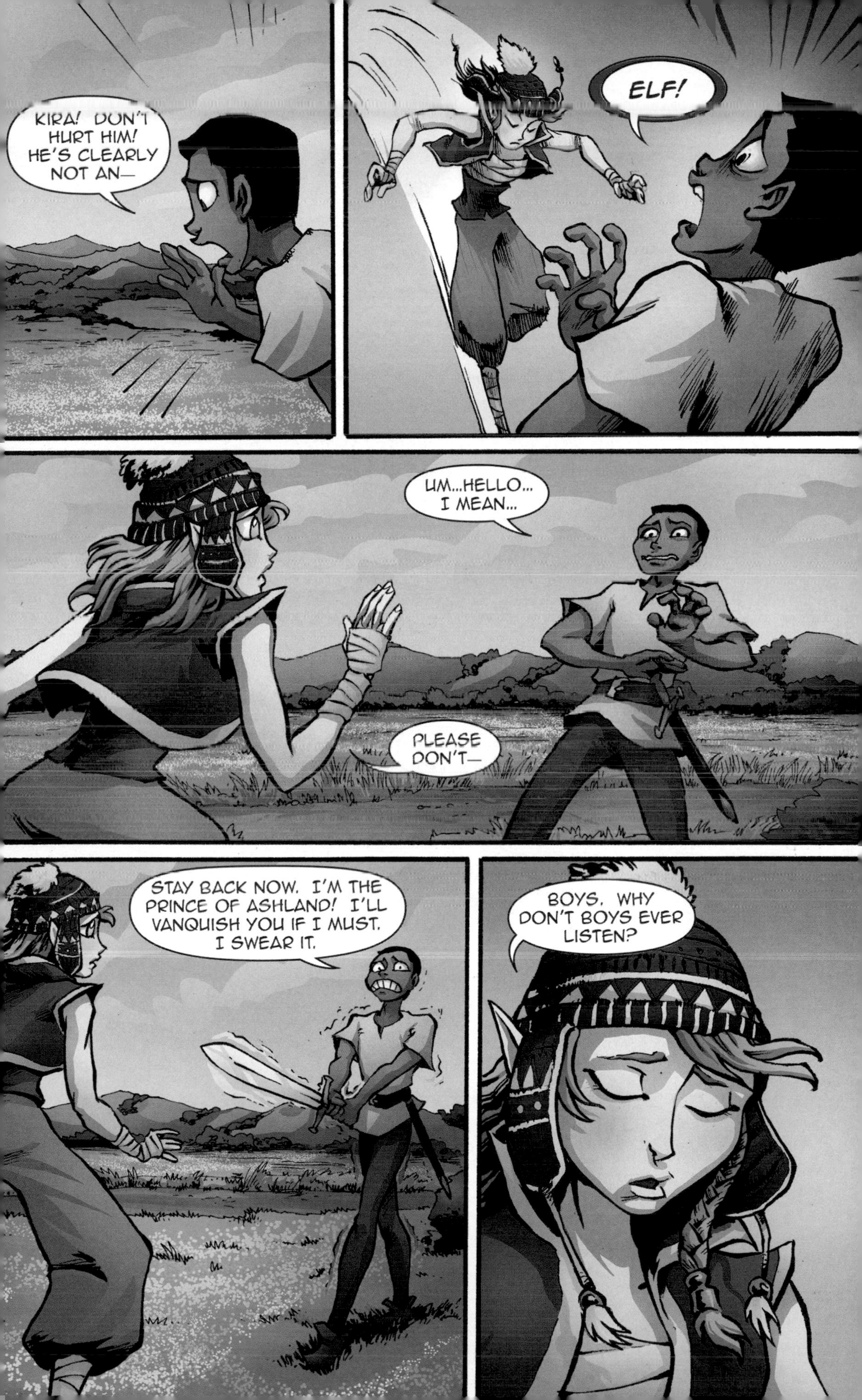
KIRA! DON'T HURT HIM! HE'S CLEARLY NOT AN—
ELF!
UM...HELLO... I MEAN...
PLEASE DON'T—
STAY BACK NOW. I'M THE PRINCE OF ASHLAND! I'LL VANQUISH YOU IF I MUST. I SWEAR IT.
BOYS. WHY DON'T BOYS EVER LISTEN?

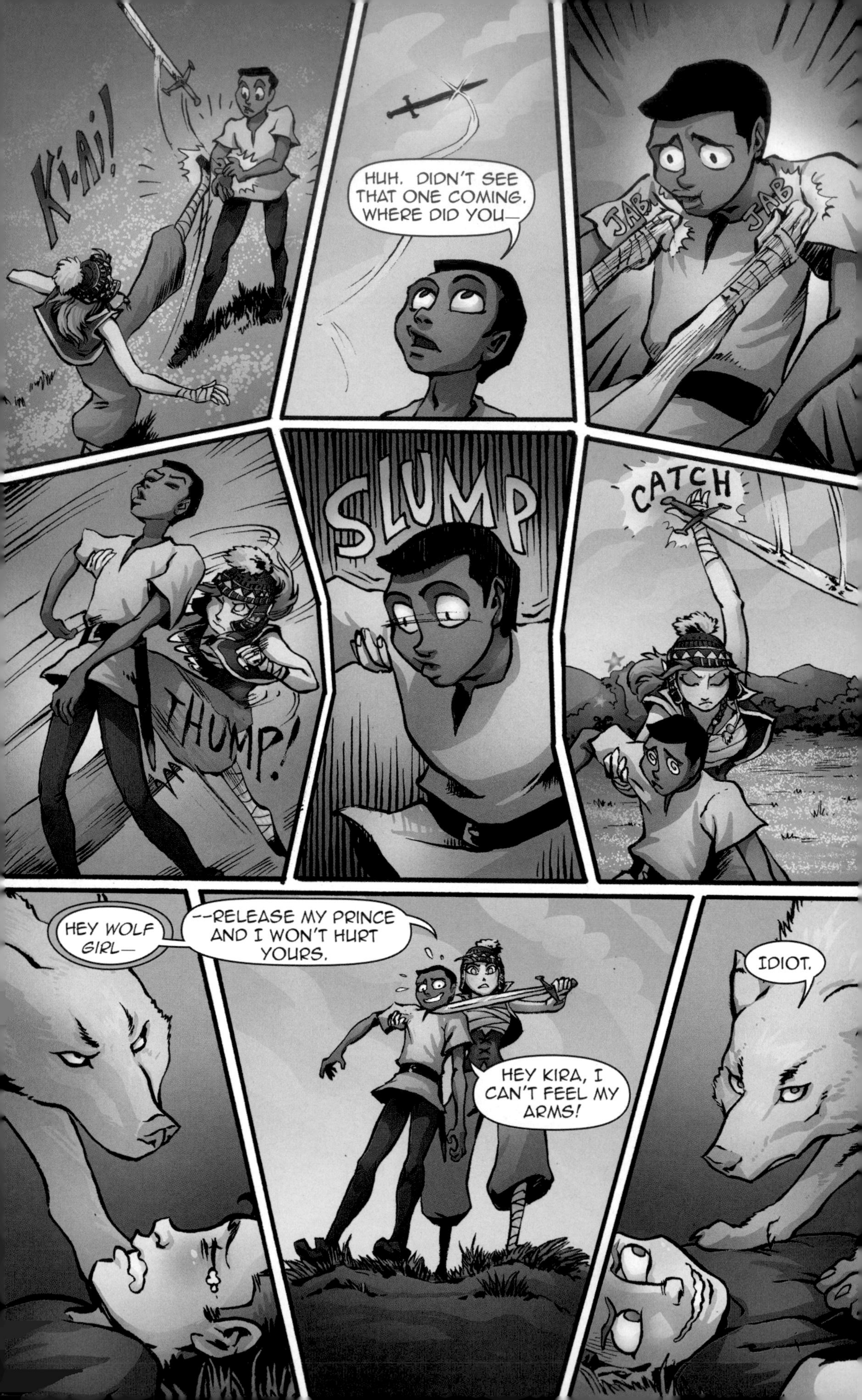
KI-AI!
HUH. DIDN'T SEE THAT ONE COMING. WHERE DID YOU—
JAB
JAB
THUMP!
SLUMP
CATCH
HEY WOLF GIRL—
--RELEASE MY PRINCE AND I WON'T HURT YOURS.
HEY KIRA, I CAN'T FEEL MY ARMS!
IDIOT.

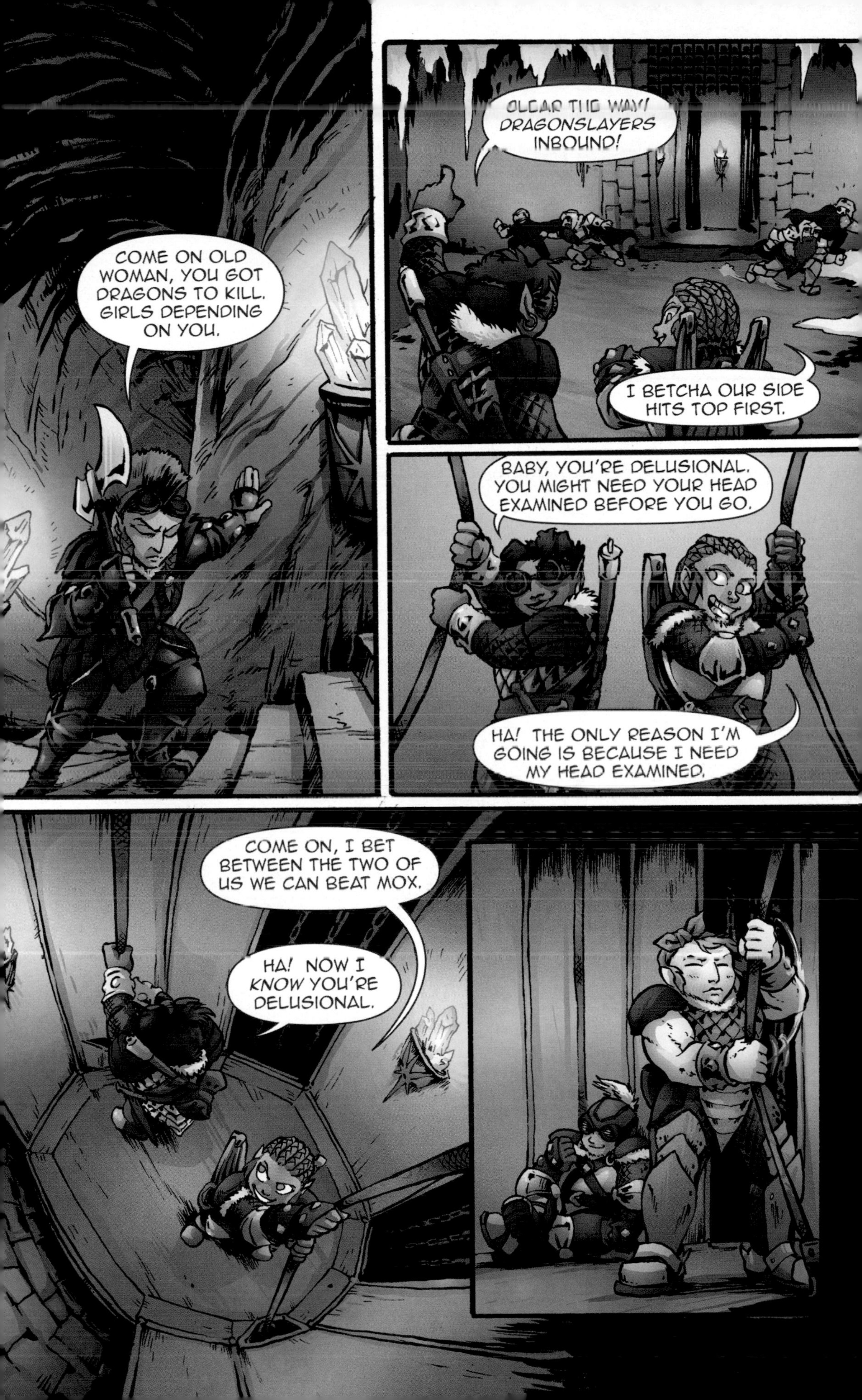
COME ON OLD WOMAN, YOU GOT DRAGONS TO KILL. GIRLS DEPENDING ON YOU.
CLEAR THE WAY! DRAGONSLAYERS INBOUND!
I BETCHA OUR SIDE HITS TOP FIRST.
BABY, YOU'RE DELUSIONAL. YOU MIGHT NEED YOUR HEAD EXAMINED BEFORE YOU GO.
HA! THE ONLY REASON I'M GOING IS BECAUSE I NEED MY HEAD EXAMINED.
COME ON, I BET BETWEEN THE TWO OF US WE CAN BEAT MOX.
HA! NOW I *KNOW* YOU'RE DELUSIONAL.

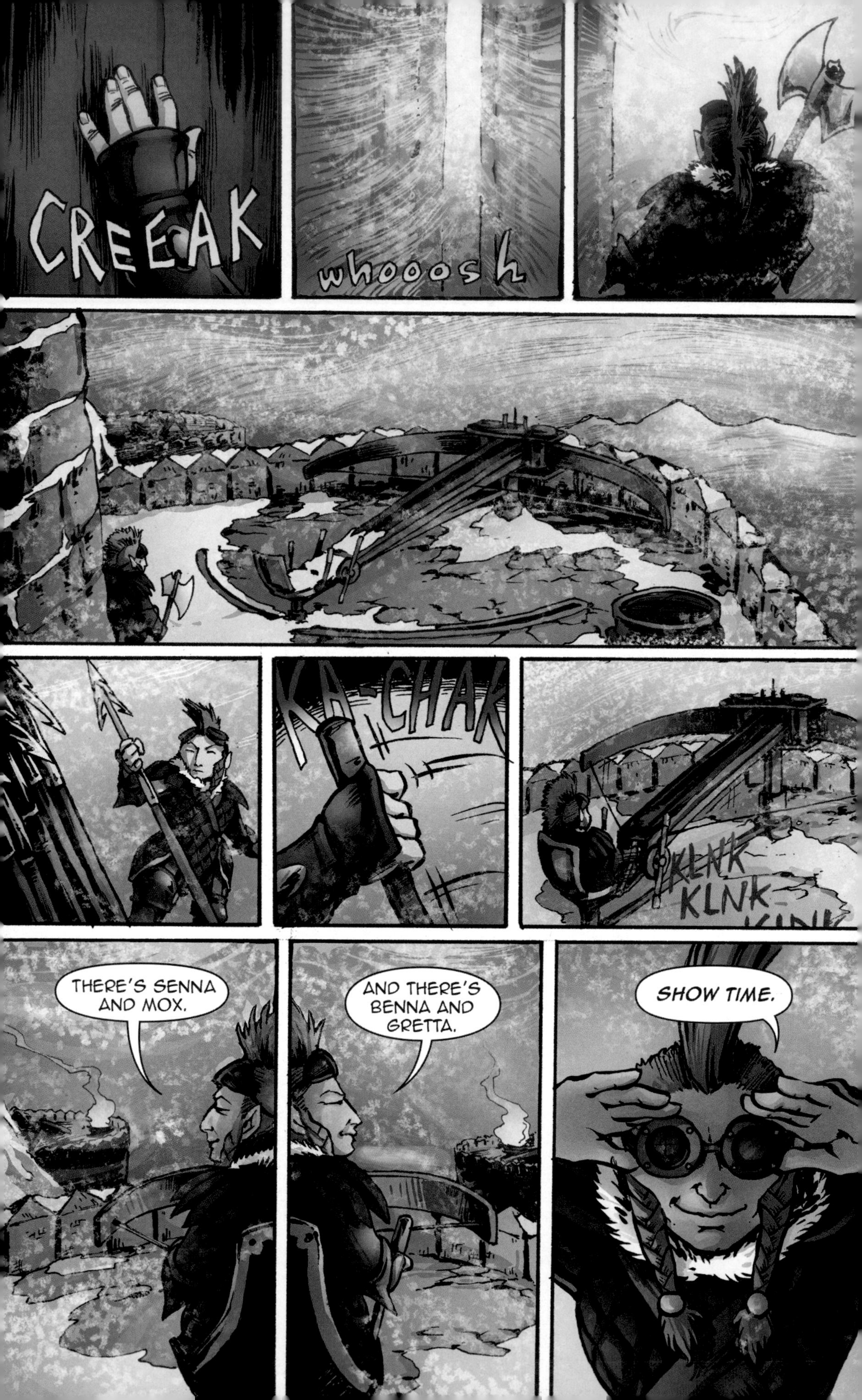
CREEAK
whoooosh
KA-CHAK
KLNK
KLNK
THERE'S SENNA AND MOX.
AND THERE'S BENNA AND GRETTA.
SHOW TIME.

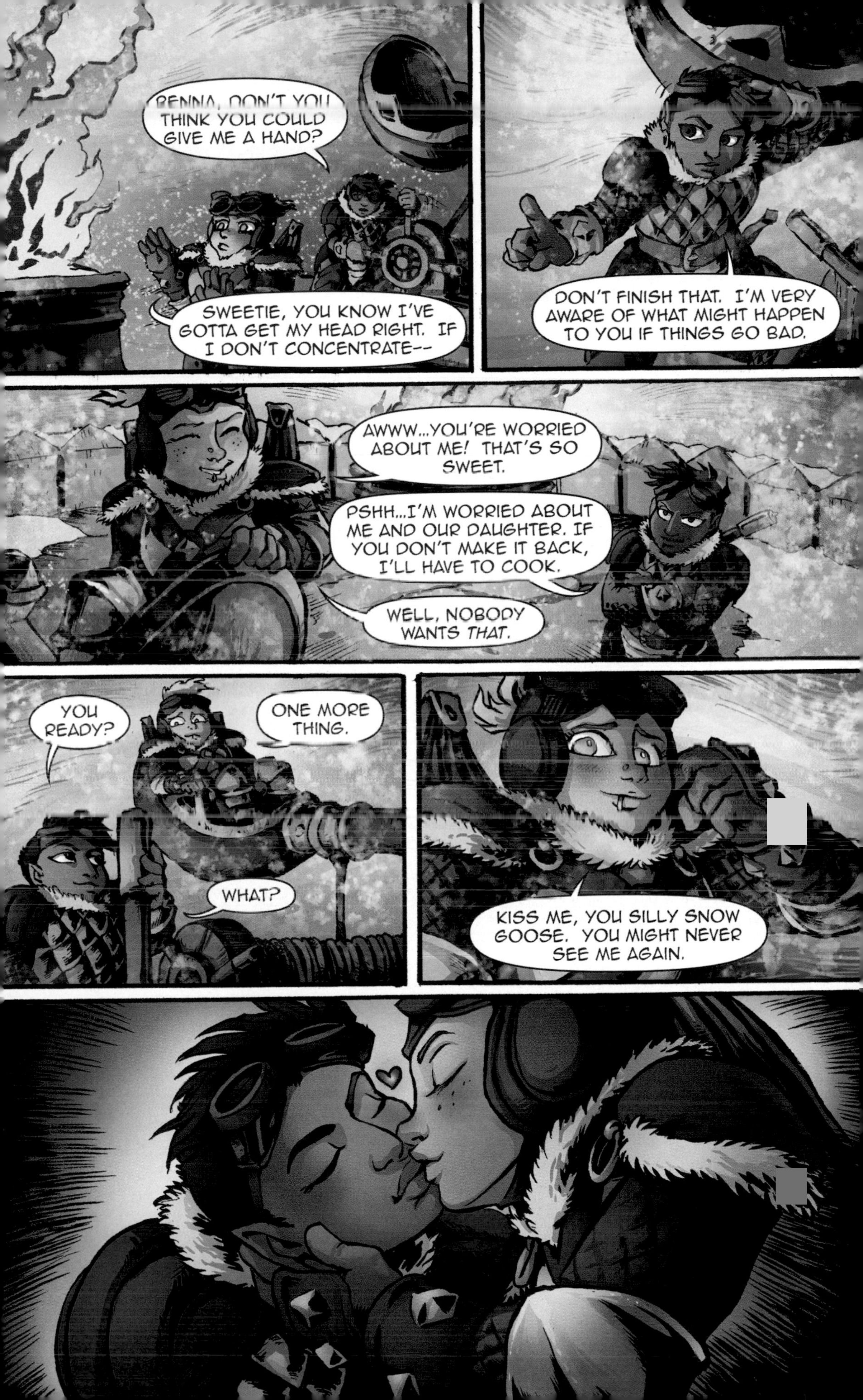
BENNA, DON'T YOU THINK YOU COULD GIVE ME A HAND?
SWEETIE, YOU KNOW I'VE GOTTA GET MY HEAD RIGHT. IF I DON'T CONCENTRATE--
DON'T FINISH THAT. I'M VERY AWARE OF WHAT MIGHT HAPPEN TO YOU IF THINGS GO BAD.
AWWW...YOU'RE WORRIED ABOUT ME! THAT'S SO SWEET.
PSHH...I'M WORRIED ABOUT ME AND OUR DAUGHTER. IF YOU DON'T MAKE IT BACK, I'LL HAVE TO COOK.
WELL, NOBODY WANTS *THAT*.
YOU READY?
ONE MORE THING.
WHAT?
KISS ME, YOU SILLY SNOW GOOSE. YOU MIGHT NEVER SEE ME AGAIN.

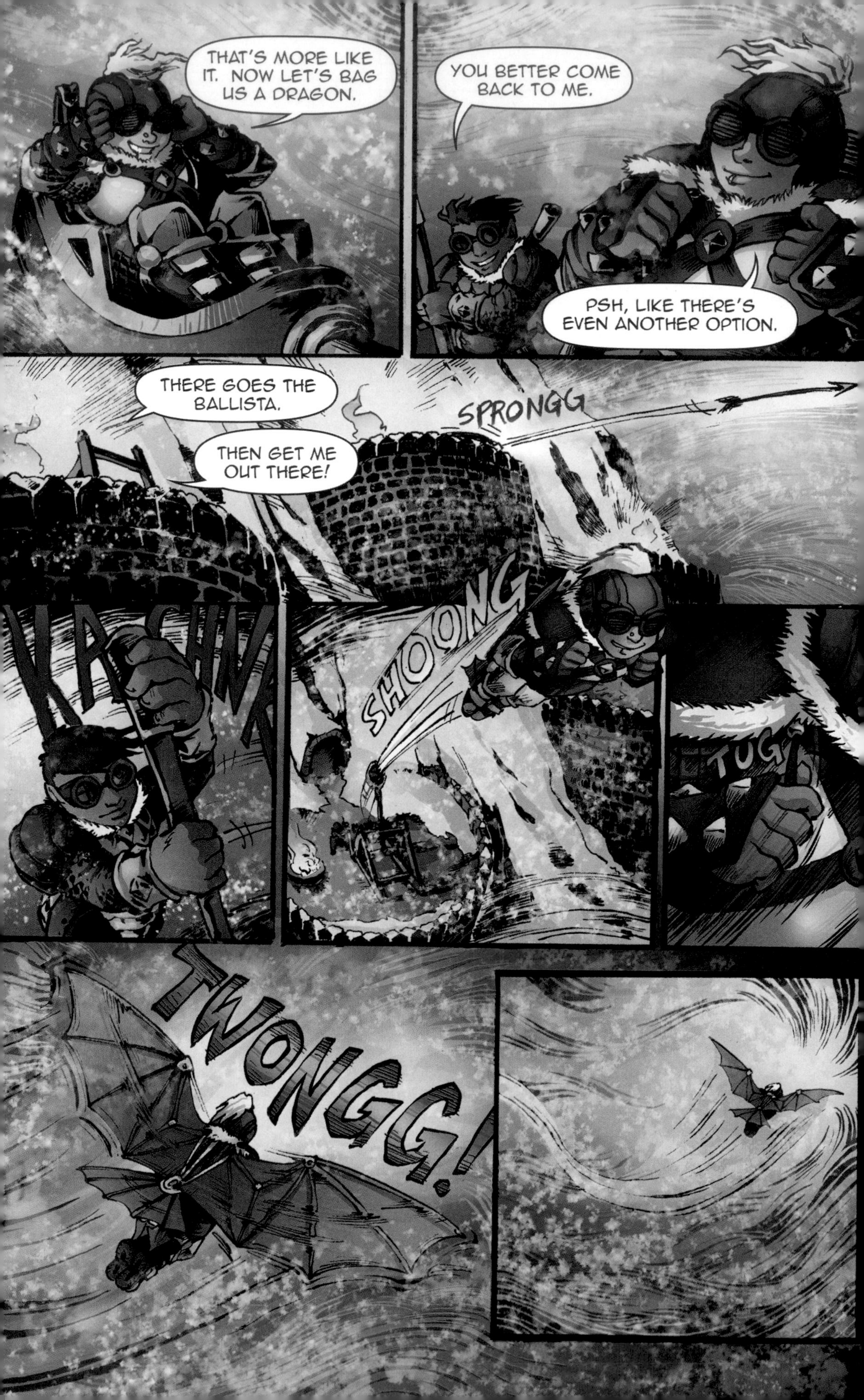
THAT'S MORE LIKE IT. NOW LET'S BAG US A DRAGON.
YOU BETTER COME BACK TO ME.
PSH, LIKE THERE'S EVEN ANOTHER OPTION.
THERE GOES THE BALLISTA.
THEN GET ME OUT THERE!
SPRONGG
KACHNK
SHOOONG
TUG
TWONGG!

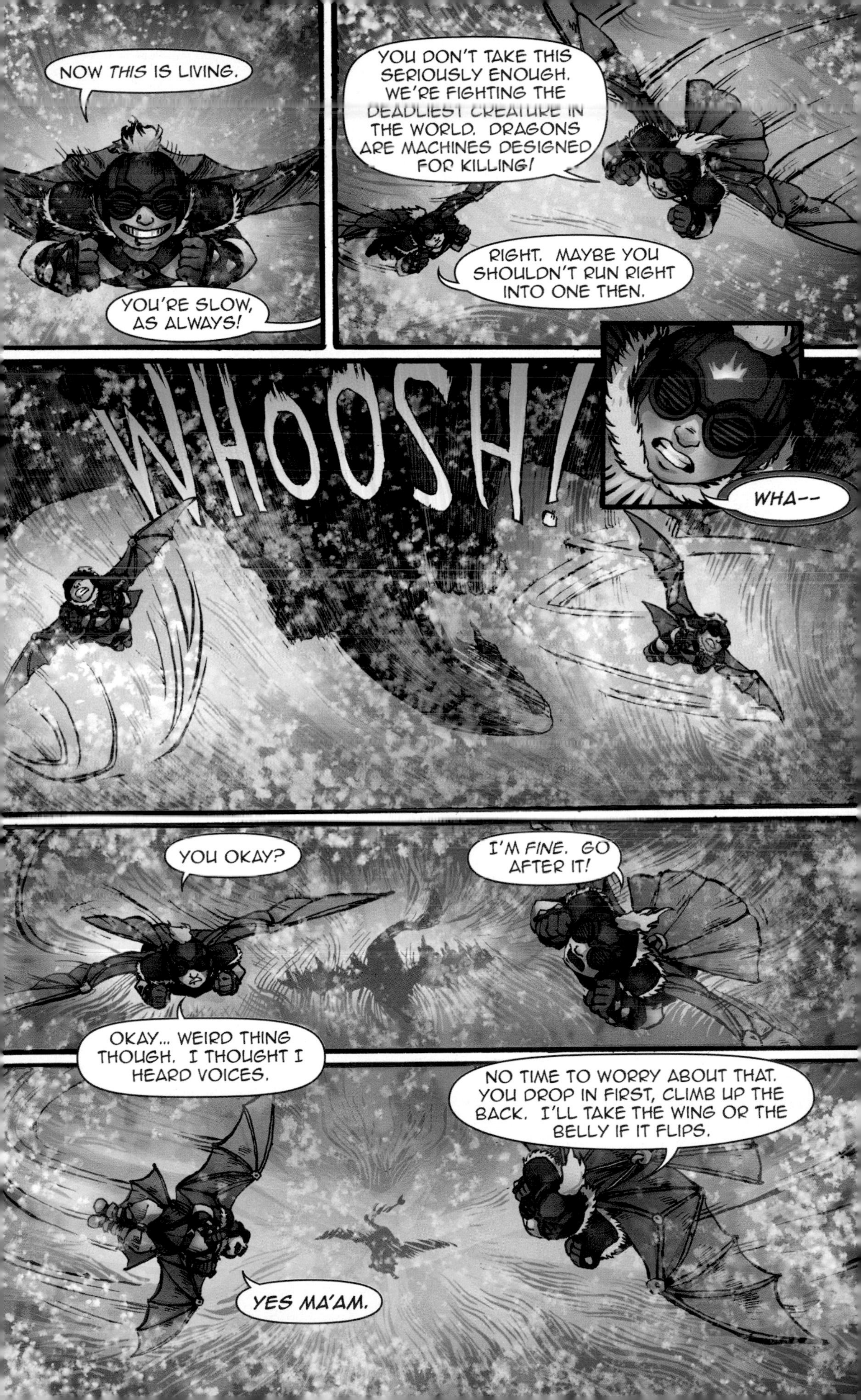

NOW THIS IS LIVING.
YOU'RE SLOW, AS ALWAYS!
YOU DON'T TAKE THIS SERIOUSLY ENOUGH. WE'RE FIGHTING THE DEADLIEST CREATURE IN THE WORLD. DRAGONS ARE MACHINES DESIGNED FOR KILLING!
RIGHT. MAYBE YOU SHOULDN'T RUN RIGHT INTO ONE THEN.
WHOOSH!
WHA--
YOU OKAY?
I'M FINE. GO AFTER IT!
OKAY... WEIRD THING THOUGH. I THOUGHT I HEARD VOICES.
NO TIME TO WORRY ABOUT THAT. YOU DROP IN FIRST, CLIMB UP THE BACK. I'LL TAKE THE WING OR THE BELLY IF IT FLIPS.
YES MA'AM.

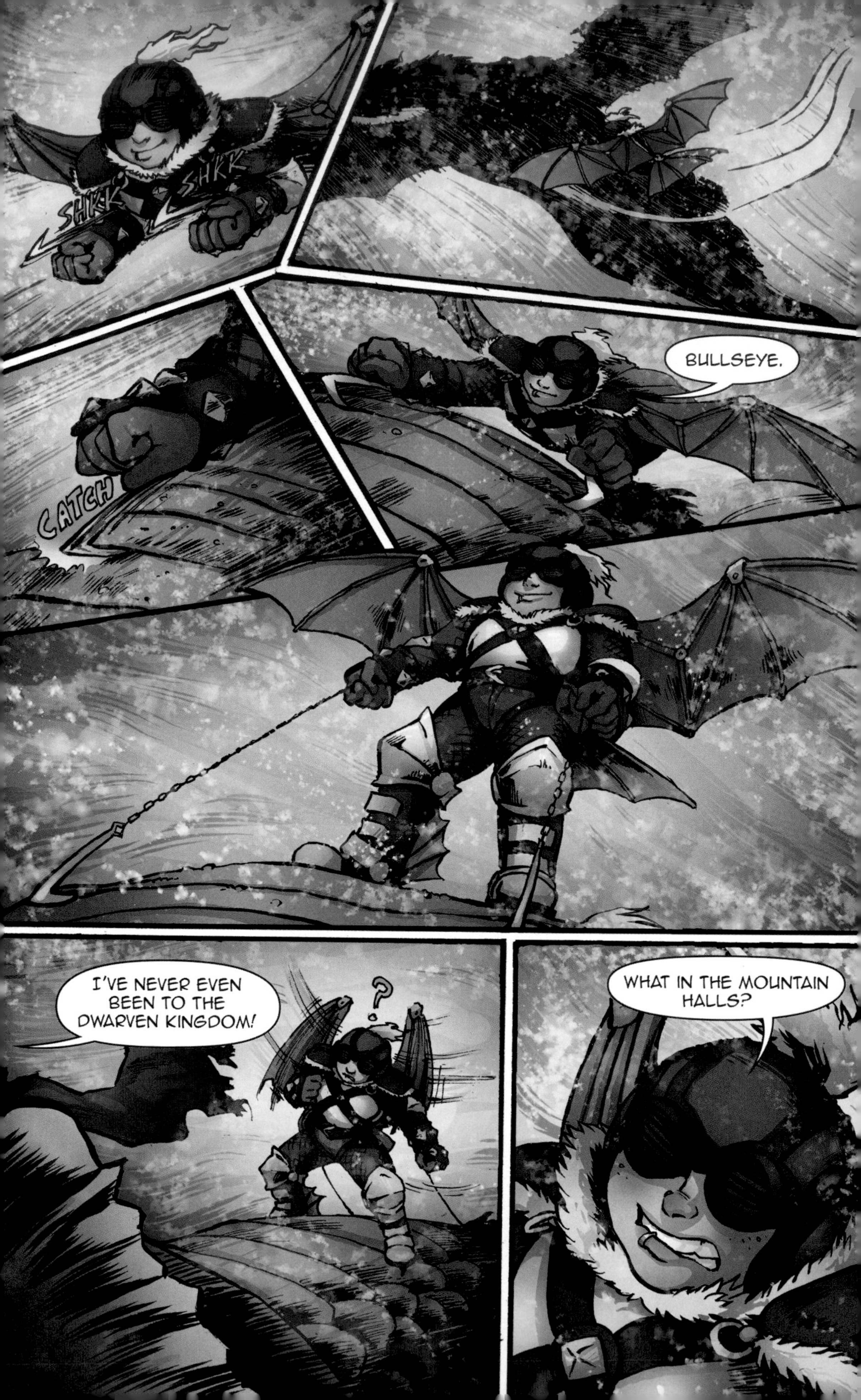
SHKK
SHKK
CATCH
BULLSEYE.
I'VE NEVER EVEN BEEN TO THE DWARVEN KINGDOM!
?
WHAT IN THE MOUNTAIN HALLS?

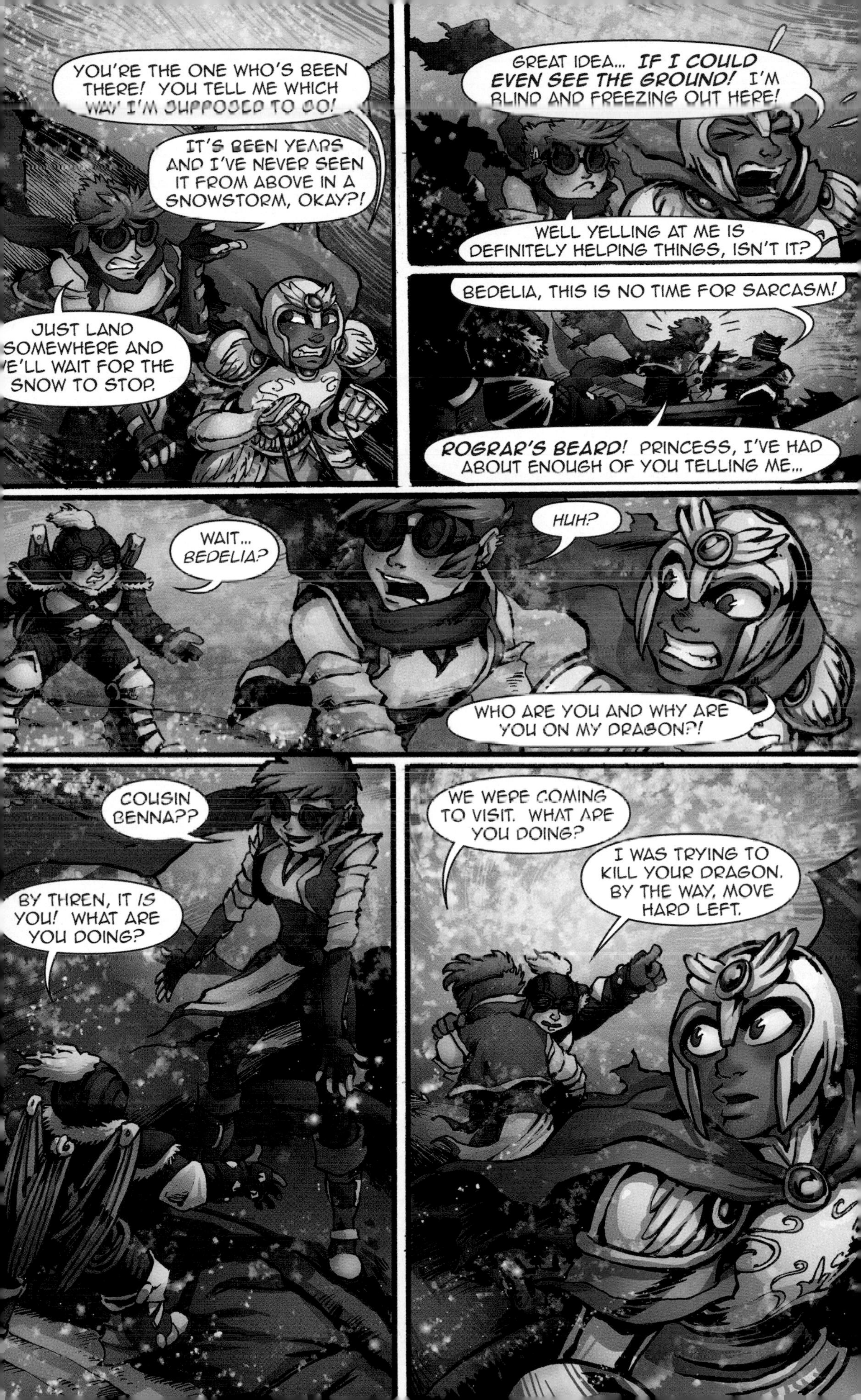

YOU'RE THE ONE WHO'S BEEN THERE! YOU TELL ME WHICH WAY I'M SUPPOSED TO GO!
IT'S BEEN YEARS AND I'VE NEVER SEEN IT FROM ABOVE IN A SNOWSTORM, OKAY?!
JUST LAND SOMEWHERE AND WE'LL WAIT FOR THE SNOW TO STOP.
GREAT IDEA... *IF I COULD EVEN SEE THE GROUND!* I'M BLIND AND FREEZING OUT HERE!
WELL YELLING AT ME IS DEFINITELY HELPING THINGS, ISN'T IT?
BEDELIA, THIS IS NO TIME FOR SARCASM!
ROGRAR'S BEARD! PRINCESS, I'VE HAD ABOUT ENOUGH OF YOU TELLING ME...
WAIT... BEDELIA?
HUH?
WHO ARE YOU AND WHY ARE YOU ON MY DRAGON?!
COUSIN BENNA??
BY THREN, IT *IS* YOU! WHAT ARE YOU DOING?
WE WERE COMING TO VISIT. WHAT ARE YOU DOING?
I WAS TRYING TO KILL YOUR DRAGON. BY THE WAY, MOVE HARD LEFT.

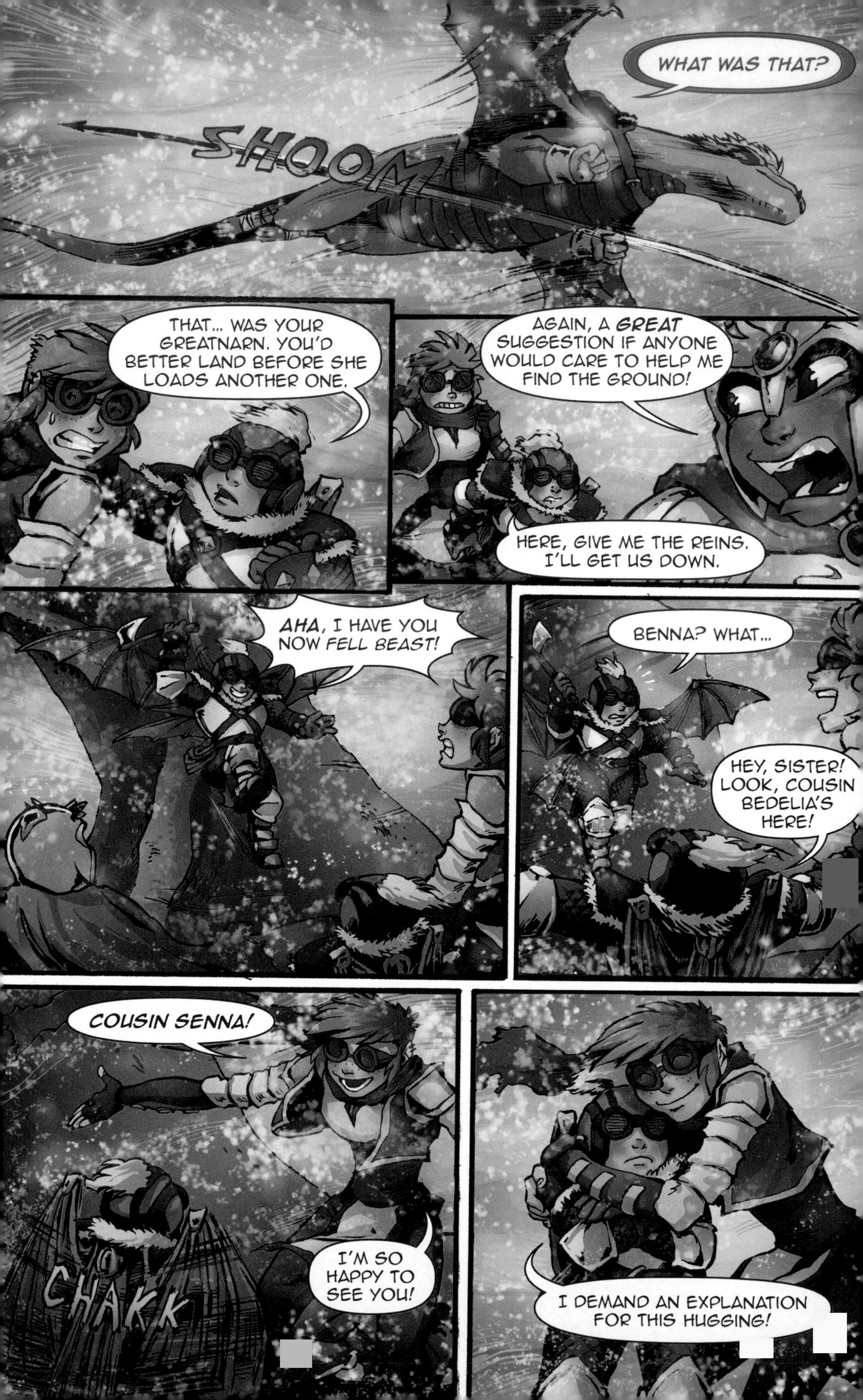
WHAT WAS THAT?
SHOOM
THAT... WAS YOUR GREATNARN. YOU'D BETTER LAND BEFORE SHE LOADS ANOTHER ONE.
AGAIN, A GREAT SUGGESTION IF ANYONE WOULD CARE TO HELP ME FIND THE GROUND!
HERE, GIVE ME THE REINS. I'LL GET US DOWN.
AHA, I HAVE YOU NOW FELL BEAST!
BENNA? WHAT...
HEY, SISTER! LOOK, COUSIN BEDELIA'S HERE!
COUSIN SENNA!
CHAKK
I'M SO HAPPY TO SEE YOU!
I DEMAND AN EXPLANATION FOR THIS HUGGING!

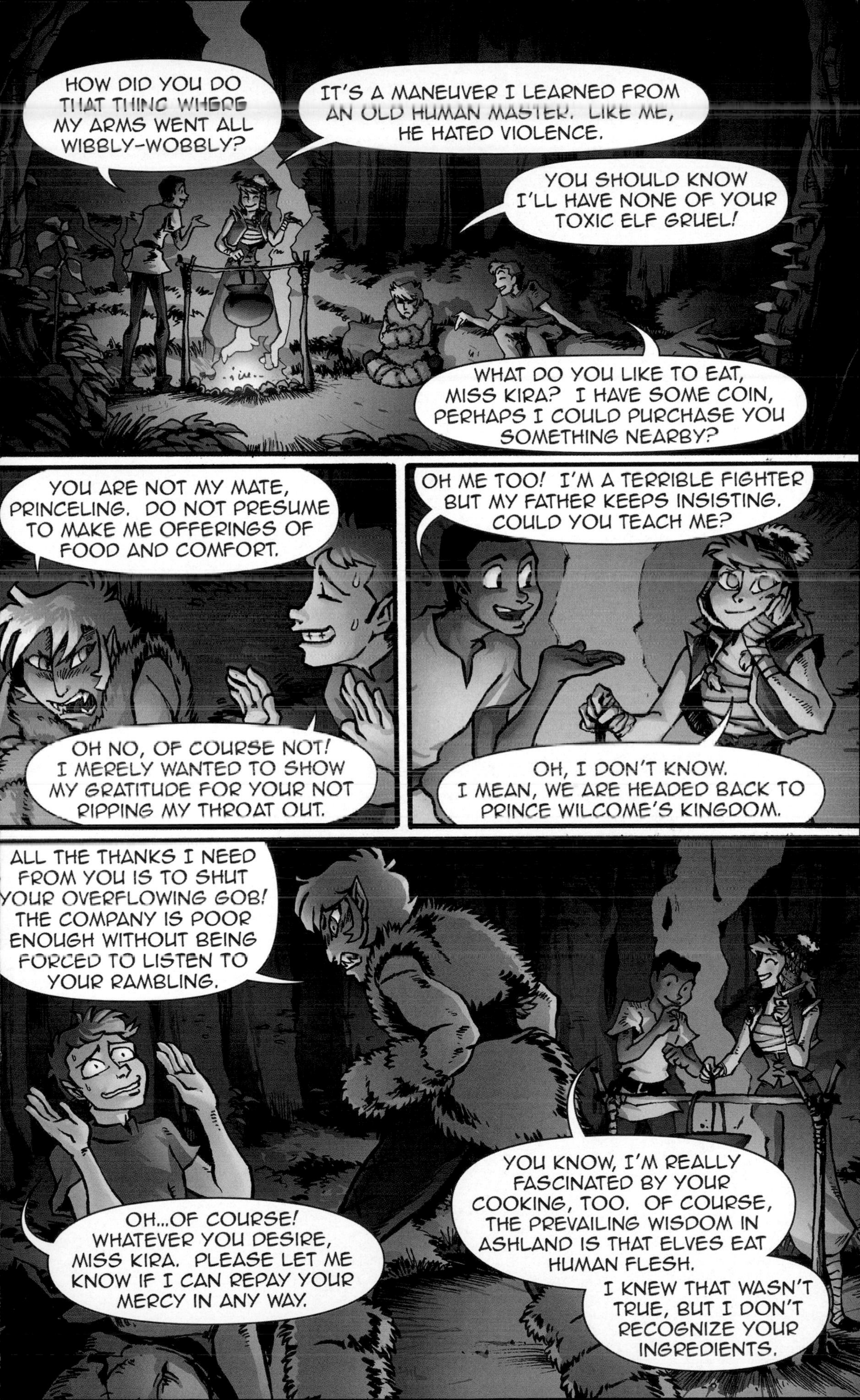
HOW DID YOU DO THAT THING WHERE MY ARMS WENT ALL WIBBLY-WOBBLY?
IT'S A MANEUVER I LEARNED FROM AN OLD HUMAN MASTER. LIKE ME, HE HATED VIOLENCE.
YOU SHOULD KNOW I'LL HAVE NONE OF YOUR TOXIC ELF GRUEL!
WHAT DO YOU LIKE TO EAT, MISS KIRA? I HAVE SOME COIN, PERHAPS I COULD PURCHASE YOU SOMETHING NEARBY?
YOU ARE NOT MY MATE, PRINCELING. DO NOT PRESUME TO MAKE ME OFFERINGS OF FOOD AND COMFORT.
OH NO, OF COURSE NOT! I MERELY WANTED TO SHOW MY GRATITUDE FOR YOUR NOT RIPPING MY THROAT OUT.
OH ME TOO! I'M A TERRIBLE FIGHTER BUT MY FATHER KEEPS INSISTING. COULD YOU TEACH ME?
OH, I DON'T KNOW. I MEAN, WE ARE HEADED BACK TO PRINCE WILCOME'S KINGDOM.
ALL THE THANKS I NEED FROM YOU IS TO SHUT YOUR OVERFLOWING GOB! THE COMPANY IS POOR ENOUGH WITHOUT BEING FORCED TO LISTEN TO YOUR RAMBLING.
OH...OF COURSE! WHATEVER YOU DESIRE, MISS KIRA. PLEASE LET ME KNOW IF I CAN REPAY YOUR MERCY IN ANY WAY.
YOU KNOW, I'M REALLY FASCINATED BY YOUR COOKING, TOO. OF COURSE, THE PREVAILING WISDOM IN ASHLAND IS THAT ELVES EAT HUMAN FLESH.
I KNEW THAT WASN'T TRUE, BUT I DON'T RECOGNIZE YOUR INGREDIENTS.

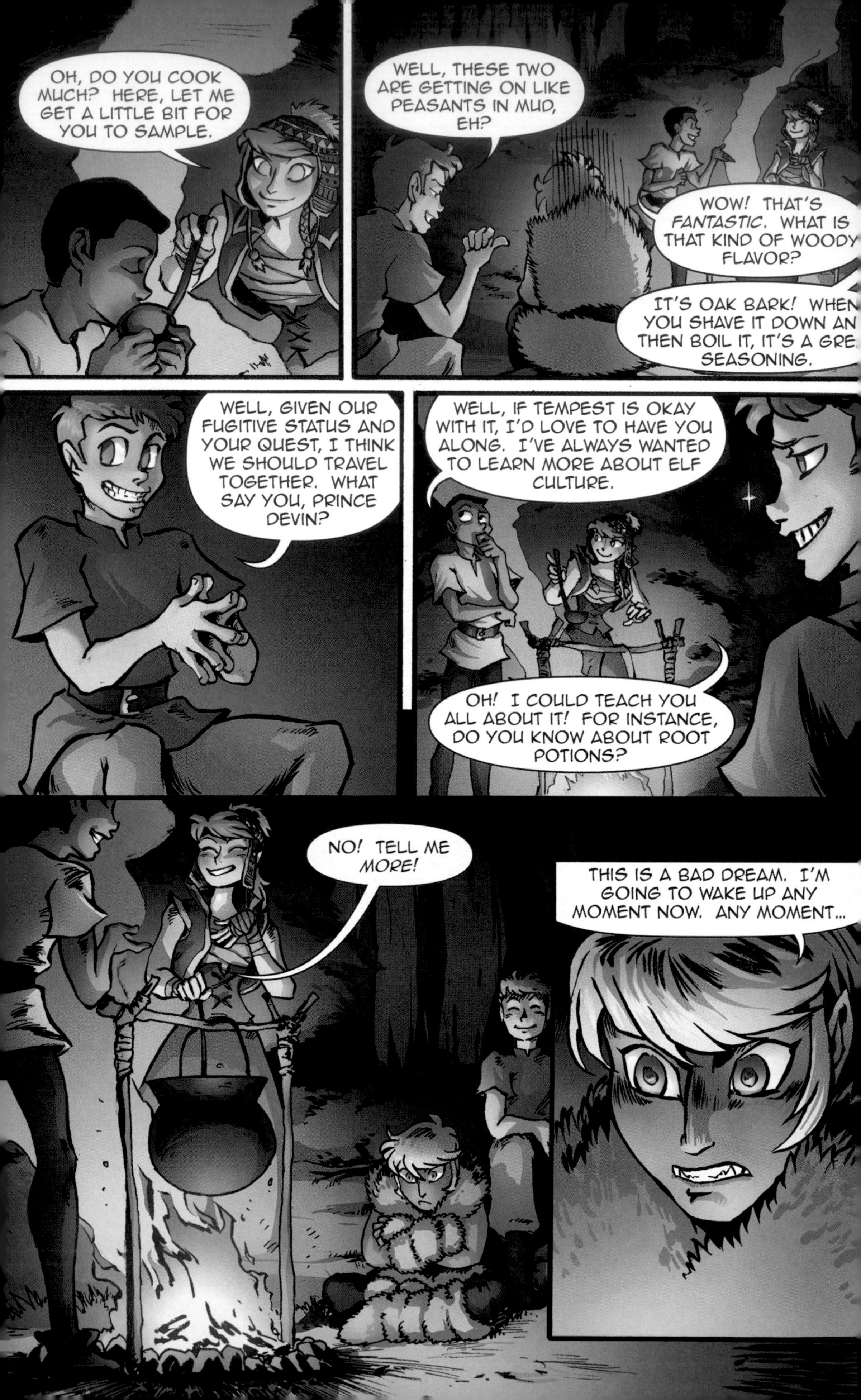
OH, DO YOU COOK MUCH? HERE, LET ME GET A LITTLE BIT FOR YOU TO SAMPLE.
WELL, THESE TWO ARE GETTING ON LIKE PEASANTS IN MUD, EH?
WOW! THAT'S *FANTASTIC*. WHAT IS THAT KIND OF WOODY FLAVOR?
IT'S OAK BARK! WHEN YOU SHAVE IT DOWN AN THEN BOIL IT, IT'S A GRE SEASONING.
WELL, GIVEN OUR FUGITIVE STATUS AND YOUR QUEST, I THINK WE SHOULD TRAVEL TOGETHER. WHAT SAY YOU, PRINCE DEVIN?
WELL, IF TEMPEST IS OKAY WITH IT, I'D LOVE TO HAVE YOU ALONG. I'VE ALWAYS WANTED TO LEARN MORE ABOUT ELF CULTURE.
OH! I COULD TEACH YOU ALL ABOUT IT! FOR INSTANCE, DO YOU KNOW ABOUT ROOT POTIONS?
NO! TELL ME *MORE*!
THIS IS A BAD DREAM. I'M GOING TO WAKE UP ANY MOMENT NOW. ANY MOMENT...

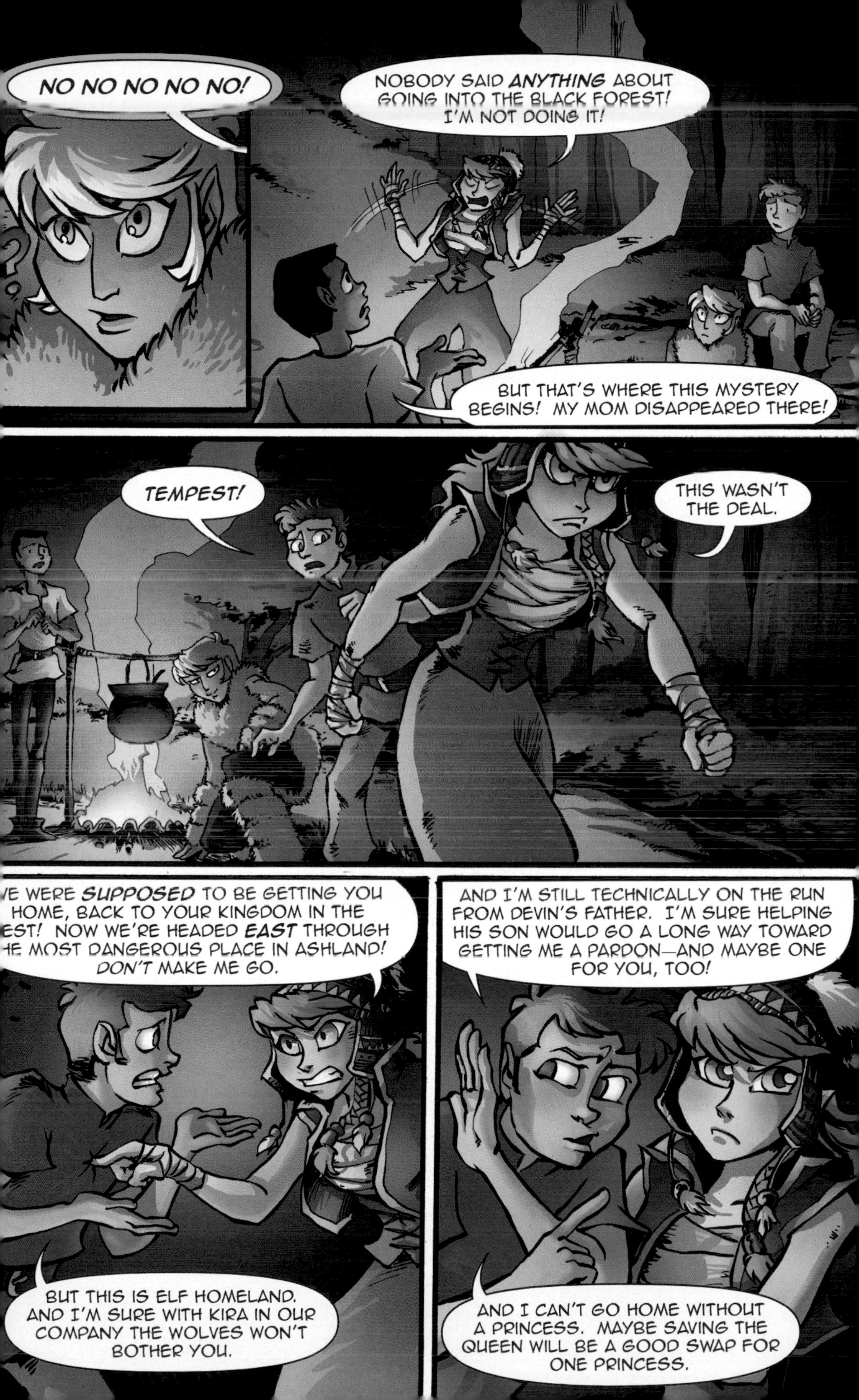
NO NO NO NO NO!
NOBODY SAID *ANYTHING* ABOUT GOING INTO THE BLACK FOREST! I'M NOT DOING IT!
BUT THAT'S WHERE THIS MYSTERY BEGINS! MY MOM DISAPPEARED THERE!
TEMPEST!
THIS WASN'T THE DEAL.
E WERE *SUPPOSED* TO BE GETTING YOU HOME, BACK TO YOUR KINGDOM IN THE EST! NOW WE'RE HEADED *EAST* THROUGH HE MOST DANGEROUS PLACE IN ASHLAND! *DON'T* MAKE ME GO.
BUT THIS IS ELF HOMELAND. AND I'M SURE WITH KIRA IN OUR COMPANY THE WOLVES WON'T BOTHER YOU.
AND I'M STILL TECHNICALLY ON THE RUN FROM DEVIN'S FATHER. I'M SURE HELPING HIS SON WOULD GO A LONG WAY TOWARD GETTING ME A PARDON—AND MAYBE ONE FOR YOU, TOO!
AND I CAN'T GO HOME WITHOUT A PRINCESS. MAYBE SAVING THE QUEEN WILL BE A GOOD SWAP FOR ONE PRINCESS.

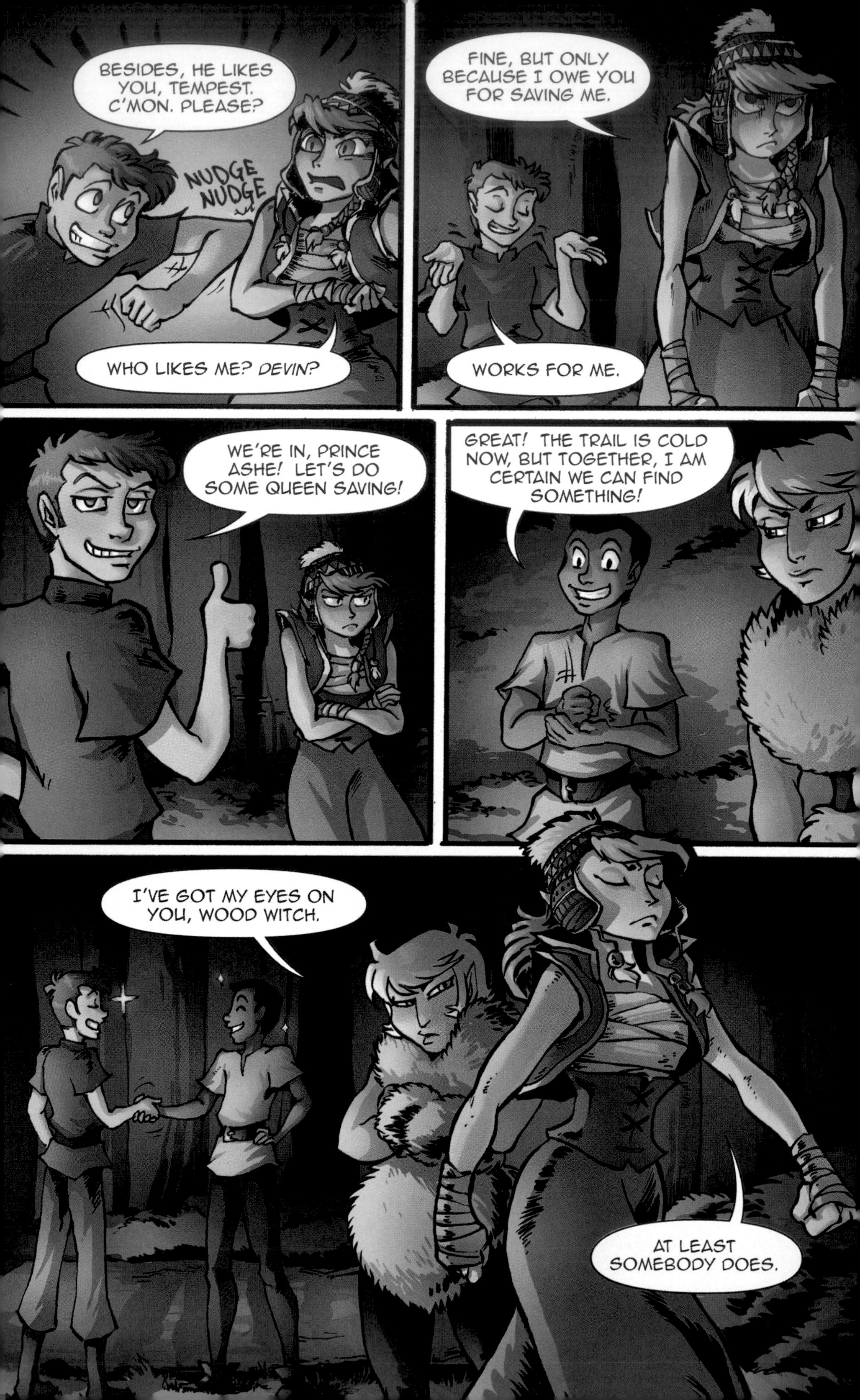
BESIDES, HE LIKES YOU, TEMPEST. C'MON. PLEASE?
NUDGE NUDGE
WHO LIKES ME? *DEVIN?*
FINE, BUT ONLY BECAUSE I OWE YOU FOR SAVING ME.
WORKS FOR ME.
WE'RE IN, PRINCE ASHE! LET'S DO SOME QUEEN SAVING!
GREAT! THE TRAIL IS COLD NOW, BUT TOGETHER, I AM CERTAIN WE CAN FIND SOMETHING!
I'VE GOT MY EYES ON YOU, WOOD WITCH.
AT LEAST SOMEBODY DOES.

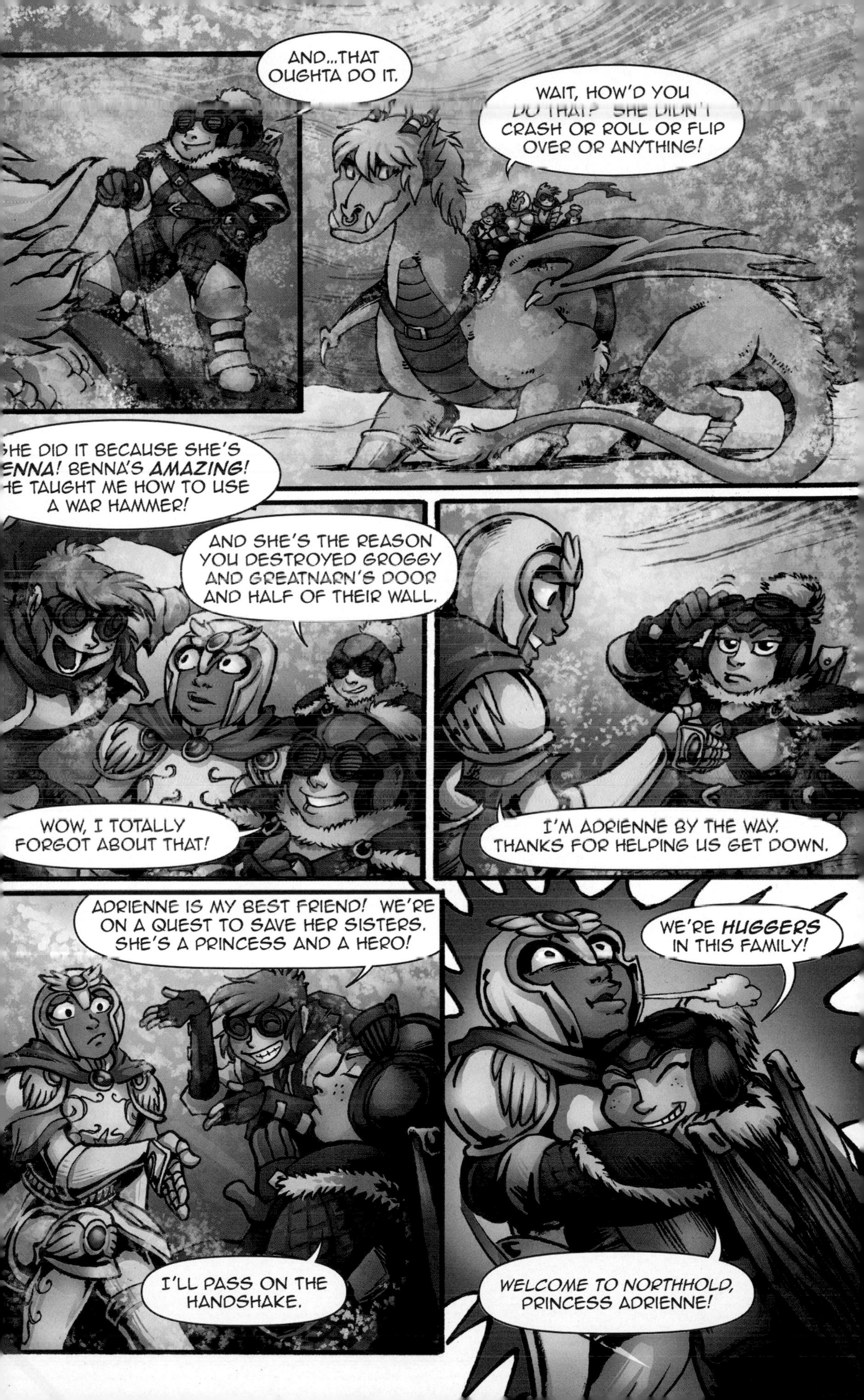
AND...THAT OUGHTA DO IT.
WAIT, HOW'D YOU DO THAT? SHE DIDN'T CRASH OR ROLL OR FLIP OVER OR ANYTHING!
HE DID IT BECAUSE SHE'S ENNA! BENNA'S AMAZING! HE TAUGHT ME HOW TO USE A WAR HAMMER!
AND SHE'S THE REASON YOU DESTROYED GROGGY AND GREATNARN'S DOOR AND HALF OF THEIR WALL.
WOW, I TOTALLY FORGOT ABOUT THAT!
I'M ADRIENNE BY THE WAY. THANKS FOR HELPING US GET DOWN.
ADRIENNE IS MY BEST FRIEND! WE'RE ON A QUEST TO SAVE HER SISTERS. SHE'S A PRINCESS AND A HERO!
I'LL PASS ON THE HANDSHAKE.
WE'RE HUGGERS IN THIS FAMILY!
WELCOME TO NORTHHOLD, PRINCESS ADRIENNE!

Bryan Seaton: Publisher • Dave Dwonch: President • Shawn Gabborin: Editor In Chief
Jason Martin: Publisher-Danger Zone • Jamal Igle: Vice-President of Marketing • Jim Dietz: Social Media Director
Nicole DAndria: Editor • Chad Cicconi: Still Waiting For His Princess • Colleen Boyd: Submissions Editor

PRINCELESS: MAKE YOURSELF #1, April 2016. Copyright Jeremy Whitley and Emily Martin, 2016. Published by Action Lab Entertainment. All rights reserved. All characters are fictional. Any likeness to anyone living or dead is purely coincidental. No part of this publication may be reproduced or transmitted without permission, except for review purposes. Printed in Canada. First Printing.

FROM SCOTT FOGG, VITO DELSANTE
ROSY HIGGINS AND TED BRANDT

ACTION LAB: DOG OF WONDER

FEATURING A COVER
BY COMICS LEGEND
NEAL ADAMS!

AVAILABLE IN FINER STORES EVERYWHERE

For five years, readers have looked at the Action Lab Entertainment logo and wondered, "Who IS that dog with the jet pack?" Wonder no more! The story you never thought would be told is now an ongoing monthly title as ACTION LAB, DOG OF WONDER, comes to comic book shelves everywhere!

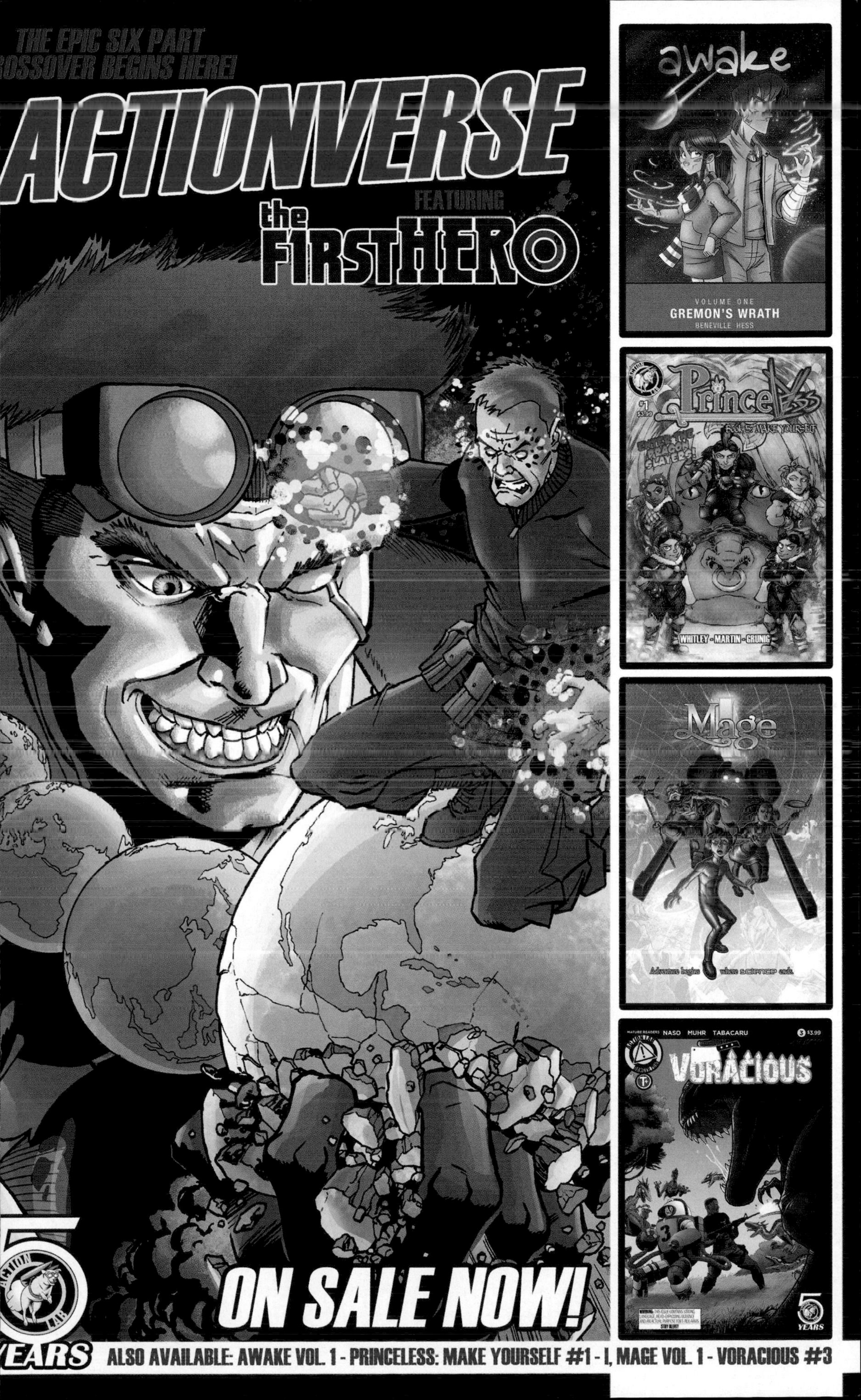
THE EPIC SIX PART
CROSSOVER BEGINS HERE!
ACTIONVERSE
FEATURING
the FIRST HERO
awake
VOLUME ONE
GREMON'S WRATH
BENEVILLE HESS
Princeless
#1
$3.99
Book 5: MAKE YOURSELF
ENTER THE DRAGON SLAYERS!
WHITLEY - MARTIN - GRUNIG
Mage
Adventure begins where science ends.
MATURE READERS NASO MUHR TABACARU
3 $3.99
VORACIOUS
STAY ALERT!
5 YEARS
ON SALE NOW!
5 YEARS
ALSO AVAILABLE: AWAKE VOL. 1 - PRINCELESS: MAKE YOURSELF #1 - I, MAGE VOL. 1 - VORACIOUS #3

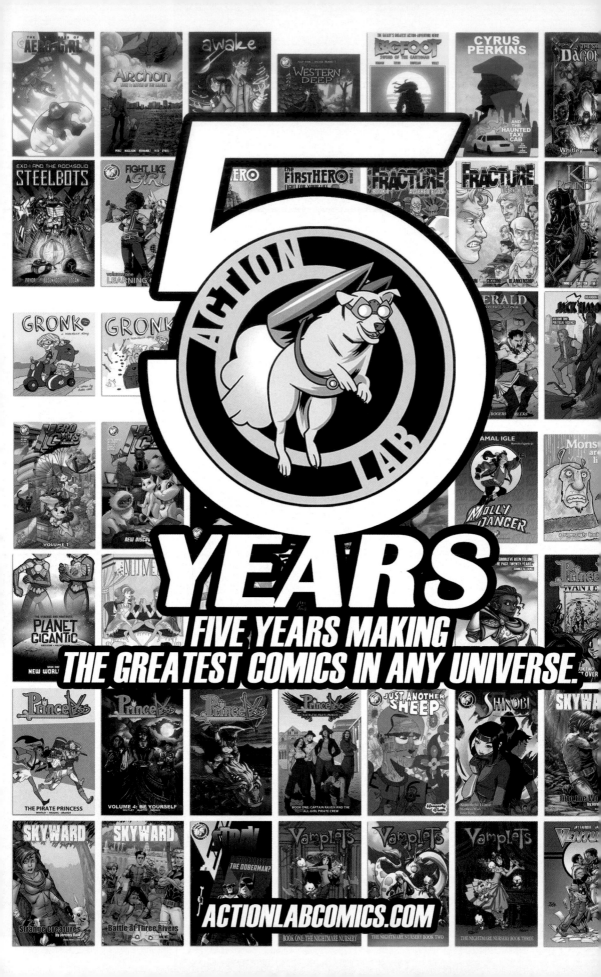

ACTION LAB

5 YEARS

FIVE YEARS MAKING
THE GREATEST COMICS IN ANY UNIVERSE.

ACTIONLABCOMICS.COM

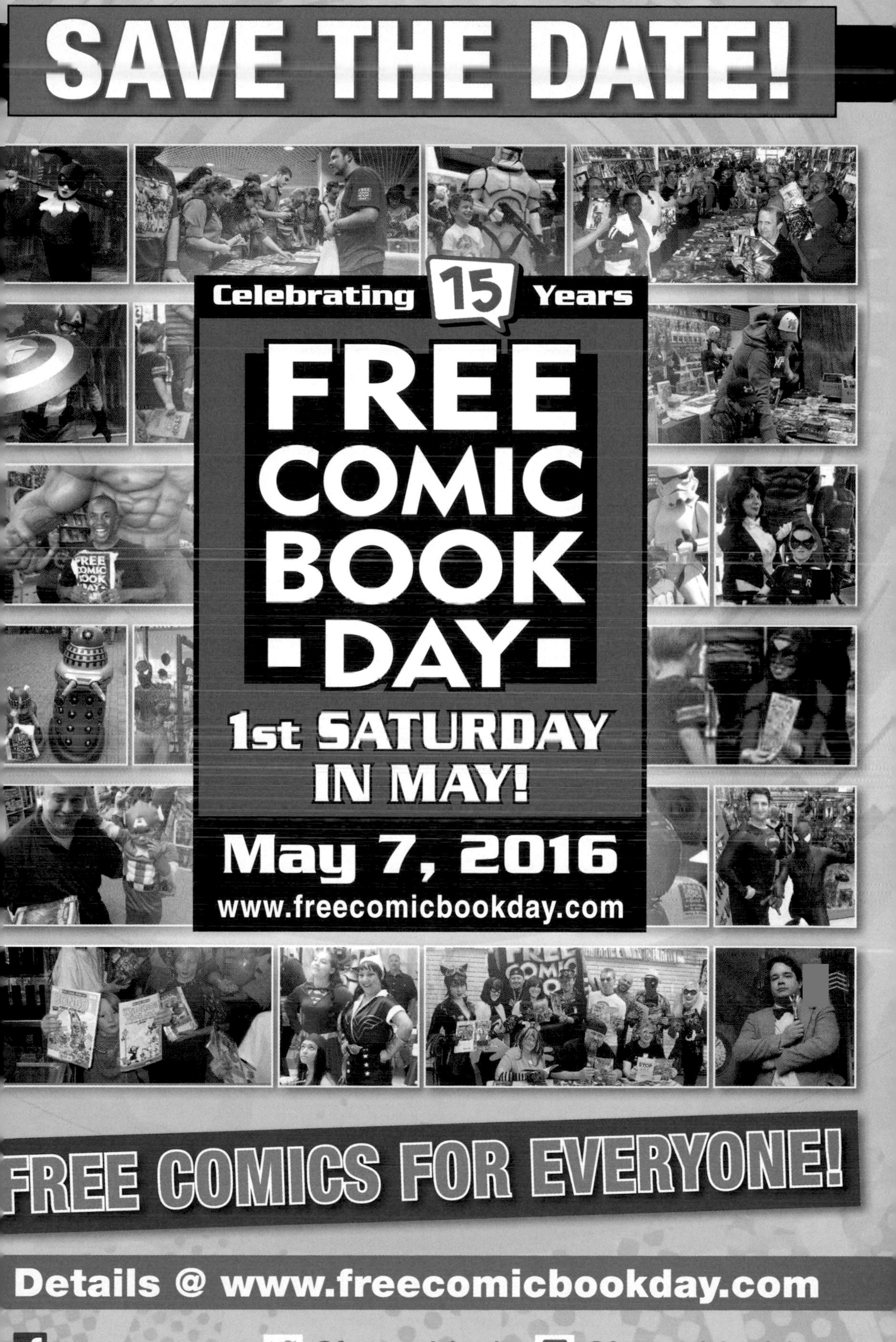
SAVE THE DATE!
Celebrating 15 Years
FREE COMIC BOOK DAY
1st SATURDAY IN MAY!
May 7, 2016
www.freecomicbookday.com
FREE COMICS FOR EVERYONE!
Details @ www.freecomicbookday.com
/freecomicbook
@freecomicbook
@freecomicbookday

Princeless: Make Yourself - Action Lab
www.actionlabcomics.com

7 02382 69115 8

00111

ACTIONLABCOMICS.COM

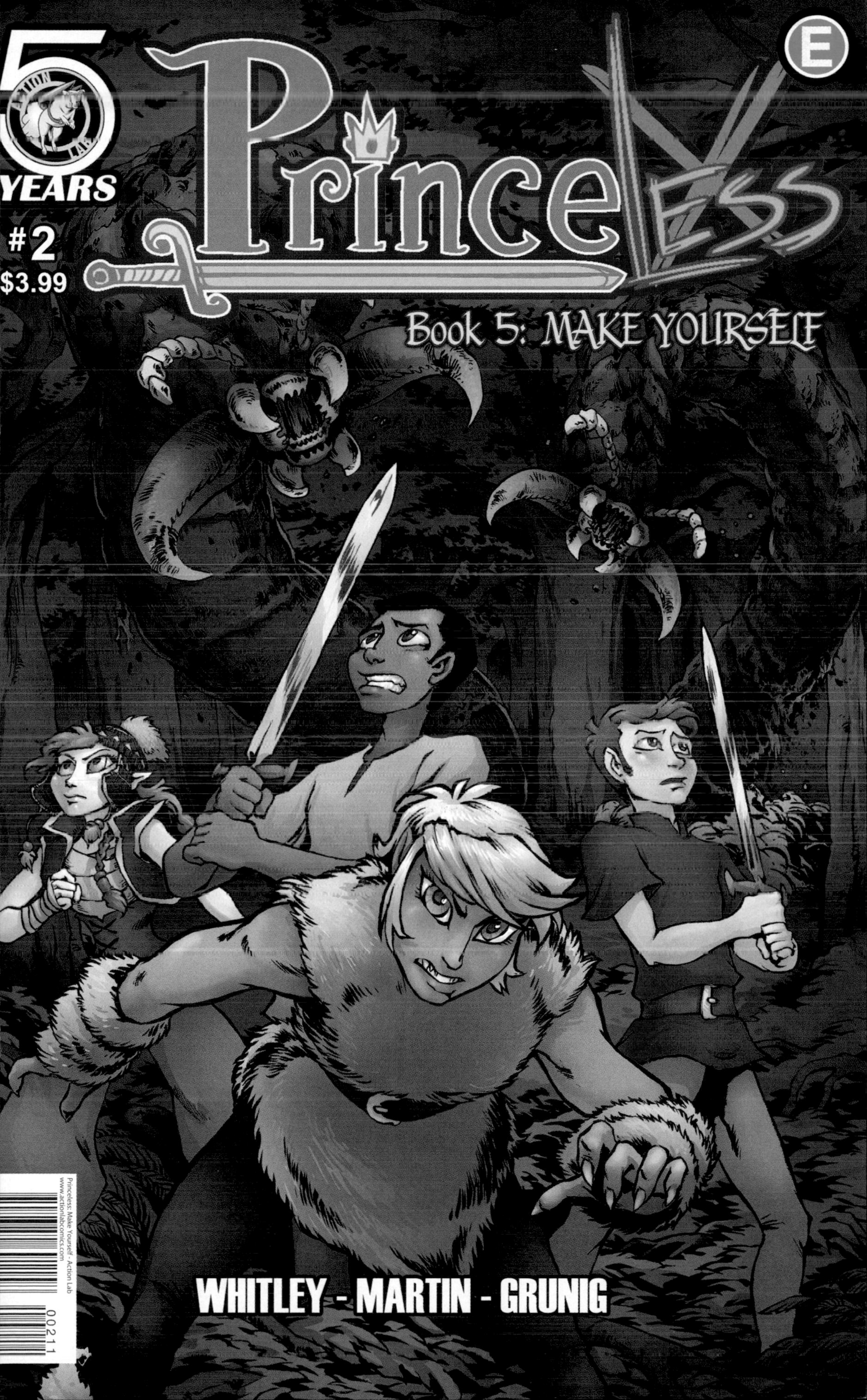
5 YEARS
#2
$3.99
Princeless
E
Book 5: MAKE YOURSELF
WHITLEY - MARTIN - GRUNIG
Princeless: Make Yourself - Action Lab
www.actionlabcomics.com

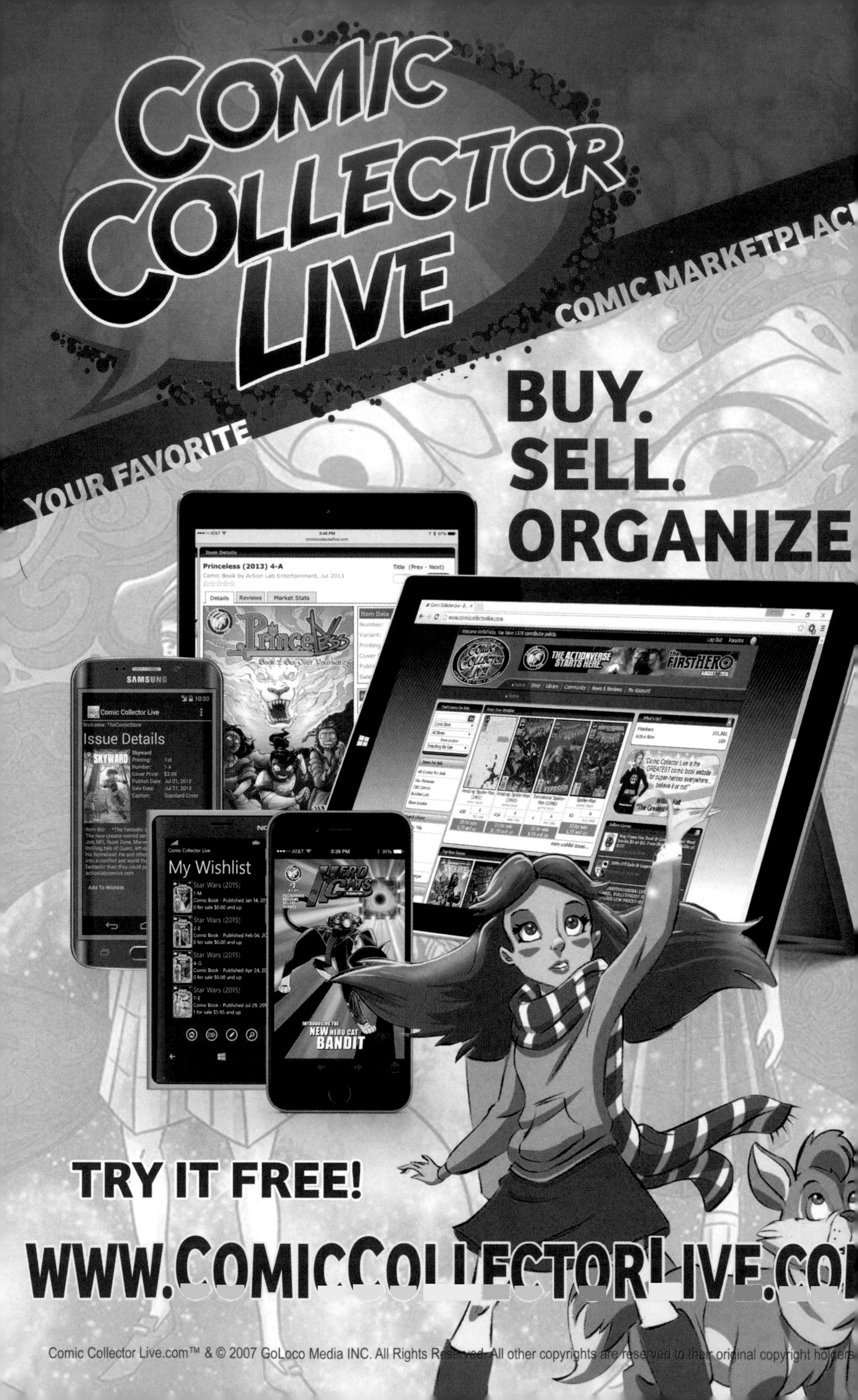
COMIC COLLECTOR LIVE
YOUR FAVORITE COMIC MARKETPLAC
BUY.
SELL.
ORGANIZE
Princeless (2013) 4-A
Issue Details
My Wishlist
TRY IT FREE!
WWW.COMICCOLLECTORLIVE.CO
Comic Collector Live.com™ & © 2007 GoLoco Media INC. All Rights Reserved. All other copyrights are reserved to their original copyright holders

CLEAR OUT! OUT OF THE WAY YOU BUNCH OF LOUTS!

GIRLS, WHAT THE *DEVIL* ARE YOU DOING BRINGING THIS BEAST DOWN OUTSIDE OF--

BEDELIA?

GREATNARN! I'M SO GLAD TO SEE YOU!

YOUR DAD...HE... HE SENT WORD THAT YOU HAD DIED IN A FIRE! I THOUGHT YOU WERE GONE!

OH YEAH, ABOUT THAT. MY FRIENDS AND I GOT INTO SOME TROUBLE AND...

SAY NO MORE! MY BEDELIA AND HER FRIENDS ARE ALWAYS WELCOME IN NORTHHOLD, EVEN IF ONE OF THEM IS A *DRAGON*.

IT'LL HAVE TO STAY OUTSIDE THE GATES THOUGH.

JNDER MISTY MOUNTAINS
TORY: Jeremy Whitley
RT: Emily Martin
OLORS/LETTERS: Brett Grunig

Bryan Seaton: Publisher ● Dave Dwonch: President ● Shawn Gabborin: Editor In Chief
Jason Martin: Publisher-Danger Zone ● Jamal Igle: Vice-President of Marketing ● Jim Dietz: Social Media Director
Nicole DAndria: Editor ● Chad Cicconi: Still Waiting For His Princess ● Colleen Boyd: Submissions Editor

ELESS: MAKE YOURSELF, #2, May 2016. Copyright Jeremy Whitley and Emily Martin, 2016. Published by Action Lab Entertainment. All rights reserved. All characters are fictional. Any likeness one living or dead is purely coincidental. No part of this publication may be reproduced or transmitted without permission, except for review purposes. Printed in Canada. First Printing.

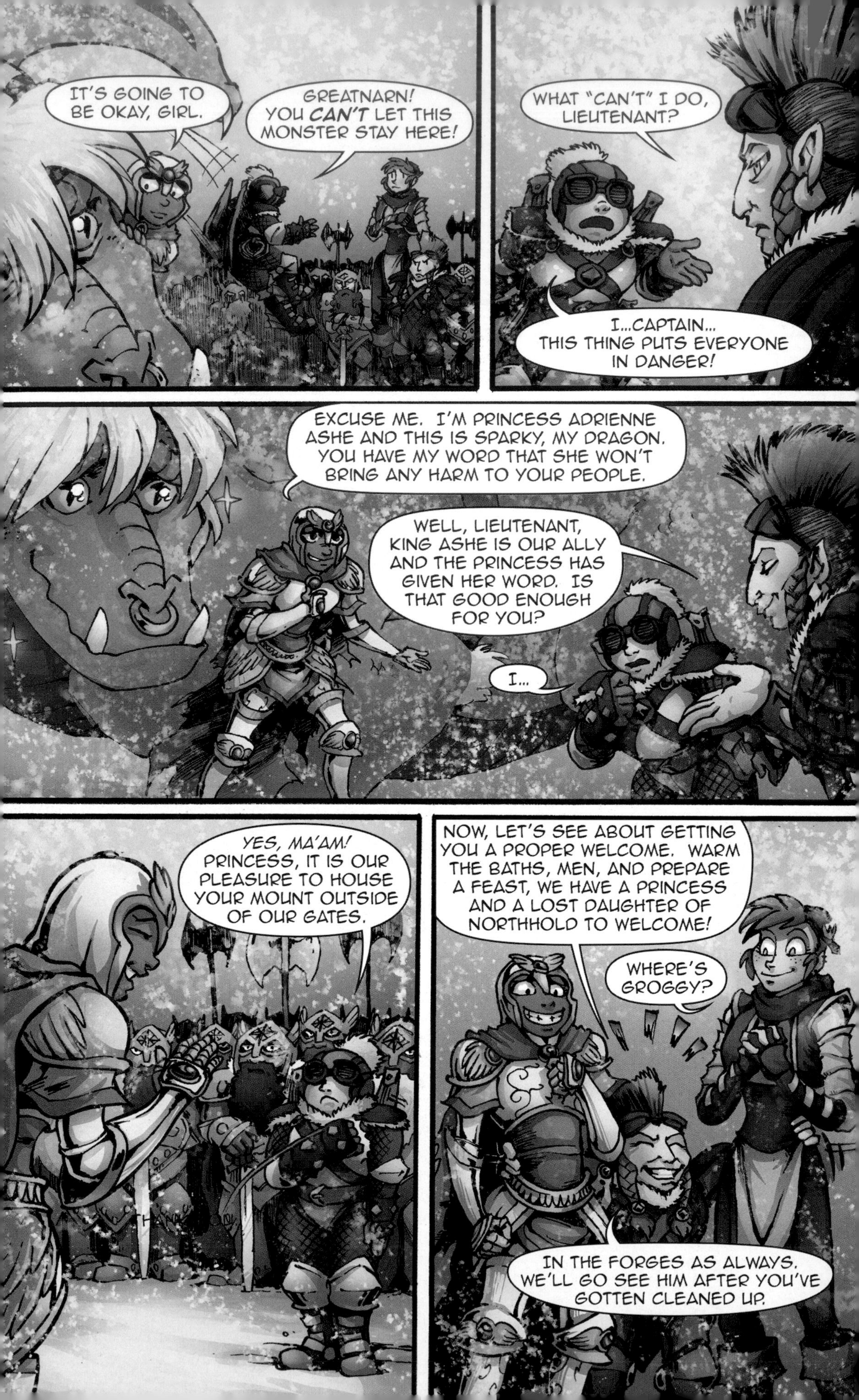

IT'S GOING TO BE OKAY, GIRL.
GREATNARN! YOU CAN'T LET THIS MONSTER STAY HERE!
WHAT "CAN'T" I DO, LIEUTENANT?
I...CAPTAIN... THIS THING PUTS EVERYONE IN DANGER!
EXCUSE ME. I'M PRINCESS ADRIENNE ASHE AND THIS IS SPARKY, MY DRAGON. YOU HAVE MY WORD THAT SHE WON'T BRING ANY HARM TO YOUR PEOPLE.
WELL, LIEUTENANT, KING ASHE IS OUR ALLY AND THE PRINCESS HAS GIVEN HER WORD. IS THAT GOOD ENOUGH FOR YOU?
I...
YES, MA'AM! PRINCESS, IT IS OUR PLEASURE TO HOUSE YOUR MOUNT OUTSIDE OF OUR GATES.
NOW, LET'S SEE ABOUT GETTING YOU A PROPER WELCOME. WARM THE BATHS, MEN, AND PREPARE A FEAST, WE HAVE A PRINCESS AND A LOST DAUGHTER OF NORTHHOLD TO WELCOME!
WHERE'S GROGGY?
IN THE FORGES AS ALWAYS. WE'LL GO SEE HIM AFTER YOU'VE GOTTEN CLEANED UP.

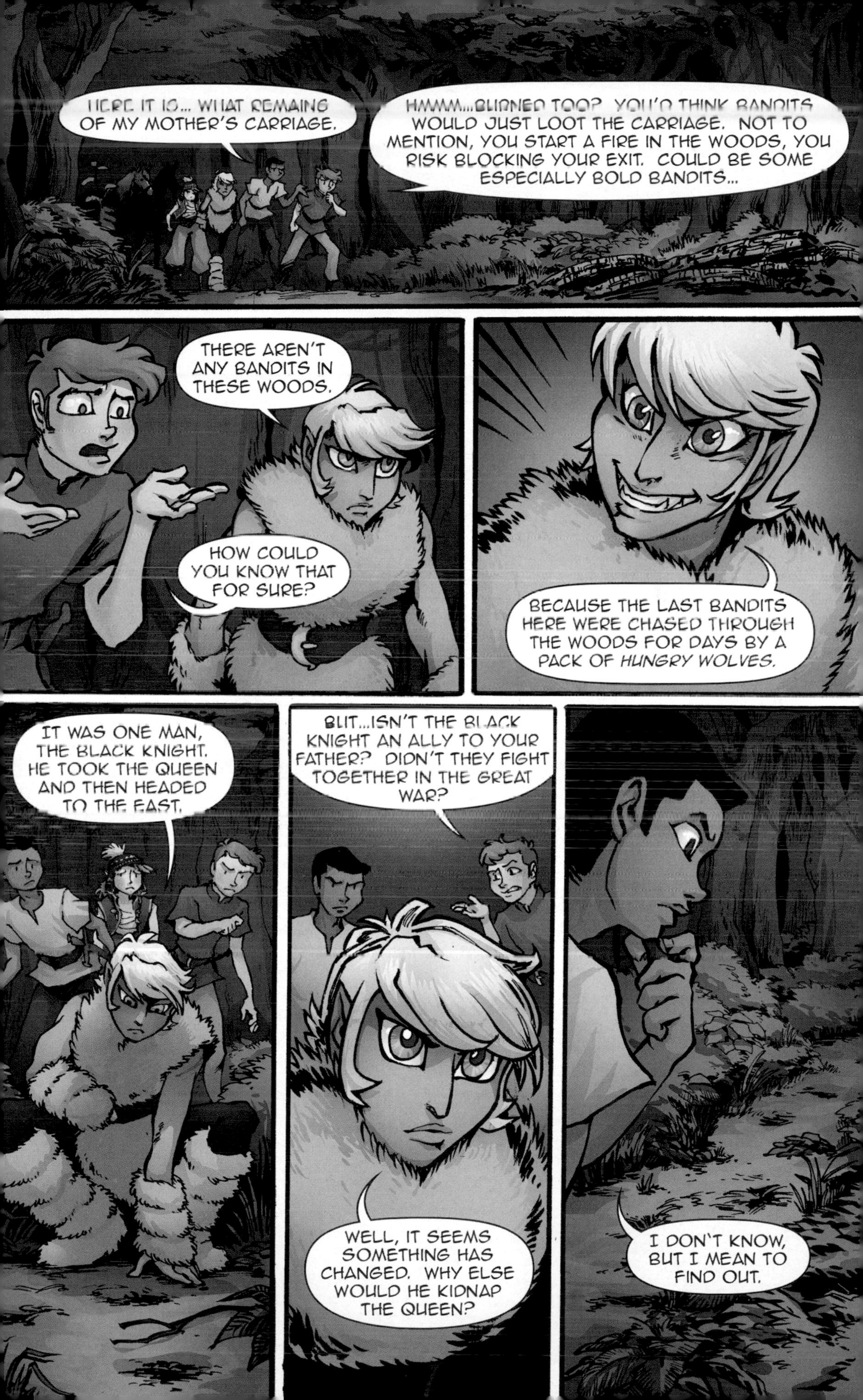
HERE IT IS... WHAT REMAINS OF MY MOTHER'S CARRIAGE.
HMMM...BURNED TOO? YOU'D THINK BANDITS WOULD JUST LOOT THE CARRIAGE. NOT TO MENTION, YOU START A FIRE IN THE WOODS, YOU RISK BLOCKING YOUR EXIT. COULD BE SOME ESPECIALLY BOLD BANDITS...
THERE AREN'T ANY BANDITS IN THESE WOODS.
HOW COULD YOU KNOW THAT FOR SURE?
BECAUSE THE LAST BANDITS HERE WERE CHASED THROUGH THE WOODS FOR DAYS BY A PACK OF *HUNGRY WOLVES.*
IT WAS ONE MAN, THE BLACK KNIGHT. HE TOOK THE QUEEN AND THEN HEADED TO THE EAST.
BUT...ISN'T THE BLACK KNIGHT AN ALLY TO YOUR FATHER? DIDN'T THEY FIGHT TOGETHER IN THE GREAT WAR?
WELL, IT SEEMS SOMETHING HAS CHANGED. WHY ELSE WOULD HE KIDNAP THE QUEEN?
I DON'T KNOW, BUT I MEAN TO FIND OUT.

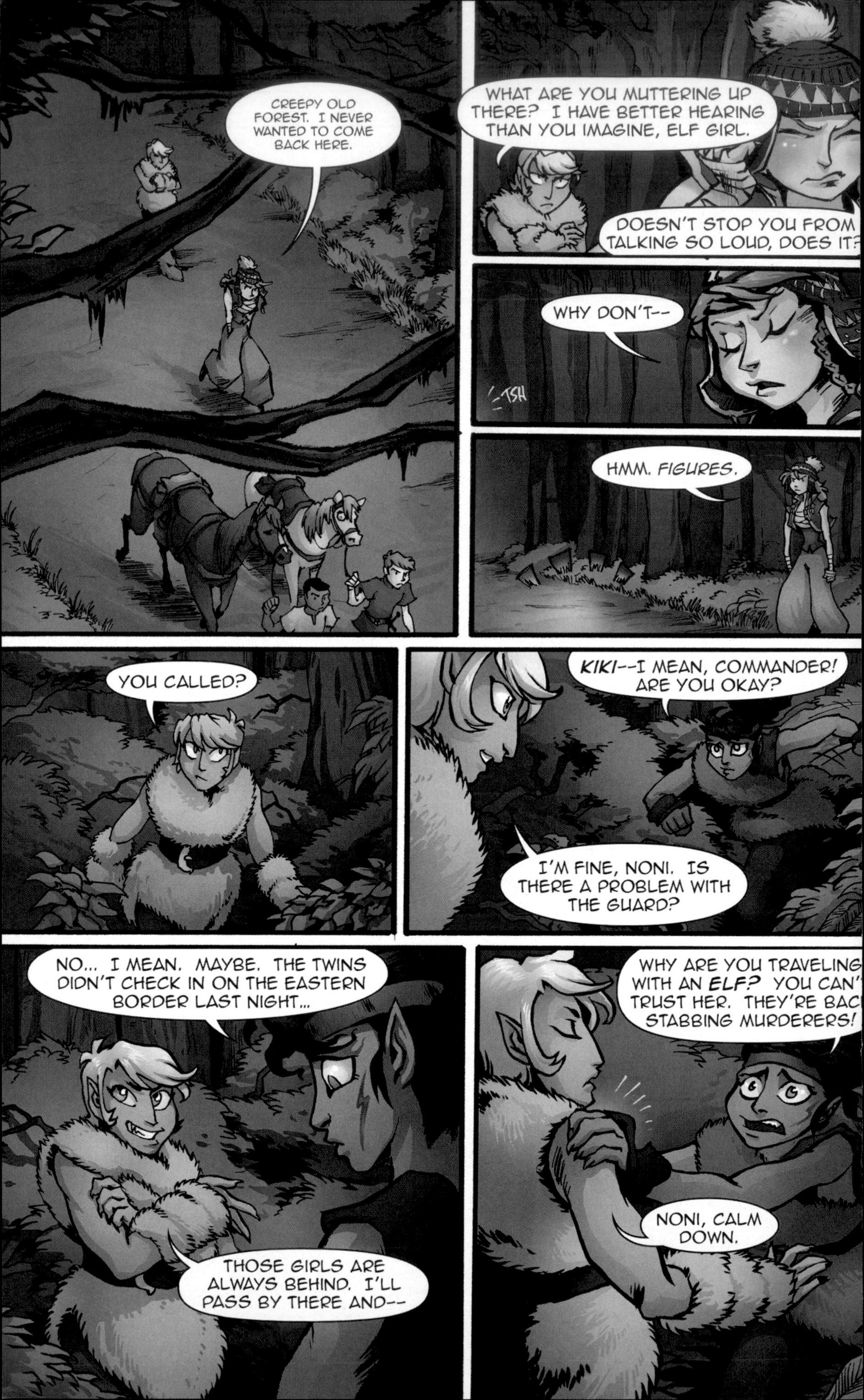
CREEPY OLD FOREST. I NEVER WANTED TO COME BACK HERE.
WHAT ARE YOU MUTTERING UP THERE? I HAVE BETTER HEARING THAN YOU IMAGINE, ELF GIRL.
DOESN'T STOP YOU FROM TALKING SO LOUD, DOES IT?
WHY DON'T--
TSH
HMM. FIGURES.
YOU CALLED?
KIKI--I MEAN, COMMANDER! ARE YOU OKAY?
I'M FINE, NONI. IS THERE A PROBLEM WITH THE GUARD?
NO... I MEAN. MAYBE. THE TWINS DIDN'T CHECK IN ON THE EASTERN BORDER LAST NIGHT...
THOSE GIRLS ARE ALWAYS BEHIND. I'LL PASS BY THERE AND--
WHY ARE YOU TRAVELING WITH AN ELF? YOU CAN'T TRUST HER. THEY'RE BACK STABBING MURDERERS!
NONI, CALM DOWN.

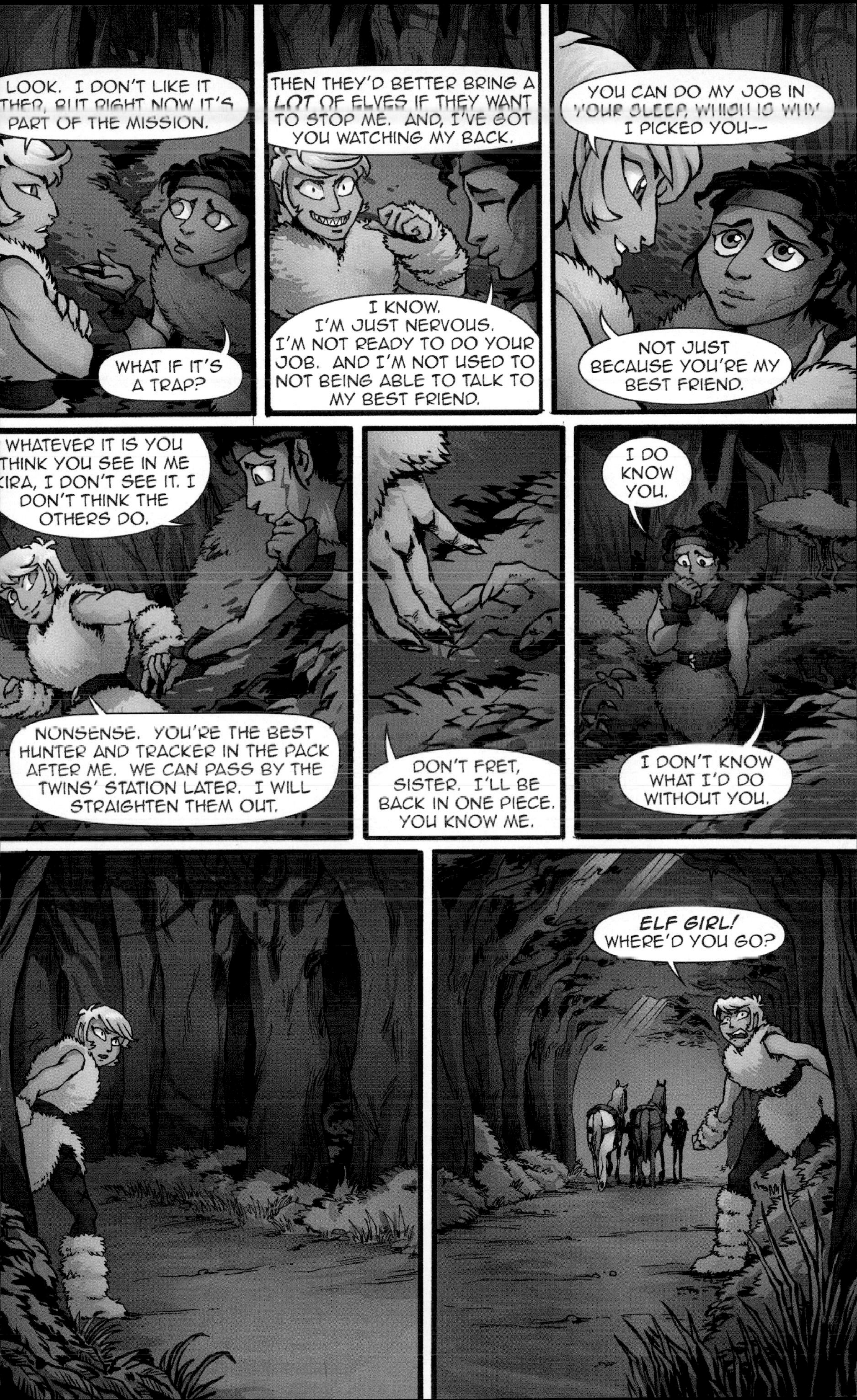
LOOK. I DON'T LIKE IT THER, BUT RIGHT NOW IT'S PART OF THE MISSION.
WHAT IF IT'S A TRAP?
THEN THEY'D BETTER BRING A *LOT* OF ELVES IF THEY WANT TO STOP ME. AND, I'VE GOT YOU WATCHING MY BACK.
I KNOW. I'M JUST NERVOUS. I'M NOT READY TO DO YOUR JOB. AND I'M NOT USED TO NOT BEING ABLE TO TALK TO MY BEST FRIEND.
YOU CAN DO MY JOB IN YOUR SLEEP, WHICH IS WHY I PICKED YOU--
NOT JUST BECAUSE YOU'RE MY BEST FRIEND.
WHATEVER IT IS YOU THINK YOU SEE IN ME KIRA, I DON'T SEE IT. I DON'T THINK THE OTHERS DO.
NONSENSE. YOU'RE THE BEST HUNTER AND TRACKER IN THE PACK AFTER ME. WE CAN PASS BY THE TWINS' STATION LATER. I WILL STRAIGHTEN THEM OUT.
DON'T FRET, SISTER. I'LL BE BACK IN ONE PIECE. YOU KNOW ME.
I DO KNOW YOU.
I DON'T KNOW WHAT I'D DO WITHOUT YOU.
ELF GIRL! WHERE'D YOU GO?

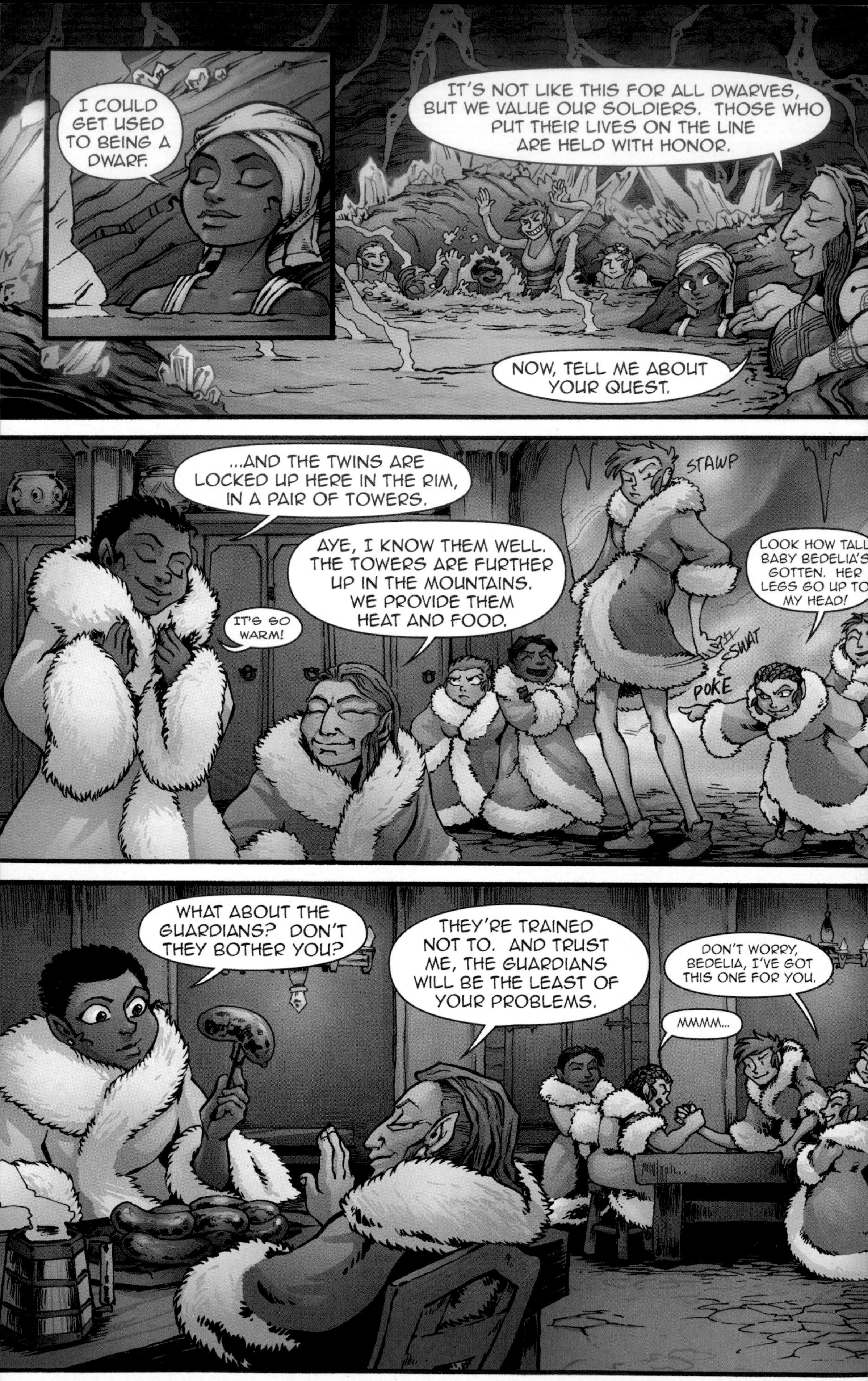
I COULD GET USED TO BEING A DWARF.
IT'S NOT LIKE THIS FOR ALL DWARVES, BUT WE VALUE OUR SOLDIERS. THOSE WHO PUT THEIR LIVES ON THE LINE ARE HELD WITH HONOR.
NOW, TELL ME ABOUT YOUR QUEST.
...AND THE TWINS ARE LOCKED UP HERE IN THE RIM, IN A PAIR OF TOWERS.
IT'S SO WARM!
AYE, I KNOW THEM WELL. THE TOWERS ARE FURTHER UP IN THE MOUNTAINS. WE PROVIDE THEM HEAT AND FOOD.
STAWP
LOOK HOW TALL BABY BEDELIA'S GOTTEN. HER LEGS GO UP TO MY HEAD!
SWAT
POKE
WHAT ABOUT THE GUARDIANS? DON'T THEY BOTHER YOU?
THEY'RE TRAINED NOT TO. AND TRUST ME, THE GUARDIANS WILL BE THE LEAST OF YOUR PROBLEMS.
MMMM...
DON'T WORRY, BEDELIA, I'VE GOT THIS ONE FOR YOU.

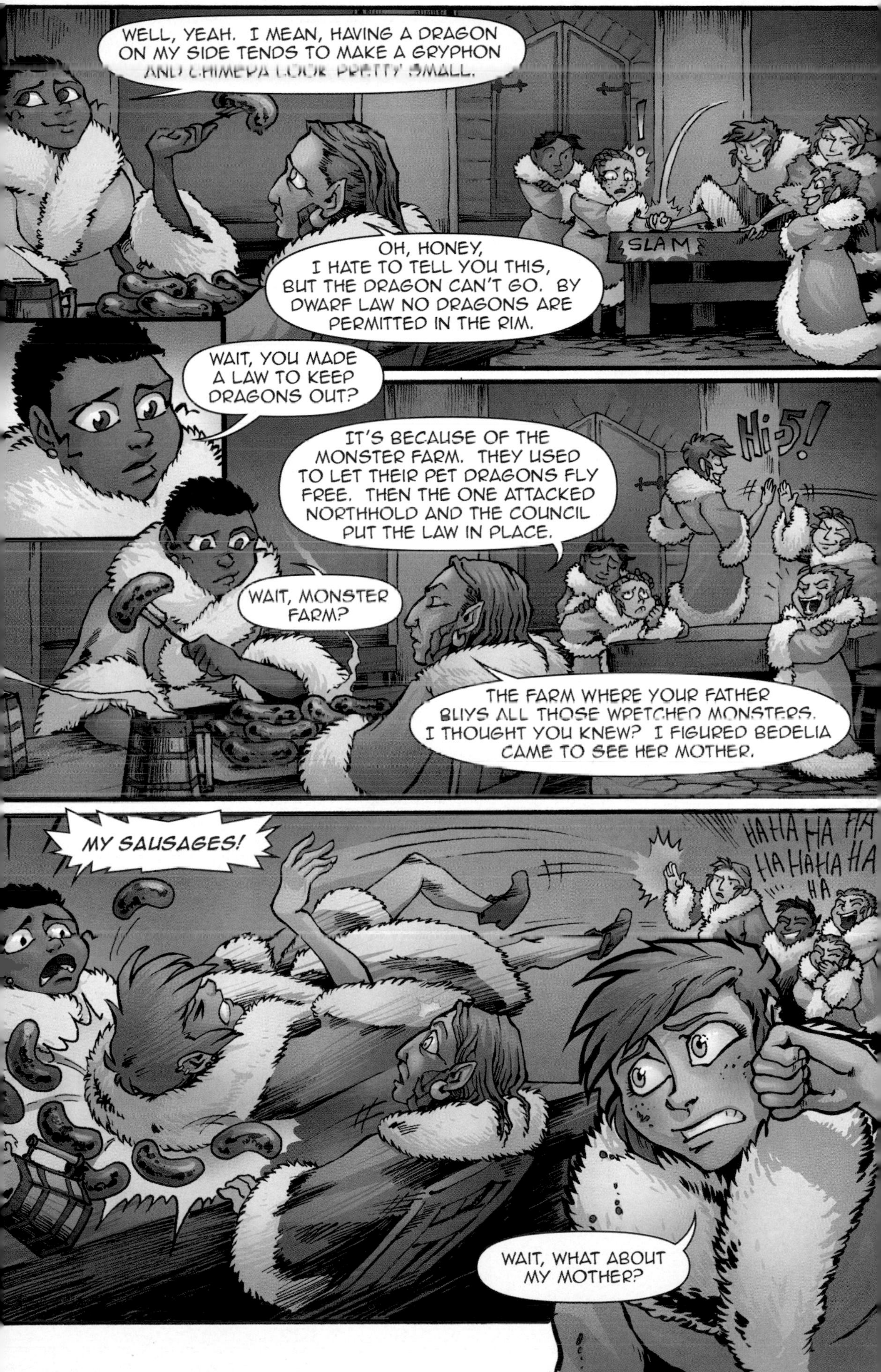
WELL, YEAH. I MEAN, HAVING A DRAGON ON MY SIDE TENDS TO MAKE A GRYPHON AND CHIMERA LOOK PRETTY SMALL.
!
SLAM
OH, HONEY, I HATE TO TELL YOU THIS, BUT THE DRAGON CAN'T GO. BY DWARF LAW NO DRAGONS ARE PERMITTED IN THE RIM.
WAIT, YOU MADE A LAW TO KEEP DRAGONS OUT?
HI-5!
IT'S BECAUSE OF THE MONSTER FARM. THEY USED TO LET THEIR PET DRAGONS FLY FREE. THEN THE ONE ATTACKED NORTHHOLD AND THE COUNCIL PUT THE LAW IN PLACE.
WAIT, MONSTER FARM?
THE FARM WHERE YOUR FATHER BUYS ALL THOSE WRETCHED MONSTERS. I THOUGHT YOU KNEW? I FIGURED BEDELIA CAME TO SEE HER MOTHER.
MY SAUSAGES!
HA HA HA HA HA HA HAHA HA HA
WAIT, WHAT ABOUT MY MOTHER?

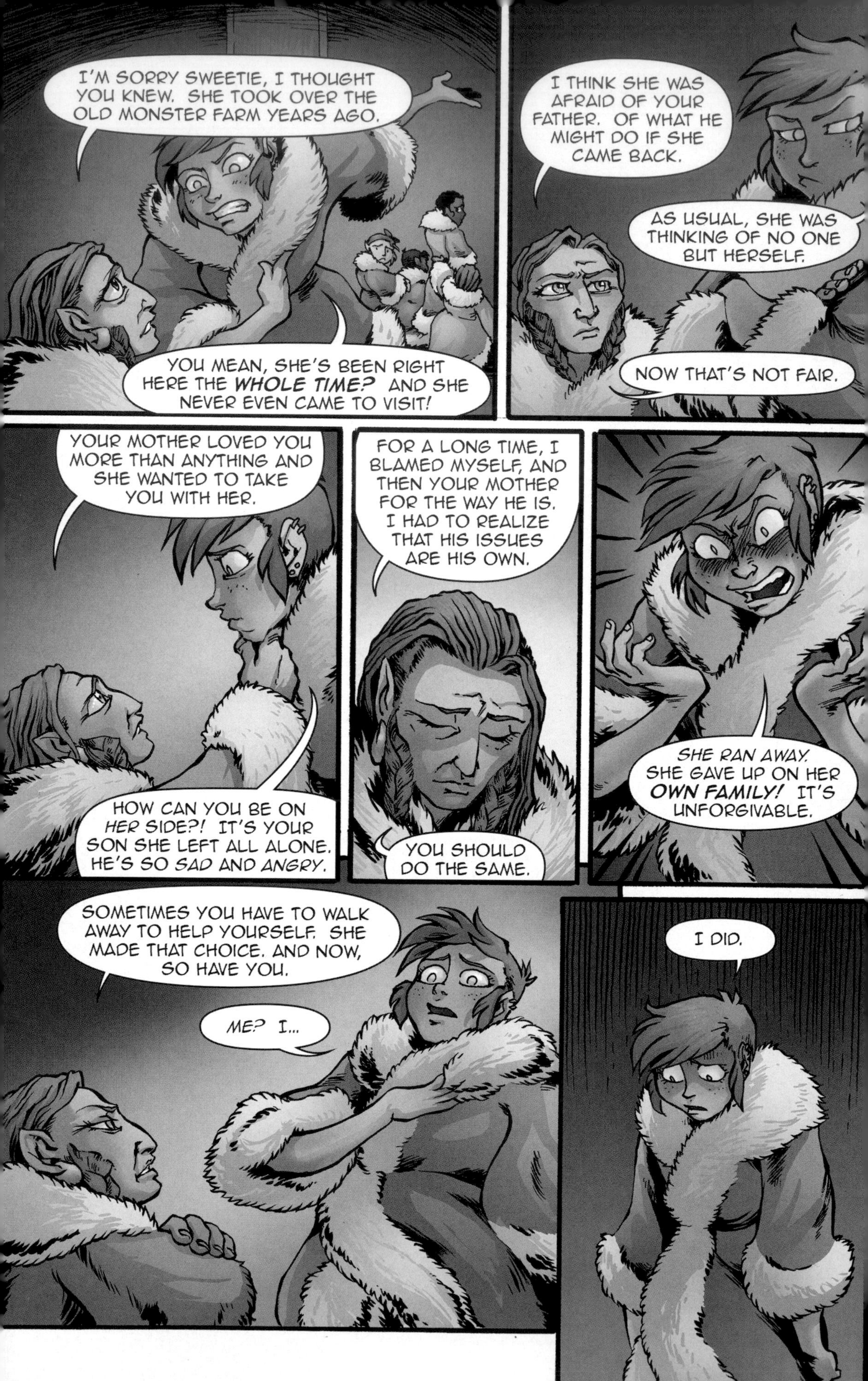
I'M SORRY SWEETIE, I THOUGHT YOU KNEW. SHE TOOK OVER THE OLD MONSTER FARM YEARS AGO.
YOU MEAN, SHE'S BEEN RIGHT HERE THE *WHOLE TIME?* AND SHE NEVER EVEN CAME TO VISIT!
I THINK SHE WAS AFRAID OF YOUR FATHER. OF WHAT HE MIGHT DO IF SHE CAME BACK.
AS USUAL, SHE WAS THINKING OF NO ONE BUT HERSELF.
NOW THAT'S NOT FAIR.
YOUR MOTHER LOVED YOU MORE THAN ANYTHING AND SHE WANTED TO TAKE YOU WITH HER.
HOW CAN YOU BE ON *HER SIDE?!* IT'S YOUR SON SHE LEFT ALL ALONE. HE'S SO *SAD* AND *ANGRY.*
FOR A LONG TIME, I BLAMED MYSELF, AND THEN YOUR MOTHER FOR THE WAY HE IS. I HAD TO REALIZE THAT HIS ISSUES ARE HIS OWN.
YOU SHOULD DO THE SAME.
SHE RAN AWAY. SHE GAVE UP ON HER ***OWN FAMILY!*** IT'S UNFORGIVABLE.
SOMETIMES YOU HAVE TO WALK AWAY TO HELP YOURSELF. SHE MADE THAT CHOICE. AND NOW, SO HAVE YOU.
ME? I...
I DID.

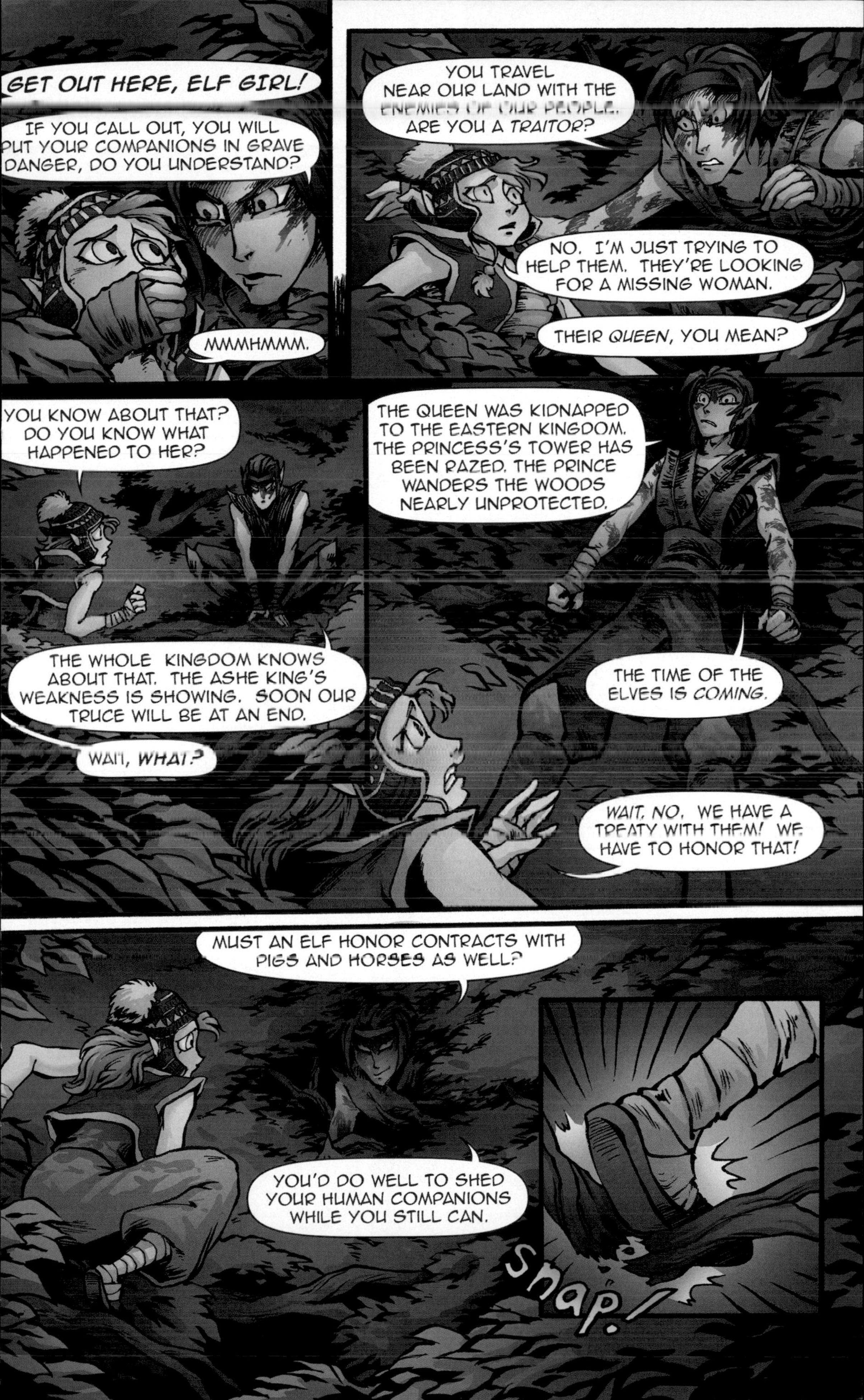
GET OUT HERE, ELF GIRL!
IF YOU CALL OUT, YOU WILL PUT YOUR COMPANIONS IN GRAVE DANGER, DO YOU UNDERSTAND?
MMMHMMM.
YOU TRAVEL NEAR OUR LAND WITH THE ENEMIES OF OUR PEOPLE. ARE YOU A TRAITOR?
NO. I'M JUST TRYING TO HELP THEM. THEY'RE LOOKING FOR A MISSING WOMAN.
THEIR QUEEN, YOU MEAN?
YOU KNOW ABOUT THAT? DO YOU KNOW WHAT HAPPENED TO HER?
THE WHOLE KINGDOM KNOWS ABOUT THAT. THE ASHE KING'S WEAKNESS IS SHOWING. SOON OUR TRUCE WILL BE AT AN END.
WAIT, WHAT?
THE QUEEN WAS KIDNAPPED TO THE EASTERN KINGDOM. THE PRINCESS'S TOWER HAS BEEN RAZED. THE PRINCE WANDERS THE WOODS NEARLY UNPROTECTED.
THE TIME OF THE ELVES IS COMING.
WAIT, NO. WE HAVE A TREATY WITH THEM! WE HAVE TO HONOR THAT!
MUST AN ELF HONOR CONTRACTS WITH PIGS AND HORSES AS WELL?
YOU'D DO WELL TO SHED YOUR HUMAN COMPANIONS WHILE YOU STILL CAN.
Snap!

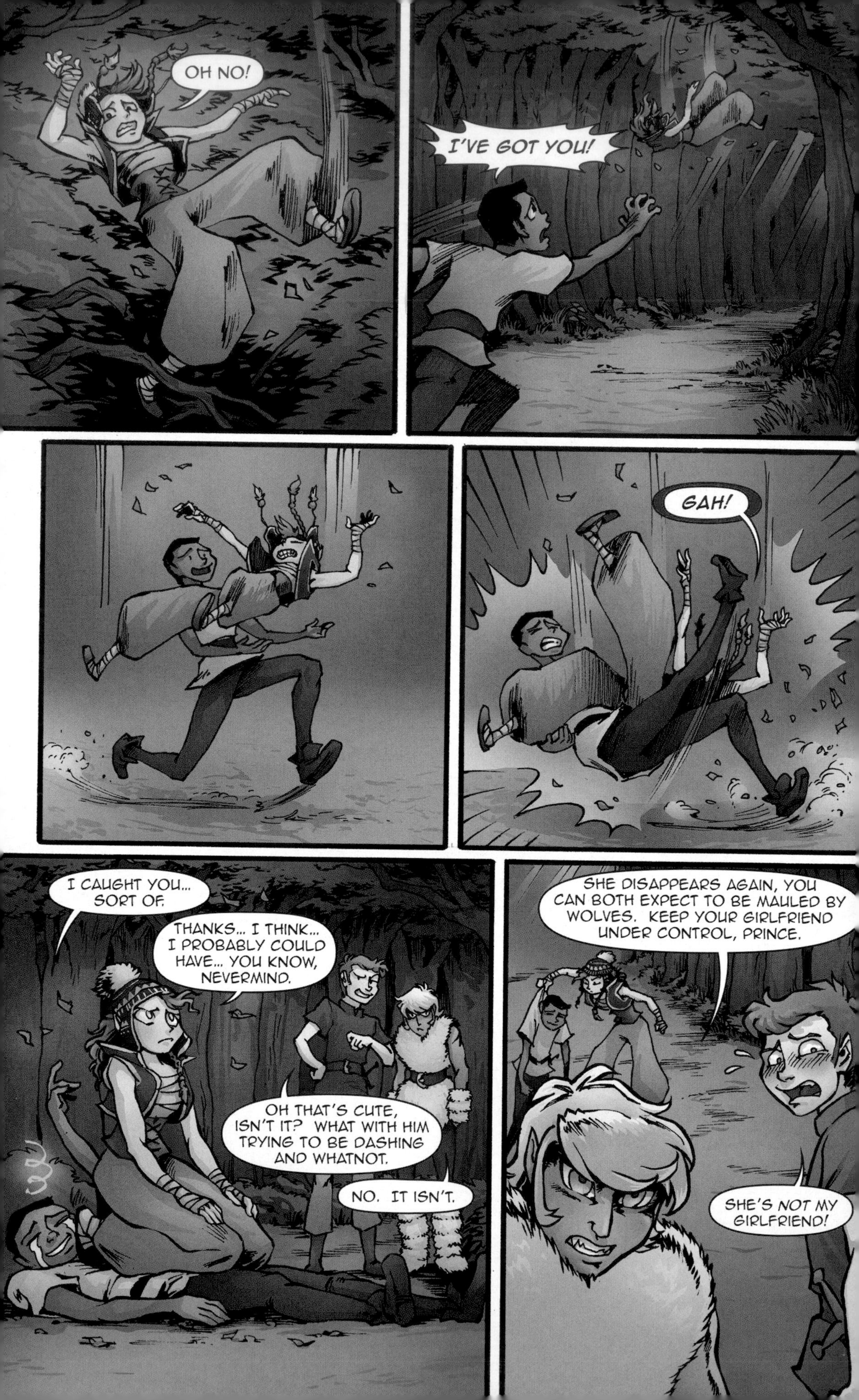
OH NO!
I'VE GOT YOU!
GAH!
I CAUGHT YOU... SORT OF.
THANKS... I THINK... I PROBABLY COULD HAVE... YOU KNOW, NEVERMIND.
OH THAT'S CUTE, ISN'T IT? WHAT WITH HIM TRYING TO BE DASHING AND WHATNOT.
NO. IT ISN'T.
SHE DISAPPEARS AGAIN, YOU CAN BOTH EXPECT TO BE MAULED BY WOLVES. KEEP YOUR GIRLFRIEND UNDER CONTROL, PRINCE.
SHE'S NOT MY GIRLFRIEND!

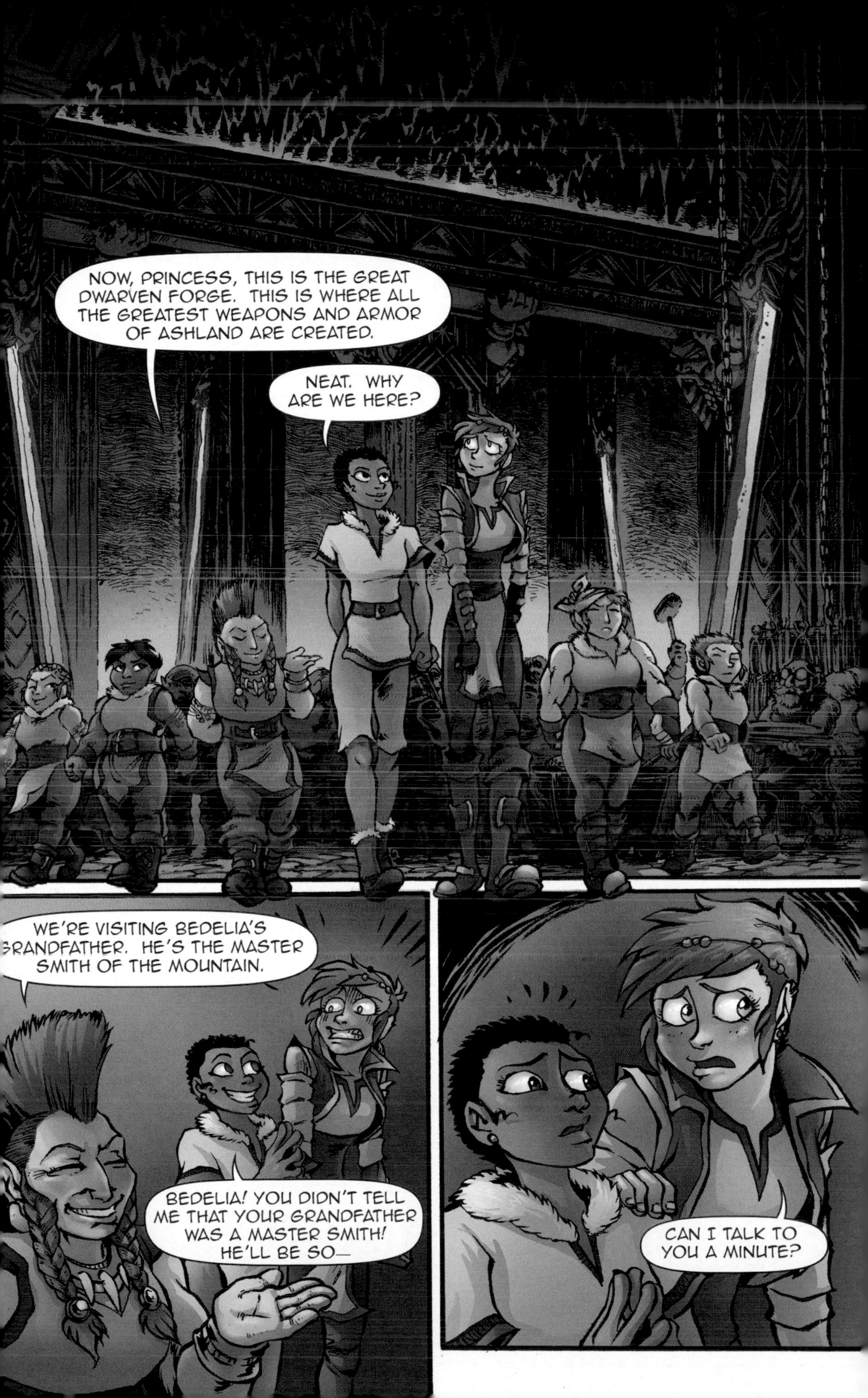
NOW, PRINCESS, THIS IS THE GREAT DWARVEN FORGE. THIS IS WHERE ALL THE GREATEST WEAPONS AND ARMOR OF ASHLAND ARE CREATED.
NEAT. WHY ARE WE HERE?
WE'RE VISITING BEDELIA'S GRANDFATHER. HE'S THE MASTER SMITH OF THE MOUNTAIN.
BEDELIA! YOU DIDN'T TELL ME THAT YOUR GRANDFATHER WAS A MASTER SMITH! HE'LL BE SO—
CAN I TALK TO YOU A MINUTE?

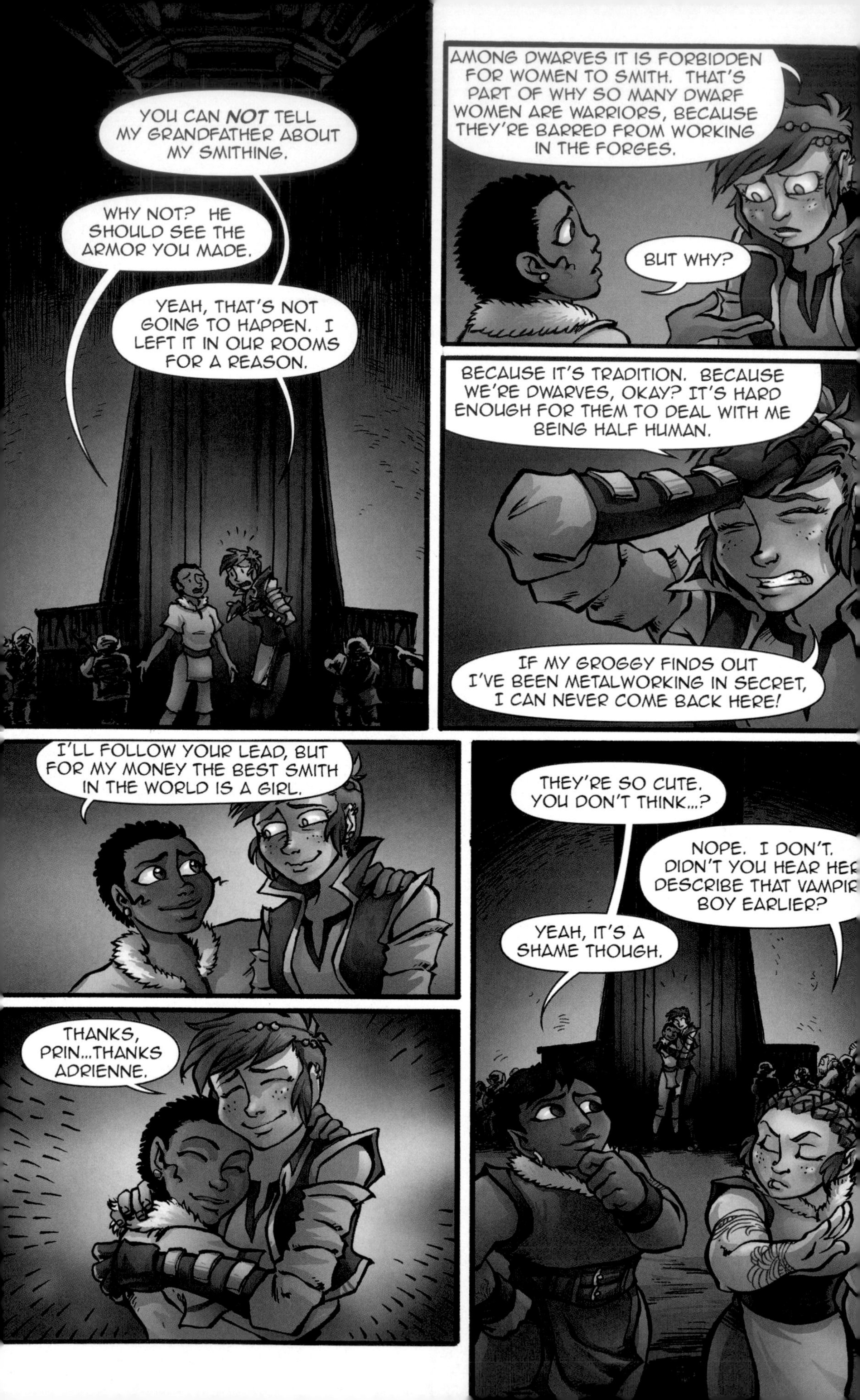
YOU CAN NOT TELL MY GRANDFATHER ABOUT MY SMITHING.
WHY NOT? HE SHOULD SEE THE ARMOR YOU MADE.
YEAH, THAT'S NOT GOING TO HAPPEN. I LEFT IT IN OUR ROOMS FOR A REASON.
AMONG DWARVES IT IS FORBIDDEN FOR WOMEN TO SMITH. THAT'S PART OF WHY SO MANY DWARF WOMEN ARE WARRIORS, BECAUSE THEY'RE BARRED FROM WORKING IN THE FORGES.
BUT WHY?
BECAUSE IT'S TRADITION. BECAUSE WE'RE DWARVES, OKAY? IT'S HARD ENOUGH FOR THEM TO DEAL WITH ME BEING HALF HUMAN.
IF MY GROGGY FINDS OUT I'VE BEEN METALWORKING IN SECRET, I CAN NEVER COME BACK HERE!
I'LL FOLLOW YOUR LEAD, BUT FOR MY MONEY THE BEST SMITH IN THE WORLD IS A GIRL.
THANKS, PRIN...THANKS ADRIENNE.
THEY'RE SO CUTE. YOU DON'T THINK...?
NOPE. I DON'T. DIDN'T YOU HEAR HER DESCRIBE THAT VAMPIRE BOY EARLIER?
YEAH, IT'S A SHAME THOUGH.

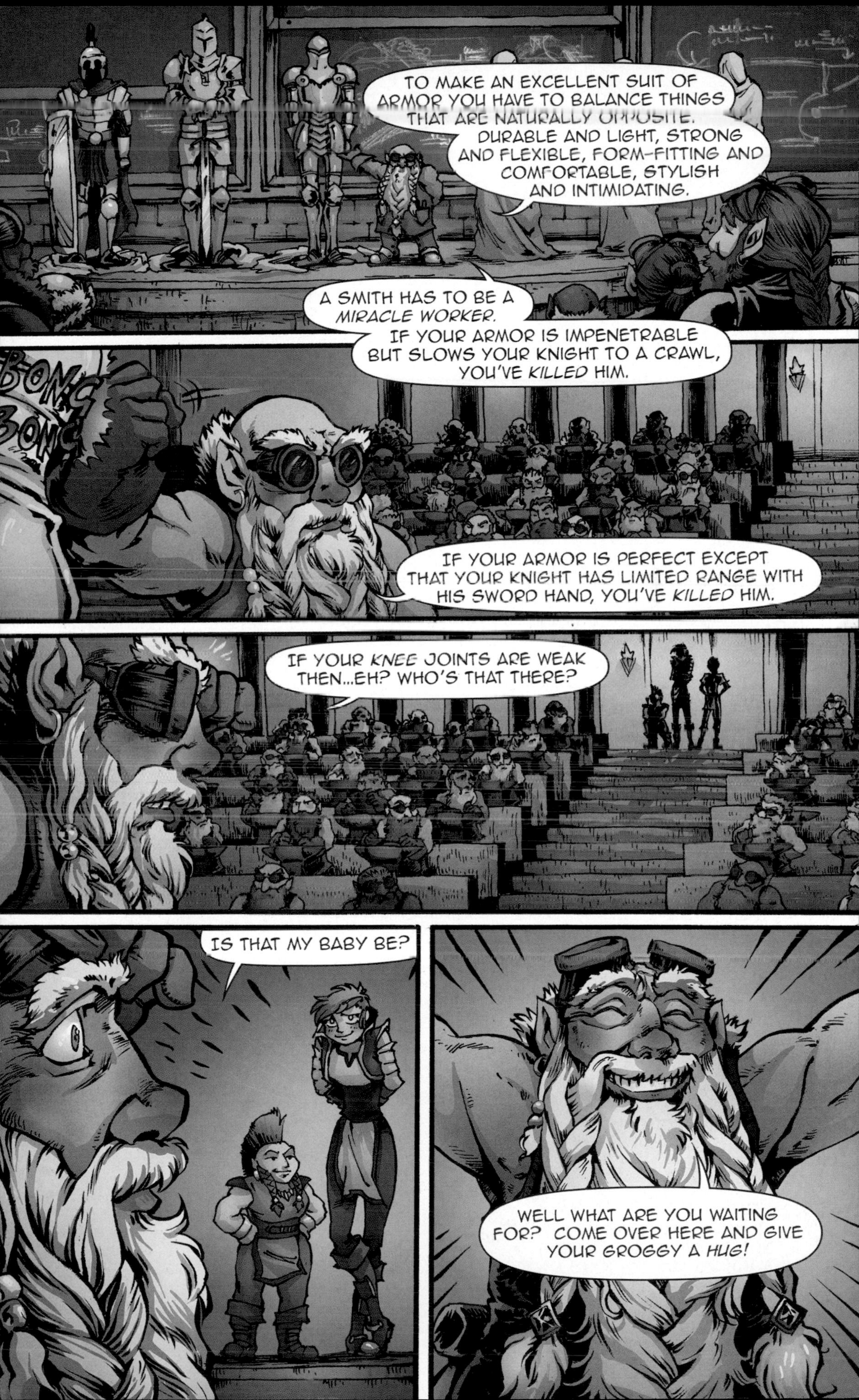
TO MAKE AN EXCELLENT SUIT OF ARMOR YOU HAVE TO BALANCE THINGS THAT ARE NATURALLY OPPOSITE. DURABLE AND LIGHT, STRONG AND FLEXIBLE, FORM-FITTING AND COMFORTABLE, STYLISH AND INTIMIDATING.
A SMITH HAS TO BE A MIRACLE WORKER.
IF YOUR ARMOR IS IMPENETRABLE BUT SLOWS YOUR KNIGHT TO A CRAWL, YOU'VE KILLED HIM.
BONG
BONG
IF YOUR ARMOR IS PERFECT EXCEPT THAT YOUR KNIGHT HAS LIMITED RANGE WITH HIS SWORD HAND, YOU'VE KILLED HIM.
IF YOUR KNEE JOINTS ARE WEAK THEN...EH? WHO'S THAT THERE?
IS THAT MY BABY BE?
WELL WHAT ARE YOU WAITING FOR? COME OVER HERE AND GIVE YOUR GROGGY A HUG!

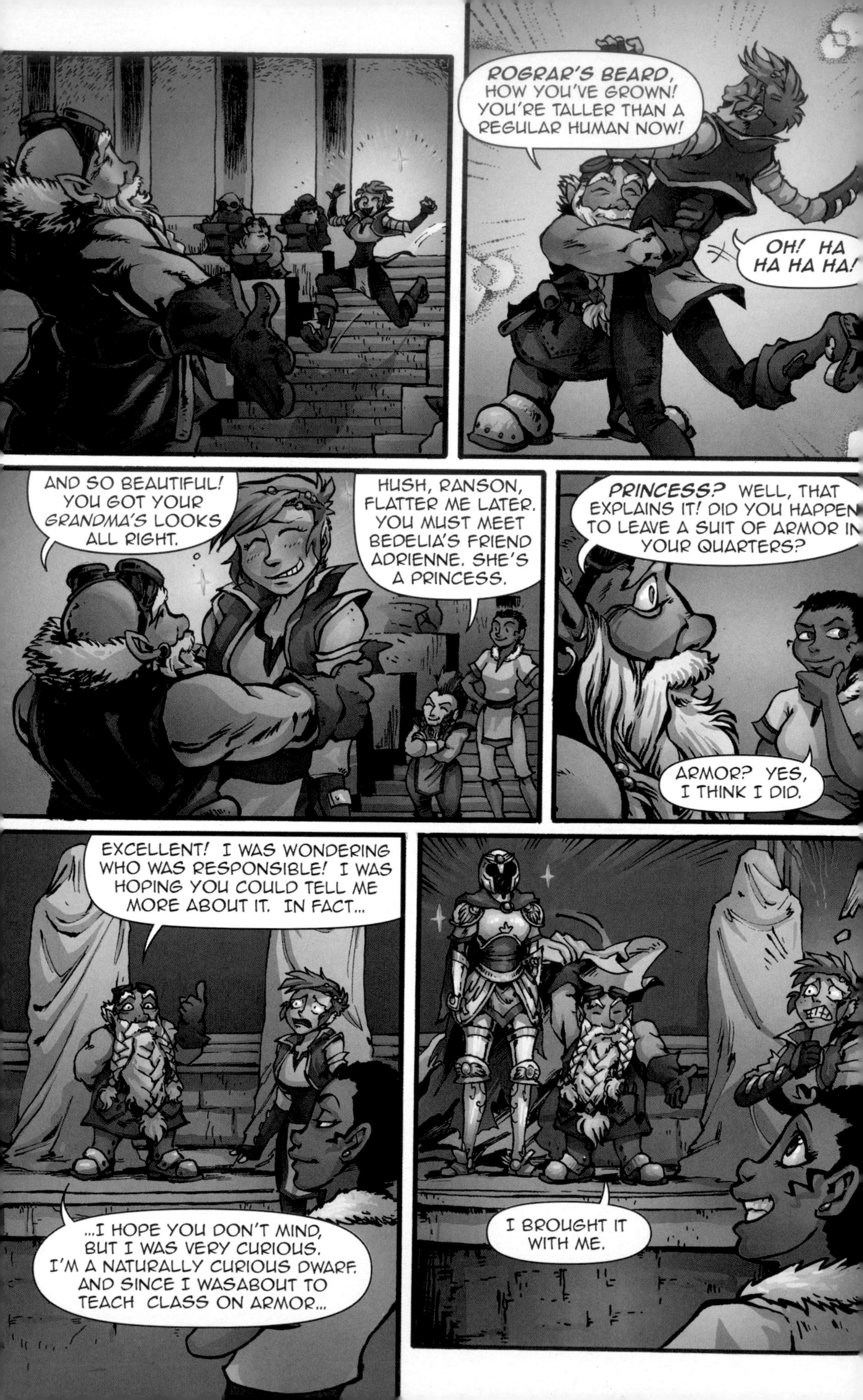
ROGRAR'S BEARD, HOW YOU'VE GROWN! YOU'RE TALLER THAN A REGULAR HUMAN NOW!
OH! HA HA HA HA!
AND SO BEAUTIFUL! YOU GOT YOUR GRANDMA'S LOOKS ALL RIGHT.
HUSH, RANSON, FLATTER ME LATER. YOU MUST MEET BEDELIA'S FRIEND ADRIENNE. SHE'S A PRINCESS.
PRINCESS? WELL, THAT EXPLAINS IT! DID YOU HAPPEN TO LEAVE A SUIT OF ARMOR IN YOUR QUARTERS?
ARMOR? YES, I THINK I DID.
EXCELLENT! I WAS WONDERING WHO WAS RESPONSIBLE! I WAS HOPING YOU COULD TELL ME MORE ABOUT IT. IN FACT...
...I HOPE YOU DON'T MIND, BUT I WAS VERY CURIOUS. I'M A NATURALLY CURIOUS DWARF. AND SINCE I WASABOUT TO TEACH CLASS ON ARMOR...
I BROUGHT IT WITH ME.

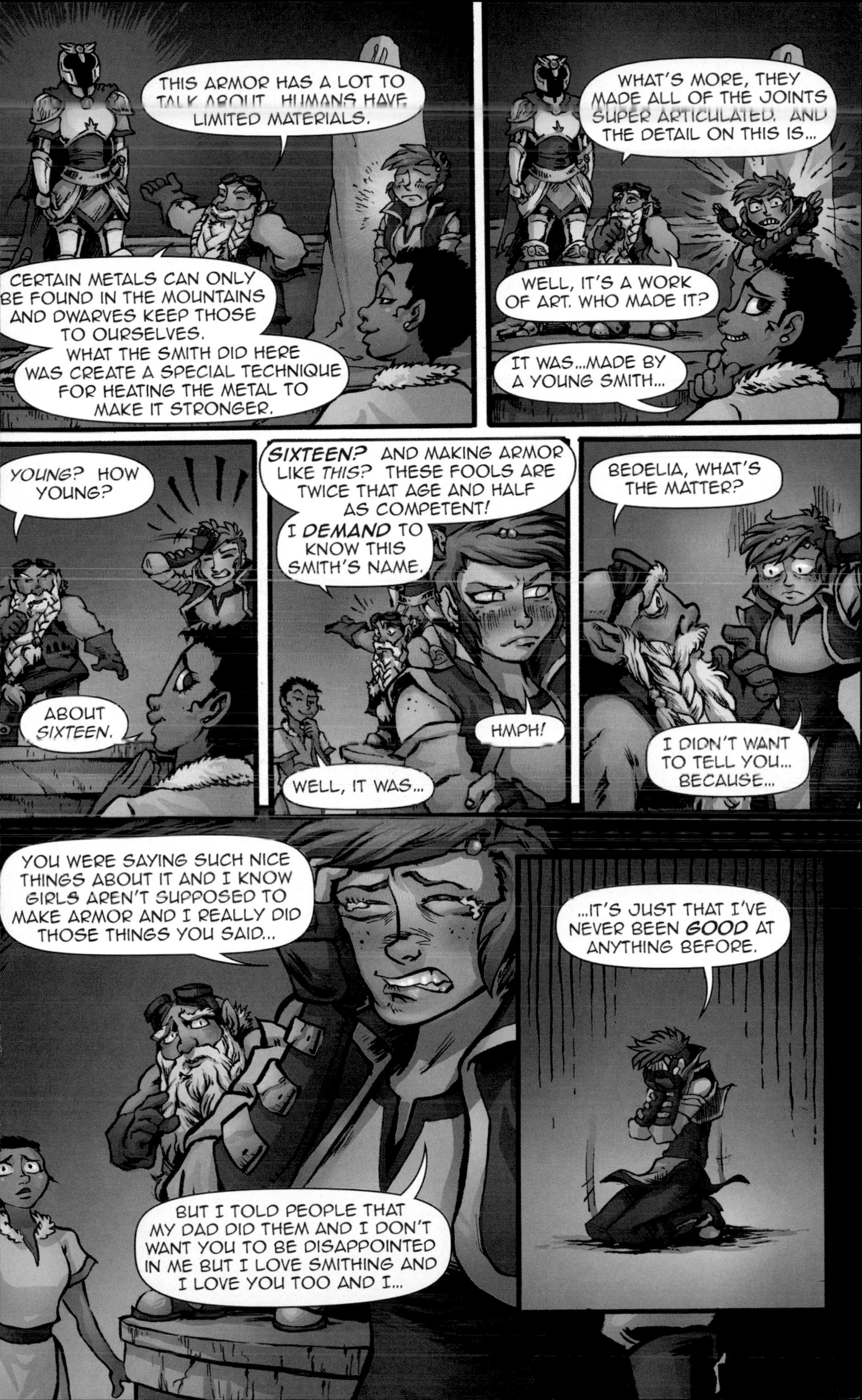
THIS ARMOR HAS A LOT TO TALK ABOUT. HUMANS HAVE LIMITED MATERIALS.
CERTAIN METALS CAN ONLY BE FOUND IN THE MOUNTAINS AND DWARVES KEEP THOSE TO OURSELVES.
WHAT THE SMITH DID HERE WAS CREATE A SPECIAL TECHNIQUE FOR HEATING THE METAL TO MAKE IT STRONGER.
WHAT'S MORE, THEY MADE ALL OF THE JOINTS SUPER ARTICULATED. AND THE DETAIL ON THIS IS...
WELL, IT'S A WORK OF ART. WHO MADE IT?
IT WAS...MADE BY A YOUNG SMITH...
YOUNG? HOW YOUNG?
ABOUT SIXTEEN.
SIXTEEN? AND MAKING ARMOR LIKE THIS? THESE FOOLS ARE TWICE THAT AGE AND HALF AS COMPETENT!
I DEMAND TO KNOW THIS SMITH'S NAME.
HMPH!
WELL, IT WAS...
BEDELIA, WHAT'S THE MATTER?
I DIDN'T WANT TO TELL YOU... BECAUSE...
YOU WERE SAYING SUCH NICE THINGS ABOUT IT AND I KNOW GIRLS AREN'T SUPPOSED TO MAKE ARMOR AND I REALLY DID THOSE THINGS YOU SAID...
BUT I TOLD PEOPLE THAT MY DAD DID THEM AND I DON'T WANT YOU TO BE DISAPPOINTED IN ME BUT I LOVE SMITHING AND I LOVE YOU TOO AND I...
...IT'S JUST THAT I'VE NEVER BEEN GOOD AT ANYTHING BEFORE.

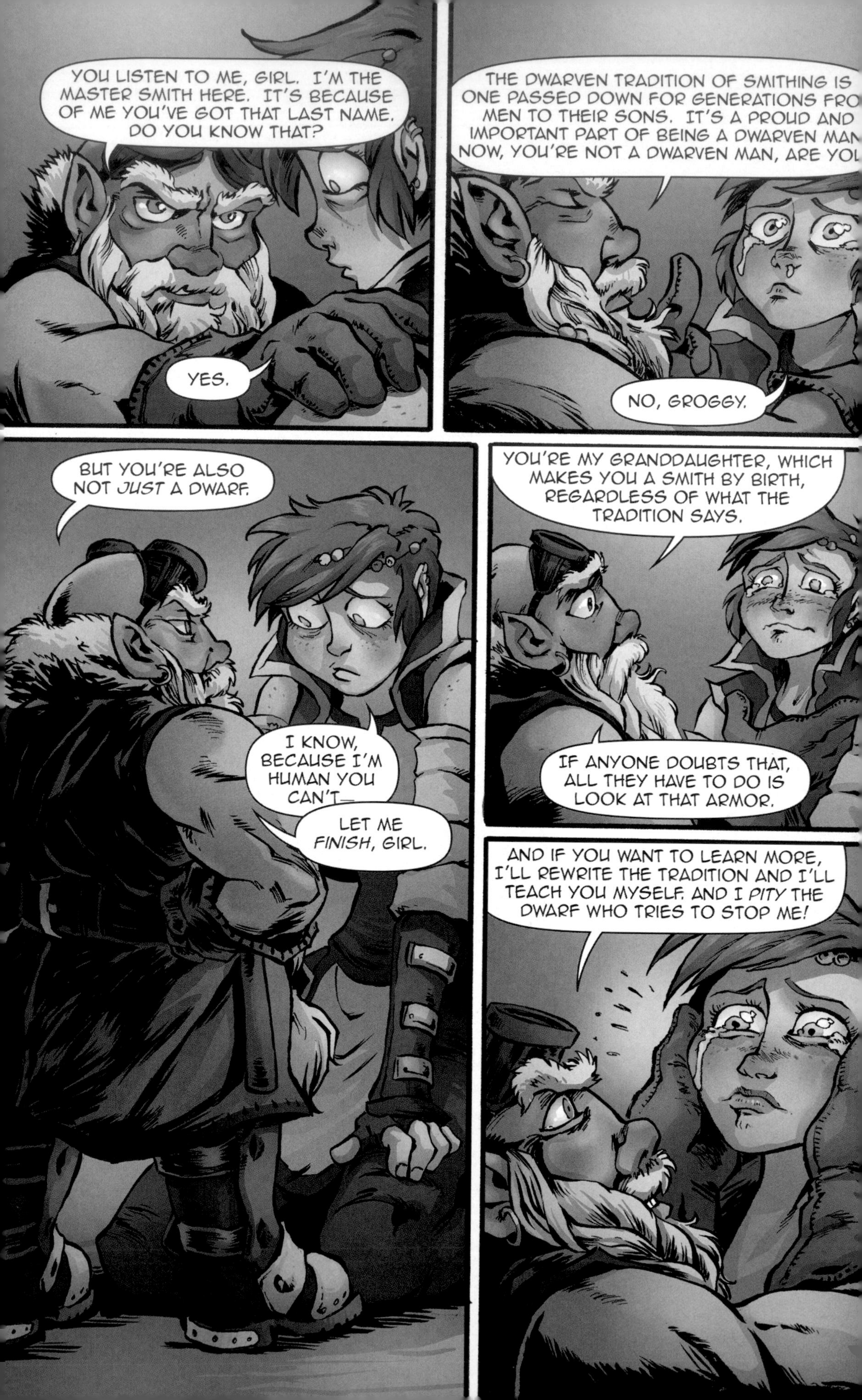
YOU LISTEN TO ME, GIRL. I'M THE MASTER SMITH HERE. IT'S BECAUSE OF ME YOU'VE GOT THAT LAST NAME. DO YOU KNOW THAT?
YES.
THE DWARVEN TRADITION OF SMITHING IS ONE PASSED DOWN FOR GENERATIONS FRO MEN TO THEIR SONS. IT'S A PROUD AND IMPORTANT PART OF BEING A DWARVEN MAN NOW, YOU'RE NOT A DWARVEN MAN, ARE YO
NO, GROGGY.
BUT YOU'RE ALSO NOT *JUST* A DWARF.
I KNOW, BECAUSE I'M HUMAN YOU CAN'T—
LET ME *FINISH*, GIRL.
YOU'RE MY GRANDDAUGHTER, WHICH MAKES YOU A SMITH BY BIRTH, REGARDLESS OF WHAT THE TRADITION SAYS.
IF ANYONE DOUBTS THAT, ALL THEY HAVE TO DO IS LOOK AT THAT ARMOR.
AND IF YOU WANT TO LEARN MORE, I'LL REWRITE THE TRADITION AND I'LL TEACH YOU MYSELF. AND I *PITY* THE DWARF WHO TRIES TO STOP ME!

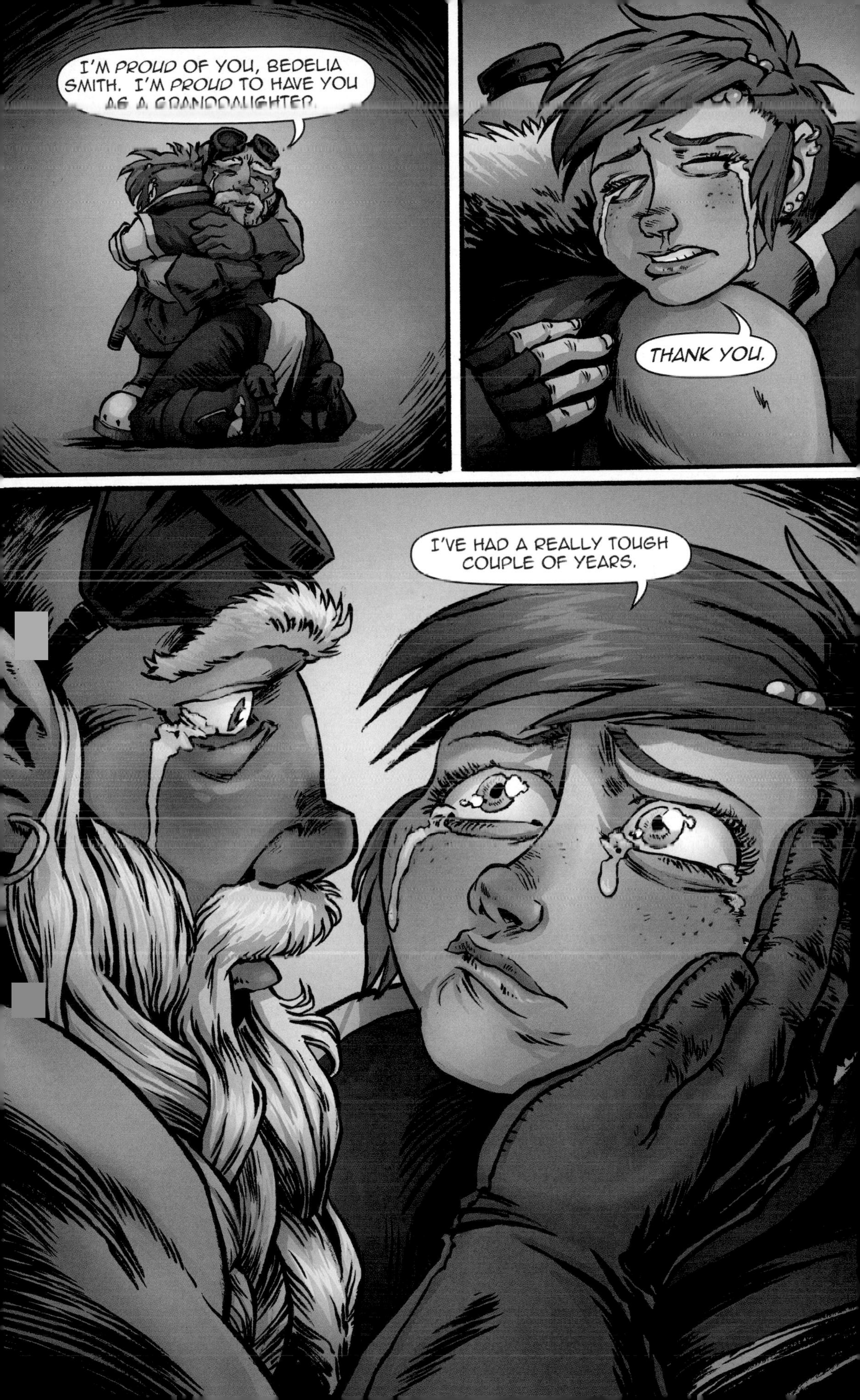
I'M PROUD OF YOU, BEDELIA SMITH. I'M PROUD TO HAVE YOU AS A GRANDDAUGHTER.
THANK YOU.
I'VE HAD A REALLY TOUGH COUPLE OF YEARS.

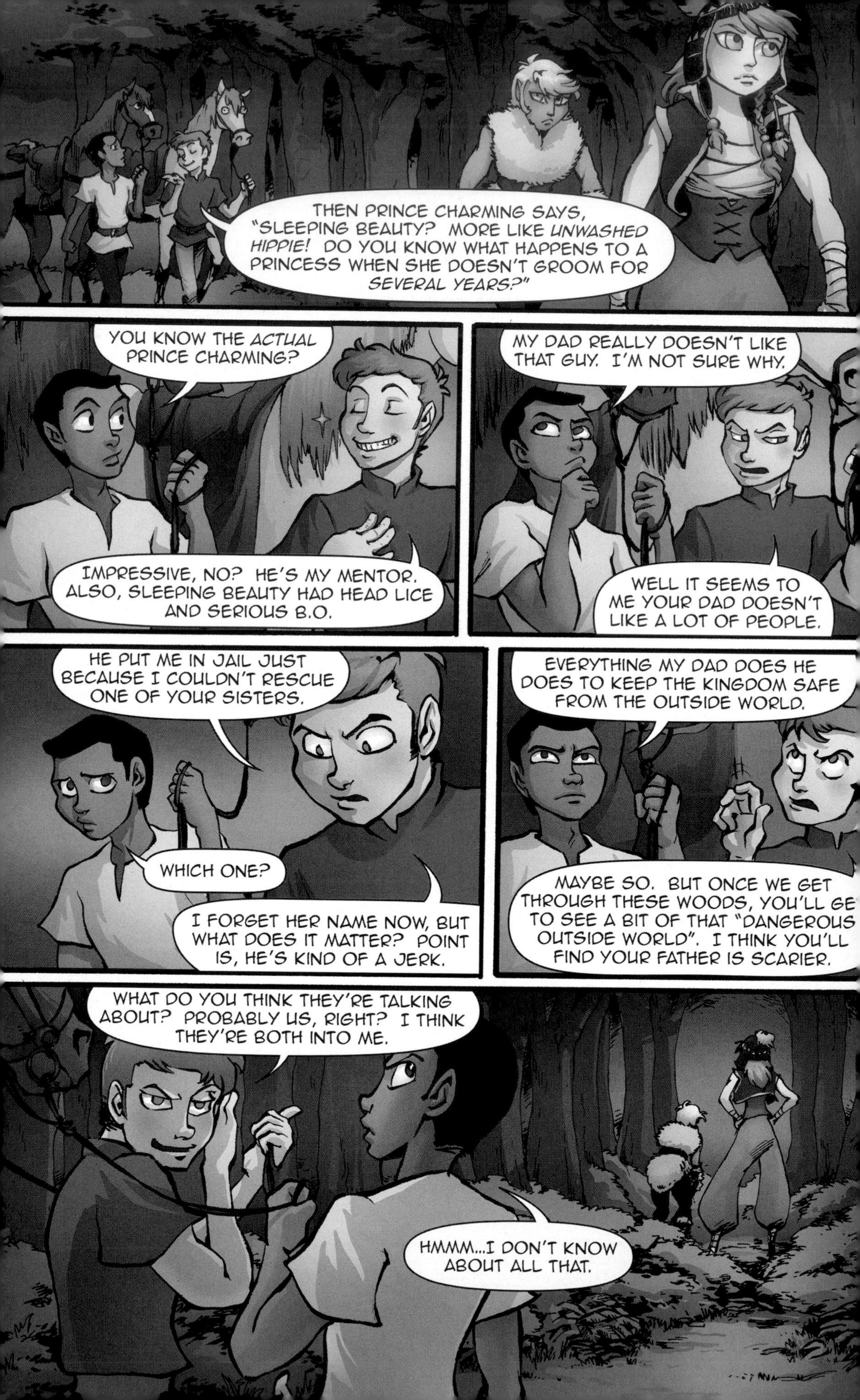
THEN PRINCE CHARMING SAYS, "SLEEPING BEAUTY? MORE LIKE *UNWASHED HIPPIE!* DO YOU KNOW WHAT HAPPENS TO A PRINCESS WHEN SHE DOESN'T GROOM FOR *SEVERAL YEARS?*"
YOU KNOW THE *ACTUAL* PRINCE CHARMING?
IMPRESSIVE, NO? HE'S MY MENTOR. ALSO, SLEEPING BEAUTY HAD HEAD LICE AND SERIOUS B.O.
MY DAD REALLY DOESN'T LIKE THAT GUY. I'M NOT SURE WHY.
WELL IT SEEMS TO ME YOUR DAD DOESN'T LIKE A LOT OF PEOPLE.
HE PUT ME IN JAIL JUST BECAUSE I COULDN'T RESCUE ONE OF YOUR SISTERS.
WHICH ONE?
I FORGET HER NAME NOW, BUT WHAT DOES IT MATTER? POINT IS, HE'S KIND OF A JERK.
EVERYTHING MY DAD DOES HE DOES TO KEEP THE KINGDOM SAFE FROM THE OUTSIDE WORLD.
MAYBE SO. BUT ONCE WE GET THROUGH THESE WOODS, YOU'LL GE TO SEE A BIT OF THAT "DANGEROUS OUTSIDE WORLD". I THINK YOU'LL FIND YOUR FATHER IS SCARIER.
WHAT DO YOU THINK THEY'RE TALKING ABOUT? PROBABLY US, RIGHT? I THINK THEY'RE BOTH INTO ME.
HMMM...I DON'T KNOW ABOUT ALL THAT.

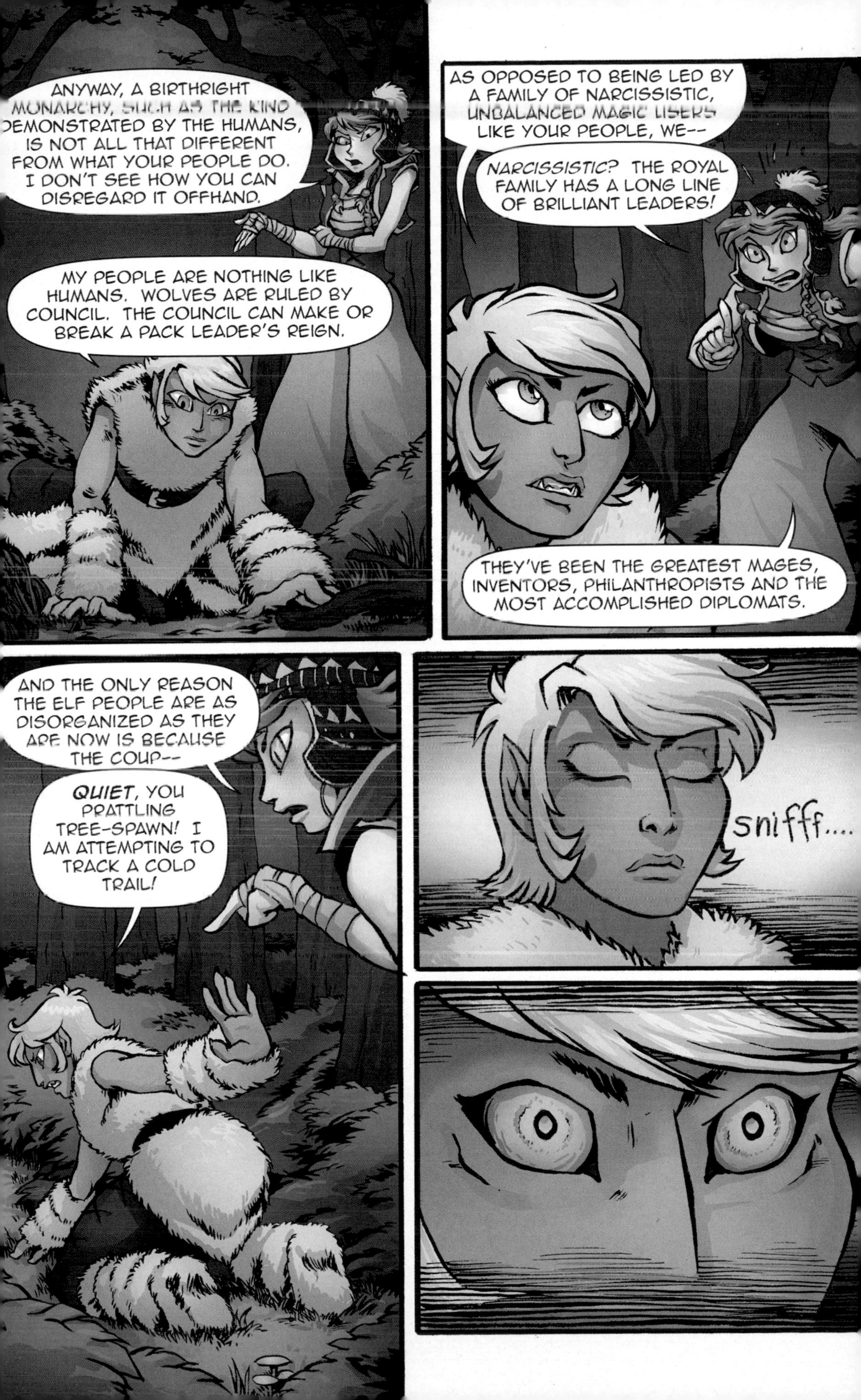
ANYWAY, A BIRTHRIGHT MONARCHY, SUCH AS THE KIND DEMONSTRATED BY THE HUMANS, IS NOT ALL THAT DIFFERENT FROM WHAT YOUR PEOPLE DO. I DON'T SEE HOW YOU CAN DISREGARD IT OFFHAND.
MY PEOPLE ARE NOTHING LIKE HUMANS. WOLVES ARE RULED BY COUNCIL. THE COUNCIL CAN MAKE OR BREAK A PACK LEADER'S REIGN.
AS OPPOSED TO BEING LED BY A FAMILY OF NARCISSISTIC, UNBALANCED MAGIC USERS LIKE YOUR PEOPLE, WE--
NARCISSISTIC? THE ROYAL FAMILY HAS A LONG LINE OF BRILLIANT LEADERS!
THEY'VE BEEN THE GREATEST MAGES, INVENTORS, PHILANTHROPISTS AND THE MOST ACCOMPLISHED DIPLOMATS.
AND THE ONLY REASON THE ELF PEOPLE ARE AS DISORGANIZED AS THEY ARE NOW IS BECAUSE THE COUP--
QUIET, YOU PRATTLING TREE-SPAWN! I AM ATTEMPTING TO TRACK A COLD TRAIL!
snifff....

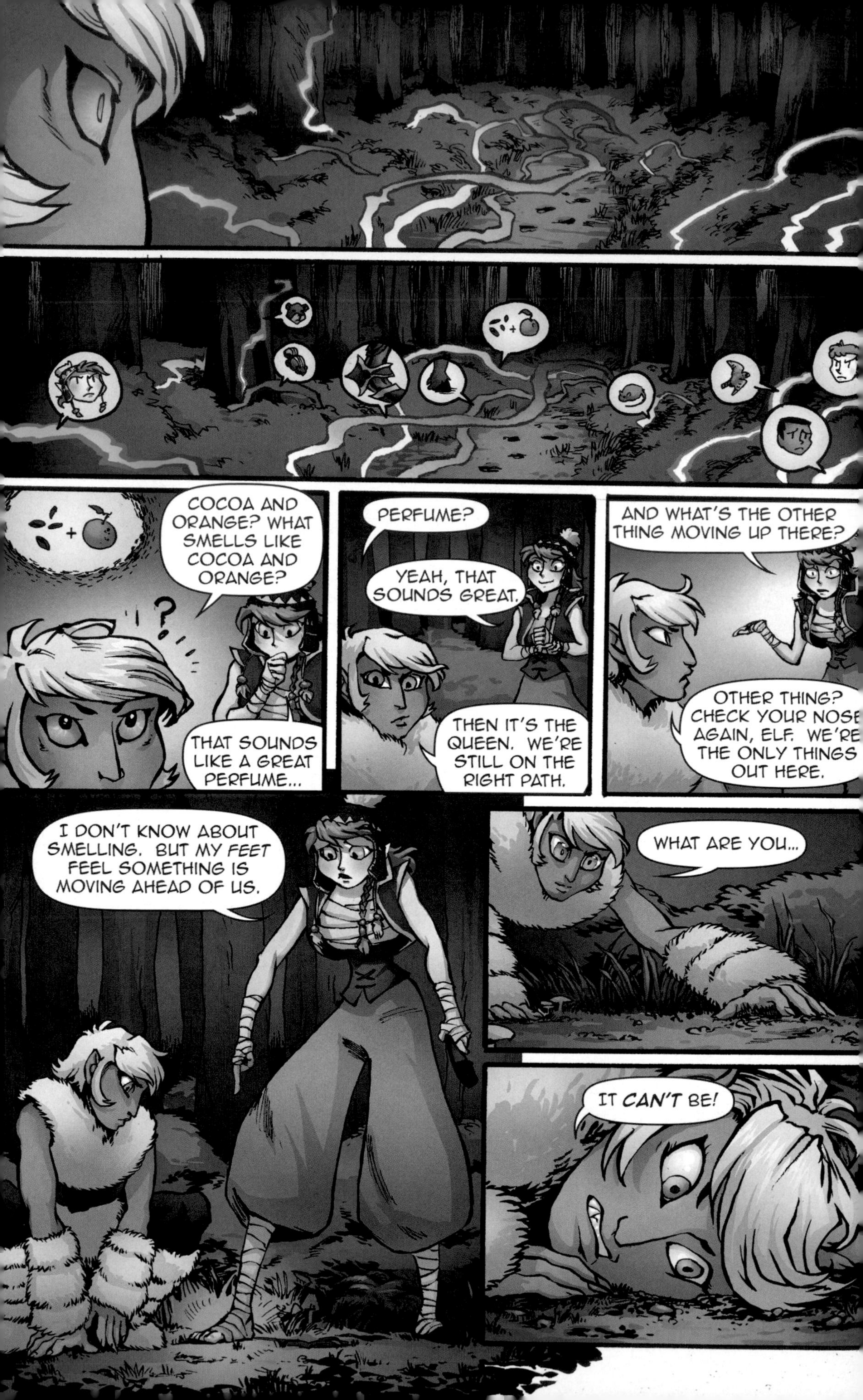
COCOA AND ORANGE? WHAT SMELLS LIKE COCOA AND ORANGE?
THAT SOUNDS LIKE A GREAT PERFUME...
PERFUME?
YEAH, THAT SOUNDS GREAT.
THEN IT'S THE QUEEN. WE'RE STILL ON THE RIGHT PATH.
AND WHAT'S THE OTHER THING MOVING UP THERE?
OTHER THING? CHECK YOUR NOSE AGAIN, ELF. WE'RE THE ONLY THINGS OUT HERE.
I DON'T KNOW ABOUT SMELLING. BUT MY *FEET* FEEL SOMETHING IS MOVING AHEAD OF US.
WHAT ARE YOU...
IT ***CAN'T*** BE!

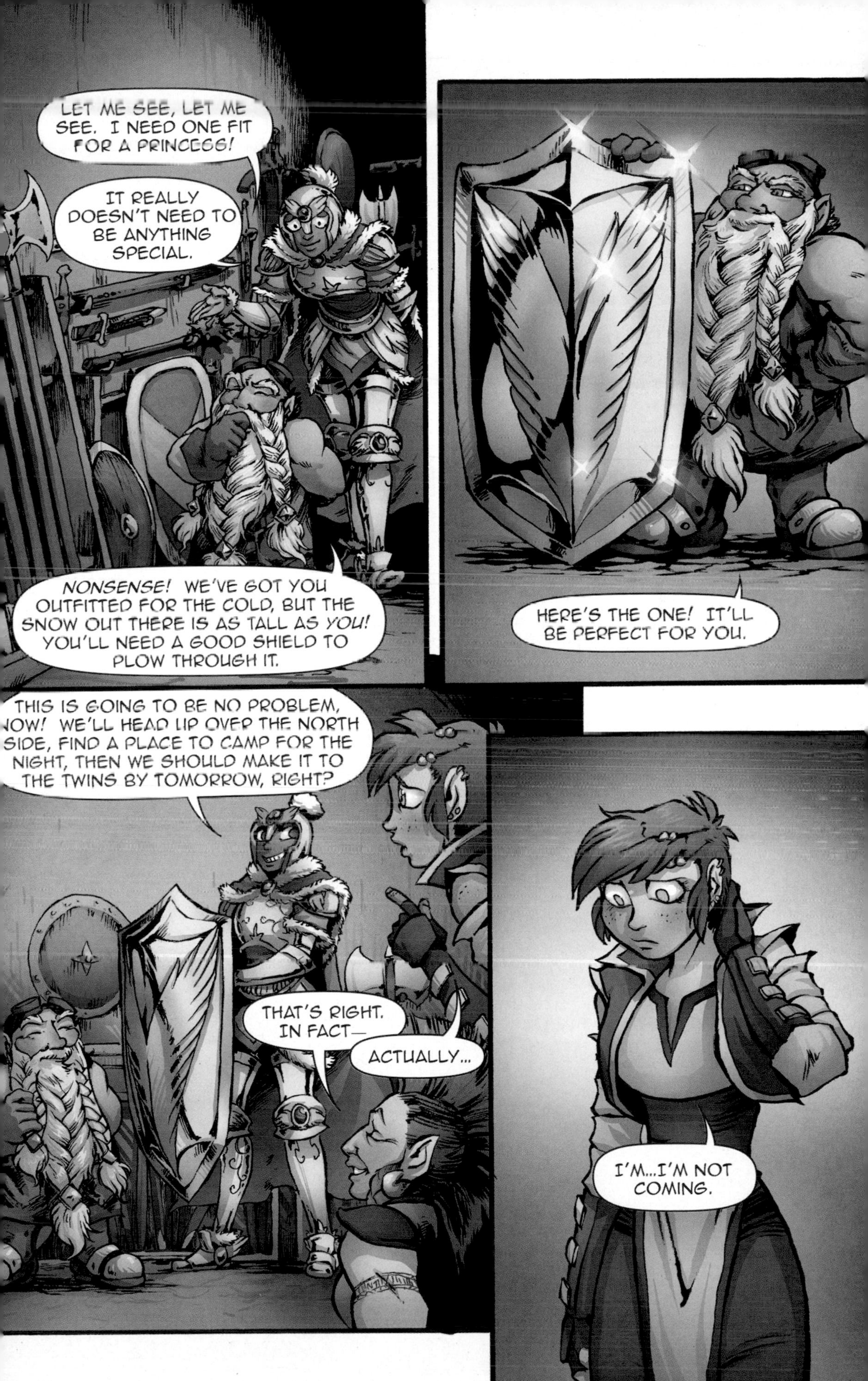
LET ME SEE, LET ME SEE. I NEED ONE FIT FOR A PRINCESS!
IT REALLY DOESN'T NEED TO BE ANYTHING SPECIAL.
NONSENSE! WE'VE GOT YOU OUTFITTED FOR THE COLD, BUT THE SNOW OUT THERE IS AS TALL AS *YOU!* YOU'LL NEED A GOOD SHIELD TO PLOW THROUGH IT.
HERE'S THE ONE! IT'LL BE PERFECT FOR YOU.
THIS IS GOING TO BE NO PROBLEM, NOW! WE'LL HEAD UP OVER THE NORTH SIDE, FIND A PLACE TO CAMP FOR THE NIGHT, THEN WE SHOULD MAKE IT TO THE TWINS BY TOMORROW, RIGHT?
THAT'S RIGHT. IN FACT—
ACTUALLY...
I'M...I'M NOT COMING.

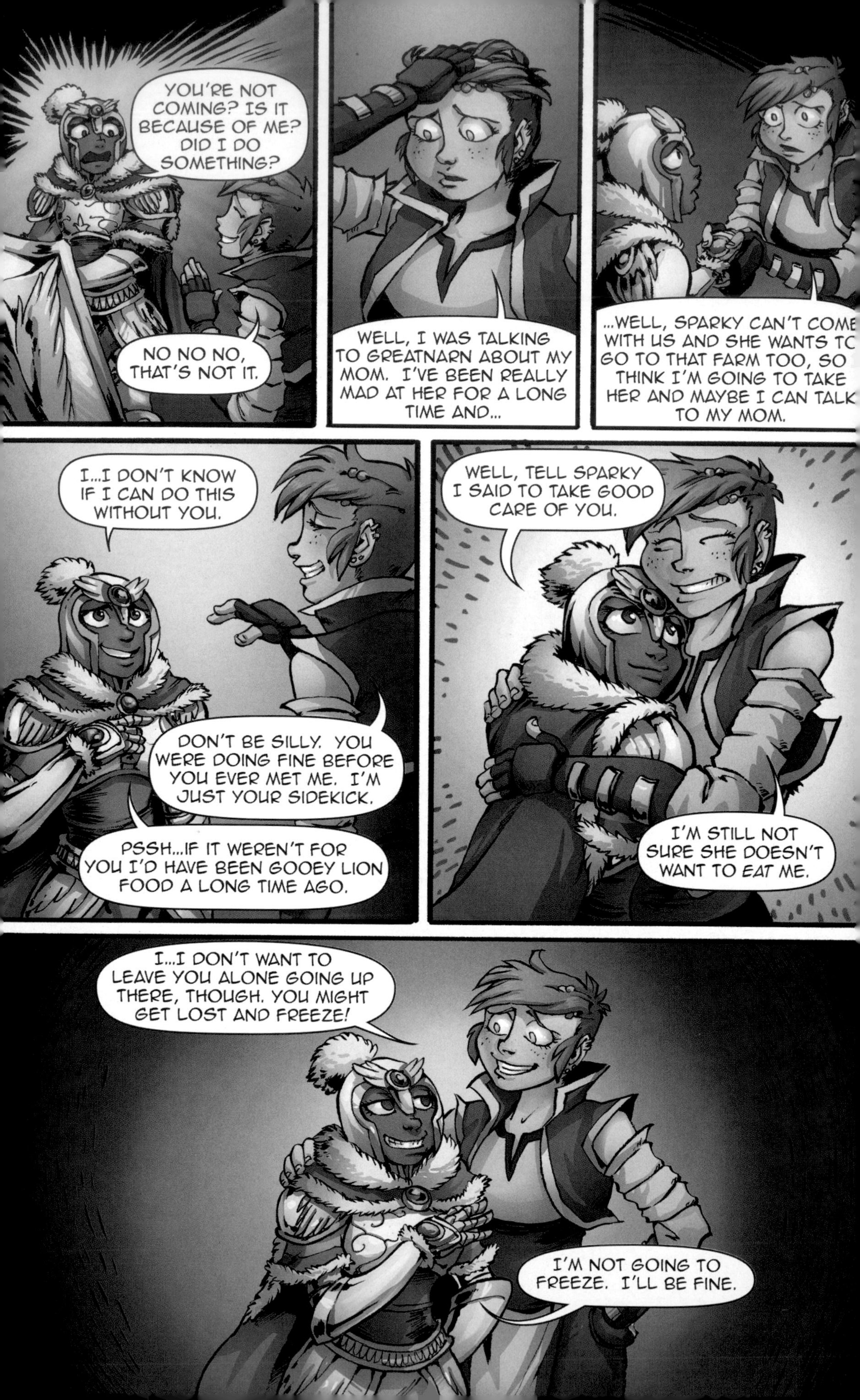
YOU'RE NOT COMING? IS IT BECAUSE OF ME? DID I DO SOMETHING?
NO NO NO, THAT'S NOT IT.
WELL, I WAS TALKING TO GREATNARN ABOUT MY MOM. I'VE BEEN REALLY MAD AT HER FOR A LONG TIME AND...
...WELL, SPARKY CAN'T COME WITH US AND SHE WANTS TO GO TO THAT FARM TOO, SO I THINK I'M GOING TO TAKE HER AND MAYBE I CAN TALK TO MY MOM.
I...I DON'T KNOW IF I CAN DO THIS WITHOUT YOU.
DON'T BE SILLY. YOU WERE DOING FINE BEFORE YOU EVER MET ME. I'M JUST YOUR SIDEKICK.
PSSH...IF IT WEREN'T FOR YOU I'D HAVE BEEN GOOEY LION FOOD A LONG TIME AGO.
WELL, TELL SPARKY I SAID TO TAKE GOOD CARE OF YOU.
I'M STILL NOT SURE SHE DOESN'T WANT TO *EAT* ME.
I...I DON'T WANT TO LEAVE YOU ALONE GOING UP THERE, THOUGH. YOU MIGHT GET LOST AND FREEZE!
I'M NOT GOING TO FREEZE. I'LL BE FINE.

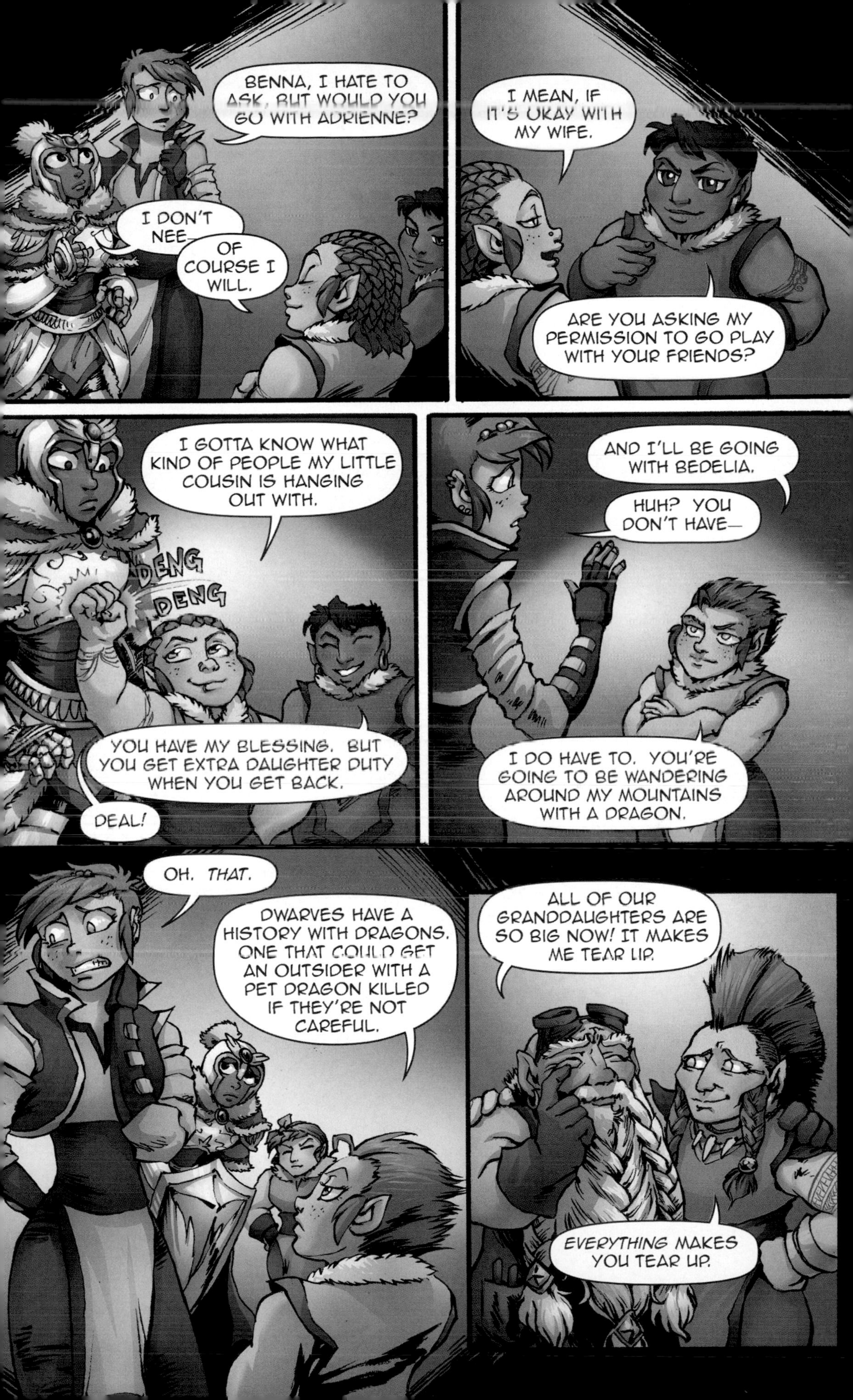

BENNA, I HATE TO ASK, BUT WOULD YOU GO WITH ADRIENNE?
I DON'T NEE—
OF COURSE I WILL.
I MEAN, IF IT'S OKAY WITH MY WIFE.
ARE YOU ASKING MY PERMISSION TO GO PLAY WITH YOUR FRIENDS?
I GOTTA KNOW WHAT KIND OF PEOPLE MY LITTLE COUSIN IS HANGING OUT WITH.
DENG
DENG
YOU HAVE MY BLESSING. BUT YOU GET EXTRA DAUGHTER DUTY WHEN YOU GET BACK.
DEAL!
AND I'LL BE GOING WITH BEDELIA.
HUH? YOU DON'T HAVE—
I DO HAVE TO. YOU'RE GOING TO BE WANDERING AROUND MY MOUNTAINS WITH A DRAGON.
OH. *THAT.*
DWARVES HAVE A HISTORY WITH DRAGONS. ONE THAT COULD GET AN OUTSIDER WITH A PET DRAGON KILLED IF THEY'RE NOT CAREFUL.
ALL OF OUR GRANDDAUGHTERS ARE SO BIG NOW! IT MAKES ME TEAR UP.
EVERYTHING MAKES YOU TEAR UP.

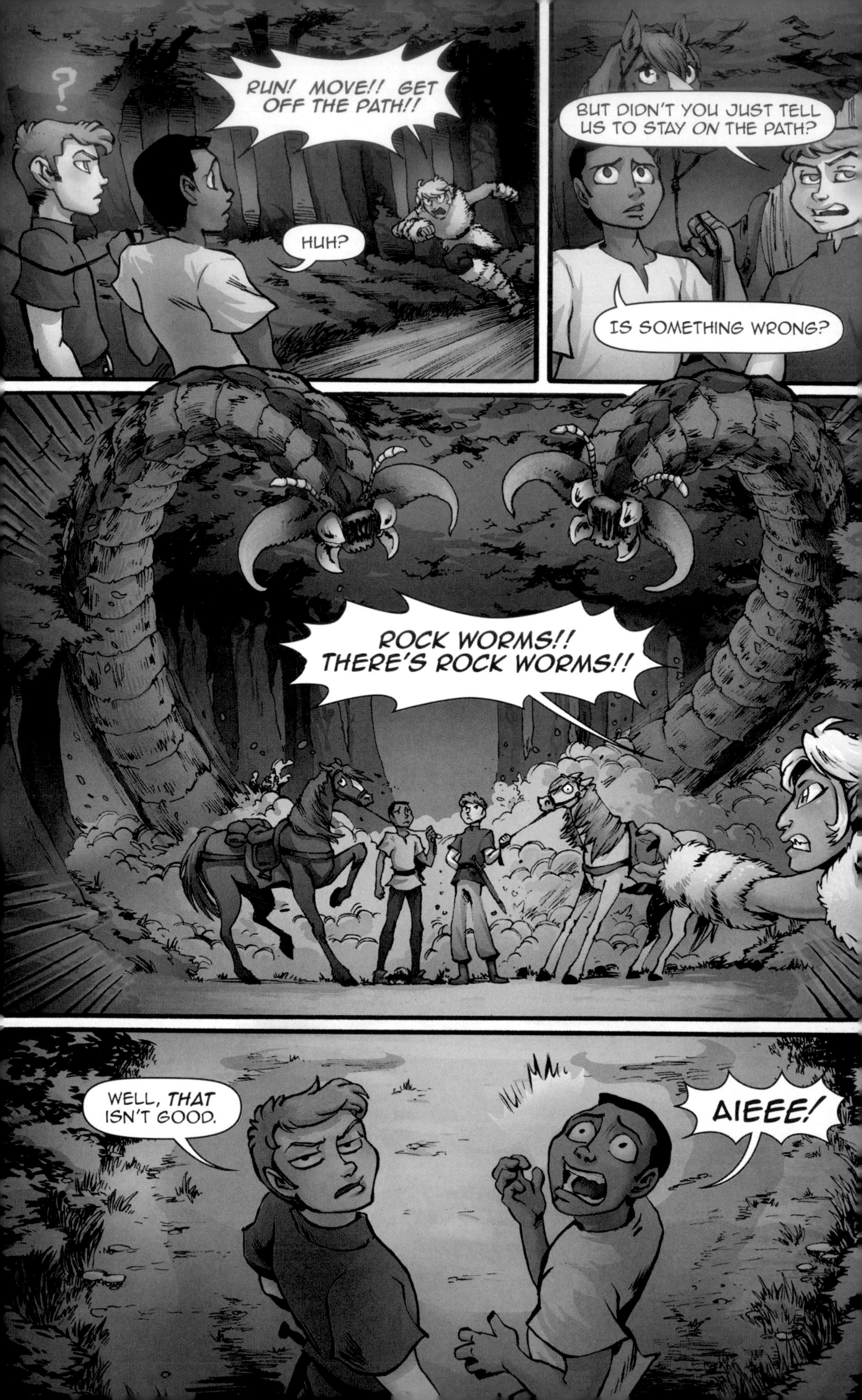
?
RUN! MOVE!! GET OFF THE PATH!!
HUH?
BUT DIDN'T YOU JUST TELL US TO STAY ON THE PATH?
IS SOMETHING WRONG?
ROCK WORMS!! THERE'S ROCK WORMS!!
WELL, THAT ISN'T GOOD.
AIEEE!

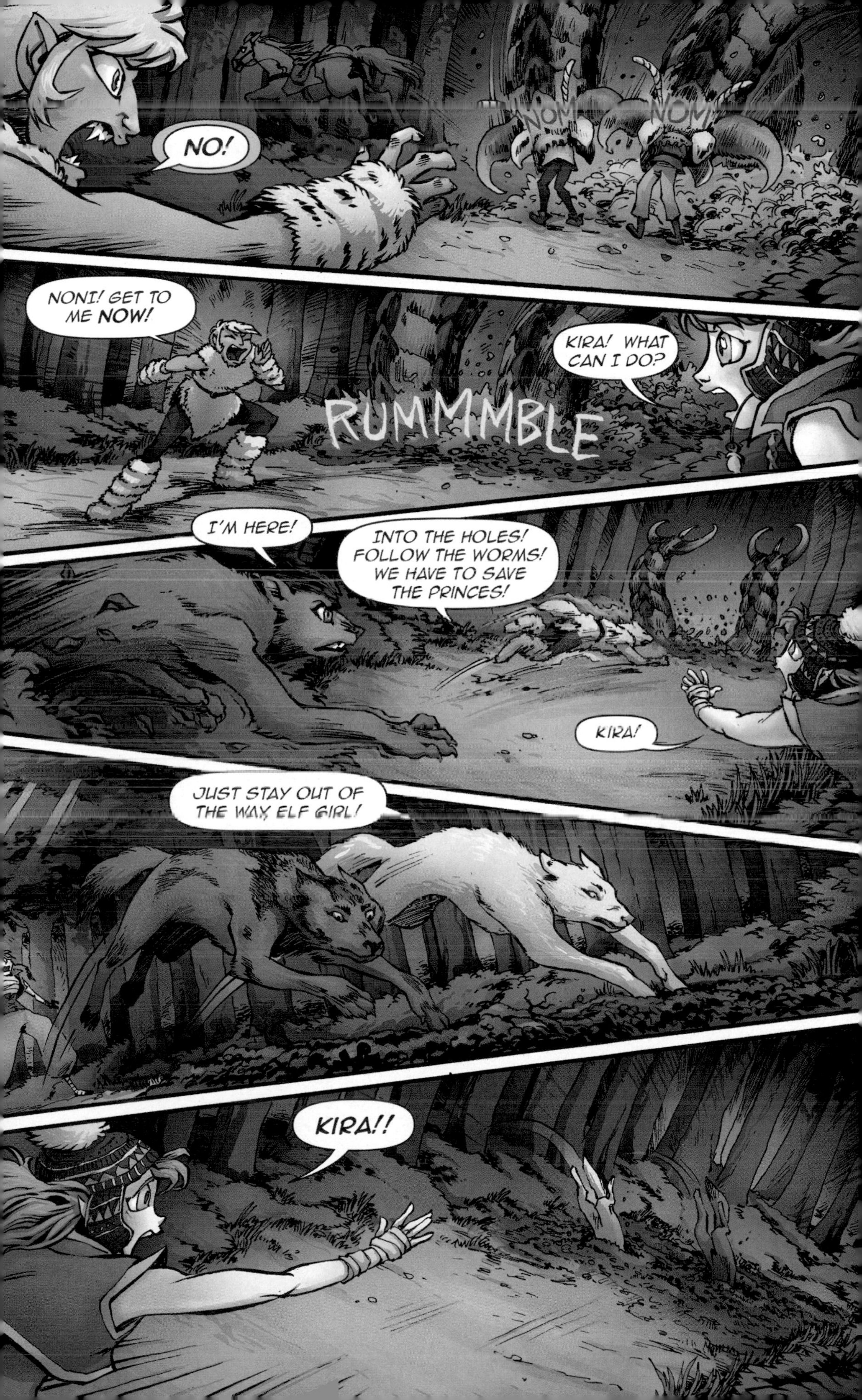
NOM
NOM
NO!
NONI! GET TO ME NOW!
KIRA! WHAT CAN I DO?
RUMMMBLE
I'M HERE!
INTO THE HOLES! FOLLOW THE WORMS! WE HAVE TO SAVE THE PRINCES!
KIRA!
JUST STAY OUT OF THE WAY, ELF GIRL!
KIRA!!

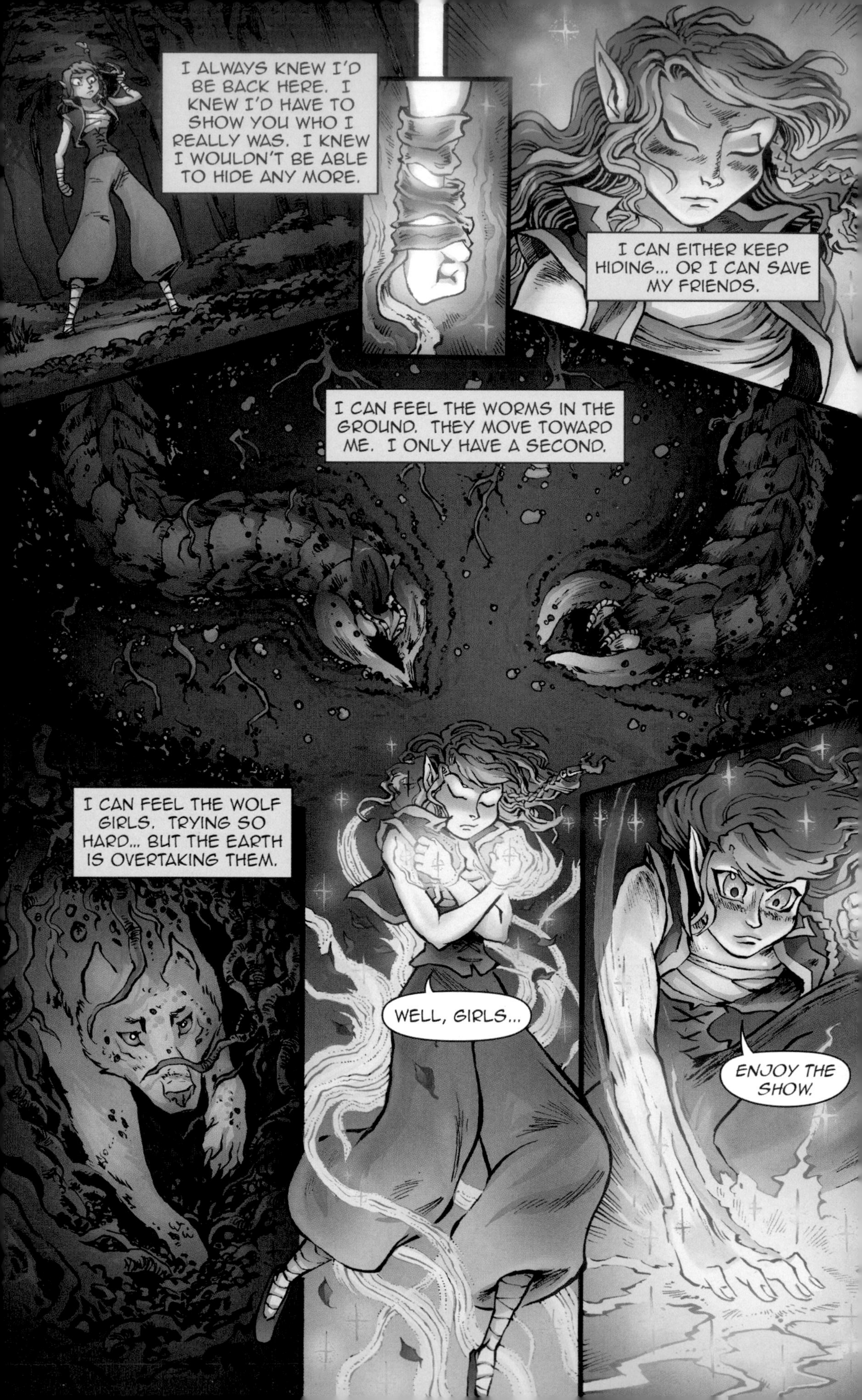
I ALWAYS KNEW I'D BE BACK HERE. I KNEW I'D HAVE TO SHOW YOU WHO I REALLY WAS. I KNEW I WOULDN'T BE ABLE TO HIDE ANY MORE.
I CAN EITHER KEEP HIDING... OR I CAN SAVE MY FRIENDS.
I CAN FEEL THE WORMS IN THE GROUND. THEY MOVE TOWARD ME. I ONLY HAVE A SECOND.
I CAN FEEL THE WOLF GIRLS. TRYING SO HARD... BUT THE EARTH IS OVERTAKING THEM.
WELL, GIRLS...
ENJOY THE SHOW.

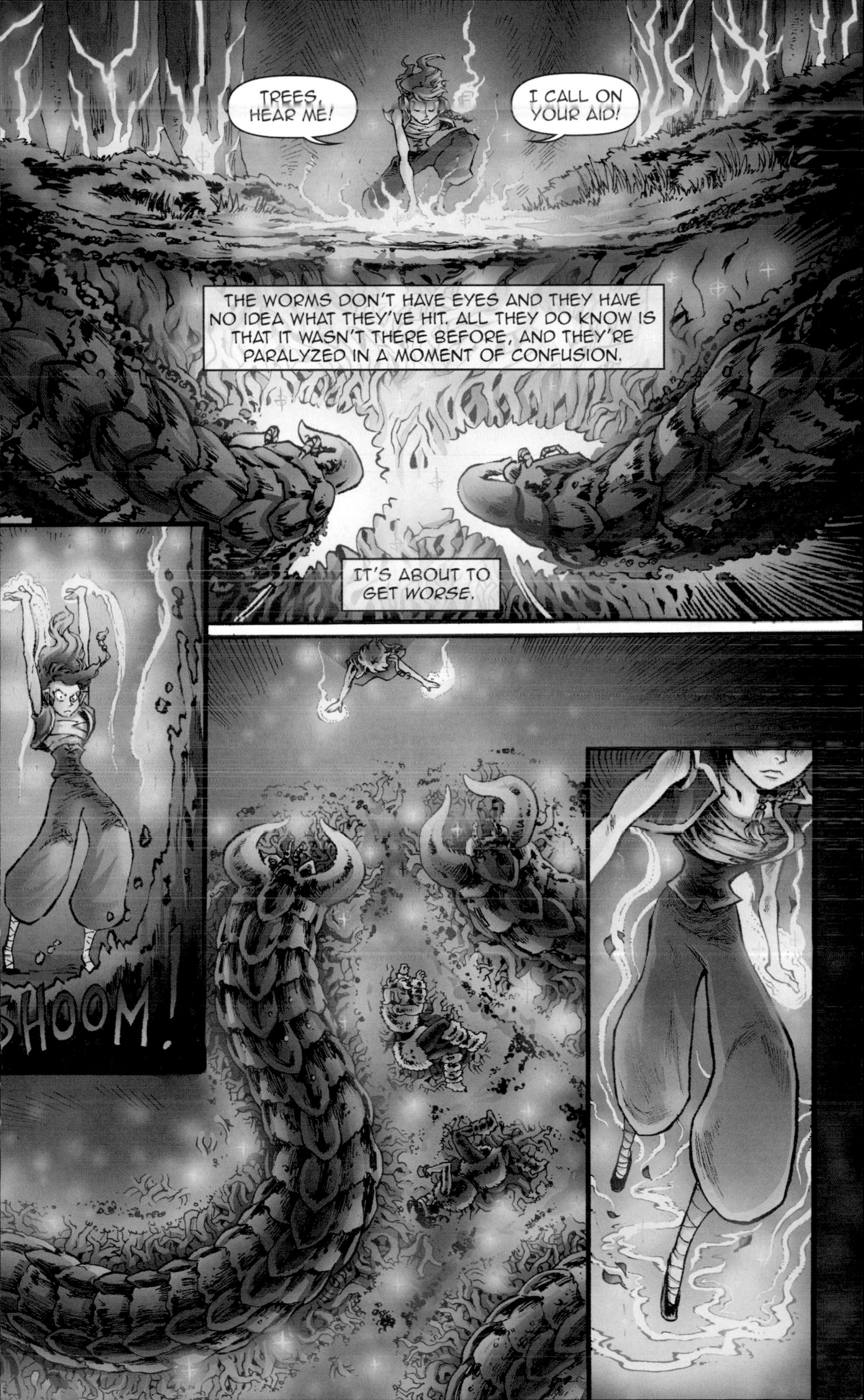
TREES, HEAR ME!
I CALL ON YOUR AID!
THE WORMS DON'T HAVE EYES AND THEY HAVE NO IDEA WHAT THEY'VE HIT. ALL THEY DO KNOW IS THAT IT WASN'T THERE BEFORE, AND THEY'RE PARALYZED IN A MOMENT OF CONFUSION.
IT'S ABOUT TO GET WORSE.
SHOOM!

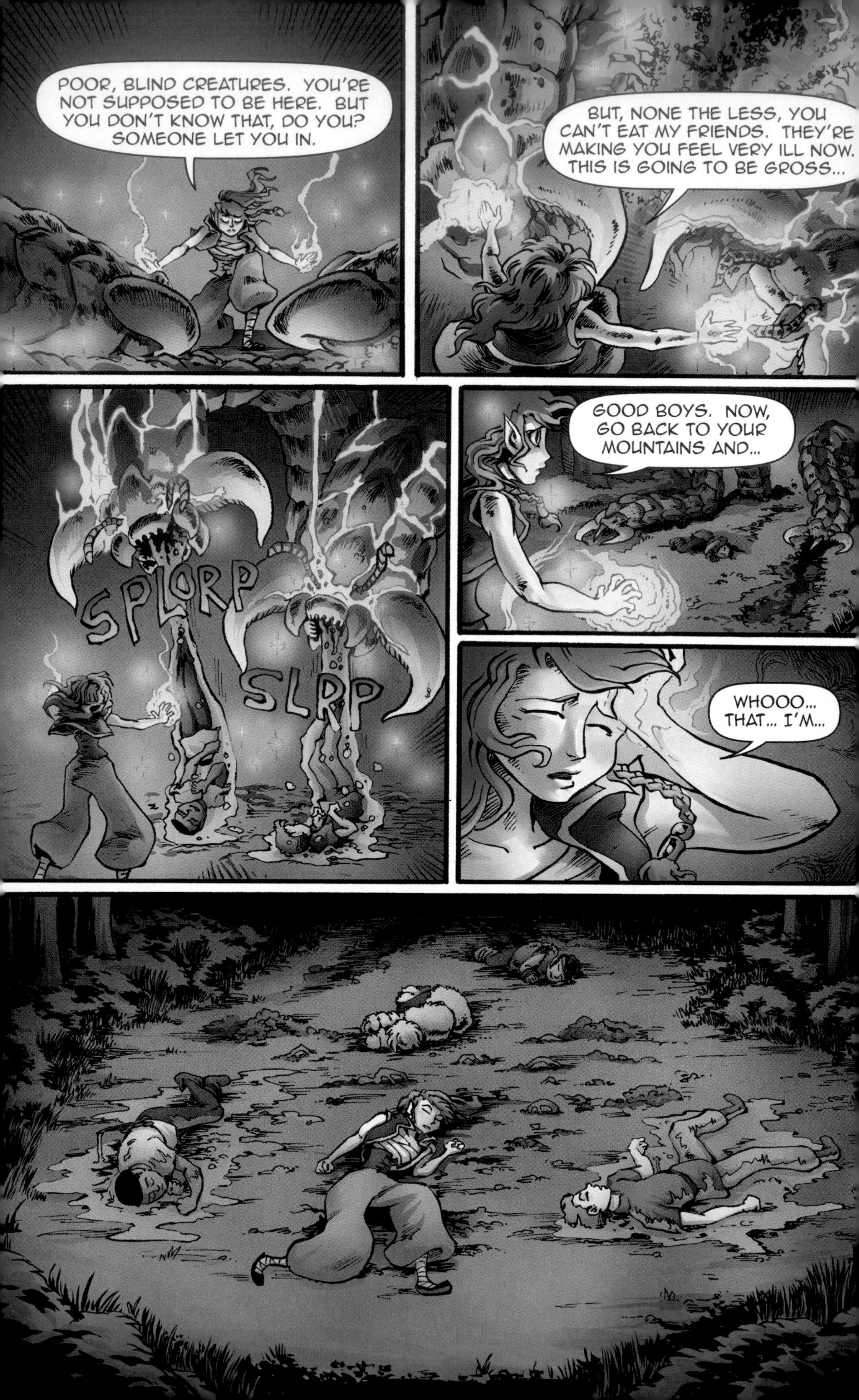
POOR, BLIND CREATURES. YOU'RE NOT SUPPOSED TO BE HERE. BUT YOU DON'T KNOW THAT, DO YOU? SOMEONE LET YOU IN.
BUT, NONE THE LESS, YOU CAN'T EAT MY FRIENDS. THEY'RE MAKING YOU FEEL VERY ILL NOW. THIS IS GOING TO BE GROSS...
SPLORP
SLRP
GOOD BOYS. NOW, GO BACK TO YOUR MOUNTAINS AND...
WHOOO... THAT... I'M...

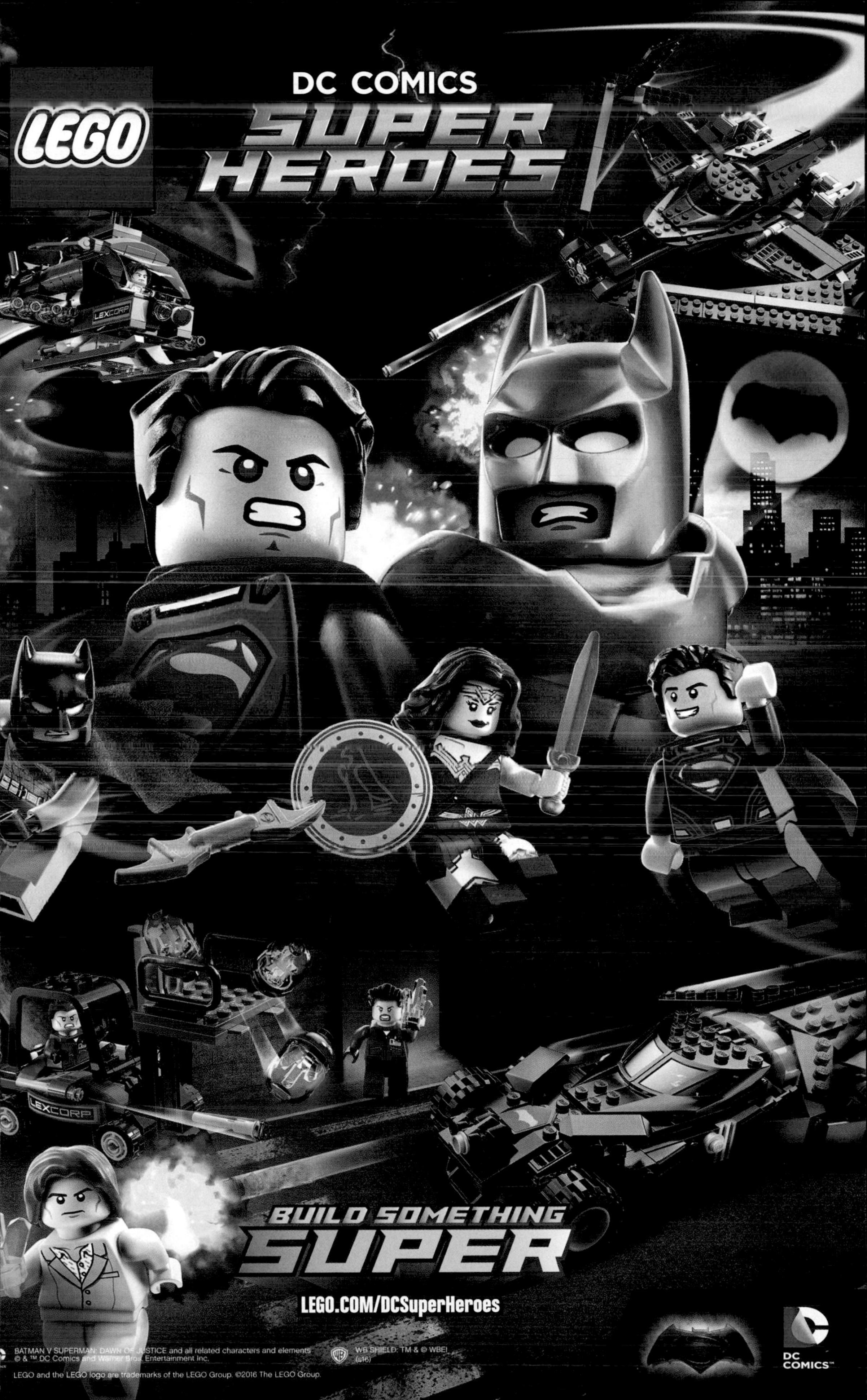
LEGO
DC COMICS
SUPER HEROES
LEXCORP
LEXCORP
BUILD SOMETHING
SUPER
LEGO.COM/DCSuperHeroes
BATMAN V SUPERMAN: DAWN OF JUSTICE and all related characters and elements © & ™ DC Comics and Warner Bros. Entertainment Inc.
WB SHIELD: TM & © WBEI (s16)
LEGO and the LEGO logo are trademarks of the LEGO Group. ©2016 The LEGO Group.
DC COMICS™

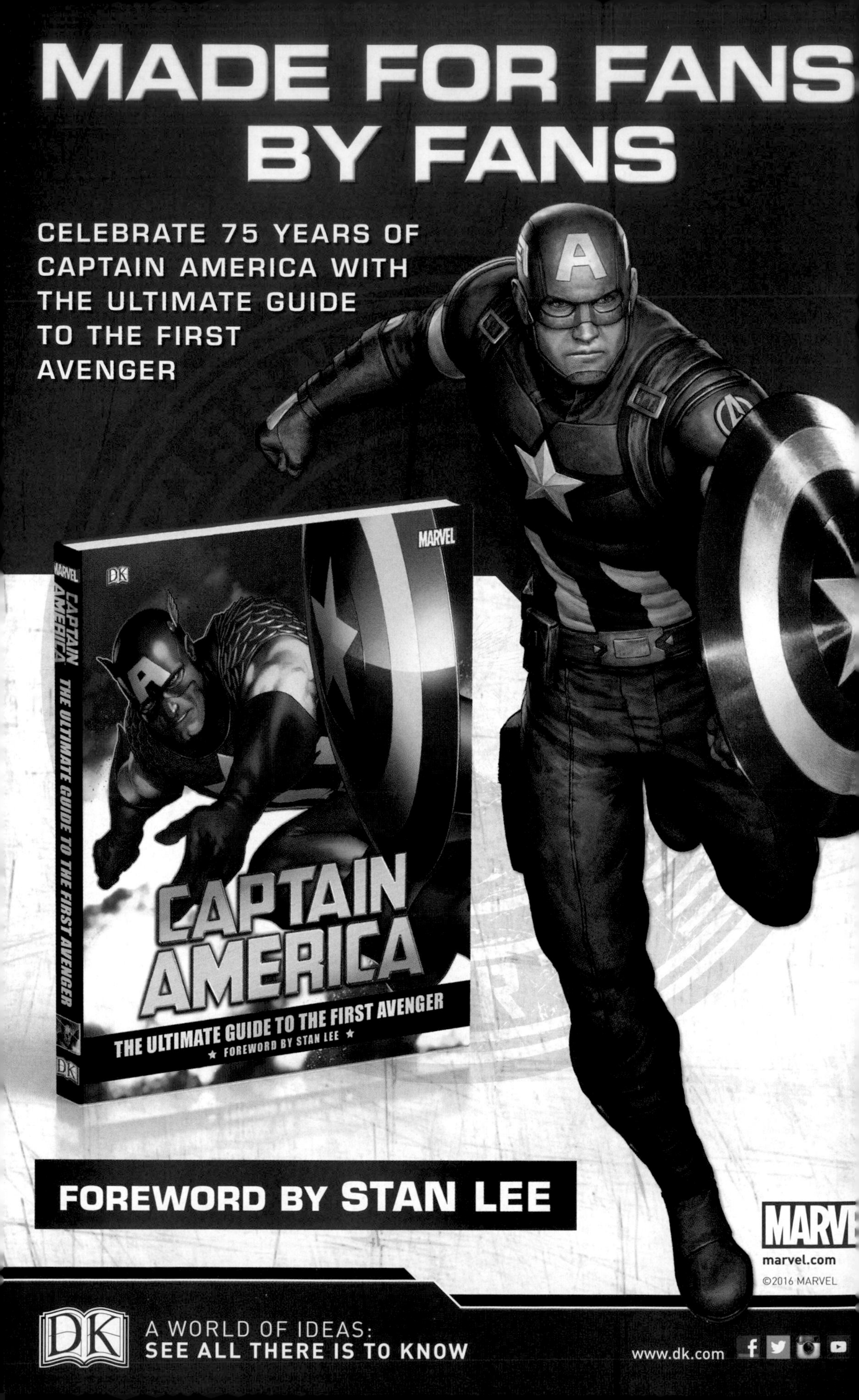
MADE FOR FANS BY FANS
CELEBRATE 75 YEARS OF CAPTAIN AMERICA WITH THE ULTIMATE GUIDE TO THE FIRST AVENGER
MARVEL
DK
CAPTAIN AMERICA
THE ULTIMATE GUIDE TO THE FIRST AVENGER
★ FOREWORD BY STAN LEE ★
FOREWORD BY STAN LEE
MARVEL
marvel.com
©2016 MARVEL
DK
A WORLD OF IDEAS:
SEE ALL THERE IS TO KNOW
www.dk.com

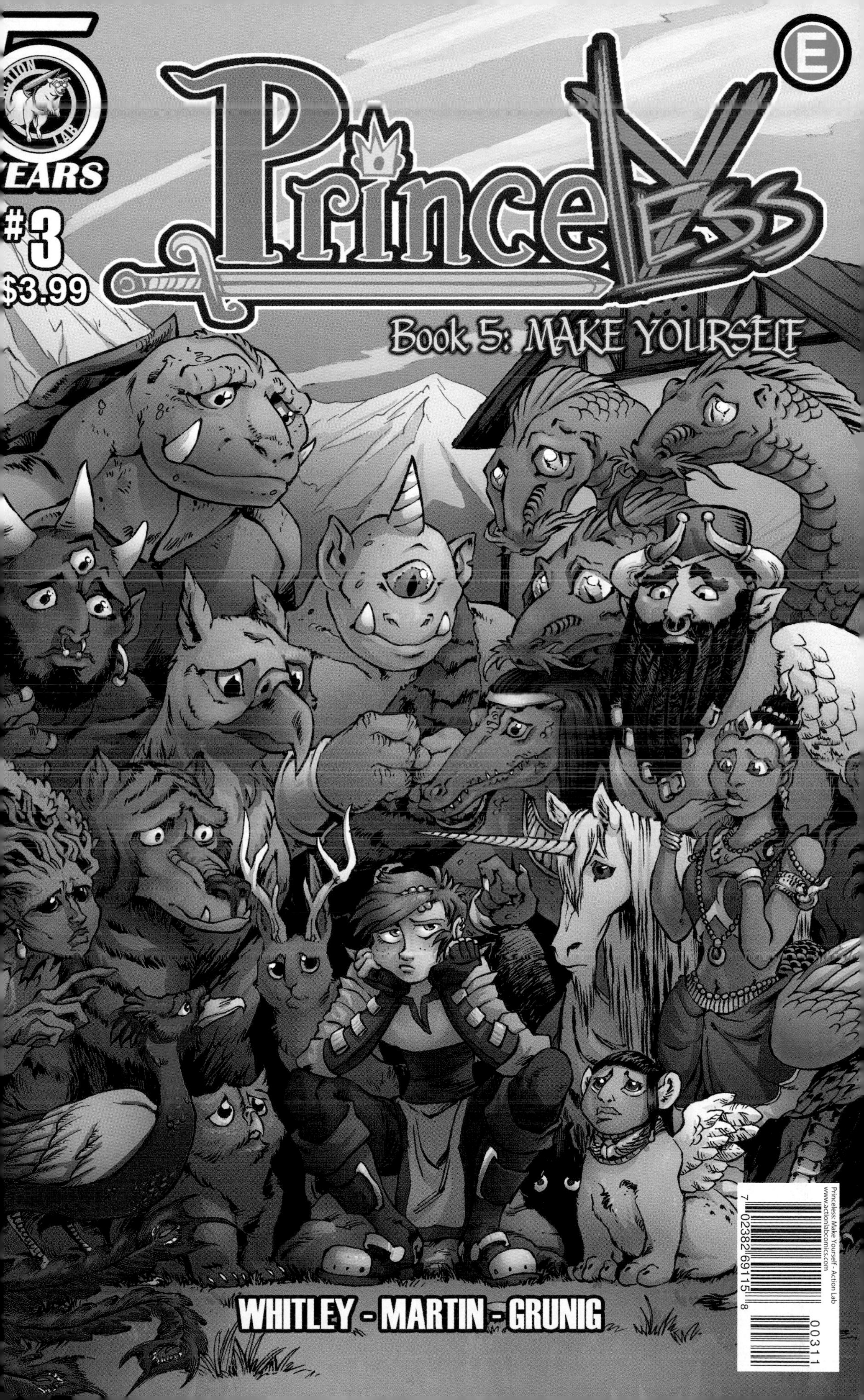
EARS
#3
$3.99
Princeless
Book 5: MAKE YOURSELF
WHITLEY - MARTIN - GRUNIG
Princeless: Make Yourself - Action Lab
www.actionlabcomics.com

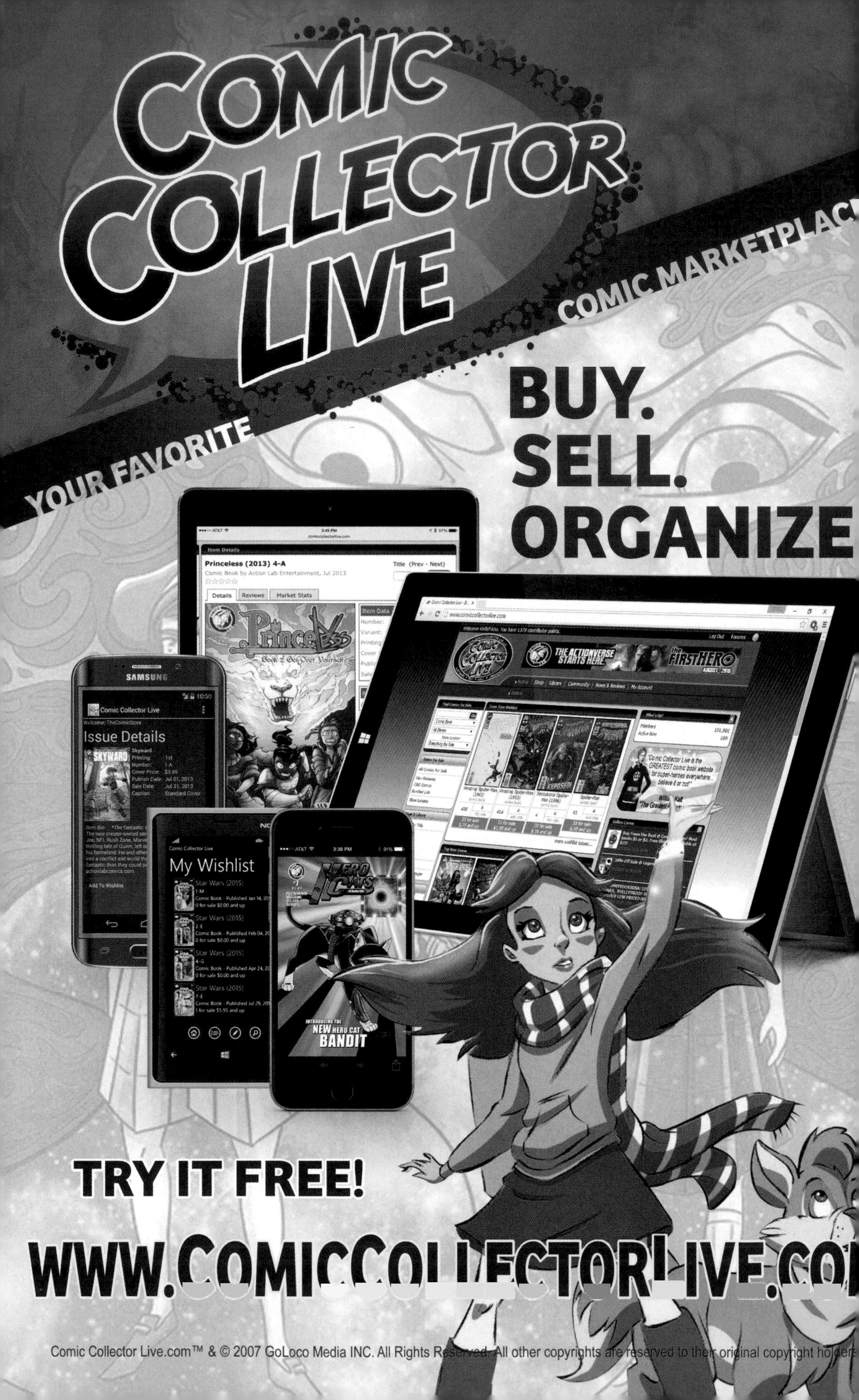
COMIC COLLECTOR LIVE
YOUR FAVORITE COMIC MARKETPLAC
BUY.
SELL.
ORGANIZE
TRY IT FREE!
WWW.COMICCOLLECTORLIVE.CO
Comic Collector Live.com™ & © 2007 GoLoco Media INC. All Rights Reserved. All other copyrights are reserved to their original copyright holders

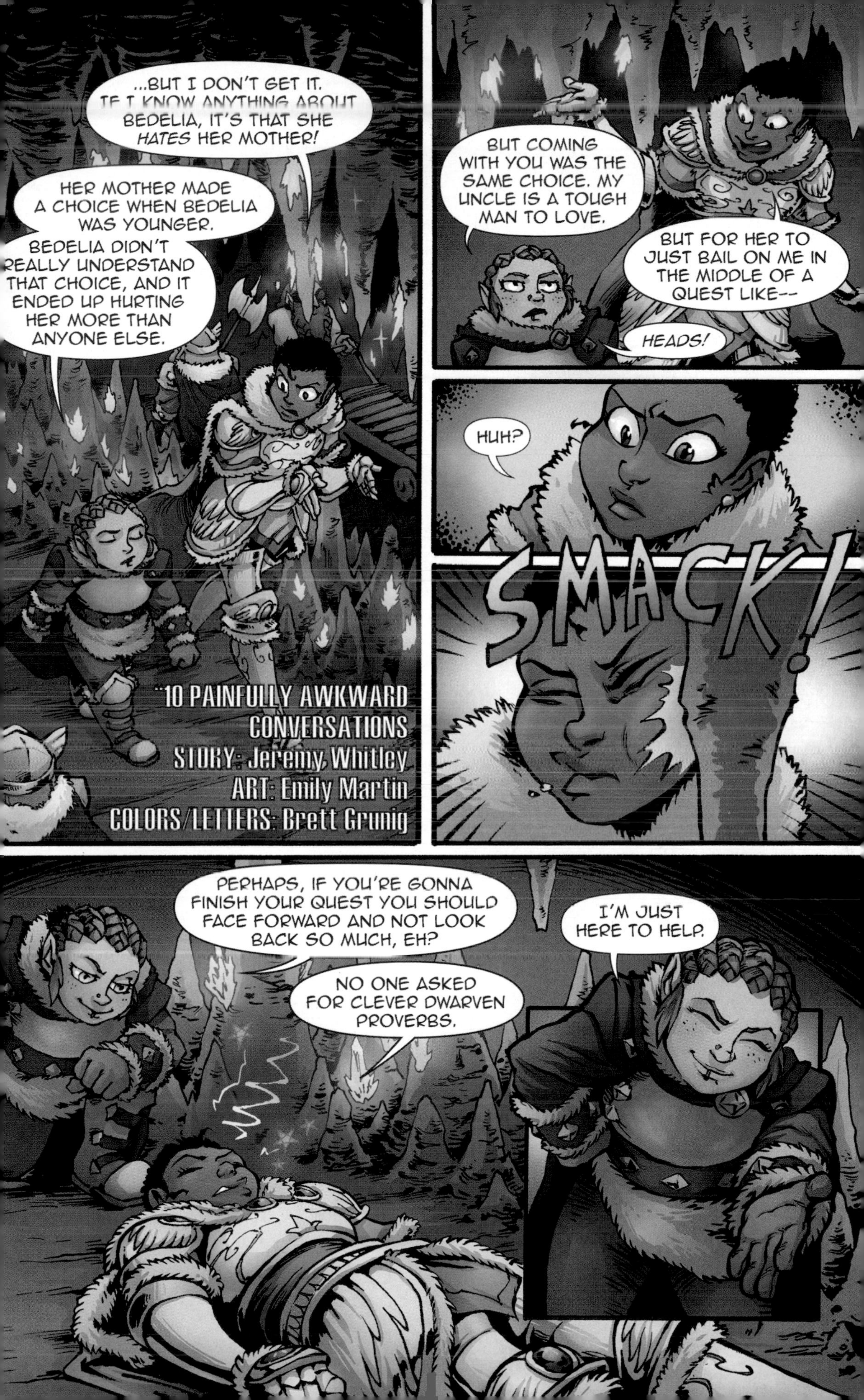
...BUT I DON'T GET IT. IF I KNOW ANYTHING ABOUT BEDELIA, IT'S THAT SHE *HATES* HER MOTHER!
HER MOTHER MADE A CHOICE WHEN BEDELIA WAS YOUNGER.
BEDELIA DIDN'T REALLY UNDERSTAND THAT CHOICE, AND IT ENDED UP HURTING HER MORE THAN ANYONE ELSE.
10 PAINFULLY AWKWARD CONVERSATIONS
STORY: Jeremy Whitley
ART: Emily Martin
COLORS/LETTERS: Brett Grunig
BUT COMING WITH YOU WAS THE SAME CHOICE. MY UNCLE IS A TOUGH MAN TO LOVE.
BUT FOR HER TO JUST BAIL ON ME IN THE MIDDLE OF A QUEST LIKE--
HEADS!
HUH?
SMACK!
PERHAPS, IF YOU'RE GONNA FINISH YOUR QUEST YOU SHOULD FACE FORWARD AND NOT LOOK BACK SO MUCH, EH?
NO ONE ASKED FOR CLEVER DWARVEN PROVERBS.
I'M JUST HERE TO HELP.

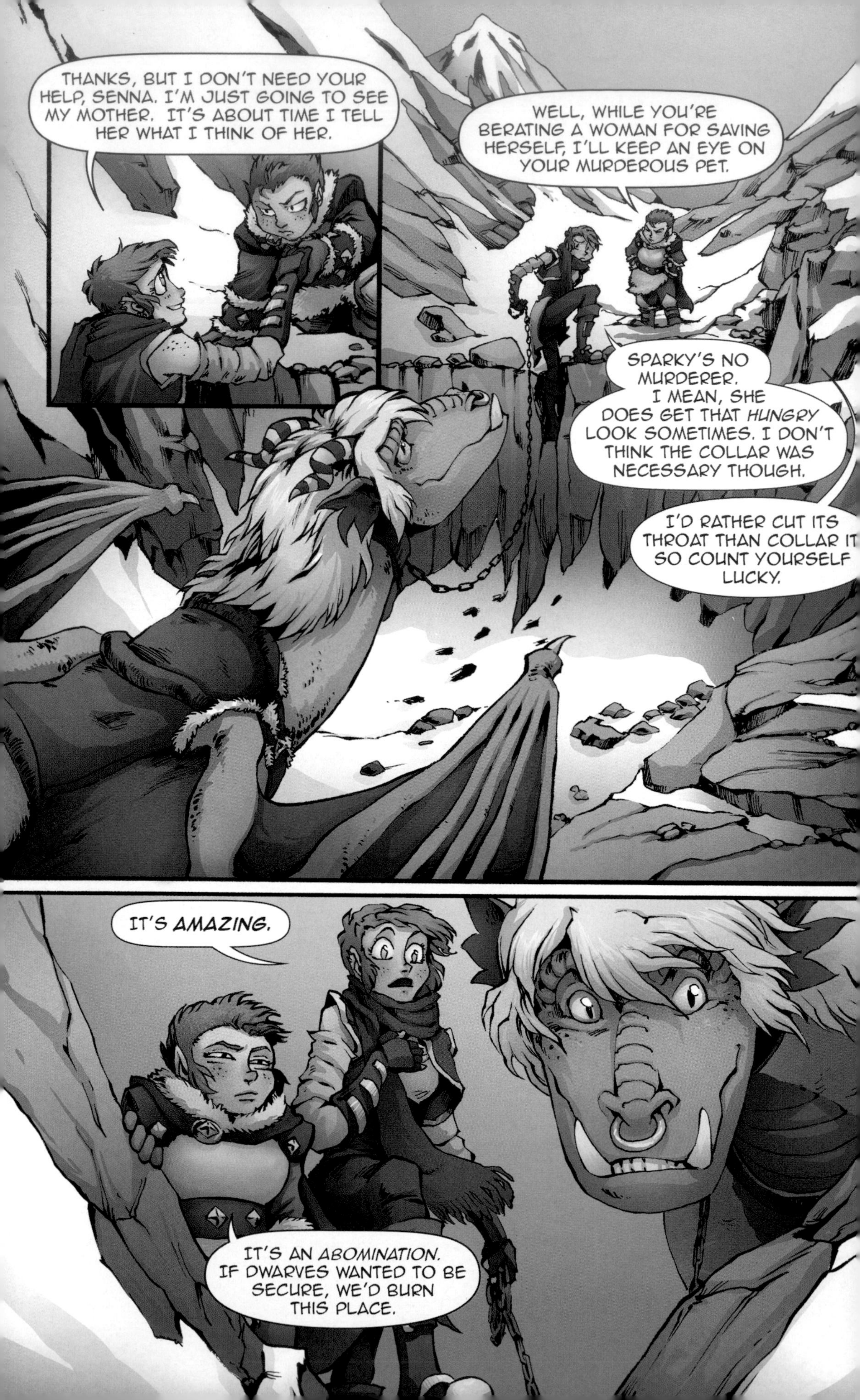
THANKS, BUT I DON'T NEED YOUR HELP, SENNA. I'M JUST GOING TO SEE MY MOTHER. IT'S ABOUT TIME I TELL HER WHAT I THINK OF HER.
WELL, WHILE YOU'RE BERATING A WOMAN FOR SAVING HERSELF, I'LL KEEP AN EYE ON YOUR MURDEROUS PET.
SPARKY'S NO MURDERER. I MEAN, SHE DOES GET THAT *HUNGRY* LOOK SOMETIMES. I DON'T THINK THE COLLAR WAS NECESSARY THOUGH.
I'D RATHER CUT ITS THROAT THAN COLLAR IT SO COUNT YOURSELF LUCKY.
IT'S **AMAZING.**
IT'S AN *ABOMINATION.* IF DWARVES WANTED TO BE SECURE, WE'D BURN THIS PLACE.

Bryan Seaton: Publisher • Dave Dwonch: President • Shawn Gabborin: Editor In Chief
Jason Martin: Publisher-Danger Zone • Jamal Igle: Vice-President of Marketing • Jim Dietz: Social Media Director
Nicole DAndria: Editor • Chad Cicconi: Still Waiting For His Princess • Colleen Boyd: Submissions Editor

:ELESS: MAKE YOURSELF #3, June 2016. Copyright Jeremy Whitley and Emily Martin, 2016. Published by Action Lab Entertainment. All rights reserved. All characters are fictional. Any likeness
one living or dead is purely coincidental. No part of this publication may be reproduced or transmitted without permission, except for review purposes. Printed in Canada. First Printing.

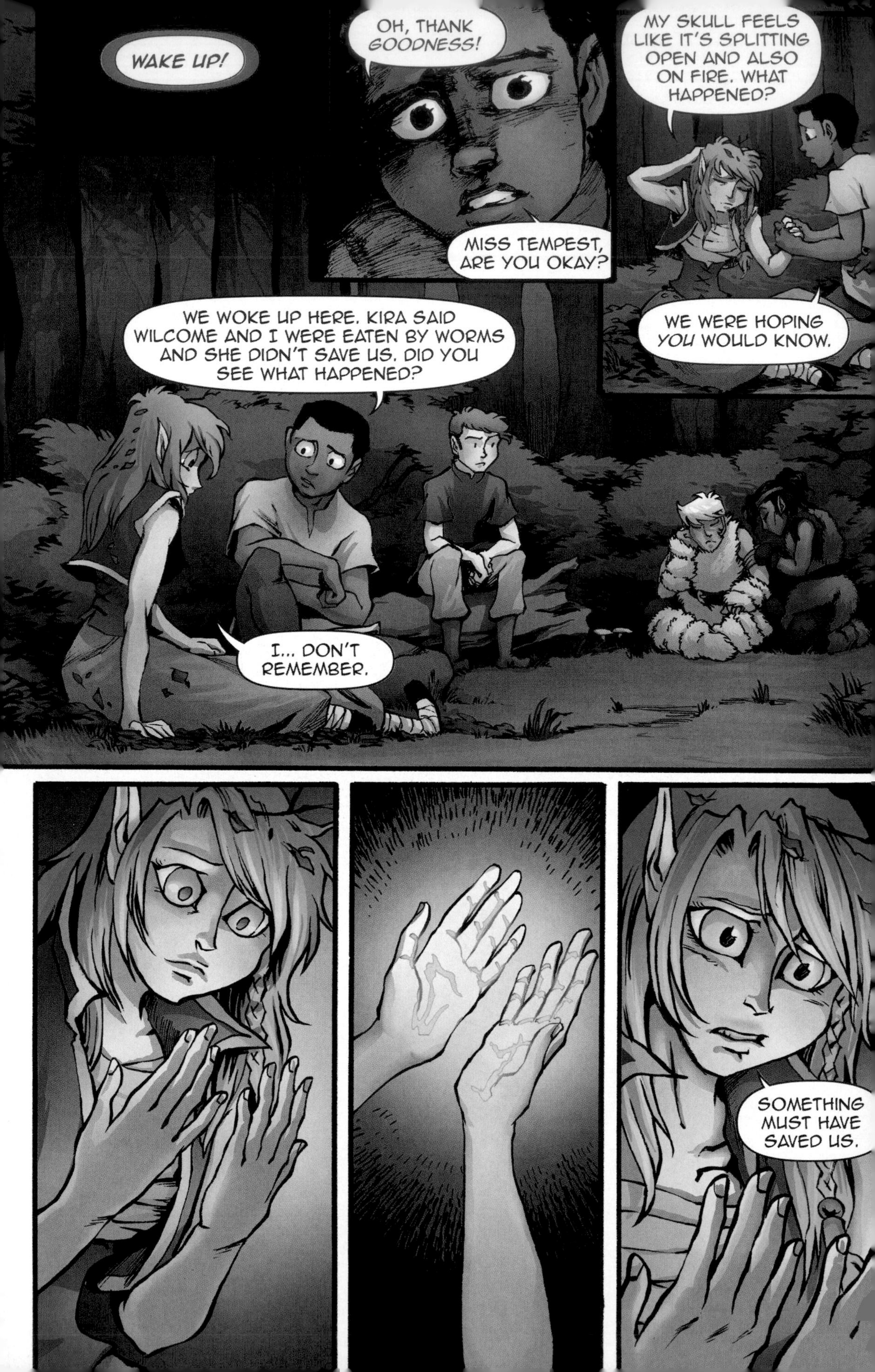
WAKE UP!
OH, THANK GOODNESS!
MISS TEMPEST, ARE YOU OKAY?
MY SKULL FEELS LIKE IT'S SPLITTING OPEN AND ALSO ON FIRE. WHAT HAPPENED?
WE WERE HOPING *YOU* WOULD KNOW.
WE WOKE UP HERE. KIRA SAID WILCOME AND I WERE EATEN BY WORMS AND SHE DIDN'T SAVE US. DID YOU SEE WHAT HAPPENED?
I... DON'T REMEMBER.
SOMETHING MUST HAVE SAVED US.

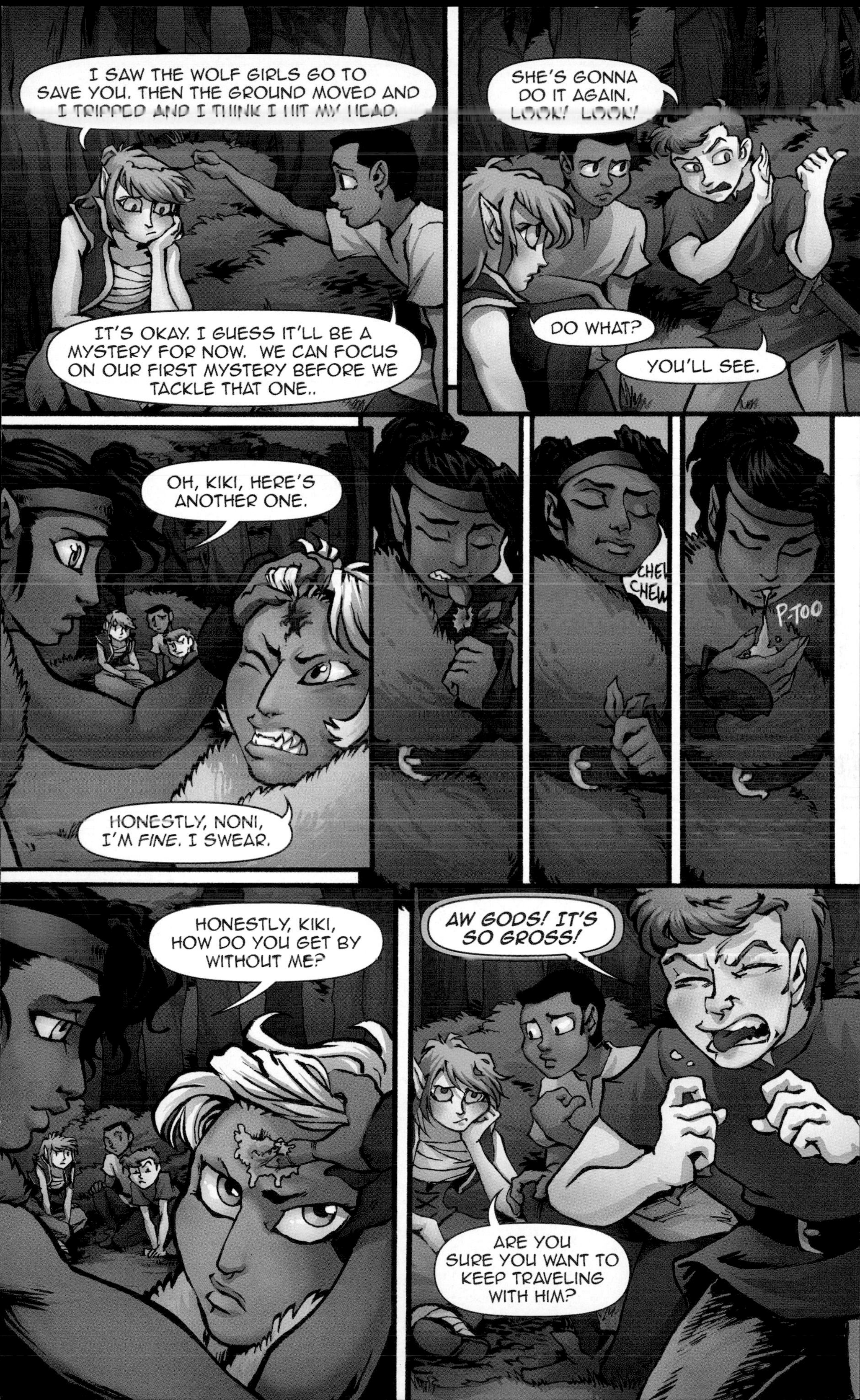
I SAW THE WOLF GIRLS GO TO SAVE YOU. THEN THE GROUND MOVED AND I TRIPPED AND I THINK I HIT MY HEAD.
IT'S OKAY. I GUESS IT'LL BE A MYSTERY FOR NOW. WE CAN FOCUS ON OUR FIRST MYSTERY BEFORE WE TACKLE THAT ONE..
SHE'S GONNA DO IT AGAIN. LOOK! LOOK!
DO WHAT?
YOU'LL SEE.
OH, KIKI, HERE'S ANOTHER ONE.
HONESTLY, NONI, I'M FINE. I SWEAR.
CHEW CHEW
P-TOO
HONESTLY, KIKI, HOW DO YOU GET BY WITHOUT ME?
AW GODS! IT'S SO GROSS!
ARE YOU SURE YOU WANT TO KEEP TRAVELING WITH HIM?

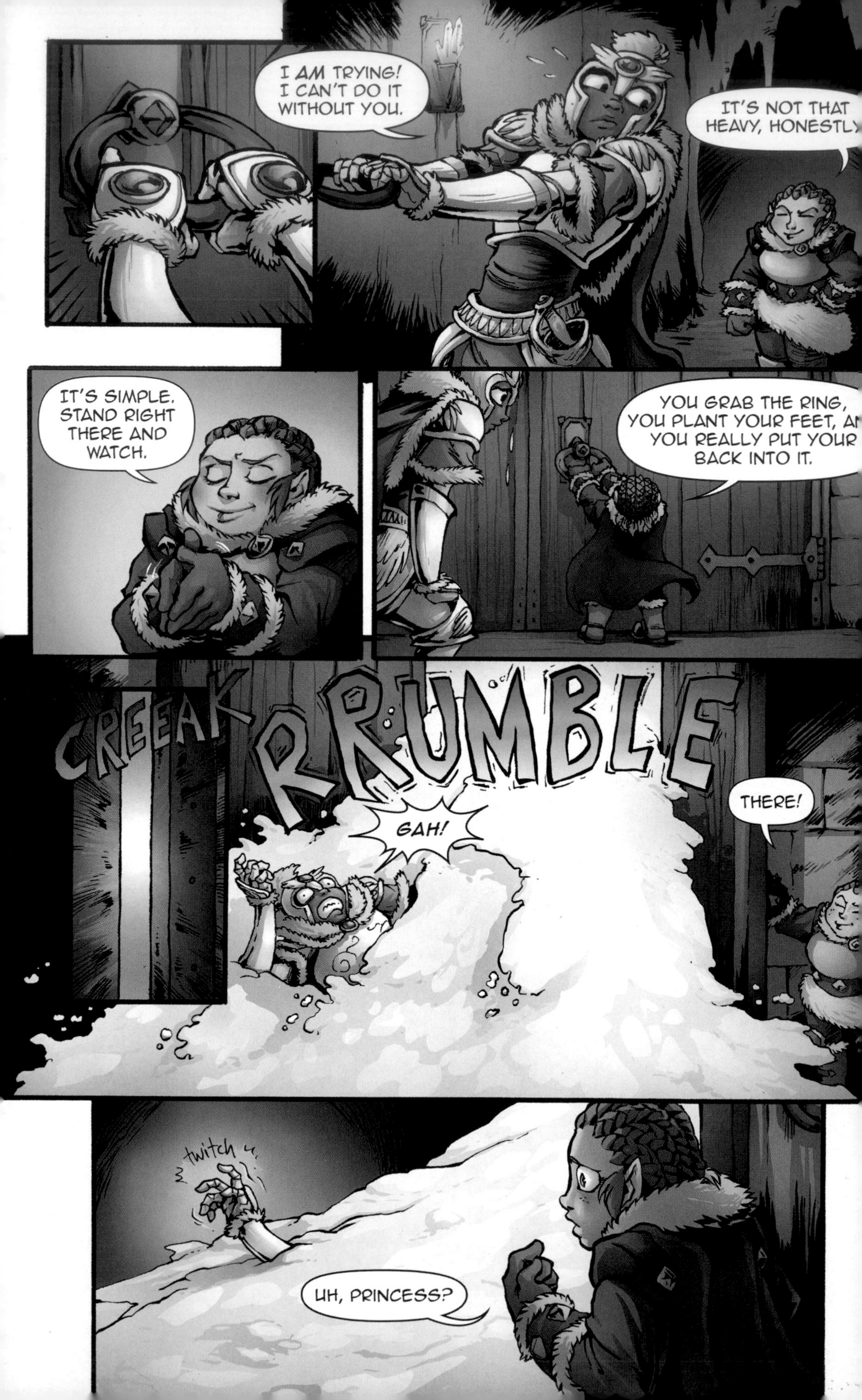
I AM TRYING! I CAN'T DO IT WITHOUT YOU.
IT'S NOT THAT HEAVY, HONESTLY
IT'S SIMPLE. STAND RIGHT THERE AND WATCH.
YOU GRAB THE RING, YOU PLANT YOUR FEET, AN
YOU REALLY PUT YOUR BACK INTO IT.
CREEAK
RRUMBLE
GAH!
THERE!
twitch
UH, PRINCESS?

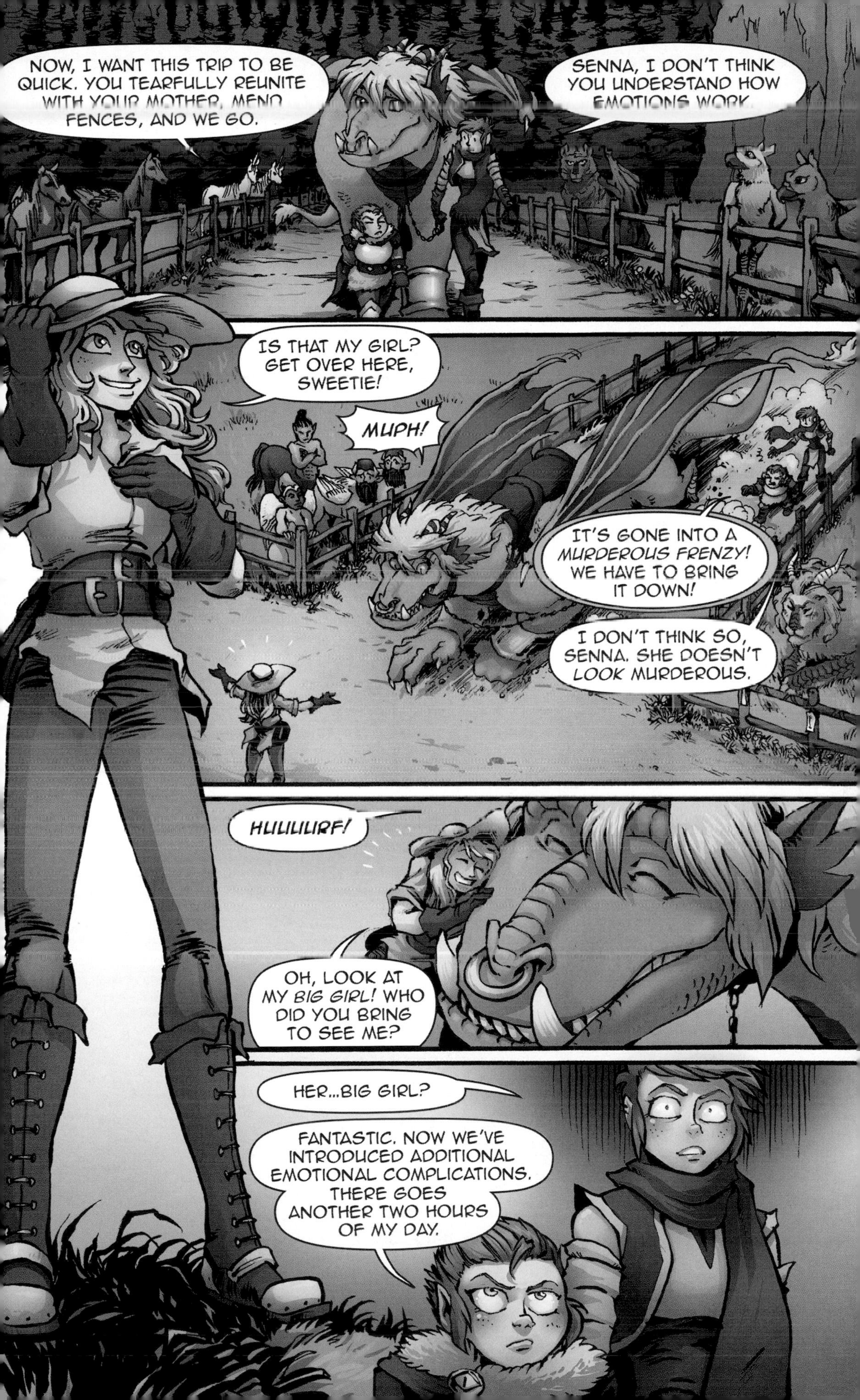
NOW, I WANT THIS TRIP TO BE QUICK. YOU TEARFULLY REUNITE WITH YOUR MOTHER, MEND FENCES, AND WE GO.
SENNA, I DON'T THINK YOU UNDERSTAND HOW EMOTIONS WORK.
IS THAT MY GIRL? GET OVER HERE, SWEETIE!
MUPH!
IT'S GONE INTO A MURDEROUS FRENZY! WE HAVE TO BRING IT DOWN!
I DON'T THINK SO, SENNA. SHE DOESN'T LOOK MURDEROUS.
HUUUURF!
OH, LOOK AT MY BIG GIRL! WHO DID YOU BRING TO SEE ME?
HER...BIG GIRL?
FANTASTIC. NOW WE'VE INTRODUCED ADDITIONAL EMOTIONAL COMPLICATIONS. THERE GOES ANOTHER TWO HOURS OF MY DAY.

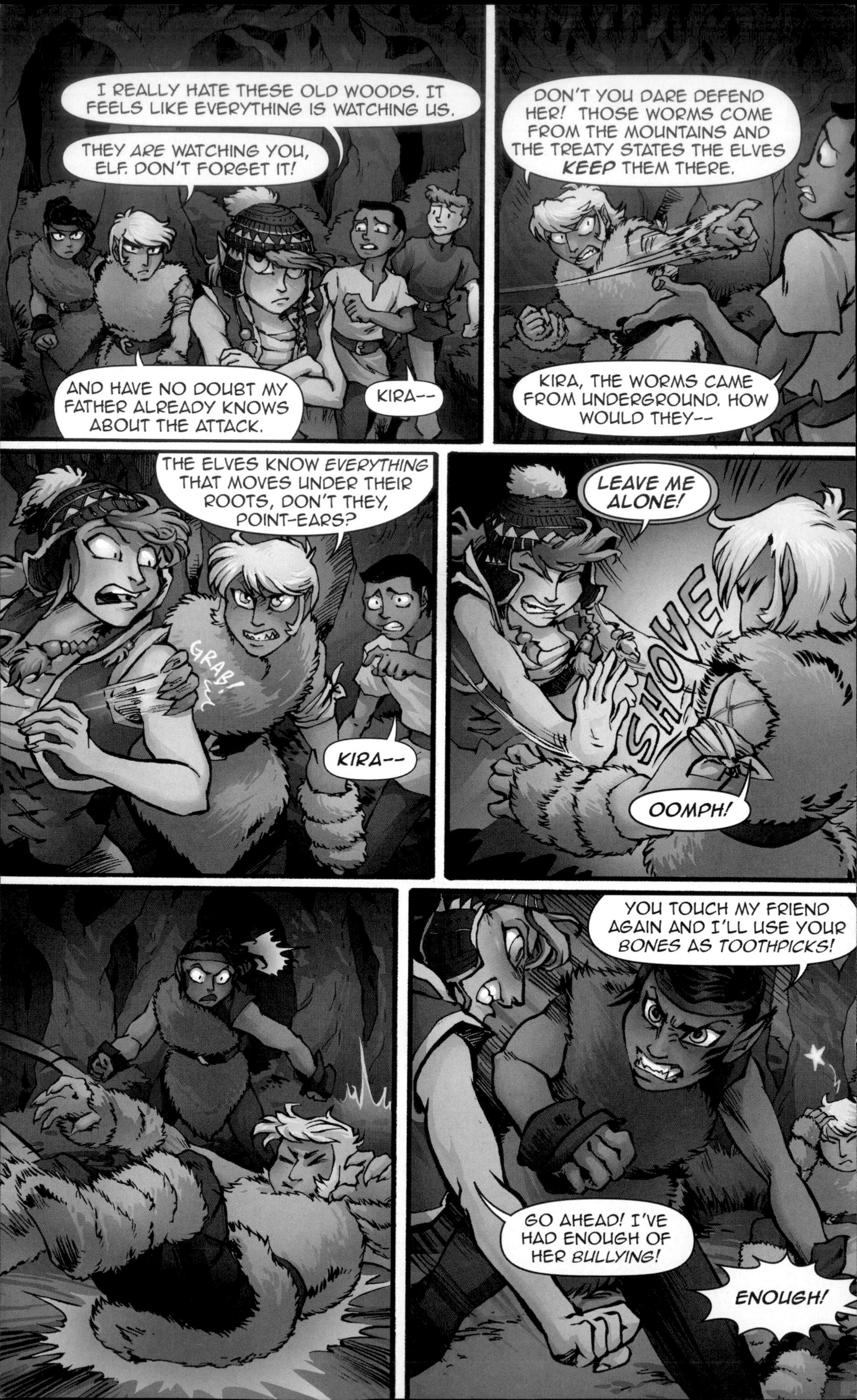
I REALLY HATE THESE OLD WOODS. IT FEELS LIKE EVERYTHING IS WATCHING US.
THEY *ARE* WATCHING YOU, ELF. DON'T FORGET IT!
AND HAVE NO DOUBT MY FATHER ALREADY KNOWS ABOUT THE ATTACK.
KIRA--
DON'T YOU DARE DEFEND HER! THOSE WORMS COME FROM THE MOUNTAINS AND THE TREATY STATES THE ELVES **KEEP** THEM THERE.
KIRA, THE WORMS CAME FROM UNDERGROUND. HOW WOULD THEY--
THE ELVES KNOW *EVERYTHING* THAT MOVES UNDER THEIR ROOTS, DON'T THEY, POINT-EARS?
GRAB!
KIRA--
LEAVE ME ALONE!
SHOVE
OOMPH!
YOU TOUCH MY FRIEND AGAIN AND I'LL USE YOUR *BONES* AS *TOOTHPICKS!*
GO AHEAD! I'VE HAD ENOUGH OF HER *BULLYING!*
ENOUGH!

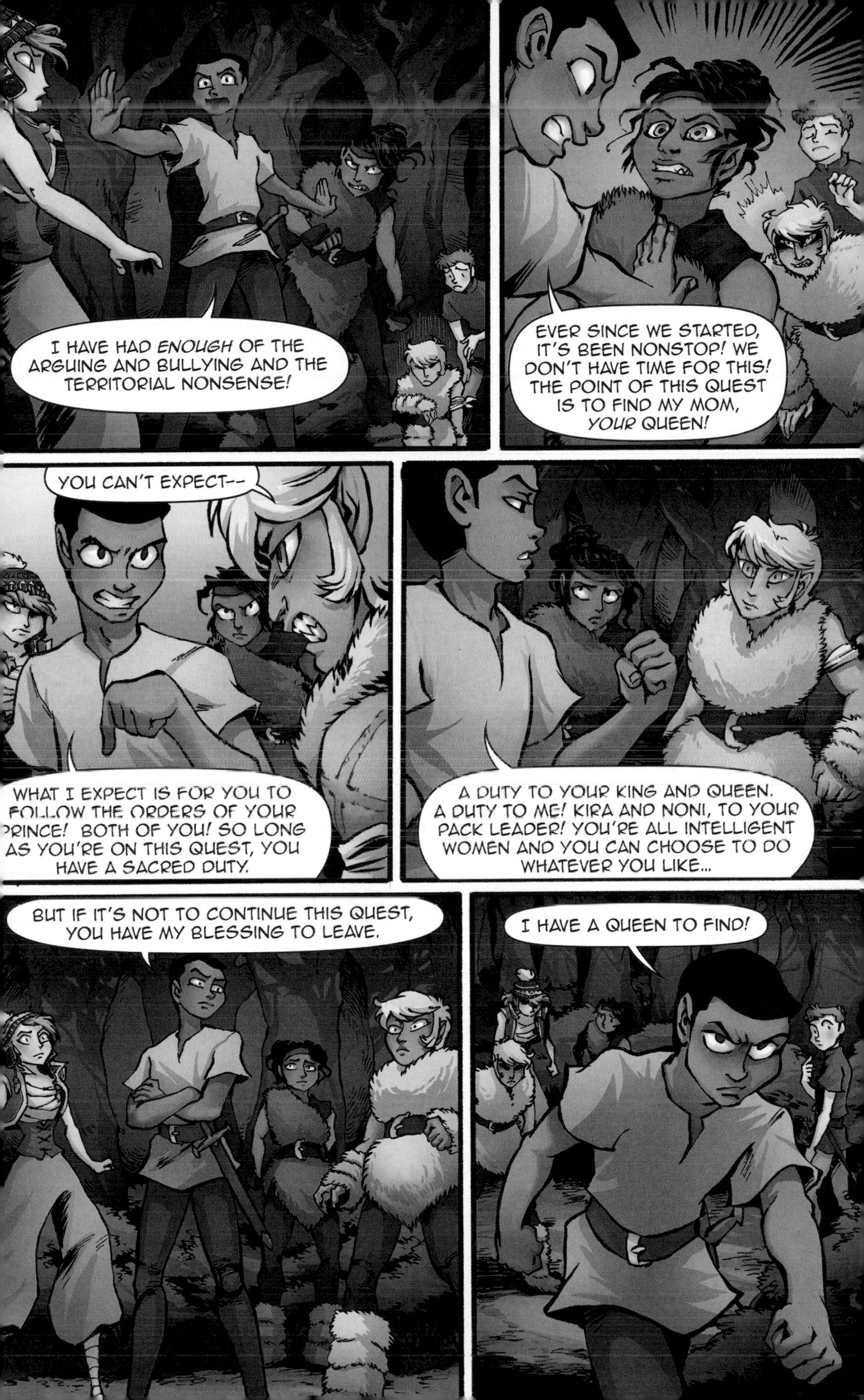
I HAVE HAD *ENOUGH* OF THE ARGUING AND BULLYING AND THE TERRITORIAL NONSENSE!
EVER SINCE WE STARTED, IT'S BEEN NONSTOP! WE DON'T HAVE TIME FOR THIS! THE POINT OF THIS QUEST IS TO FIND MY MOM, *YOUR* QUEEN!
YOU CAN'T EXPECT--
WHAT I EXPECT IS FOR YOU TO FOLLOW THE ORDERS OF YOUR PRINCE! BOTH OF YOU! SO LONG AS YOU'RE ON THIS QUEST, YOU HAVE A SACRED DUTY.
A DUTY TO YOUR KING AND QUEEN. A DUTY TO ME! KIRA AND NONI, TO YOUR PACK LEADER! YOU'RE ALL INTELLIGENT WOMEN AND YOU CAN CHOOSE TO DO WHATEVER YOU LIKE...
BUT IF IT'S NOT TO CONTINUE THIS QUEST, YOU HAVE MY BLESSING TO LEAVE.
I HAVE A QUEEN TO FIND!

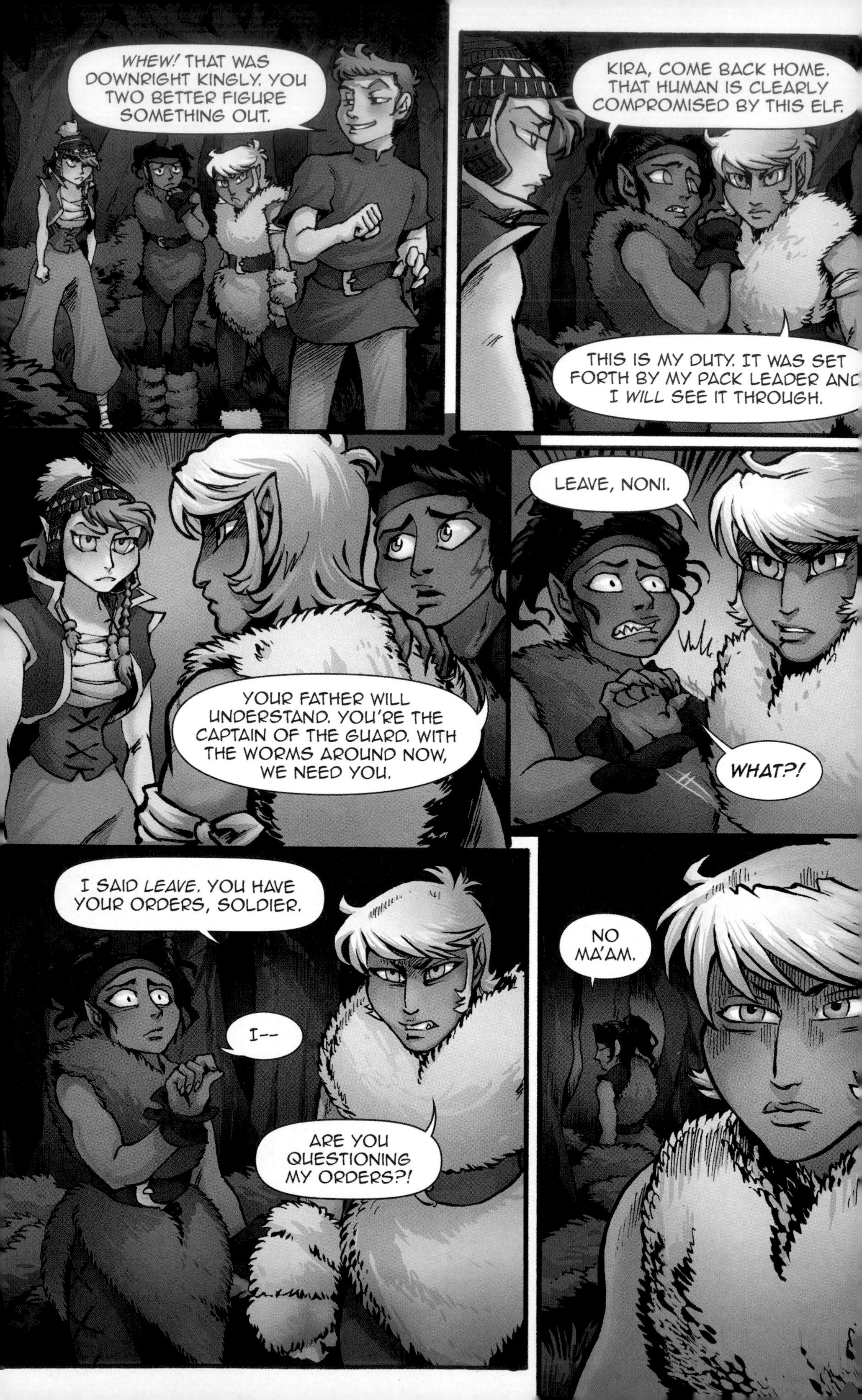
WHEW! THAT WAS DOWNRIGHT KINGLY. YOU TWO BETTER FIGURE SOMETHING OUT.
KIRA, COME BACK HOME. THAT HUMAN IS CLEARLY COMPROMISED BY THIS ELF.
THIS IS MY DUTY. IT WAS SET FORTH BY MY PACK LEADER AND I WILL SEE IT THROUGH.
YOUR FATHER WILL UNDERSTAND. YOU'RE THE CAPTAIN OF THE GUARD. WITH THE WORMS AROUND NOW, WE NEED YOU.
LEAVE, NONI.
WHAT?!
I SAID LEAVE. YOU HAVE YOUR ORDERS, SOLDIER.
I--
ARE YOU QUESTIONING MY ORDERS?!
NO MA'AM.

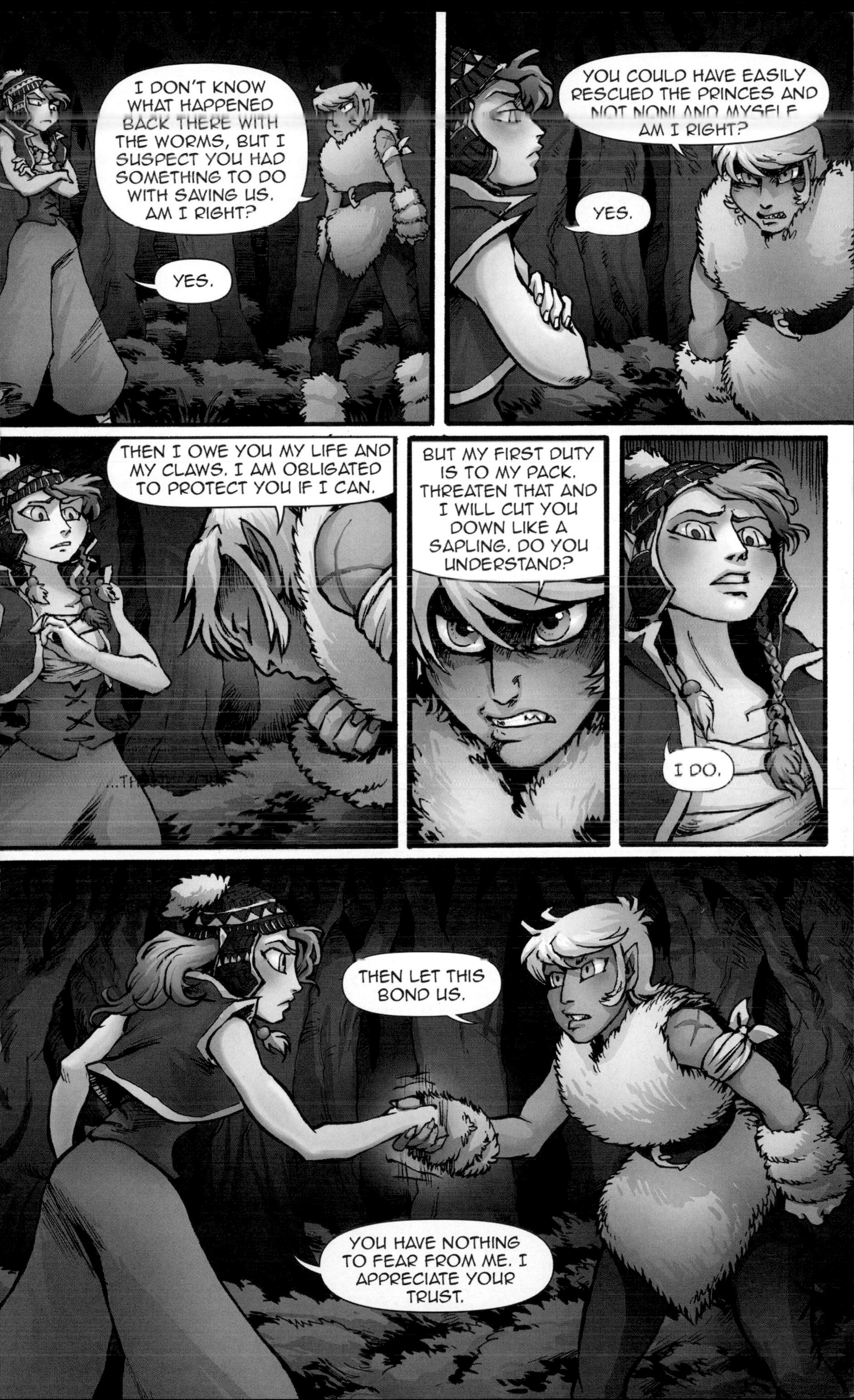
I DON'T KNOW WHAT HAPPENED BACK THERE WITH THE WORMS, BUT I SUSPECT YOU HAD SOMETHING TO DO WITH SAVING US. AM I RIGHT?
YES.
YOU COULD HAVE EASILY RESCUED THE PRINCES AND NOT NONI AND MYSELF. AM I RIGHT?
YES.
THEN I OWE YOU MY LIFE AND MY CLAWS. I AM OBLIGATED TO PROTECT YOU IF I CAN.
BUT MY FIRST DUTY IS TO MY PACK. THREATEN THAT AND I WILL CUT YOU DOWN LIKE A SAPLING. DO YOU UNDERSTAND?
I DO.
THEN LET THIS BOND US.
YOU HAVE NOTHING TO FEAR FROM ME. I APPRECIATE YOUR TRUST.

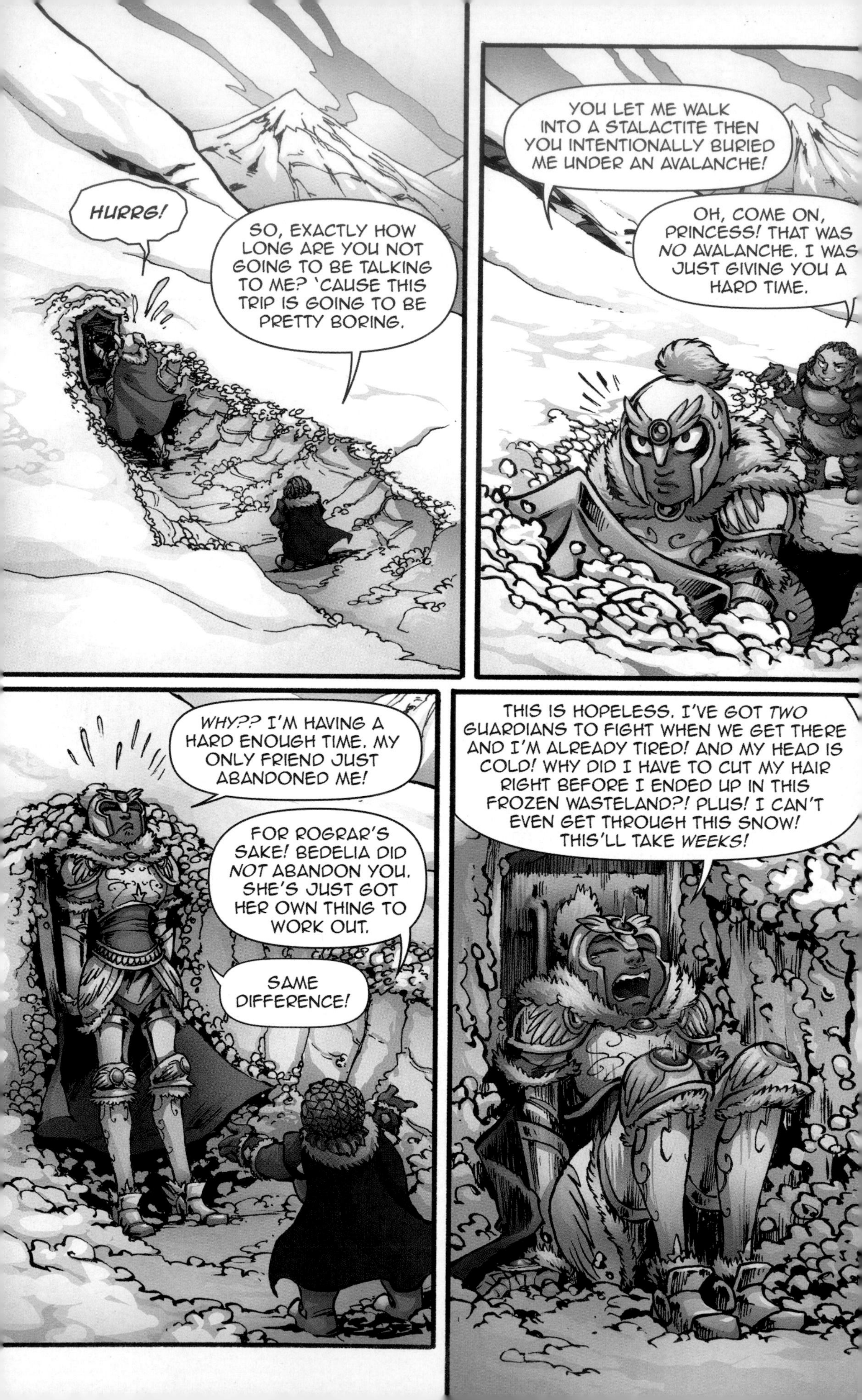
HURRG!
SO, EXACTLY HOW LONG ARE YOU NOT GOING TO BE TALKING TO ME? 'CAUSE THIS TRIP IS GOING TO BE PRETTY BORING.
YOU LET ME WALK INTO A STALACTITE THEN YOU INTENTIONALLY BURIED ME UNDER AN AVALANCHE!
OH, COME ON, PRINCESS! THAT WAS *NO* AVALANCHE. I WAS JUST GIVING YOU A HARD TIME.
WHY?? I'M HAVING A HARD ENOUGH TIME. MY ONLY FRIEND JUST ABANDONED ME!
FOR ROGRAR'S SAKE! BEDELIA DID *NOT* ABANDON YOU. SHE'S JUST GOT HER OWN THING TO WORK OUT.
SAME DIFFERENCE!
THIS IS HOPELESS. I'VE GOT *TWO* GUARDIANS TO FIGHT WHEN WE GET THERE AND I'M ALREADY TIRED! AND MY HEAD IS COLD! WHY DID I HAVE TO CUT MY HAIR RIGHT BEFORE I ENDED UP IN THIS FROZEN WASTELAND?! PLUS! I CAN'T EVEN GET THROUGH THIS SNOW! THIS'LL TAKE *WEEKS!*

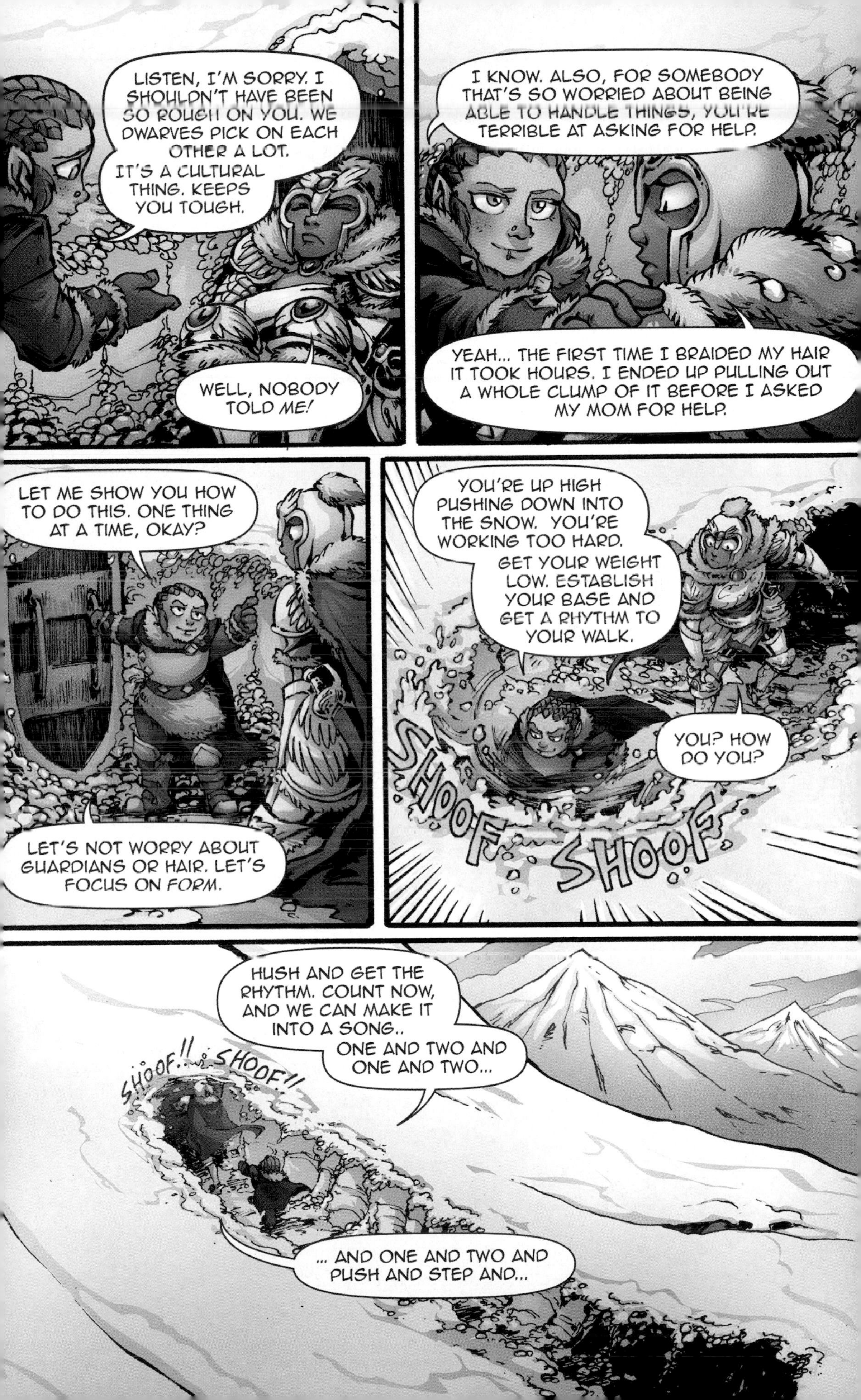
LISTEN, I'M SORRY. I SHOULDN'T HAVE BEEN SO ROUGH ON YOU. WE DWARVES PICK ON EACH OTHER A LOT.
IT'S A CULTURAL THING. KEEPS YOU TOUGH.
WELL, NOBODY TOLD *ME!*
I KNOW. ALSO, FOR SOMEBODY THAT'S SO WORRIED ABOUT BEING ABLE TO HANDLE THINGS, YOU'RE TERRIBLE AT ASKING FOR HELP.
YEAH... THE FIRST TIME I BRAIDED MY HAIR IT TOOK HOURS. I ENDED UP PULLING OUT A WHOLE CLUMP OF IT BEFORE I ASKED MY MOM FOR HELP.
LET ME SHOW YOU HOW TO DO THIS. ONE THING AT A TIME, OKAY?
LET'S NOT WORRY ABOUT GUARDIANS OR HAIR. LET'S FOCUS ON *FORM.*
YOU'RE UP HIGH PUSHING DOWN INTO THE SNOW. YOU'RE WORKING TOO HARD.
GET YOUR WEIGHT LOW. ESTABLISH YOUR BASE AND GET A RHYTHM TO YOUR WALK.
YOU? HOW DO YOU?
SHOOF
SHOOF
HUSH AND GET THE RHYTHM. COUNT NOW, AND WE CAN MAKE IT INTO A SONG..
ONE AND TWO AND ONE AND TWO...
SHOOF!! SHOOF!!
... AND ONE AND TWO AND PUSH AND STEP AND...

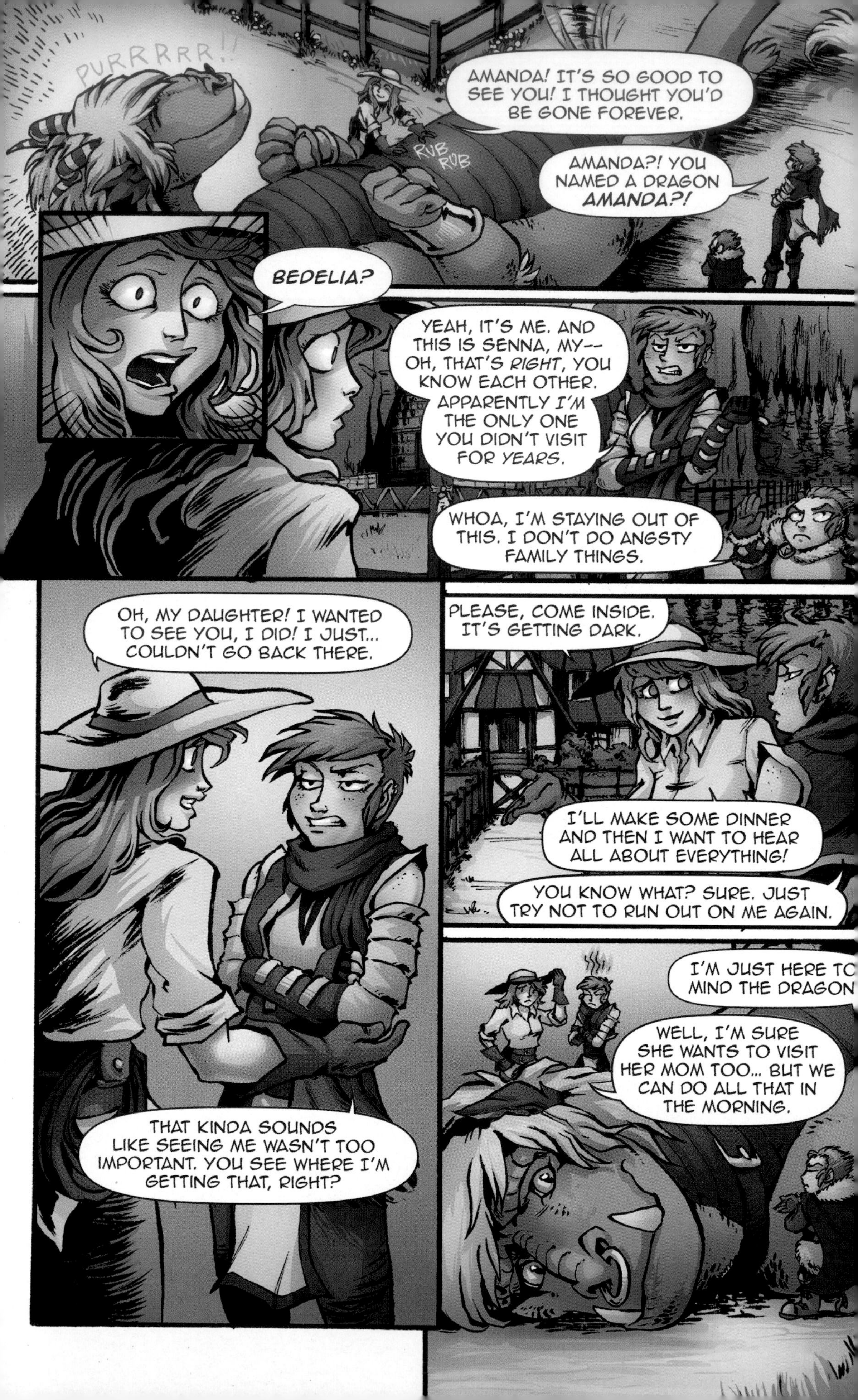
PURRRRR!!
AMANDA! IT'S SO GOOD TO SEE YOU! I THOUGHT YOU'D BE GONE FOREVER.
RUB RUB
AMANDA?! YOU NAMED A DRAGON AMANDA?!
BEDELIA?
YEAH, IT'S ME. AND THIS IS SENNA, MY-- OH, THAT'S RIGHT, YOU KNOW EACH OTHER. APPARENTLY I'M THE ONLY ONE YOU DIDN'T VISIT FOR YEARS.
WHOA, I'M STAYING OUT OF THIS. I DON'T DO ANGSTY FAMILY THINGS.
OH, MY DAUGHTER! I WANTED TO SEE YOU, I DID! I JUST... COULDN'T GO BACK THERE.
THAT KINDA SOUNDS LIKE SEEING ME WASN'T TOO IMPORTANT. YOU SEE WHERE I'M GETTING THAT, RIGHT?
PLEASE, COME INSIDE. IT'S GETTING DARK.
I'LL MAKE SOME DINNER AND THEN I WANT TO HEAR ALL ABOUT EVERYTHING!
YOU KNOW WHAT? SURE. JUST TRY NOT TO RUN OUT ON ME AGAIN.
I'M JUST HERE TO MIND THE DRAGON
WELL, I'M SURE SHE WANTS TO VISIT HER MOM TOO... BUT WE CAN DO ALL THAT IN THE MORNING.

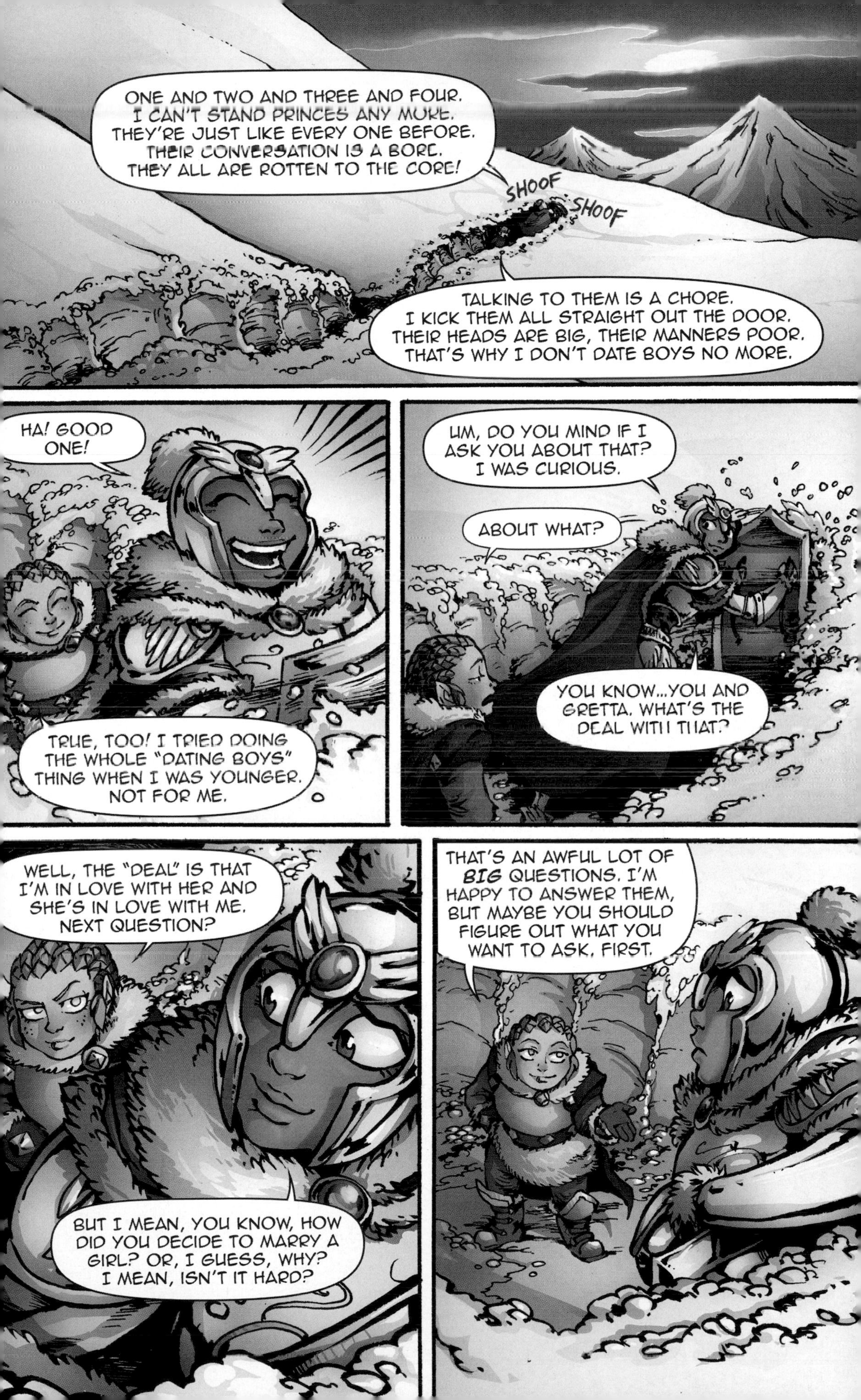
ONE AND TWO AND THREE AND FOUR. I CAN'T STAND PRINCES ANY MORE. THEY'RE JUST LIKE EVERY ONE BEFORE. THEIR CONVERSATION IS A BORE. THEY ALL ARE ROTTEN TO THE CORE!
SHOOF SHOOF
TALKING TO THEM IS A CHORE. I KICK THEM ALL STRAIGHT OUT THE DOOR. THEIR HEADS ARE BIG, THEIR MANNERS POOR. THAT'S WHY I DON'T DATE BOYS NO MORE.
HA! GOOD ONE!
TRUE, TOO! I TRIED DOING THE WHOLE "DATING BOYS" THING WHEN I WAS YOUNGER. NOT FOR ME.
UM, DO YOU MIND IF I ASK YOU ABOUT THAT? I WAS CURIOUS.
ABOUT WHAT?
YOU KNOW...YOU AND GRETTA. WHAT'S THE DEAL WITH THAT?
WELL, THE "DEAL" IS THAT I'M IN LOVE WITH HER AND SHE'S IN LOVE WITH ME. NEXT QUESTION?
BUT I MEAN, YOU KNOW, HOW DID YOU DECIDE TO MARRY A GIRL? OR, I GUESS, WHY? I MEAN, ISN'T IT HARD?
THAT'S AN AWFUL LOT OF *BIG* QUESTIONS. I'M HAPPY TO ANSWER THEM, BUT MAYBE YOU SHOULD FIGURE OUT WHAT YOU WANT TO ASK, FIRST.

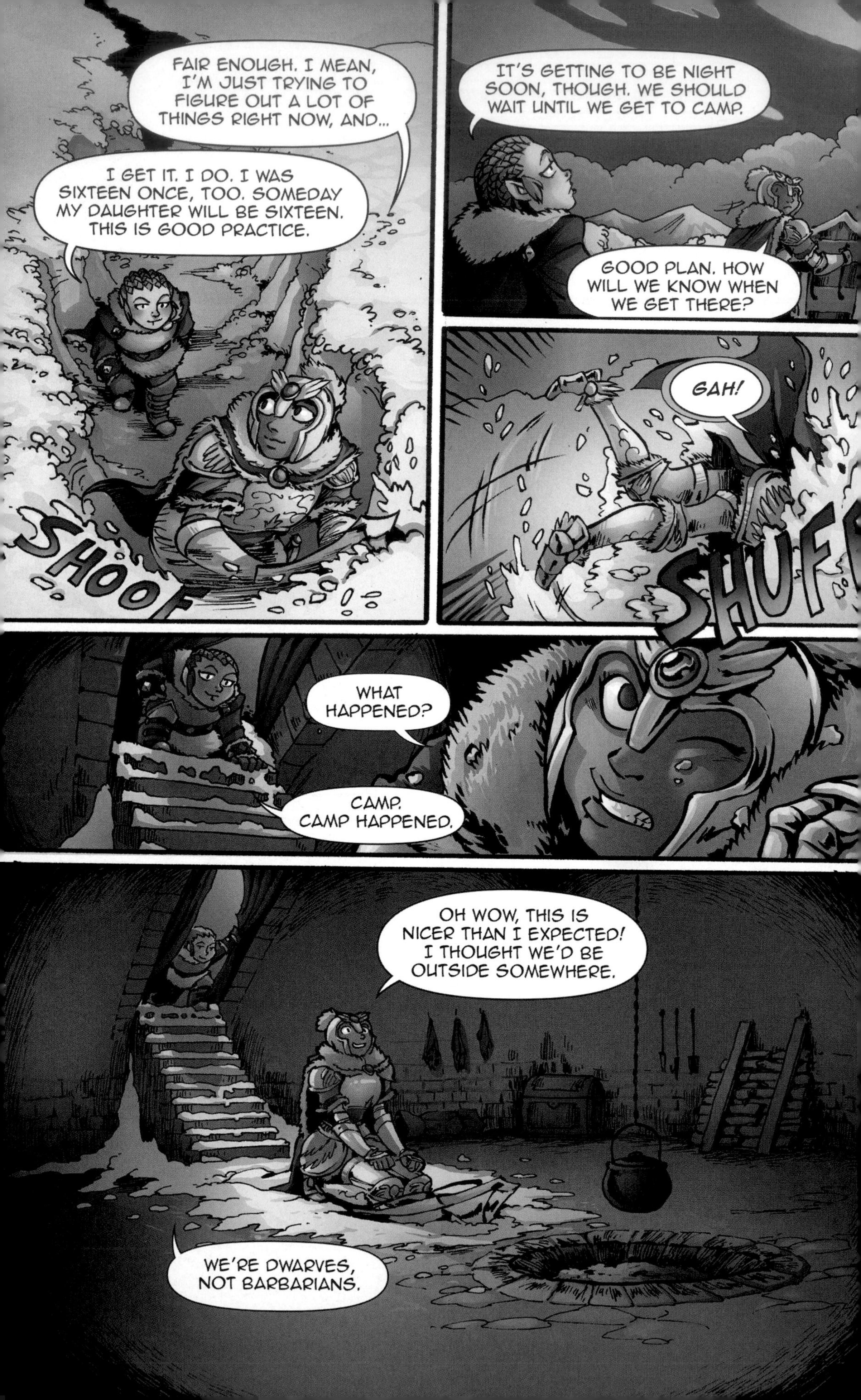
FAIR ENOUGH. I MEAN, I'M JUST TRYING TO FIGURE OUT A LOT OF THINGS RIGHT NOW, AND...
I GET IT. I DO. I WAS SIXTEEN ONCE, TOO. SOMEDAY MY DAUGHTER WILL BE SIXTEEN. THIS IS GOOD PRACTICE.
SHOOF
IT'S GETTING TO BE NIGHT SOON, THOUGH. WE SHOULD WAIT UNTIL WE GET TO CAMP.
GOOD PLAN. HOW WILL WE KNOW WHEN WE GET THERE?
GAH!
SHUF
WHAT HAPPENED?
CAMP. CAMP HAPPENED.
OH WOW, THIS IS NICER THAN I EXPECTED! I THOUGHT WE'D BE OUTSIDE SOMEWHERE.
WE'RE DWARVES, NOT BARBARIANS.

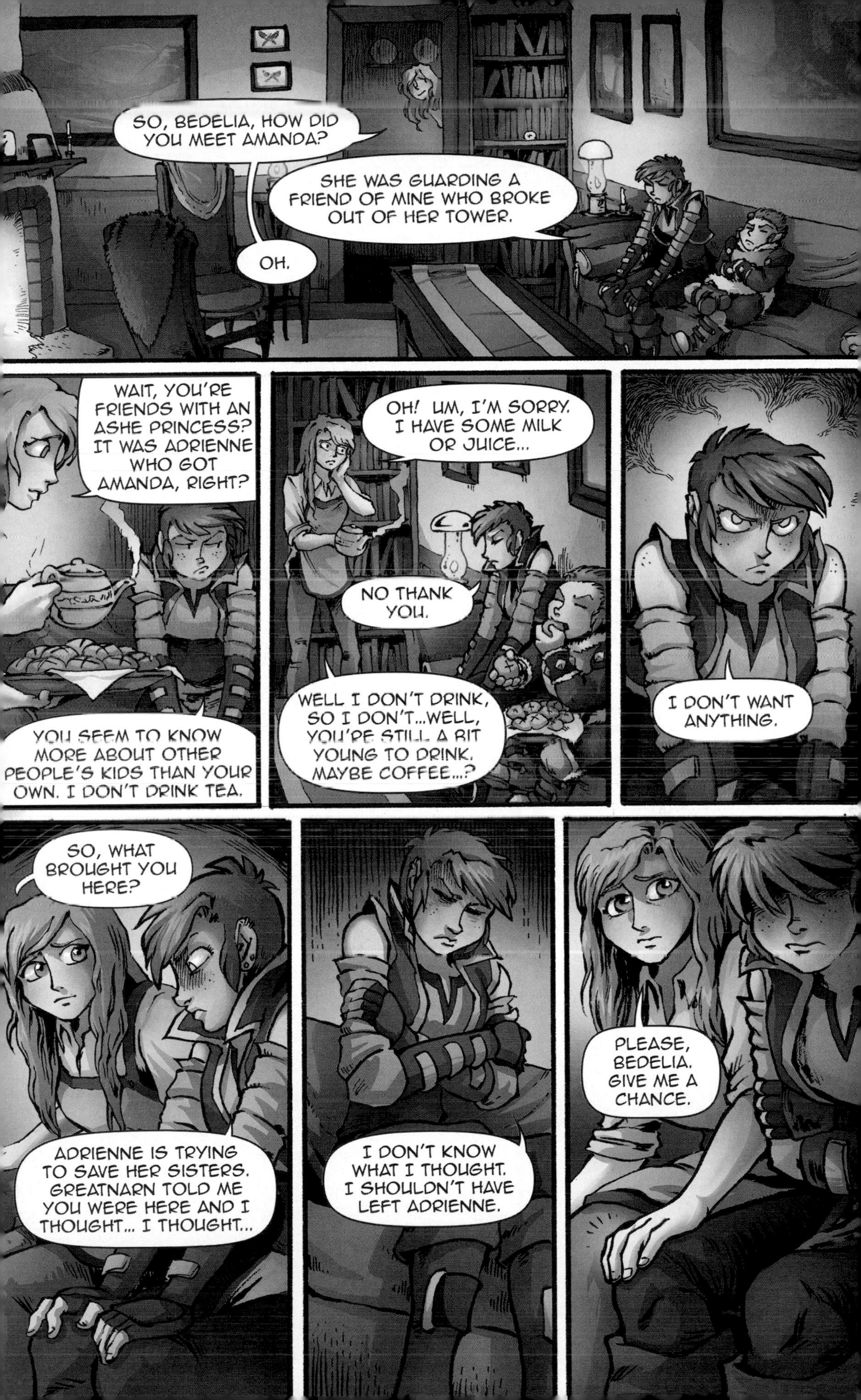
SO, BEDELIA, HOW DID YOU MEET AMANDA?
SHE WAS GUARDING A FRIEND OF MINE WHO BROKE OUT OF HER TOWER.
OH.
WAIT, YOU'RE FRIENDS WITH AN ASHE PRINCESS? IT WAS ADRIENNE WHO GOT AMANDA, RIGHT?
YOU SEEM TO KNOW MORE ABOUT OTHER PEOPLE'S KIDS THAN YOUR OWN. I DON'T DRINK TEA.
OH! UM, I'M SORRY. I HAVE SOME MILK OR JUICE...
NO THANK YOU.
WELL I DON'T DRINK, SO I DON'T...WELL, YOU'RE STILL A BIT YOUNG TO DRINK. MAYBE COFFEE...?
I DON'T WANT ANYTHING.
SO, WHAT BROUGHT YOU HERE?
ADRIENNE IS TRYING TO SAVE HER SISTERS. GREATNARN TOLD ME YOU WERE HERE AND I THOUGHT... I THOUGHT...
I DON'T KNOW WHAT I THOUGHT. I SHOULDN'T HAVE LEFT ADRIENNE.
PLEASE, BEDELIA. GIVE ME A CHANCE.

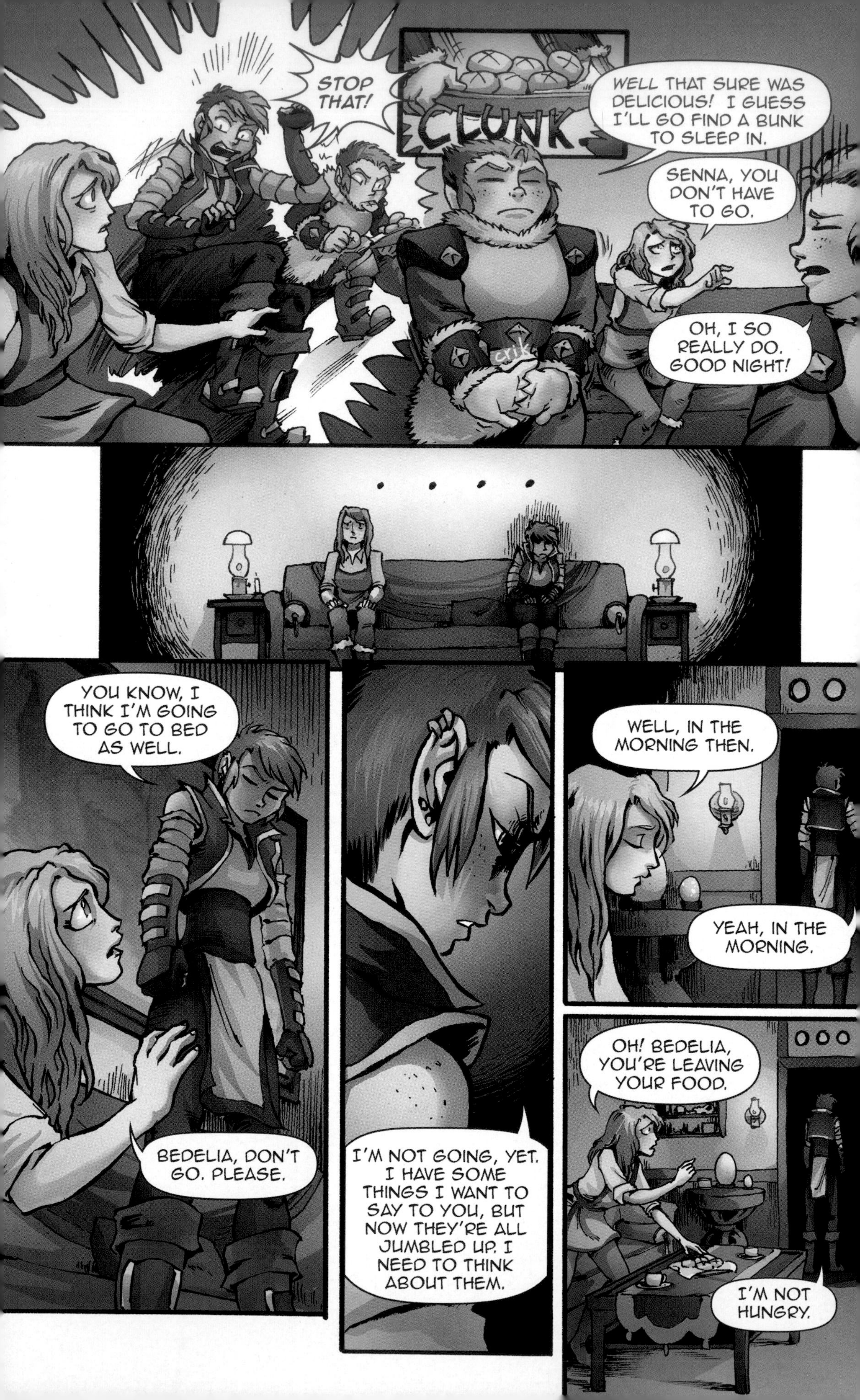
STOP THAT!
CLUNK
WELL THAT SURE WAS DELICIOUS! I GUESS I'LL GO FIND A BUNK TO SLEEP IN.
SENNA, YOU DON'T HAVE TO GO.
OH, I SO REALLY DO. GOOD NIGHT!
crik
. . . .
YOU KNOW, I THINK I'M GOING TO GO TO BED AS WELL.
BEDELIA, DON'T GO. PLEASE.
I'M NOT GOING, YET. I HAVE SOME THINGS I WANT TO SAY TO YOU, BUT NOW THEY'RE ALL JUMBLED UP. I NEED TO THINK ABOUT THEM.
WELL, IN THE MORNING THEN.
YEAH, IN THE MORNING.
OH! BEDELIA, YOU'RE LEAVING YOUR FOOD.
I'M NOT HUNGRY.

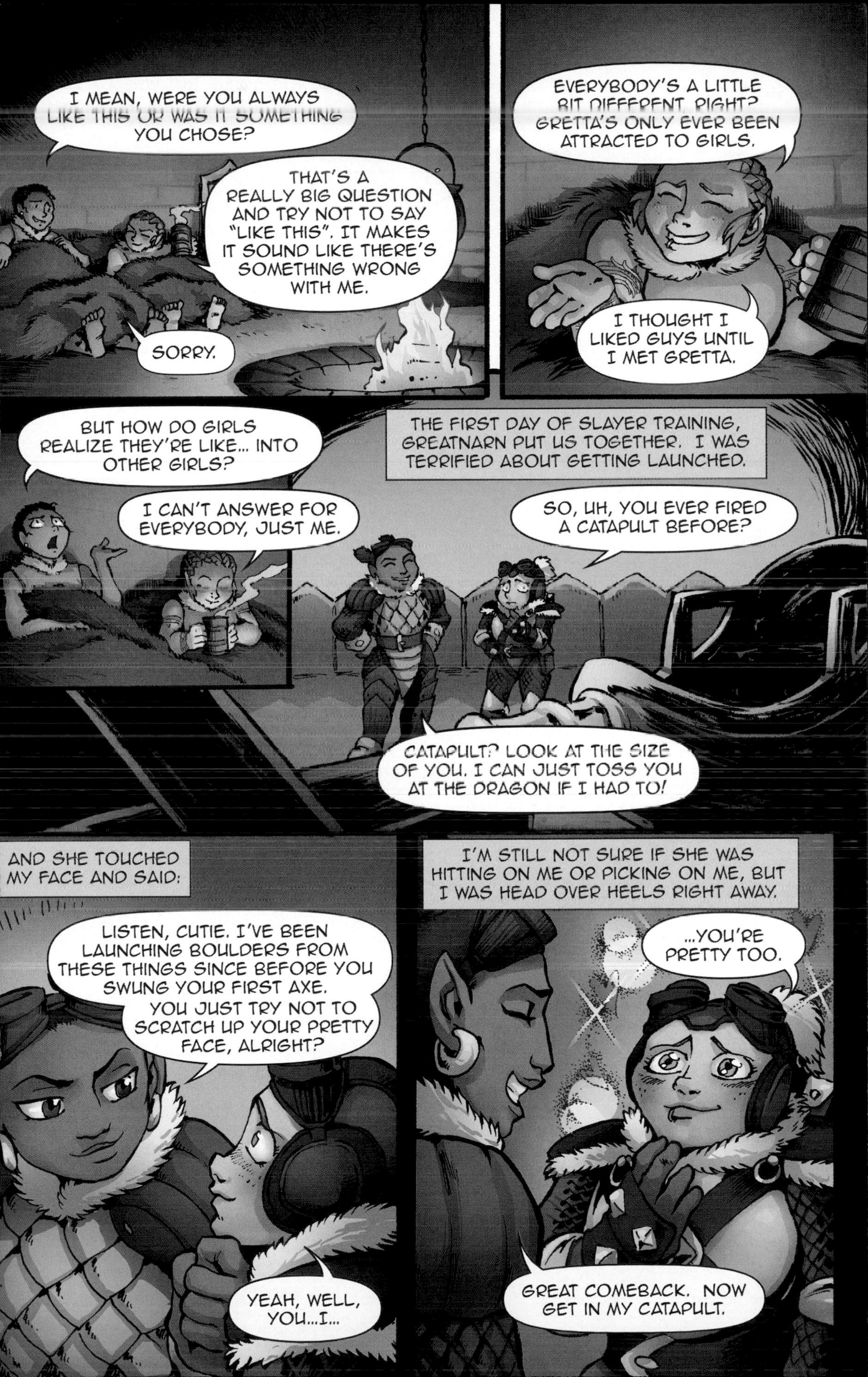
I MEAN, WERE YOU ALWAYS LIKE THIS OR WAS IT SOMETHING YOU CHOSE?
THAT'S A REALLY BIG QUESTION AND TRY NOT TO SAY "LIKE THIS". IT MAKES IT SOUND LIKE THERE'S SOMETHING WRONG WITH ME.
SORRY.
EVERYBODY'S A LITTLE BIT DIFFERENT, RIGHT? GRETTA'S ONLY EVER BEEN ATTRACTED TO GIRLS.
I THOUGHT I LIKED GUYS UNTIL I MET GRETTA.
BUT HOW DO GIRLS REALIZE THEY'RE LIKE... INTO OTHER GIRLS?
I CAN'T ANSWER FOR EVERYBODY, JUST ME.
THE FIRST DAY OF SLAYER TRAINING, GREATNARN PUT US TOGETHER. I WAS TERRIFIED ABOUT GETTING LAUNCHED.
SO, UH, YOU EVER FIRED A CATAPULT BEFORE?
CATAPULT? LOOK AT THE SIZE OF YOU. I CAN JUST TOSS YOU AT THE DRAGON IF I HAD TO!
AND SHE TOUCHED MY FACE AND SAID:
LISTEN, CUTIE. I'VE BEEN LAUNCHING BOULDERS FROM THESE THINGS SINCE BEFORE YOU SWUNG YOUR FIRST AXE.
YOU JUST TRY NOT TO SCRATCH UP YOUR PRETTY FACE, ALRIGHT?
YEAH, WELL, YOU...I...
I'M STILL NOT SURE IF SHE WAS HITTING ON ME OR PICKING ON ME, BUT I WAS HEAD OVER HEELS RIGHT AWAY.
...YOU'RE PRETTY TOO.
GREAT COMEBACK. NOW GET IN MY CATAPULT.

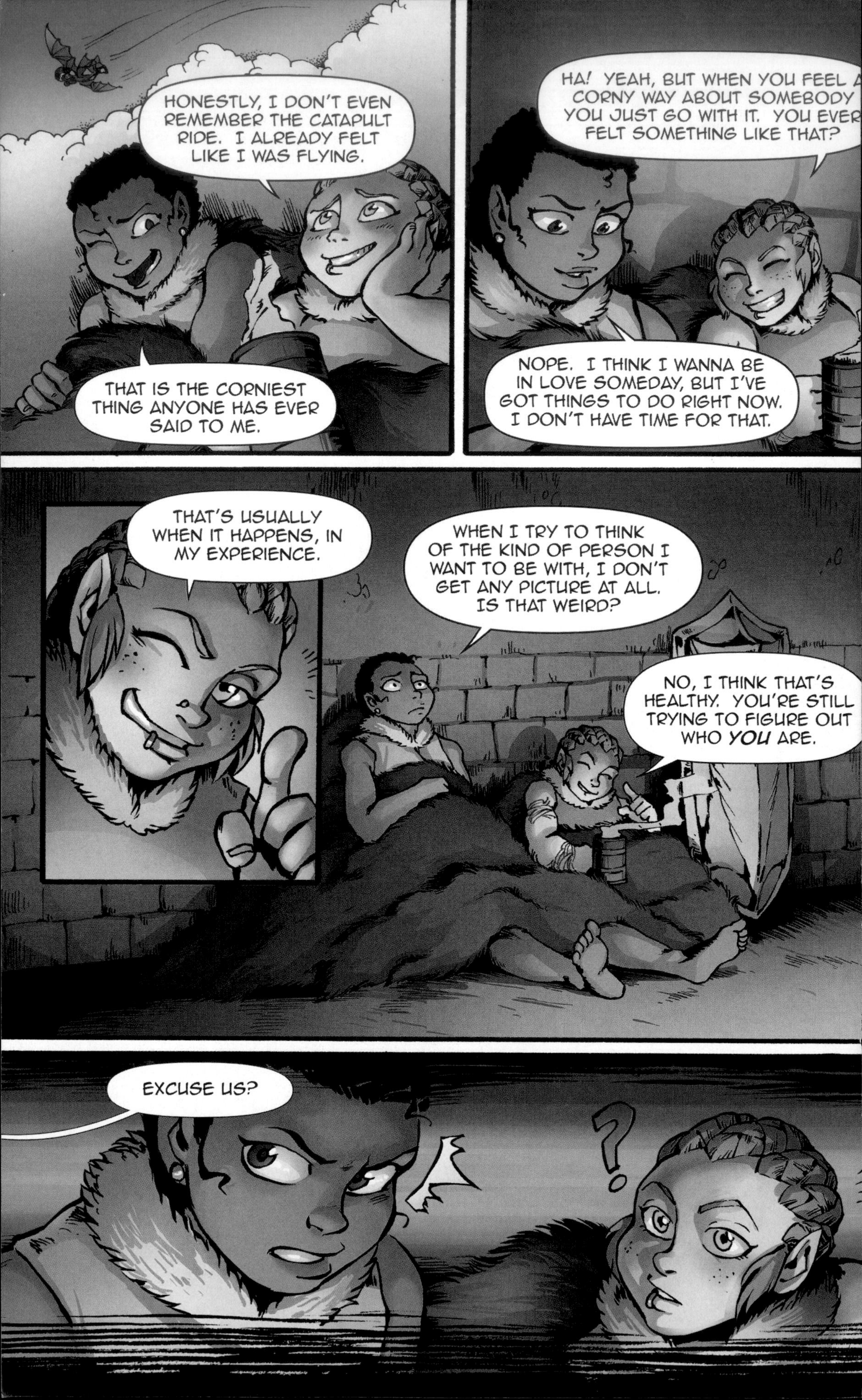
HONESTLY, I DON'T EVEN REMEMBER THE CATAPULT RIDE. I ALREADY FELT LIKE I WAS FLYING.
THAT IS THE CORNIEST THING ANYONE HAS EVER SAID TO ME.
HA! YEAH, BUT WHEN YOU FEEL A CORNY WAY ABOUT SOMEBODY YOU JUST GO WITH IT. YOU EVER FELT SOMETHING LIKE THAT?
NOPE. I THINK I WANNA BE IN LOVE SOMEDAY, BUT I'VE GOT THINGS TO DO RIGHT NOW. I DON'T HAVE TIME FOR THAT.
THAT'S USUALLY WHEN IT HAPPENS, IN MY EXPERIENCE.
WHEN I TRY TO THINK OF THE KIND OF PERSON I WANT TO BE WITH, I DON'T GET ANY PICTURE AT ALL. IS THAT WEIRD?
NO, I THINK THAT'S HEALTHY. YOU'RE STILL TRYING TO FIGURE OUT WHO *YOU* ARE.
EXCUSE US?
?

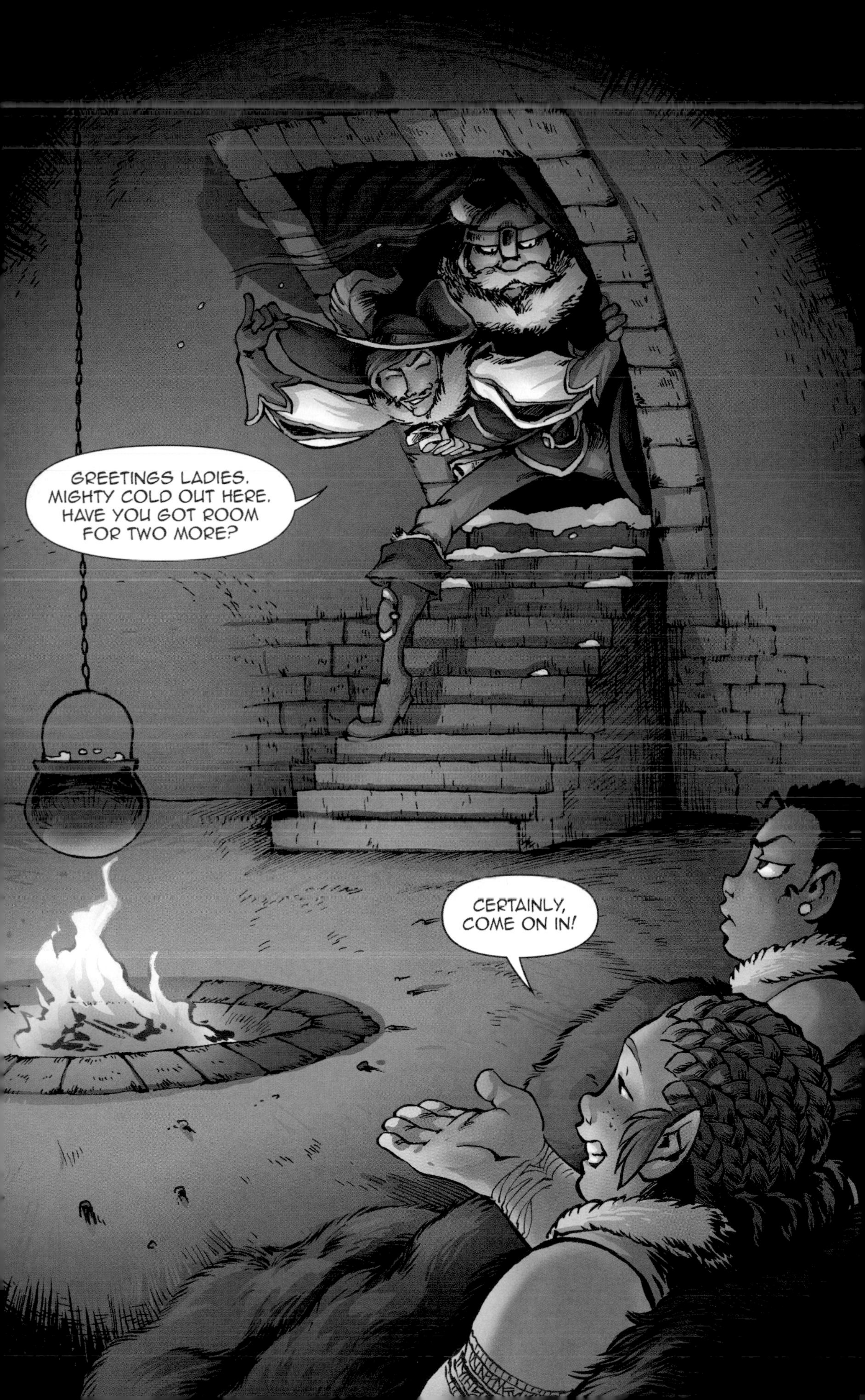
GREETINGS LADIES. MIGHTY COLD OUT HERE. HAVE YOU GOT ROOM FOR TWO MORE?
CERTAINLY, COME ON IN!

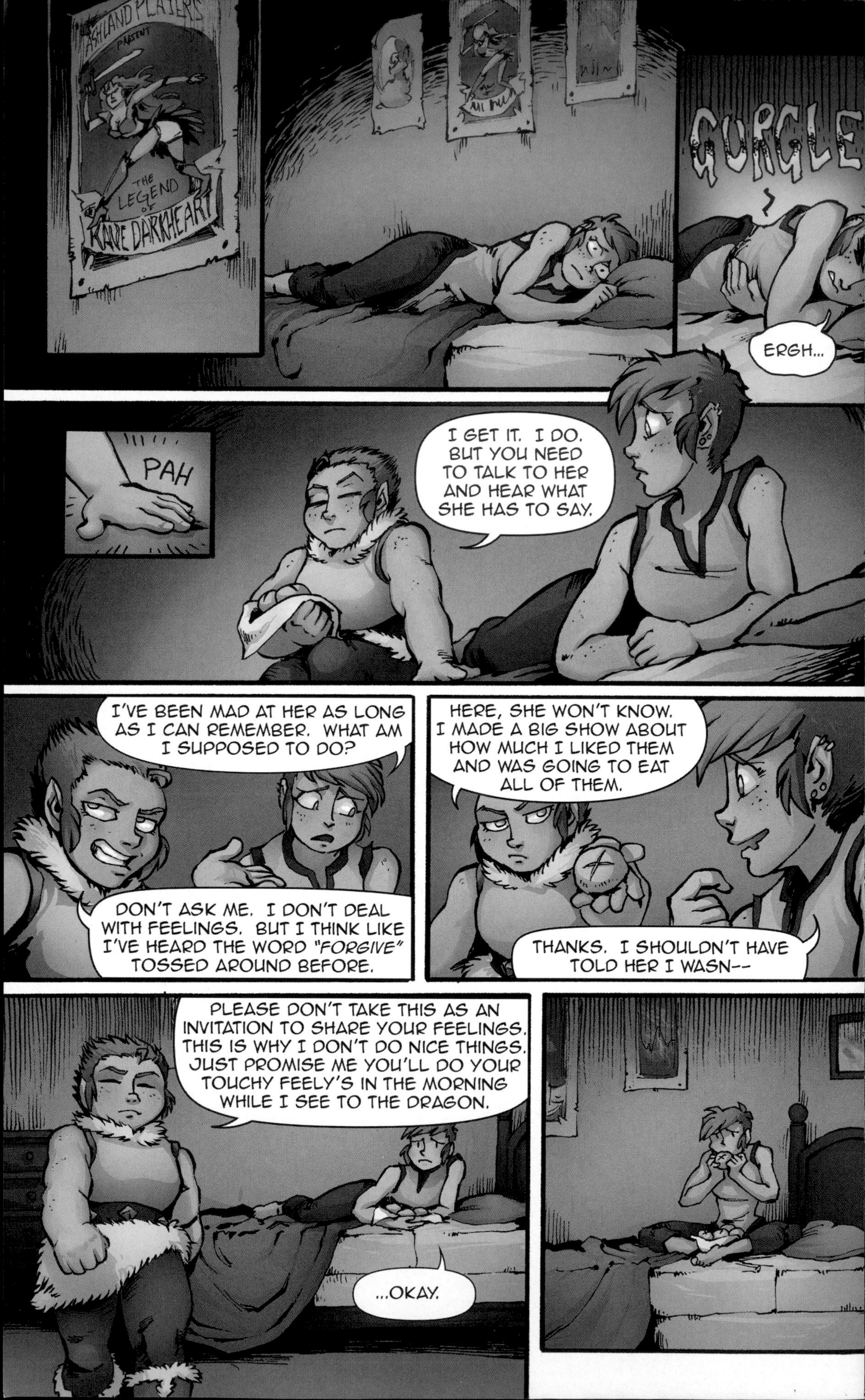
ASHLAND PLAYERS PRESENT THE LEGEND OF KADE DARKHEART
GURGLE
ERGH...
PAH
I GET IT. I DO. BUT YOU NEED TO TALK TO HER AND HEAR WHAT SHE HAS TO SAY.
I'VE BEEN MAD AT HER AS LONG AS I CAN REMEMBER. WHAT AM I SUPPOSED TO DO?
DON'T ASK ME. I DON'T DEAL WITH FEELINGS. BUT I THINK LIKE I'VE HEARD THE WORD *"FORGIVE"* TOSSED AROUND BEFORE.
HERE, SHE WON'T KNOW. I MADE A BIG SHOW ABOUT HOW MUCH I LIKED THEM AND WAS GOING TO EAT ALL OF THEM.
THANKS. I SHOULDN'T HAVE TOLD HER I WASN--
PLEASE DON'T TAKE THIS AS AN INVITATION TO SHARE YOUR FEELINGS. THIS IS WHY I DON'T DO NICE THINGS. JUST PROMISE ME YOU'LL DO YOUR TOUCHY FEELY'S IN THE MORNING WHILE I SEE TO THE DRAGON.
...OKAY.

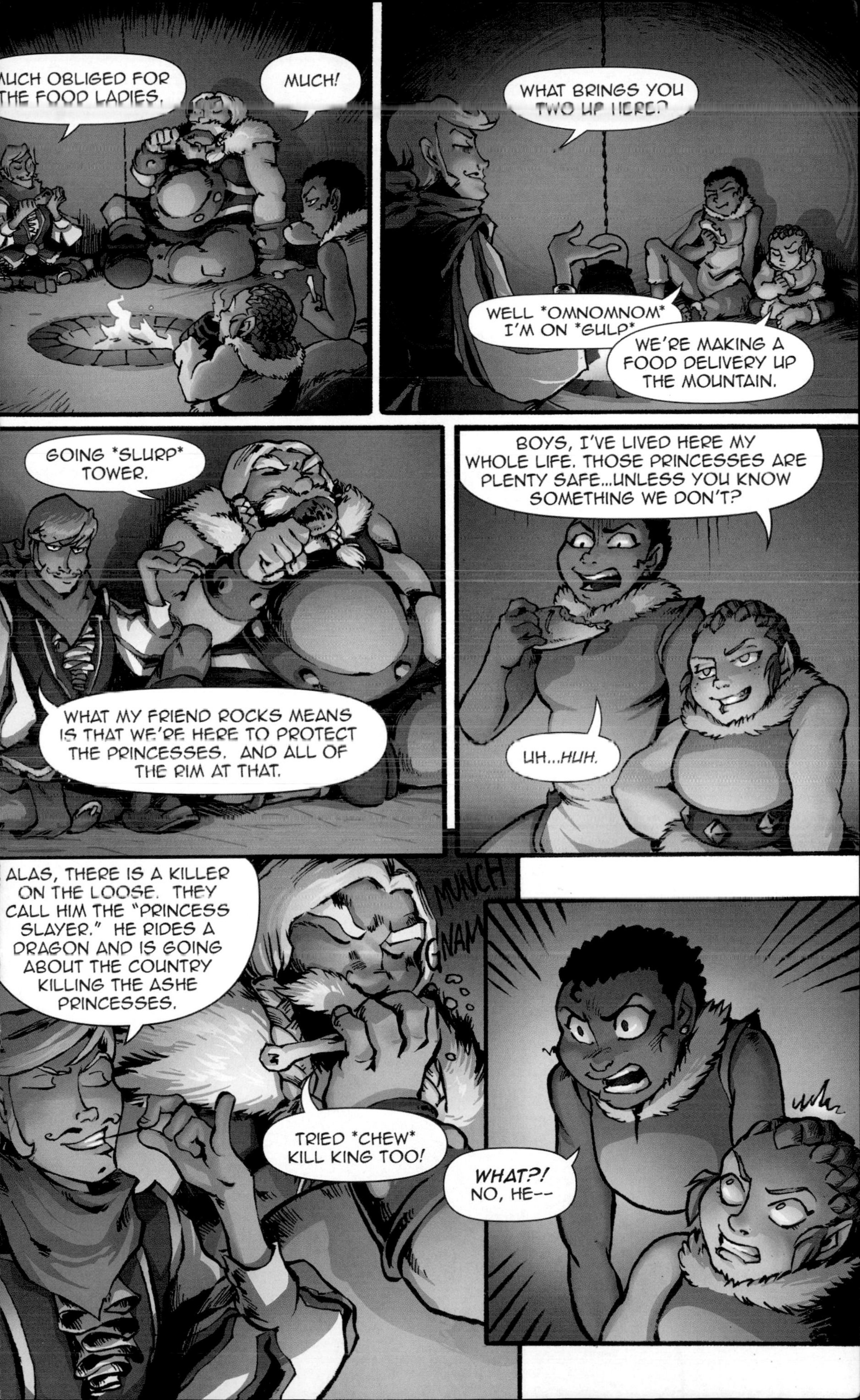
MUCH OBLIGED FOR THE FOOD LADIES.
MUCH!
WHAT BRINGS YOU TWO UP HERE?
WELL *OMNOMNOM* I'M ON *GULP*
WE'RE MAKING A FOOD DELIVERY UP THE MOUNTAIN.
GOING *SLURP* TOWER.
WHAT MY FRIEND ROCKS MEANS IS THAT WE'RE HERE TO PROTECT THE PRINCESSES. AND ALL OF THE RIM AT THAT.
BOYS, I'VE LIVED HERE MY WHOLE LIFE. THOSE PRINCESSES ARE PLENTY SAFE...UNLESS YOU KNOW SOMETHING WE DON'T?
UH...HUH.
ALAS, THERE IS A KILLER ON THE LOOSE. THEY CALL HIM THE "PRINCESS SLAYER." HE RIDES A DRAGON AND IS GOING ABOUT THE COUNTRY KILLING THE ASHE PRINCESSES.
MUNCH
GNAM
TRIED *CHEW* KILL KING TOO!
WHAT?! NO, HE--

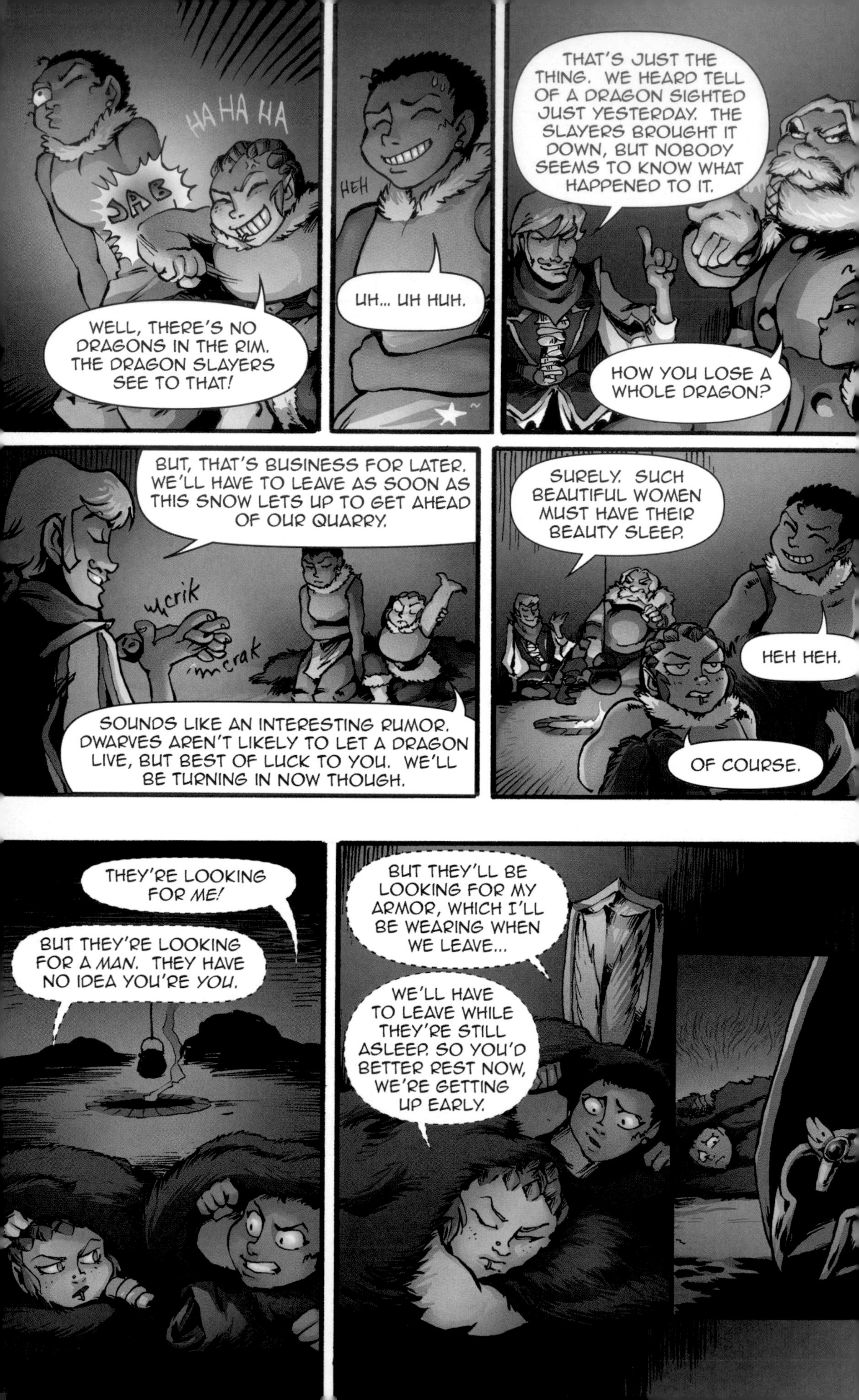
HA HA HA
JAB
WELL, THERE'S NO DRAGONS IN THE RIM. THE DRAGON SLAYERS SEE TO THAT!
HEH
UH... UH HUH.
THAT'S JUST THE THING. WE HEARD TELL OF A DRAGON SIGHTED JUST YESTERDAY. THE SLAYERS BROUGHT IT DOWN, BUT NOBODY SEEMS TO KNOW WHAT HAPPENED TO IT.
HOW YOU LOSE A WHOLE DRAGON?
BUT, THAT'S BUSINESS FOR LATER. WE'LL HAVE TO LEAVE AS SOON AS THIS SNOW LETS UP TO GET AHEAD OF OUR QUARRY.
crik
crak
SOUNDS LIKE AN INTERESTING RUMOR. DWARVES AREN'T LIKELY TO LET A DRAGON LIVE, BUT BEST OF LUCK TO YOU. WE'LL BE TURNING IN NOW THOUGH.
SURELY. SUCH BEAUTIFUL WOMEN MUST HAVE THEIR BEAUTY SLEEP.
HEH HEH.
OF COURSE.
THEY'RE LOOKING FOR ME!
BUT THEY'RE LOOKING FOR A MAN. THEY HAVE NO IDEA YOU'RE YOU.
BUT THEY'LL BE LOOKING FOR MY ARMOR, WHICH I'LL BE WEARING WHEN WE LEAVE...
WE'LL HAVE TO LEAVE WHILE THEY'RE STILL ASLEEP. SO YOU'D BETTER REST NOW, WE'RE GETTING UP EARLY.

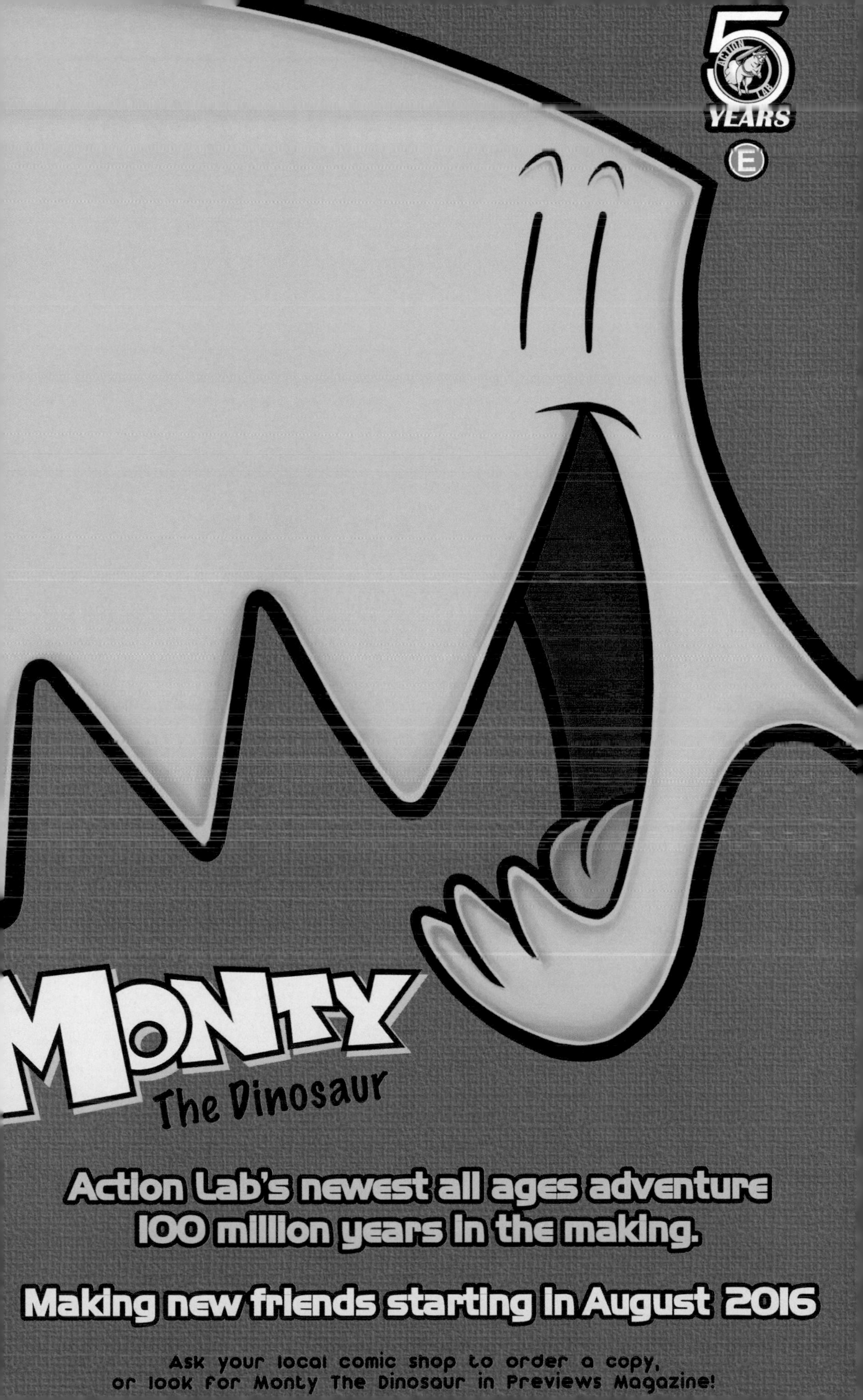
5 YEARS
ACTION LAB
E
MONTY
The Dinosaur
Action Lab's newest all ages adventure
100 million years in the making.
Making new friends starting in August 2016
Ask your local comic shop to order a copy,
or look for Monty The Dinosaur in Previews Magazine!

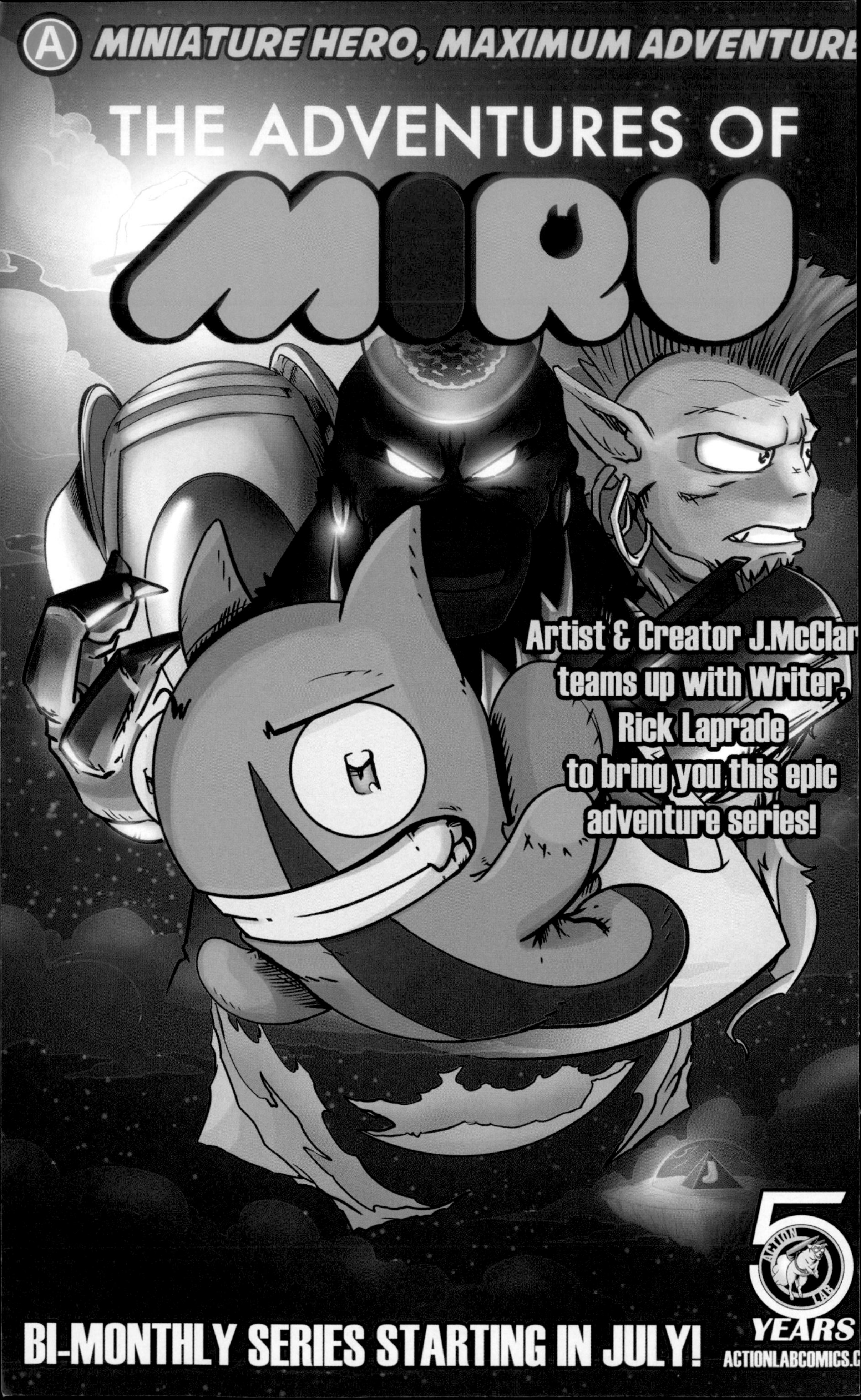
MINIATURE HERO, MAXIMUM ADVENTURE
THE ADVENTURES OF
MIRU
Artist & Creator J.McClar
teams up with Writer,
Rick Laprade
to bring you this epic
adventure series!
BI-MONTHLY SERIES STARTING IN JULY!
5 YEARS
ACTIONLABCOMICS.C

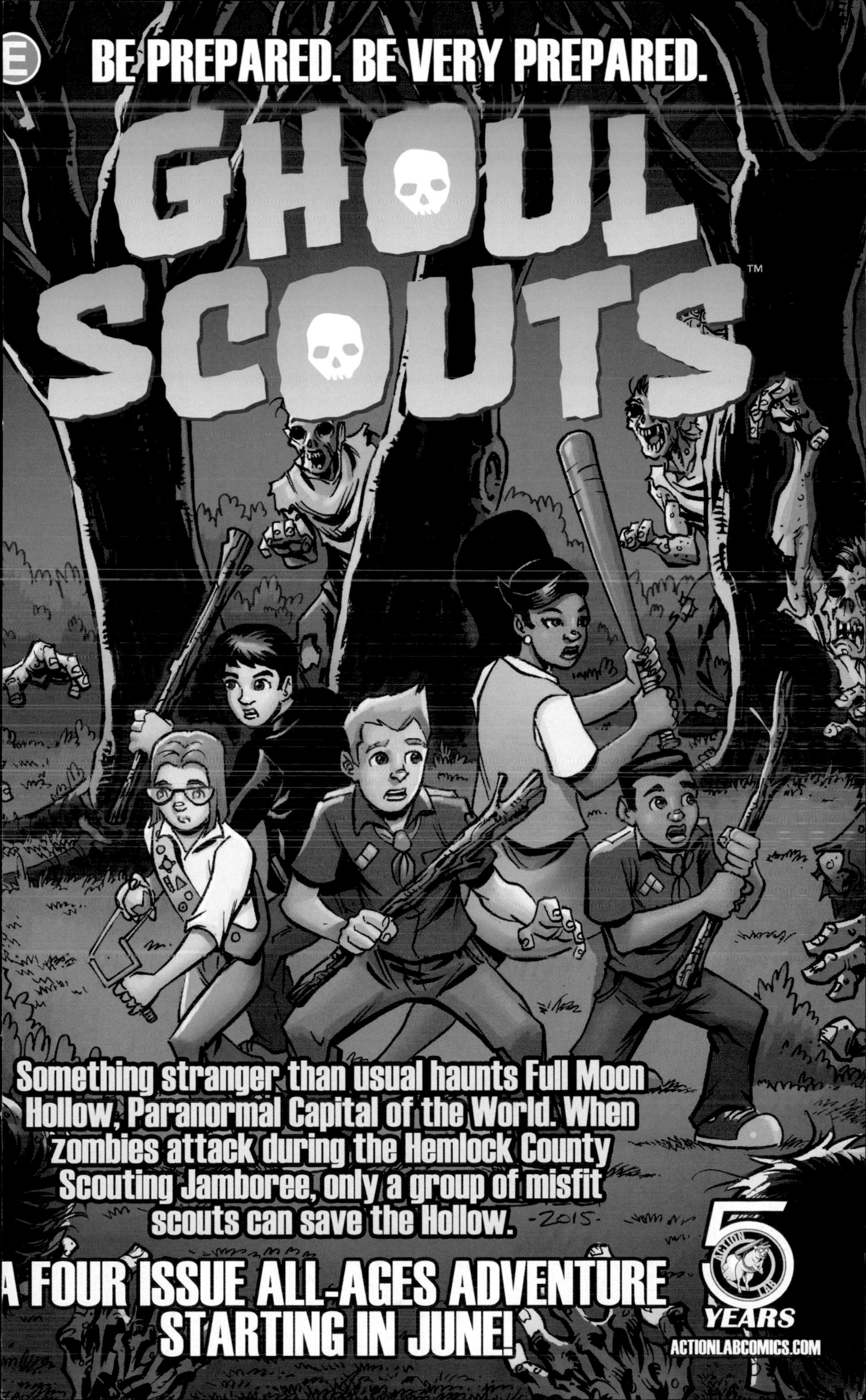
E
BE PREPARED. BE VERY PREPARED.
GHOUL SCOUTS™
Something stranger than usual haunts Full Moon Hollow, Paranormal Capital of the World. When zombies attack during the Hemlock County Scouting Jamboree, only a group of misfit scouts can save the Hollow.
-2015-
A FOUR ISSUE ALL-AGES ADVENTURE STARTING IN JUNE!
5 YEARS
ACTION LAB
ACTIONLABCOMICS.COM

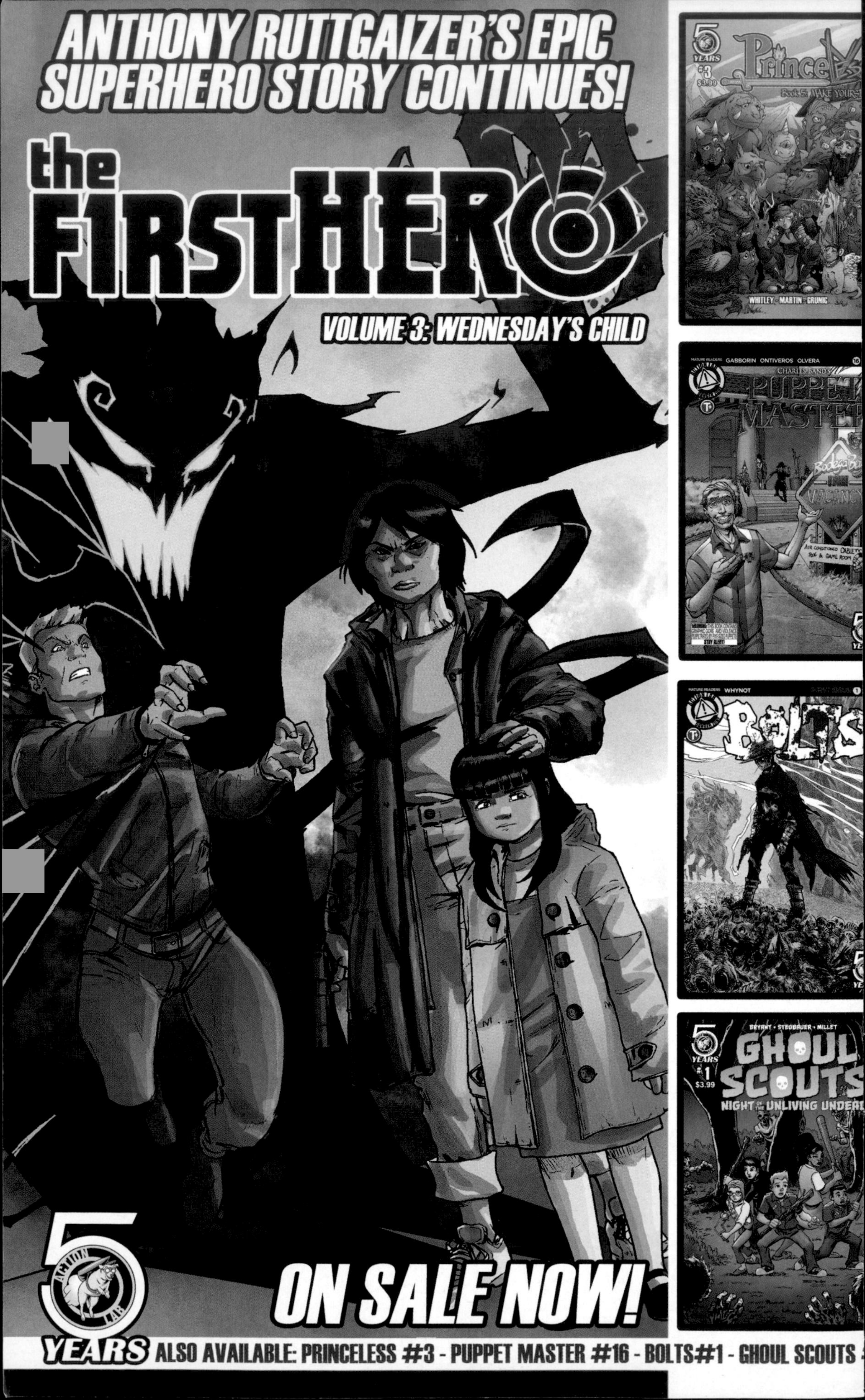
ANTHONY RUTTGAIZER'S EPIC SUPERHERO STORY CONTINUES!
the FIRST HERO
VOLUME 3: WEDNESDAY'S CHILD
ON SALE NOW!
5 ACTION LAB YEARS
ALSO AVAILABLE: PRINCELESS #3 - PUPPET MASTER #16 - BOLTS#1 - GHOUL SCOUTS
5 YEARS #3 $3.99
WHITLEY MARTIN GRUNIG
MATURE READERS GABBORIN ONTIVEROS OLVERA 16
MATURE READERS WHYNOT
BRYANT • STEGBAUER • MILLET
#1 $3.99

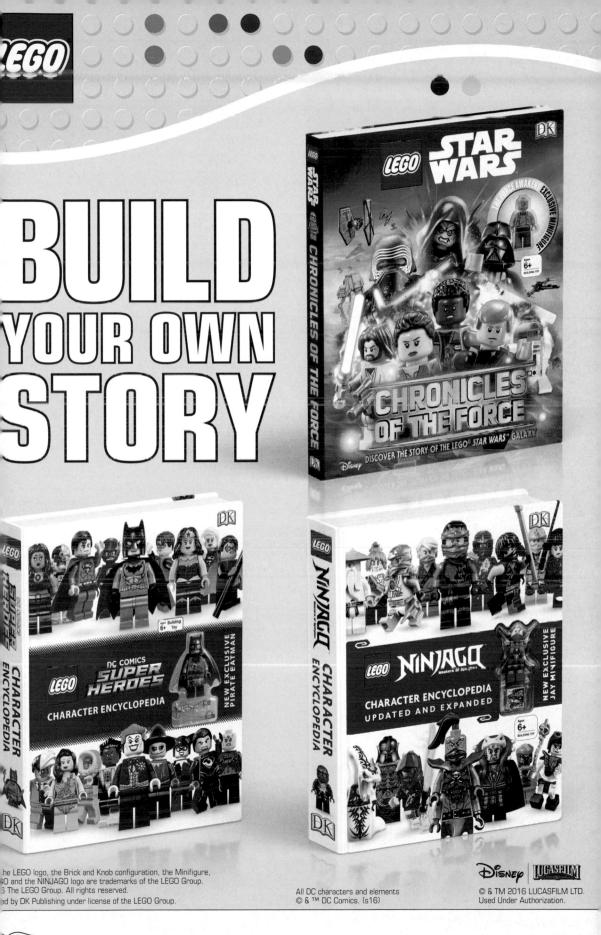

BUILD YOUR OWN STORY

LEGO STAR WARS

CHRONICLES OF THE FORCE

DISCOVER THE STORY OF THE LEGO® STAR WARS™ GALAXY

DC COMICS SUPER HEROES
LEGO CHARACTER ENCYCLOPEDIA

NEW EXCLUSIVE PIRATE BATMAN

LEGO NINJAGO
CHARACTER ENCYCLOPEDIA
UPDATED AND EXPANDED

NEW EXCLUSIVE JAY MINIFIGURE

he LEGO logo, the Brick and Knob configuration, the Minifigure,
D and the NINJAGO logo are trademarks of the LEGO Group.
The LEGO Group. All rights reserved.
d by DK Publishing under license of the LEGO Group.

All DC characters and elements
© & ™ DC Comics. (s16)

© & ™ 2016 LUCASFILM LTD.
Used Under Authorization.

A WORLD OF IDEAS:
SEE ALL THERE IS TO KNOW

www.dk.com

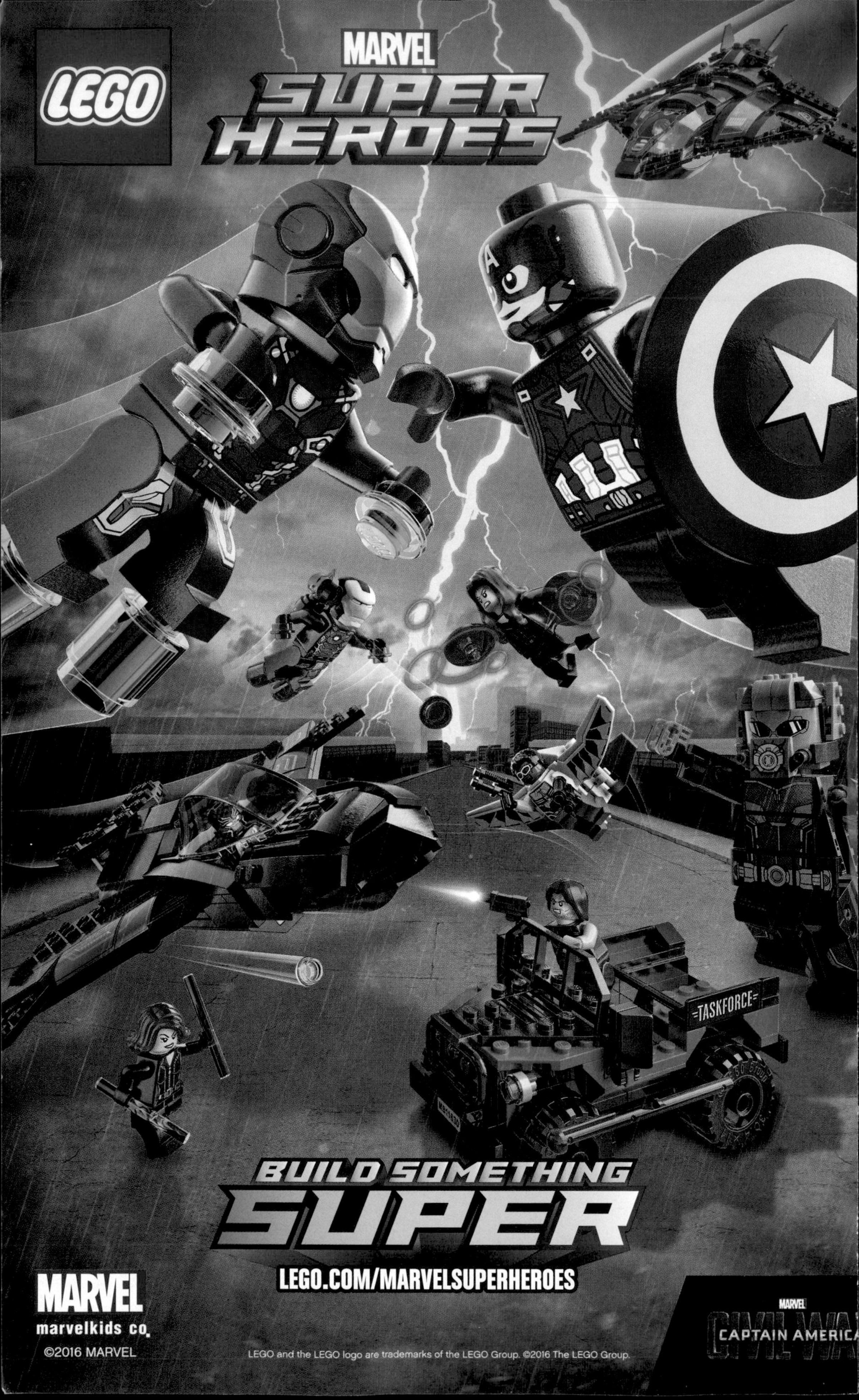
LEGO
MARVEL
SUPER HEROES
TASKFORCE
BUILD SOMETHING SUPER
LEGO.COM/MARVELSUPERHEROES
MARVEL
marvelkids com
©2016 MARVEL
MARVEL
LEGO and the LEGO logo are trademarks of the LEGO Group. ©2016 The LEGO Group.